PROCEED, SERGEANT LAMB

The British Regiments of the Line which are here mentioned as serving in America now bear the following names:

4th Foot:	The King's Own Royal Lancaster Regiment
7th Foot:	The Royal Fusiliers, City of London Regiment
8th Foot:	The King's Liverpool Regiment
9th Foot:	The Royal Norfolk Regiment
14th Foot:	The Prince of Wales' Own West Yorkshire Regiment
20th Foot:	The Lancashire Fusiliers
23rd Foot:	The Royal Welch Fusiliers
33rd Foot:	The Duke of Wellington's West Riding Regiment
47th Foot:	The Loyal North Lancashire Regiment
62nd Foot:	The Duke of Edinburgh's Wiltshire Regiment
71st Foot:	The Highland Light Infantry, First Battalion
74th Foot:	The Highland Light Infantry, Second Battalion
82nd Foot:	The South Lancashire Regiment, The Prince of Wales' Volunteers

PROCEED, SERGEANT LAMB

ROBERT GRAVES

INTRODUCTION BY

MADISON SMARTT BELL

SEVEN STORIES PRESS
NEW YORK · OAKLAND · LONDON

First Seven Stories Press edition December 2023.

Seven Stories Press
140 Watts Street
New York, NY 10013
www.sevenstories.com

Library of Congress Cataloging-in-Publication Data

Names: Graves, Robert, 1895-1985 author. | Bell, Madison Smartt, writer of
  introduction.
Title: Proceed, Sergeant Lamb / Robert Graves ; introduction by Madison
  Smartt Bell.
Description: First Seven Stories Press edition. | New York : Seven Stories
  Press, 2023.
Identifiers: LCCN 2023039406 | ISBN 9781644213186 (paperback)
Subjects: LCSH: Lamb, Roger, 1756-1830--Fiction. | United
  States--History--Revolution, 1775-1783--Fiction. | United
  States--History--Revolution, 1775-1783--Participation, Irish--Fiction. |
  Great Britain--History, Military--18th century--Fiction. | Irish--United
  States--Fiction. | LCGFT: Biographical fiction. | Historical fiction. |
  War fiction. | Novels.
Classification: LCC PR6013.R35 P7 2023 | DDC 823/.912--dc23/eng/20230919
LC record available at https://lccn.loc.gov/2023039406

College professors and high school and middle school teachers may order free examination copies of Seven Stories Press titles. Visit https://www.sevenstories.com/pg/resources-academics or email academic@sevenstories.com.

Printed in the USA.

9 8 7 6 5 4 3 2 1

CONTENTS

INTRODUCTION TO
THE 2025 EDITION

In the conclusion of his World War I memoir, *Goodbye to All That*, Robert Graves writes, "I made several attempts during these years to rid myself of the poison of war memories by finishing my novel, but had to abandon it—ashamed of having distorted my material with a plot, and yet not sure enough of myself to turn it back into undisguised history, as here." Supplying raw material with a plot is what novelists do, though they don't usually talk about it in such a contemptuous manner. Years after liberating his memoir from an abortive fiction, Graves performed this exact same operation on the raw material of Roger Lamb's 1809 military memoir.

The plot of Graves's personal life had thickened considerably by the time he began writing his first Lamb novel in 1939. His marriage to Nancy Nicholson had ended, though without (yet) benefit of divorce. The marriage had first been fractured by Graves's turbulent affair with the American poet Laura Riding (coauthor of three of the thirty-five books Graves had published since the end of World War I), but by 1939 he and Riding had split, and Graves was living with another woman, Beryl Hodge, who would become his second wife. All these adventures were expensive (Graves had four children by Nancy Nicholson and Beryl was pregnant with the first of four he'd have with her) and Graves needed, badly, to earn. An American Revolutionary War novel was suggested by an editor at Methuen, the then-publisher of Graves's two Claudius novels. Graves fell upon Roger Lamb's memoirs as a ready-made source, and once the writing was well underway, he became so entranced by his protagonist that he would sometimes half-consciously set a place for Sergeant Lamb at his and Beryl's table for two.

The plot of Graves's Lamb novels reflects his personal situation by presenting marriage as an obstacle to romance. Fictional Lamb, while his regiment is quartered in an Irish village, prior to shipping out to North America, falls in love with a local lass, Kate Weldone, but through much chicanery he ends up facilitating her elopement with a fellow soldier, Richard Harlowe, who soon proves to be an utter cad. Like many actual military wives of the period, Kate travels to America in support of her husband, who supports her but little. Though Kate's unhappiness in the marriage is soon apparent, Lamb is more scrupulous than Graves in the matter of seducing married women, so their romance remains blighted until Lamb, dispatched to learn the ways of Britain's Iroquois allies, discovers that Kate has fled the abuses of Harlowe to join an enemy tribe. Lamb's (wholly fictional) mission to the Iroquois being a lengthy one, he has time to marry her according to tribal custom; when the time comes for him to return to his regiment, she is pregnant. Kate eventually gives up her child to a forest-dwelling Quaker, and returns to her adoptive tribe rather than rejoin the wicked Harlowe. Lamb might reunite this little family if he would leave his regiment to permanently join the tribe, but his conscience will not permit him to "bear the disgraceful name of deserter."

This aspect of the story (continued to a tragic finale in *Proceed, Sergeant Lamb*) is a vaudevillian melodrama that would have embarrassed James Fenimore Cooper, but the military narrative of both novels is much more durably compelling (and also more solidly grounded in fact). For American readers, then and now, Graves presents a contrarian view of our founding revolution. Graves's Lamb, much like his real-life prototype, is an unquestioning but not unthinking loyalist to Britain and the Crown. His sympathies are with colonial loyalists who have been styled by the revolutionaries as Tories and traitors and energetically persecuted as such. One of the most striking aspects of the Lamb novels is their admiring (and persuasive) portrait of Benedict Arnold, whose name is simply synonymous with treason in Americans' conventionally received ideas of our own national origin. Then too, both novels are rich with perceptive and insightful observations of the culture, manners, and mores of the colonies as they fought their way to nationhood, of the style that would be published by Fanny Trollope and Alexis de Tocqueville a few decades after Lamb's American adventure.

Graves had a notion that his Lamb novels would become standard in the teaching of history in the United States. Something of the sort probably did happen with his Claudius novels, which offer a user-friendly point of entry to the phase of the Roman Empire they depict. Given the truism that winners write the history, stateside course adoptions of the Lamb novels may not seem any more likely now than previously. On the other hand, this republication occurs at a moment when our usual beliefs about our nation's foundation are getting some very radical challenges. There may, after all, be room for more than one different perspective.

Madison Smartt Bell, 2024

FOREWORD

Proceed, Sergeant Lamb is the sequel and conclusion to my *Sergeant Lamb of The Ninth.* Lamb's own rather disjointed *Journal* and *Memoir,* published in Dublin in 1809 and 1811, provide the bones of the story: the body has been built up from a mass of contemporary records, British, American, French and German. No incident of any historical importance has been invented or distorted. There has been too much, rather than too little, material to draw upon: for a start, no less than three officers of Lamb's regiment, The Twenty-Third, or Royal Welch Fusiliers, kept journals of the American War—Captains Julian and de Saumarez, and Colonel Mackenzie.

The frontispiece,* reproduced by kind permission of the Lieutenant-Governor of the Royal Hospital, Chelsea, is in Lamb's own handwriting—the first sheet of a Memorial sent in 1809 to the Duke of York, applying for a veteran's pension. It concludes:

> 'That Memorialist, being now far advanced in life, humbly solicits your Royal Highness to recommend him for a military pension, which would smooth his declining years and be most gratefully received as a remuneration for the many times he has risked his life and limbs in His Majesty's service.
>
> That for the truth of these facts, he most humbly refers to General H. Calvert and Colonel Mackenzie.'

Colonel Mackenzie (the one who kept the journal) had been adjutant of The Twenty-Third at Boston and Deputy-Adjutant-General at New York. Lamb had reported to him in New York when in 1782 he escaped there from captivity for the second time. General Sir Harry Calvert, as a newly joined second-lieutenant, had been helped

---

* Not reproduced in this edition.

through his first guard-mounting at New York in 1779 by Lamb, an experienced sergeant. He was now Adjutant-General of the Army and saw to it at once that Lamb was awarded an out-pension of one shilling a day—a generous amount at that time—and excused the formality of coming to Chelsea to establish his identity. The official reason for the award in the Hospital ledger is 'worn out'.

There is no record at the Hospital of Lamb's death. However, a reference to him by the Reverend W. B. Lumley in a mid-Victorian memorial volume of the Methodist Church in Ireland shows that 'worn out' referred only to Lamb's capacity for further soldiering. He was still alive and working hard fifteen years later, at the age of seventy. 'The best known of the teachers of Whitefriar Street Day School was Mr. Roger Lamb, who for nearly forty years superintended it with great fidelity and great advantage to the boys under his care. The grandson of this good man is now the eloquent and learned Dr. Chadwick, Dean of Armagh.'

A descendant, Miss E. Chadwick of Armagh, has kindly searched among family papers for a portrait or other record of Roger Lamb, but without success.

Lamb's story has come close to me in several ways. My paternal great-grandfather and grandfather, possibly even my father—if Lamb survived for a few years after his retirement—were Dubliners of Lamb's day. Admirals Samuel and Thomas Graves, who successively commanded the British fleet in American waters, were cousins of my great-grandfather, who was Chief of Police at Dublin and subscribed to Lamb's *Journal* before publication. (The well-known Massachusetts family of Graves, stemming from Thomas Graves of Hatfield, the town on the Connecticut River through which Lamb passed as a prisoner, have a common ancestry with the Irish branch to which in the War of Independence they were 'fratricidally opposed'.) But the chief link that I have with Lamb is that I had the honour of serving, like him, in the Royal Welch Fusiliers during a long and bloody war; and found their character as a regiment, and their St. David's Day customs, happily unaltered since his day.

R. G., *Galmpton-Brixham, Devon*, 1940

PROCEED, SERGEANT LAMB

CHAPTER I

In the first volume of this authentic relation of my career as a soldier, I told of my birth at Dublin in the year 1753, my enlistment in the Ninth Regiment of Foot at the age of seventeen, my peace-time service in various barracks of Ireland, and my campaigning in Canada and the State of New York in the years 1776 and 1777. For the benefit of those who have not been able to peruse the first book, I will now give a short Detail of other matters that will give them a running start into this second and concluding volume of my adventures.

I was fellow-recruit with four men, who afterwards fought by my side. These were: my good friend Terence Reeves, who had been a link-boy in the city of Belfast before his enlistment and was therefore nick-named 'Moon-Curser'; Alexander, called 'Smutchy', Steel who had once kept a Limerick gin-shop, and when I first served with him was but a clumsy slouch; Brooks the Dipper, a bad and dirty soldier, who had been recruited in a jail; and lastly Richard Pearce, the felonious son of an Ulster nobleman, who had taken refuge in the ranks of The Ninth, under the assumed name of Harlowe, from the just vengeance of the Law.

This Pearce, or Harlowe, married Kate Weldone, the woman whom I loved, and took her with him to Canada on campaign; but when he proved faithless, she ran off into the woods from Fort Niagara where he was stationed. Kate then for a while lived with me as my 'squaw', while I was by my officer's permission absent from my regiment and learning the Indian arts of battle from certain Mohican warriors, led by their gifted war-chief, Thayendanegea, or Captain Brant. A girl child was later born to Kate at the house of a Dry Quaker in the wilderness by the foot of Lake George. The wild untrammelled life of the Indians had not only fired my fancy but also satisfied my judgment as offering the philosophic mind far more for admiration than for disgust. However, the call of military duty restrained me from following my passionate inclination, which

3

*was to continue with Kate (and the sweet fruit of our illicit love) as a
member of the Mohican nation into which I had been duly initiated by
the aforesaid Thayendanegea. I continued a loyal soldier of King George
III. Kate and the child, when last I had news of them, were the guests of
Thayendanegea's wife, Miss Molly, at Genesee village in the territory of
the Six Nations—far beyond the confines of New York State.*

*Another fellow-soldier of mine was a veteran, Mad Johnny Maguire,
who had fought in America with The Ninth when Savannah Town was
taken from the Spaniards. His elder brother, Cornelius, was a farmer
of Norwalk in Connecticut; the two met by chance, at the close of my
narrative, after a battle in which, each unknown to the other, they were
fratricidally opposed. It was Mad Johnny who had done a good service to
Steel, Harlowe, Reeves and myself, when, being all recruits together, we
repented in time of a desperate plan to desert the Army, which we had
almost put into execution. Johnny let us return through his sentry post
before we were apprehended, the reason for our rash decision to desert
having been the ill-usage we suffered from the corporal of our mess, a
petty tyrant by name Buchanan.*

*The above particulars I reckon sufficient to afford my readers a knowl-
edge of the names and characters of such of my fellow-soldiers as have
principally figured in the history hitherto. Now two other persons of
civilian status, must be presented to them: the first, a young, slightly formed
woman, Jane Crumer, the wife of a private soldier of The Ninth. Mrs.
Crumer attended very devotedly to our wounded after we captured Fort
Anna, below Lake Champlain, and later risked her life at Saratoga to fetch
water from a creek under the rifle-gun fire of American marksmen posted
on the opposing bank. The remaining character is difficult of description:
he was a lean, lantern-jawed Irishman, with a black wet forelock and a
cajoling tongue. His name was the Reverend John Martin. He appeared to
me first on the day of my enlistment in the year 1770 at a cockfight, where
I lost money that was not mine to lose; he wore no clerical garb on that
occasion but carried a dark-winged cock under his arm. Later he appeared
in the guise of a Romish chaplain at Newgate Jail in Dublin, the day that
one Pretty Murphy, a murderer, was hanged, and myself acted Sergeant of
the Guard. Finally this Reverend John Martin was seen by Terry Reeves in*

the year 1777, on the day before we took the fortress of Ticonderoga; he was then garbed as a Chaplain of the Forty-Seventh Regiment, and was reading a leather-bound book close to the enemy's works. Terry Reeves believed this fantastical personage to be the Father of Lies himself; nor would I myself now swear that he was indeed human flesh, rather than a conjoint fancy of our disordered brains.

Now for the circumstances in which I found myself in November 1777, the month in which this new volume opens. I had attained to the rank of corporal, and was performing the duties of a sergeant, in the Light Infantry company of The Ninth. The Ninth formed part of Lieutenant-General Sir John Burgoyne M.P.'s army. This army, consisting of British regular troops and some German mercenaries, had in the summer of 1777 invaded New York State by way of the Canadian Lakes and Hudson's River. In October of that year, we were cut off and forced to capitulate, at Saratoga on Hudson's River, by an American army outnumbering us by four to one, commanded by General Horatio Gates, a renegade Briton. However, so evident was our resolve to fight on to the death rather than surrender ignominiously, that General Burgoyne succeeded in wresting from General Gates far better terms than we had a right to hope; namely, a pledge to send us home safely to Great Britain in return merely for our laying down our arms and undertaking not to serve again in the American continent while the war was still in progress. We duly yielded up our muskets and ammunition and what remained of our artillery; thereupon marching through wild country, under the escort of our enemies, to Boston, the so-called 'City of Saints', which lay some two hundred miles away to the east. Here, according to the Convention signed between the two opposing generals, transports were to be sent from New York, which was in British hands, for our repatriation. Pending the arrival of these ships, we British were crowded into miserable derelict huts on Prospect Hill, a few miles from Boston; yet, in the confident hope of speedy relief, we did not allow our present hardships to daunt us. We numbered about two thousand whole men, and some hundreds of sick and wounded. The German prisoners had been sent by the Americans to better quarters, in the hope that they would desert our cause.

THE WEATHER was very bad, the rain pelting in at the open windows; we were saucy and improvident enough on the first night to tear down some of the rafters to keep the fire alive in the grate—an act for which our guards greatly abused us. But this was still November, before we settled into the full misery of winter. When December came, those of us who could lie down at night, and the many who sat up from the cold, were obliged frequently to rise and shake the snow from our clothes, which the wind drifted in at the openings. Our officers were removed from us and quartered in the University town of Cambridge, become an arsenal for military stores, where but few students remained at their Latin studies—for war is the enemy of the Humanities—and those were little boys. Our officers' accommodation was scarcely better than ours, though many fine houses, the property of American loyalists, lay empty there as the common prey of plunderers.

Officers, quartermaster-sergeants and soldiers' wives were given passes, renewed each month, to go from their quarters for a distance of a few miles; but none was allowed any nearer the city of Boston, that emporium of rebellion, than Bunker's Hill and Breed's Hill (where the battle was fought) on the hither bank of the Charles River. That the common soldiers were not allowed out of the barracks was considered a great hardship, the more so since Colonel David Henley, the American commandant of the camp, forced us to buy all our provisions at two store-houses which he set up there for his own profit. By him we were charged greatly above the market price for every sort of commodity.

Our upkeep and support was paid in paper by Congress, who demanded to be reimbursed by General Burgoyne in gold and silver at the nominal value of the notes! When General Burgoyne protested at this fraud, the answer came: 'General Burgoyne supposes his solid coin to be worth three times as much as our currency. But what an opinion must he have of the authority of these States, to suppose that his money could be received at any higher rate than our own in public payment! Such payment would be at once depreciating our currency with a witness.'

What was worse, we soldiers had huge stoppages made from our pay on account of pretended damage done by us during our passage through the State of Massachusetts; it was alleged that we had burned fences, destroyed hay, grain and flax, and plundered houses of furniture. There was no redress against this plain lie and grievous injustice, for we were prisoners; and the claimants, who eagerly caught at the chance of recovering, by a recital of invented losses, real losses caused them by the war, would not be denied. General Gates was heartily cursed by the rank and file for his condonation of this smart dealing.

I was appointed by Lieut.-Colonel Hill to be temporary Surgeon to the Regiment, for Surgeon Shelly, captured in the fighting at Fort Anna, had not been returned to us; and thus I became in a manner an officer. Yet I was not asked for my parole as the officers were, and remained with my comrades on Prospect Hill. I frequently needed to visit the townships of Watertown, Mystic and Cambridge to purchase drugs and comforts for our sick. The better sort of Americans whom I met on these occasions treated me with hospitality, but I was often insulted by those whose business had been ruined by the war, or who had lost relatives in the fighting. What seemed to puzzle them was that I could be an Irishman and yet loyal to King George who, I was persistently told, governed my country with monstrous oppression.

I was often urged to desert and to take up the profession which in New England, and indeed in most colonies of America, was practically engrossed by my fellow-countrymen—namely, that of travelling schoolmaster. It was said, I could pick up a good living by going from one out-of-the-way township to another and teaching the boys and girls to read, write and cipher. My pay would be 'country pay' that is, payment in kind: my board would be found, my clothes and boots kept in repair and in addition I would, each schooling season, receive a barrel or two of flour, some lengths of yarn, a few fleeces, a keg of molasses and so many cords of wood. There was great store set here upon education and much reading done, though religious and political argument in tract and newspaper comprised the greater part of this. Thrifty parents who could not afford to pay the Irish schoolmaster would often smuggle their children into the back rows

of his class and bid them learn all they could before the cheat was discovered. I was smilingly warned that I must be a pretty slick man to
avoid being overreached by my prospective pupils and their parents.

In order to avoid offence, I would tell those who urged me on
this course that if ever I took to the profession it would be at home
in Ireland, where ignorance was far more prevalent than in their
enlightened country, and the need for Irish school-masters correspondingly greater.

I came upon many sights that interested me greatly. In the streets
of Cambridge, for instance, I saw an entire house being rolled on
logs, fitted with wheels, to another situation. The house had been
raised on four screws placed at the corners and the logs thrust underneath. I had the courage to ask the owner the reason for his removal,
and, says he very frankly: 'My wife's mother is a scold, yet I can get
no satisfaction against her from the deacons, who fear her tongue as
much as I do. I am a peaceable man and am therefore removing to a
distance beyond the tether of her infirmities.'

Many young women rode by me, unescorted, eyeing me with
remarkable boldness. They were mounted upon the horses peculiar
to New England—a fine-headed, long-maned, goose-rumped, cat-
hammed breed, with switch tails. When the snow lay thick on the
ground I passed on the road many large sleighs, to seat a dozen persons, drawn by two or four horses and jingling with bells, but not
decorated in the pleasant manner of the Canadian cariole. In these
sleighs, large parties of young men and women were accustomed on
moonlight nights to go out for a drive of two or three hours to a distant rendezvous with a similar party from another town: they drank,
danced and caroused all night and returned to their common avo-
cations the next morning without taking any sleep. In Ireland such
a custom would be judged very imprudent, but here they thought
nothing of it.

The most disagreeable part of my outings was when I must pass
the American sentinels at the camp gates. They were militiamen, of
an age either too advanced or too immature for more active service.
The granddads, as we generically named the bushy-wigged elder sort,

were in the main cold-blooded, querulous and slow; whereas the grandchildren, as we named the fifteen- and sixteen-year-olds, were hot-blooded, self-important and impatient to be doing great deeds on the field of battle. The granddads usually kept us waiting on some excuse or other, pretending that our passes were forged or that we were not the persons named in them; and if we showed impatience they protracted the delay yet further. The grandchildren threatened and insulted us, but were not so slow about their business.

One sentry, a Select-man (or church-elder) of Cambridge, held me up for three days in succession. On the third day I said to him: 'Surely, my friend, we need not run through that long rigmarole yet again?'

'I thot I told you to halt!' he drawled, presenting his piece at my breast. 'I swear now, if you attempt to pass, I'll blow you to pieces with my blazing-iron. I do not know you from Adam, you rascal.'

Now supervened a laughable yet somewhat disgusting incident which has been recounted by Lieutenant Anburey in phrases which I could not better for delicacy. A soldier's wife of the tough breed, who had followed the drum for thirty years, and could carry burdens like an ox, cook like a witch, forage like a Hessian, and outswear Mortal Harry himself at his prime, came bustling out from the camp, a short clay pipe in her mouth, and a dirty pass in her hand. Long Winifried was her name and some years before she had borne without flinching a sentence of one hundred lashes laid on her bare back: for the crime of stealing the Town Bull of Boston, slaughtering him and hacking him into beefsteaks. Long Winifried waved the paper in the old Select-man's face and was for passing on. He flew into a passion and called on her to halt, or he would fire. She turned back and gave him Billingsgate oratory in a scorching flood, to the effect that she was hastening to buy a little milk for her sick grandchild and he would cut his pranks at his own peril—she would not be halted. As the Lieutenant writes: 'When the old man was so irritated as to present his firelock, the woman immediately ran up, snatched it from him, knocked him down and, striding over the prostrate hero in the exultation of triumph, profusely besprinkled him not with Olympian dew but, 'faith, with something more natural. Nor did she quit her post till a file of sturdy ragamuffins marched valiantly to his relief, dispossessed the Amazon and enabled the knight of the grisly caxon to look fierce and reshoulder his musket.' But, for myself, I did not wait for this concluding scene, hurriedly snatching up my fallen pass and running away down the path, lest I be cited as an accessory after the fact.

On the morning of December 13th, I went out from the camp to Cambridge, which lay two miles off, in order to attend upon Lieut.-Colonel Hill. He was sick and had desired me to come and bleed him. The sentinel that day was a young sickly boy who gave me no difficulty at the gate, and I therefore looked forward to a pleasant excursion, it being a clear Sunday morning, with the church bells pealing and the sun shining brilliantly across the thin snow.

I had crossed Willis Creek and nearly reached the Colonel's house at the outskirts of Cambridge, when I was stopped by my enemy, 'the knight of the grisly caxon', but in his quality not of sentinel but of Select-man. He informed me that I was contravening three of the oldest and most venerated laws in the province at one and the same time: the first, by carrying a bundle upon the Sabbath Day—for I had in my hand a little canvas case containing cupping instruments; the second, by being seen in the streets during the hour of Divine Service; and the third, by proceeding along a road for more than the Sabbath Day's journey allowed to the Jews by the prophet Moses.

I pleaded that I was going upon an errand of mercy and obeying the orders of my superior officer; but he was very fierce and would not listen to me. He confined me instantly to a dungeon in the town jail, which was dark, empty and very cold, and kept me there upon bread and water until the next day; drily remarking, as the key was turned upon me, that I was but a young bear with all my troubles before me. Two small doors with double locks and bolts shut me from the exercise yard; two small windows, strong grated with iron, introduced a gloomy light to the apartment and were without a single pane of glass. I slept upon a little damp straw. In this place I was kept for two days and nights, without even being able to go outside for the necessities of nature; but must add my sum to the noisome litter deposited in the corner by previous malefactors. Nor was

I permitted to send a message to my commanding officer, explaining why I had not waited upon him; no, they marched me back to the Camp, where they cast me into the prison-hut, next the guard-room, where our people were confined for slight or imagined faults by the American guards, without prior reference to our own officers. This prison-hut was a worse place than the Cambridge jail, being very damp and verminous, but at least I had company. The first to greet me there was Terry Reeves, who had been arrested in my absence. He asked me with surprise what brought me into confinement; and indeed it was the first time in my whole service that I had found myself in that disgrace. 'The Book of Deuteronomy, I believe,' I said. 'And what brought you here?'

'Tobacco-juice,' he answered with equal brevity, and told me his story. He had been suffering greatly of a toothache and the only relief he could find was in rum, of which he drank above a pint upon an empty stomach. As he was walking from his hut to the guard-room, where he was about to put in a report on men fallen sick, he saw a person approach him dressed in a rough frieze overcoat with a woollen cap upon his head. This person, who was chewing tobacco, squirted the juice from the corner of his mouth across Terry's path, wetting his boot. Terry cried in vexation: 'Hold hard and keep your yellow spittle off my feet, damn you!' The man replied: 'I squirt where I please, you scoundrel. I am a major in the Massachusetts service.'

To which Terry made answer: 'If that be so, which I doubt, you are no credit to the Provincial service. To spit on a soldier's boot is a beastly habit in an officer.' Whereupon the officer arrested Terry.

Corporal Buchanan was also confined. His charge was: 'being found in possession of a spade, knowing it to be stolen from the guard.'

The Commandant of the Camp, this Colonel David Henley, was a very drunken, passionate person, and the author of most of our troubles, by inflaming his subordinates to cruel treatment of us. On the day after I was confined in this prison-hut, a number of quartermaster-sergeants attended the Deputy-Adjutant-General's office for the monthly renewal of their passes. He railed at them all for the disorderly noise which, so the guards informed him, had arisen on the previous night from the huts. Sergeant Fleming of The Forty-Seventh stating, as an excuse, that none of us had been able to sleep because of the cold—which was very true—Colonel Henley clenched his fist and shook it at the Sergeant crying: 'You rascals, I'll make damnation fly out of ye. For I will myself one of these nights go the rounds and if I hear the least word or noise in your barracks, I'll pour shot amongst ye and make flames of Hell leap out of ye and turn your barracks inside out. Moreover, my merry men, the sentinels inform me that when they stop ye for your passes, you look sulky at 'em. Were I a sentinel, and you did so to me, I would blow your brains out, aye, were you Whaley, Goffe or the Devil himself.'*

Three days later this Colonel Henley came on horseback with some other militia officers to release several of us who were prisoners, in order to make room for others, the prison-hut being overcrowded. He called us out in order of rank, myself first, then the two corporals. Having read out our crimes he made many very scurrilous remarks to the three of us, which I heard with indifference, Corporal Buchanan with feigned awe, but Terry Reeves with indignation. Finally he told us that the Ninth Regiment gave more trouble than any other corps. Terry Reeves, who could never hold his tongue, then remarked archly: 'I believe, Sir, that General Schuyler and General Gates were both of your opinion during the last campaign.'

Colonel Henley, feeling his dignity challenged, grew very angry, and began to thunder at Terry.

Says he: 'You hired cut-throat, how dare you insult a Provincial officer, as you insulted Major McKissock yesterday? Do you venture to tell your British majors that they are a discredit to their service?'

---

* This expression, often heard in New England, refers to the two famous Swordsmen and Regicides from whom the general pardon was withheld at the Restoration. They had fled to New England, where they lived under assumed names in the town of Hadley. Goffe once routed a swaggering fencing-master who came to give a display at Boston, himself armed with only a wet mop and a cheese, tied in a napkin, which he used as a shield. The fencing-master, whose sword was at each lunge received in the cheese, and his face dabbed with the mop, cried out: 'Who are you in the name of God? You must be either Whaley, Goffe or the Devil himself.' R. L.

'No, sir,' replied Terry unabashed, 'for I tell no lies.'

This was as much of the conversation as I heard, for Colonel Henley catching a smile as it stole across my face, ordered me back to close confinement.

I am informed that, after I had gone, Terry continued: 'However, Sir, I am sorry if I insulted the Major; but I could not have known him to be of field rank because of his civilian dress and his unofficerlike habit of chewing and spitting. I own that I was in liquor, owing to a toothache, and therefore I am ready to beg his pardon if I seemed disrespectful in manner.'

Colonel Henley in a rage: 'By God, Sir, had it been me you served so, I would have run you through the body. You're a great rascal, I guess.'

Terry Reeves remained undaunted. He replied: 'Sir, I am no rascal, but a good soldier, and my officers know it.'

'Silence, you coward Englishman!' cried Colonel Henley. Another officer, Major Sweasey, called Terry a rascal and raised a whip to strike him.

But Terry Reeves would not be silenced. 'I am no coward, Colonel Henley, and I will not be so abused by you. If I had arms and ammunition I should soon be with General Howe, fighting for my King and Country.'

'Damn your King and Country! When you had arms, you were willing enough to lay them down,' was Colonel Henley's strange rejoinder.

Terry Reeves cried: 'Sir, I tell you, I will not hear my King abused.'

Colonel Henley again called him to silence, and then Corporal Buchanan must put in his oar with: 'Hold your tongue, Corporal Reeves, when the officer bids you.'

Terry in disgust turned on Corporal Buchanan: 'Damn you, you fawning fellow, why don't you stick up for your King and Country?'

'Be silent, Terry, or you'll be getting us all into trouble,' muttered Buchanan.

Terry would not be silent. 'God damn them all,' he cried in a loud voice. 'I'll stand by my King till I die.'

Colonel Henley in great scorn: 'This is a free country, rascal. We acknowledge no Kings here.'

'No, I believe not,' said Terry, 'or none but King Hancock.'

This excited a laugh among the grandchildren on guard, which so infuriated the Colonel that he cried to them: 'Silence, boys, and let one of you run him through for a scoundrel!'

None of them stirred, for in America there is a tribute of respect always paid to a ready tongue, and they reckoned that Terry Reeves should not be murdered for his.

Colonel Henley then leaping off his horse, seized a firelock with a fixed bayonet from one of the lads, and ran at Terry. Terry leapt back a pace, so that the steel did no more than prick him in the left breast.

Colonel Henley white with passion: 'Another word, and I'll drive it through your body.'

'I don't care,' cried brave Terry. 'For I'll stand by King and Country till I die.'

The Colonel made another push at Terry's heart with the bayonet; but Smutchy Steel, who was one of the new prisoners waiting for accommodation in the hut, leaped forward to the rescue, calling to Buchanan to do the same. The two of them knocked up the firelock, and the bayonet passed harmlessly over Terry's shoulder.

Thereupon an ancient corporal of the guard drawlingly interposed, saying to the Colonel: 'No, I swear, Neighbour Henley, you shan't kill this man, for he was committed to my charge by Major McKissock whom he insulted. You may do as you like with the other rogues, but this Corporal Reeves is my prisoner and I'm answerable for him to Major McKissock, who's my own company officer.'

Major Sweasey then dismounted and besought Colonel Henley to return Terry to the prison-hut; in which plea he was seconded by another officer present. Colonel Henley at last consented.

Terry was brought back into the hut, bleeding profusely from an upward stab three inches long. He exclaimed still in unquenched indignation: 'Damn them all, I'll never allow my King to be abused while I live!' I was fast by the legs, but he came to me and I could dress his wound with the bandages which I carried in my canvas case.

CHAPTER II

THE CRUEL excesses of an individual such as Colonel Henley, and their effect upon several of his subordinates, cannot be enlarged into an indictment of the whole American nation, and I may here note that in time of war the greatest magnanimity towards the enemy seems always to be shown by the troops most directly engaged in the fighting, whereas the meanest and most inhumane feelings prevail in the bases and camps far remote from the hostile scene. Nor would I disguise from my readers that at New York, where the prisoners taken from the Americans were confined in hulks in the harbour, the treatment that they received, it is said, greatly exceeded in malignity what we were now experiencing. It should be observed that the Commissary of Prisoners was an American Tory, as were most of the prison-guards, and these revenged themselves for past injuries upon their unfortunate fellow-countrymen. Nevertheless, the negligence of the high British officers responsible for the well-being of these prisoners cannot escape censure; and the Provost-Marshal, Major Cunningham, a beast in human form, was (I regret to record) an Irishman. When charity supplied a vessel of broth to his starving captives, he would divert himself by kicking it over, and watching the poor creatures lap the liquor from the foul floor with their tongues. The rulers of Massachusetts when they learned of the barbarities which had been done on the hulks, and at Major Cunningham's jail in Walnut Street, New York, naturally retaliated upon us.

I will not therefore enlarge at inordinate length upon our sufferings at Colonel Henley's hands, merely relating an incident that occurred early in the new year of 1778, while a number of our people, myself among them, were watching a parade of the American militia. Their unhandiness with arms was the subject of a silent merriment among such veteran spectators as ourselves, though we contrived to keep straight faces. Colonel Henley, who commanded the parade, became aware of our close interest and shouted: 'Off, you rascals, and clear the parade; or it will be the worse for you.'

We immediately turned about and began to pick our way carefully through the mud, those of us who were behind waiting for the rest of the crowd to get clear before following them. 'Damn you,' cried Colonel Henley, 'I'll make you mend your pace!'

At that moment, Corporal Buchanan, looking over his shoulder, saw the militia soldier who was performing the manual exercise as fugleman to the rest, by a maladroit movement drop his musket to the ground. Buchanan could not restrain his mirth, but gave way to a roaring laugh. Colonel Henley, setting spurs to his horse, ran at him with his sword. Buchanan avoided the thrust and made good his escape, but the sword wounded in the left side a corporal of another regiment. Colonel Henley then rode back to his men. He was straightening, as he went, the sword which, being of inferior make, had bent nearly double against the corporal's ribs. He then ordered his men to load and come back with him to hunt Buchanan down and blaze at him when found. Though unarmed ourselves, we all felt ourselves in honour bound to protect our comrade from death, and shouted to the Colonel that he would only catch his man by a general massacre of us all.

Colonel Henley had already given the first order for a volley in our midst; but Major Sweasey, who then fortunately appeared, implored him to desist. The Major proposed instead that the British officer in command of our huts be asked to arrest Buchanan and confine him for trial. Colonel Henley unwillingly consented, and we dispersed. In the end Buchanan was given up as a prisoner and sentenced to a few days' imprisonment for disrespect.

When, however, two more of our soldiers were wounded by the instigation of Colonel Henley, separately, on a single day, General Burgoyne demanded a special court-martial of this infamous person. The plea was granted and he himself acted as prosecutor, speaking very eloquently and sharply and calling the Americans to a reminder of that due sense of the rights of mankind that they had expressed so

ably in their Declaration of Independence. Yet it will readily be imagined that Colonel Henley was acquitted of the four crimes charged
against him, the court being composed of his associates, and the evidence of the militiamen (who had been well rehearsed beforehand)
being preferred to that of British eye-witnesses. It was alleged in his
defence that we had daily and hourly offered insult and insolence to
our guards, and to the Colonel himself by our resolution to protect
Buchanan; and that the Colonel was a warm-blooded but benevo-
lent officer animated only by a desire to protect his country from
affront. The perjury was unashamed. Terry Reeves' rejoinder on the
subject of King Hancock was distorted into the absurd statement:
'King Hancock is come to Town. Don't you think him a saucy fellow
for coming so near to General Burgoyne?'

General Burgoyne's prosecution of this American colonel was
much spoken of, and that the verdict was an acquittal was used
against him by Americans and by his enemies at home as putting
him in the light of a mischief-maker. Yet we soldiers loved him for his
warm championship of our cause, and his action was on the whole
successful: for though Colonel Henley 'for public honour' was for-
mally reinstated in his command after the trial, he was removed a
week later, and a more humane colonel named Lee replaced him.
Colonel Lee did away with one great evil: he granted our people
passes for the purchase of provisions, so that the extravagant price
of commodities at the two stores on the hill dropped down to the
market rate.

On January 10th, two days after this incident upon the parade
ground, I walked over to Charlestown Neck to make a few small
purchases from the farmers in the neighbourhood of the burned village of Charlestown. Terry Reeves, who had recovered of his stabbing
wound, had been chosen to act quartermaster-sergeant of The Ninth
and provided with a pass to accompany me.

I said to him: 'Let us now pass over Bunker's Hill and Breed's
Hill and see how the battle went.' This we did, and we were resting
in the ruined redoubt which had been the scene of the fiercest
fighting in this battle when we heard footsteps approach. Looking

over the parapet, we found ourselves confronted with a person whose disagreeable aspect will by this time be so familiar to readers of my former volume that I will spare them a fresh account of it, as being unchanged. It was, let me ask them to believe, once more the Reverend John Martin, but this time dressed as an American Congregational minister.

I silently gripped Terry's shoulder to impress upon him that I would face the thing out boldly and that I expected him to stand by me; but I could feel, by the shudder that took him, that he was almost dead with fear.

'Good day to you, holy man,' I cried. 'And who pray, may you be? For this is the third time that you and I have met, yet we are still unacquainted.'

'I disremember any such meeting,' said he in an off-hand way. 'Yet to be sure, you have an Irish accent.'

'So had my father,' I replied sternly. 'But that is neither here nor there. I asked you your name. Then give it!'

'I am the Reverend John Martin,' he said, suddenly very humble, 'a chaplain of the Rhode Island militia. I see that you belong to the captured, or Convention, Army. Many of your British comrades were killed hereabouts three years ago. Do you happen to be acquainted with a charming play, *The Downfall of British Tyranny*? I am not the author, but I mended a few lines, you know.'

'A wretched, patched production, they tell me,' I said, though I had never heard of it before.

'No, no,' the false priest persisted. 'An altogether delightful one. It hits them all off. Admiral Tombstone (meaning Admiral Graves, ha, ha!) relates in tarry-trousered style: 'Many powdered *beaux, petits maîtres,* fops, fribbles, skip-jackets, macaronies, jack-puddings, noble-men's bastards and whores' sons fell that day.'

'No more of that,' said I, 'or with my fists I shall resent the insult to the Army.'

'No offence was intended,' he said hurriedly, 'A play is but a play, a harmless thing. But, good Sergeant, I myself took part in the battle. Indeed, it was I who, the night before, in the absence of Colonel

Gridley, the patriot Engineer, oversaw the construction of this very redoubt. I had above a thousand men at work.'

'Tell me more,' said I, staring into his eyes, 'and I'll believe less.'

But he would not meet my gaze, and tried instead to fascinate Terry, who was now quaking like a man in a fit.

'Oh,' said he, when I repeated my injunction in a louder voice. 'Just as you wish. Well, then, on the next morning I went down into Charlestown yonder with a spy-glass, for a look at the foe. A cannon-ball came hurtling through the house where I was taking refreshment, the property of a Mr. Cary. It fetched off my hat, without touching me, and I returned to the Hill. There I sent a message back to General Ward at Cambridge for reinforcements, judging the force in the redoubt to be weak; and, in answer a little after noon, up comes Colonel Putnam with the Connecticut men.'

'So,' said I, 'you took quite a prominent part, you say, in directing the battle?' I sneered at him, for I could see that every word was a fabrication, and shook off all my fanciful terrors.

'That was nothing to what followed,' he continued, in hurried tones, his voice gradually rising. 'I returned in person to headquarters at Cambridge, in order to press General Ward there to send forward wagons for the safe conveyance of the wounded. On my return the fighting was very warm. I stood down by that fence,' [pointing to the left, as we faced Boston] 'where the Connecticut men, intermixed with some Irish companies, were engaged with the Welch Fusiliers. The Irish inadvertently fired upon our line, but I ran forward and called on them in the Old Irish tongue to desist. The Connecticut men, not understanding this language, suspected treachery; but the Irish listened to me, and all was well.'

'So you too are an Irishman,' I said, very severe, as if I had learned this for the first time. 'Now we can discourse on common ground. Continue!'

He went on, his eyes flickering about like a candle-flame in a draught, 'I had girded on an Irish long sword that day, and it was well that I came so armed. The British pushed around the end of the fence by the water, and damned me for a clerical dog, saying that they would have my life. A Welchman fired point-blank at me and rushed upon me with his bayonet. I let out his bowels with my sword. Then I engaged, cut and thrust, with an officer who drew his hanger; I slew him too with a stroke on the neck. I lost but a button sliced off my coat.'

Then I said to this parson: 'Did I believe that you were either an honest man, or a clerk in Holy Orders, which I do not, I would spare you punishment. But you have sailed under too many false colours and proved a bird of ill omen to my comrade and myself on too many occasions. Now I am about to 'change my luck' in Indian fashion by making your feathers fly.'

I turned to Terry. 'Terry,' said I, 'for the honour of our Army, and of Ireland, I am resolved to give this liar a thrashing—"be he Whaley, Goffe or the Devil himself". Lend me the loan of that little hickory club you were carrying.'

Terry cried: 'No, no, Gerry. Let be! He will do us some mischief.' But I snatched up the club notwithstanding, from where it lay in the trench, and swung at the false priest's head.

He dodged, and leaped nimbly over the parapet—I tripped, felt curiously numbed, as if I had touched a catfish, and was slow in following. When I had surmounted the parapet and gazed about me, he had disappeared as cleanly as if he had never been!

Terry stared at me in a dazed way. 'Oh, Gerry,' he faltered, 'it's a brave boy you are, surely. When I meet that Devil I feel always like a frog before a black snake, and there's no hiding it. I am sure now that when we return to Camp there'll be black news waiting for us.'

I reproved him with: 'Terry, you must not allow these sick thoughts to weigh with you. Take a stick to the Devil and he leaps off and vanishes; for there is no power or force in lies. That you are a gallant man we know, from your defiance of Colonel Henley. I think that his Reverence will not show himself again to us in a hurry.'

'If he were mortal flesh,' said Terry, still in a whimpering voice, 'I should not care. But he is as old as the wickedness of the world.'

On our return to the Camp we found that Terry's gloomy prediction was justified, and confirmation given to the headless rumours that had for long been flying through the Camp. The Convention of Saratoga, solemnly entered into by General Gates, was not to be ratified by Congress, and we were therefore to be kept prisoners for an indefinite time!

Here, as always, when treating of the American Congress, a distinction must be made between the real motives guiding their policy, and their professed motives. Their excuse for not ratifying the Convention was that General Burgoyne had called American public faith in question by unjustly charging a militia colonel with attempted murder, and by complaining further that the wretched accommodation given his officers at Cambridge and to ourselves at Prospect Hill did not agree with what had been stipulated; and that therefore if he could express himself so warmly, he might well be himself meditating a breach of the Convention! Furthermore, we had retained our empty cartouche boxes and our cross-belts when delivering up our arms at Saratoga, and this (though it had not been insisted upon by General Gates that we should do so) was a failure to conform with the spirit of the agreement. Nor, they complained, had our officers supplied them with a personal description of all our non-commissioned officers and men—for which no express demand had, either, been made. Finally, when because of the danger and difficulties of bringing transports into Boston during the winter months, it had been demanded of Congress that we should be permitted to march to Providence in Rhode Island, where the harbourage was more convenient, and be fetched off from there, they pretended to regard this as an attempted evasion of the Convention, and the preparation for an offensive movement.

The fact of the matter was that Americans in general, and New Englanders in particular, hate to be overreached in a bargain, and when it became known to Congress that General Gates, with our army surrounded and outnumbered by five to one, had yet yielded to General Burgoyne's menace of a desperate attack and let us go freely, they felt cheated and looked for a legal loophole by which to escape. General Lafayette, a young French officer of fortune who, with the rank of major-general, was now one of General Washington's military family, told Congress that it would be a very foolish action to ratify the Convention. He pointed out that even if we were not sent back to America we could still serve as garrison troops elsewhere in the Empire, and release other regiments to take our places. Further, we might thereupon be actively employed against the French, whom the news of our surrender would surely now encourage into an open alliance with the Americans against us. General Lafayette urged these military considerations more readily because the proposed breach of faith affected only the American Republic, not his own country. It is said that General Washington and other men of honour were not of his way of thinking. They remonstrated indignantly at the weak and futile pretexts used by Congress to avoid their obligations. Nevertheless, General Lafayette succeeded in overriding all scruples by advancing as precedent an alleged breach, by our Government, many years before, of the Convention of Kloster Seben, where the French were the losers.

The Convention being not yet directly repudiated, we still had hope at least of being exchanged against American prisoners. Meanwhile, there were rumours running among our guards of an attempt on the part of Admiral Howe to enter Boston with his fleet and rescue us; and great excitement was caused one night by the lighting of a chain of beacons from hill to hill, which brought the militia up from a great distance to repel an attack. However, it was but a false alarm designed by the Americans to stimulate popular distrust in the public faith of Britain.

Our captivity had begun to grow very wearisome, from the lack of employment and hope deferred, but we comforted ourselves with an assurance that the Spring would soon be upon us, and that the new campaign would be decisive for British arms. It was notorious that General Washington, who alone of American generals kept an army in the field during this winter, had been reduced to great straits by his enemies in Congress, who starved him of supplies, and by the desertion of his militia, who were impatient of the discipline that he imposed upon them. Less than three thousand men remained under arms with him in the camp at Valley Forge by the Schuylkill River, and General Howe, snug in Philadelphia, refrained from attack only because he believed that the force of the Revolution was already broken by the jealousies and rivalries of its leaders.

Our watchword was 'Patience'.

However, before the year was much older, news came that the Colonists had done what we never believed them capable of doing—they had signed an armed alliance with our mortal enemies the French and thus renounced for ever the name and tradition of Englishmen! France from the beginning of the contest had secretly encouraged the Americans in their opposition and supplied them with munitions of war, while at the same time amusing Great Britain with declarations of the most pacific intentions. What made matters worse was that the traitors of our Opposition were in constant treaty with the American agents in France and openly rejoiced when news reached them of General Burgoyne's capitulation at Saratoga.

I am sorry to relate that the American agents who visited our camp, and constantly pestered us with threats and cajolements in an attempt to make us desert, had considerable success with some regiments even thus early in our captivity; though but little with The Ninth. We were promised our freedom, citizenship and liberty to pursue our trade in any State in which we chose to settle; and, if we cared to enter their army, the rank and pay of an officer for every man of three years' service and upwards! Even the newest recruit of ours could turn a large fee by becoming a deserter; for the well-to-do farmers or manufacturers called out as militiamen now found it next to impossible to engage substitutes and were willing to offer almost any price for such. Remarkable it is how few men took this bait, and how many of those who did were but pretended deserters, and crossed over into New York at the earliest opportunity. However, the whole band of The Sixty-Second was seduced except the Master, and went to dispense *Yankee Doodle* and other patriotic airs to a Boston regiment; and once we recognized a soldier of The Forty-Seventh, who had deserted three years previously, riding up to the camp in major's uniform at the head of a supply column. Our officers had the mortification of taking orders from him.

On April 15th, when the Spring had suddenly appeared, and we saw green grass again for the first time since our captivity, our brigade (which consisted of the Artillery, the Advanced Troops and The Ninth) was paraded one morning and told to prepare for a march to Rutland in the interior of the province; because the Council of Boston had decided that we should fare better there. It happened very fortunately for us that a vessel under a flag of truce had arrived at Boston from New York two days previously with some necessaries for us, including blankets, linen and medicaments; else we should have been in a wretched state. We were marched along the same Worcester road which we had taken on our journey to Boston and halted about midday at a place called Weston, our destination that night being Westborough which lay at twenty-five miles' distance from the camp. I was resting by the roadside, avoiding as far as possible any converse with the inhabitants of the place, who were exercising their wit at our expense, when I heard my name called and an American militia sergeant came forward from the crowd and gripped my hand.

I did not at first recognize him but he swore that, being indebted to me for his life, he must at least insist on my taking refreshment with him at a tavern near by. He was one Gershom Hewit, whose wounds I had dressed after the fight at Fort Anna. I declined at first to go with him, lest I might be apprehended for quitting the column, but he undertook to write me out a pass, and his offer of a glass of mimbo—that is to say, hot rum and water sweetened with molasses—was very inviting; so I went with him up the hill to the tavern.

Hewit took me into a private apartment where the mimbo was set before us. When the landlord had departed, he clapped me on the back in a very cordial manner, and told me that we had met again in a fortunate hour, since it now lay in his power to do me a very considerable service; in quittance of his debt to me.

When I asked him what that could be, he told me in evident expectation of my acceptance, that if I would desert the King's service and a cause which was, I must admit, both an evil and a lost one, he had it in his power to make me the surgeon of his regiment, at very good pay—for he had been commissioned that very day to find a man to fill the vacancy!

Said I: 'Sergeant Gershom Hewit, you have formed a mistaken opinion of my character. I thank you for your offer of this surgeon's commission and for your present hospitality, but I must decline to talk treason with you, even in a private apartment.' I took up my smoking glass and toasted the health of King George, adding, 'If you will not drink with me, I must drink alone.'

I drank alone, for he arose and left me without another word. I stayed a minute or two more in the room, reading a well-thumbed copy of *Poor Richard's Almanack,* for the year 1744, published at Philadelphia by Dr. Benjamin Franklin, that lay upon the chimney-shelf.

There was a rhyme in it that struck my eye, and I memorized it for the edification of my comrades. It referred to the New England custom of 'bundling', namely the supposedly chaste lying in bed together of young, affectionate, unmarried persons of opposite sexes for the sake of company and the saving of fuel; this was still universally practised among the common people hereabouts, who held that the man and woman (being already sanctified by Grace) could not yield to temptation. The mother of the girl concerned would usually tuck the pair in bed herself and blow out the light. It may be remarked here that love-children were frequent in America; but the man almost invariably married the woman whom he had seduced, and the advantage of a large population in so extensive and rich a country excused the fault even if it were not repaired by subsequent wedlock; so long as it was not incestuous or too often repeated by the same woman. Bundling was the subject of much raillery, and I found that if ever, while in American company, I looked grave at jests on this head, I was adjudged a person of evil imagination who doubted the innocence of my hosts.

The rhyme ran:

> Biblis does solitude admire,
> A wondrous Lover of the Dark:
> Each night puts out her Chamber Fire
> And just *keeps in a single Spark*;
> 'Till four she keeps herself alive,

Warmed by her piety, no doubt;
Then, tired with kneeling, just at five
She sighs—and lets that Spark *go out*.

I thought: 'These are a people whom I will never come to understand. If the practice be indeed blameless, how come the country people to take such delight in salacious jokes on the subject? Or, if it be vicious, how do the ministers, who hold such a sway over the people, tolerate and even encourage it as innocent?'

At this point of my reflexion there came a noise of angry shouting from the common tap-room of the inn, crashes as if a battle were in progress, and screams of grief and indignation from the women of the house. I learned later that a company of our artillerymen had followed me to the tavern for a drink of mimbo, and that Sergeant Hewit, after leaving my presence, had attached himself to their company and attempted to wean them from the Service. They had made scornful replies, which the Americans present had resented, and a battle was joined with stools and fists. Three drinking-glasses were broken, but no injuries done to the contestants beyond a few bruises. The artillerymen had made good their retreat and rejoined their column just as it marched off.

The landlord, fearing that he would get no satisfaction, cried out in my hearing, just as I was quietly taking my departure: 'I have a hostage, wife, never fear. I'll squeeze payment out of him, I swear.' He ran up to me, catching at the collar of my jacket and, says he: 'You rogue of a Britonian, you will pay me for these broken glasses, or I'll have the Law on you.'

I replied: 'Landlord, you know as well as myself that I was not in this room while the stools were flying, but in the parlour.'

'O what a wicked falsehood!' cried his dutiful wife and daughters; 'You were the ringleader of the party, O fie! O fie! We saw you with our own eyes.'

'This will cost you sixty dollars, young man,' said the landlord very severely. 'You see, there are witnesses.'

I turned to the landlord's wife and asked in a smooth voice: 'Can you tell me, Madam, for I have been long parted from my Bible by the accidents of war, which is the number of the Commandment—is it the Tenth or the Ninth?—which prohibits the bearing of false witness?'

Yet she was not abashed. 'The Commandment prohibits only the bearing of false witness against a neighbour, and the Gospel makes it nation plain (in the chapter concerning the good Samaritan) that only he is a neighbour who does a man a friendly service. You have done us no such friendly service. You have come into our land to lay it waste and destroy our young men, as the Assyrians came into the Land of Israel; and I have neither love for you nor pity.'

'Summon Sergeant Gershom Hewit, then, Madam,' said I, 'for he can call me neighbour, and he will testify that I am not culpable of these breakages.'

'No, no,' exclaimed the landlord, 'you can't escape us that a way. Neighbour Hewit, though he brot you here, is greatly obliged to me and would not injure my trade. The Commandment forbids the giving of false witness against a neighbour, but it does not insist that one should volunteer to give true witness even when called upon. Come, come, don't be het up, but pay me my sixty dollars. Nay, I'll be content with fifty, for the sake of peace.'

I could not by any means prevail on them to summon Sergeant Hewit, who had returned to his own house with a bruised head; for all were aware of the obligation under which Sergeant Hewit stood to me.

Now, I had four guineas in gold concealed in my shoes, each one of which was now worth at least fifty Continental paper dollars. Rather than be committed to jail and separated from my comrades, I would willingly have drawn on this hoard to pay the fine. Though the injustice was monstrous, the landlord had me in his power. Unfortunately, however, this way out was barred: once I discovered my hoard, the landlord would take it all away, and even make a virtue of his great benevolence in compounding with me for twenty odd dollars instead of fifty.

Fifty dollars in paper was not so stiff a price as appears at first sight, perhaps only double the value of the broken glasses. For the

Americans had been dependent on Britain and Ireland for almost the whole of their glass-ware and crockery; therefore three years of war, and (before the war) the strong associations of colonists to avoid the use of English manufactured goods, and finally the rapid depreciation of the paper-currency, had sent up the value of the simplest household utensils from halfpence to dollars. Breakages were almost impossible to renew, and I may mention here that when General Gates, after the capitulation of Saratoga, had entertained General Burgoyne and his staff at a banquet, no more than four plates and two drinking-glasses could be found for this purpose in the whole American camp.

In short, I refused to pay, but told them that they were at liberty to take me to a magistrate where they might prove the crime against me if they could. There was a deal of whispering together among the men who had been engaged in the brawl with the artillerymen, and presently one of them came forward and asked me: 'Say, you rascal lobster, kin you clip?'

I told him I was no barber, but he angrily bade me not to be witty at his expense. He then explained that he wished to know whether or no I was fleet of foot.

'Is this a challenge?' I asked.

'No,' he said very slowly, 'not exactly a challenge, but a tarnal provocation.'

The mob guffawed at this rejoinder and it was now borne upon me that they had concerted to make me 'run the gauntlet' to the nearest magistrate's house. Running the gauntlet, or gantlope, between the ranks of a regiment, of which each man was armed with a switch or strap, was a punishment lately borrowed from the British Army by General Washington for introduction into his own; together with the more formal punishments of flogging and riding the wooden horse. The last-named very painful punishment (which consisted of setting the offender a-straddle upon the edge of a board six feet above the ground, with muskets tied to his feet) was only awarded for serious offences, such as horse-stealing and desertion. General Washington discarded it, in the end, because of the permanent injuries it often occasioned; but by permission of Congress, the legitimate allowance of stripes in flogging was at the same time raised from the Mosaic limit of thirty-nine to that of five hundred—though, I believe, seldom more than two hundred were awarded. Running the gauntlet, which combined entertainment with castigation, was the sentence usually inflicted throughout the American forces upon soldiers who failed in their duty. The whole regiment being made the executioner, the drummers were relieved of the peculiar odium which their disagreeable duty as floggers brings upon them in every army; and there was also this advantage, that the criminal was left to the mercy of his comrades, who laid on lightly or heavily according to their estimation of the gravity of the crime and his character as a soldier.

I was kindly excused the precaution usually taken to ensure that the victim did not escape lightly, viz. a sergeant with a bayonet placed at the runner's breast walking slowly backwards to check his pace. They took me to the tavern door, and pointing out the magistrate's house at a hundred yards' distance down the hill, which was conspicuous for an American flag flying from a staff, 'There, damn you,' one cried, 'Look at the Stripes of Liberty!' Presently their leader gave me the word 'Go!' I instantly darted off. I was young and active and the slope accelerated my pace, so that I received but few blows, though a score of people, armed with hickory sticks, aimed to strike me as I passed.

The magistrate himself, a red-faced man wearing a monstrous corn-yellow wig, was on the stoep, or raised platform, which surrounded his house; he appeared to be enjoying the fun very heartily. As I leaped into the sanctuary of his parlour, he pretended surprise at my unceremonious haste, and asked me gruffly, where were my manners? The landlord soon arrived, carrying the broken glasses on a tray for a testimony against me, and claimed the fifty dollars from my pocket. But he said: 'Come now, I swear I'm a merciful man. I'll accept forty, and that's dog-cheap.'

The magistrate called me a rogue and a common brawler and, without hearing my defence, threatened me with the hulks at

Boston, where I should be fed on bread and water, did I not instantly pay. I persisted in declaring that I had no part in the outrage and challenged any person to come forward and prove it against me, demanding fair play. I observed that I had evidently raised a scruple in the conscience of the landlord's wife and daughters: for they did not venture to swear against me. Yet, the landlord himself being very insistent, the magistrate rejected my plea and repeated that to the hulks I must go, unless I laid down the mulct upon the table.

Then I said: 'As for the money, Sir, you cannot either by squeezing or threats get blood from a flint, or coin from a pauper. You are at liberty to search my pockets, and take what you find, but more cannot be effected. I have always understood the folk of Massachusetts to be a reasonable people.' Then I produced two dollars in Continental paper and an English sixpence, all of which I laid upon the table. 'As for sending me to Boston, that will only cause you trouble; nor will it pay for the drinking-glasses, which (I repeat) I did not break; and so Sergeant Gershom Hewit, who owns himself under an obligation to me for the saving of his life, would be glad to testify, were he summoned.'

The magistrate, I judged, was chary of offending Gershom Hewit. After some consultation among themselves, the matter was arranged to the general satisfaction. The price of the glasses was to be made up by a voluntary contribution of the whole company, who demanded in return the pleasure of striking at me once more, having succeeded so ill on the former occasion.

I was therefore brought to the door and held by the magistrate and his sons until my enemies were each man posted between the house and the Westborough road, all prepared to strike me. The magistrate asked for the word 'ready'; and when they gave it I was let go. Once more I darted along the line, though the ground did not favour me as before; and despite that the number of my assailants was greatly increased by the news of my arrest, which had spread through the town, I did not receive in all more than a dozen blows. Their confusion and eagerness to deal strokes upon my unprotected head spoilt their aim, and I dodged, checked and ducked with an agility that surprised even myself. They did not pursue me after I had gained the road and by rapid marching I was enabled to join my companions. However, I felt my body and head sore for many days afterwards.

CHAPTER III

ON OUR arrival at Rutland, ten miles beyond the township of Worcester, we found no preparation made for us. In a region of forest remote from any houses, we were given axes with which to fell a great number of trees, and to cut pickets from them of the length of five and twenty feet, sharpened at either end. These pickets we were then ordered to drive firmly into the earth, very close together, so that a pen was made enclosing a space of two or three acres. Only when this was accomplished were we allowed to build log huts for our shelter and accommodation; to procure boards for which we must fell more timber and convey it to a saw-mill some miles away. We were, however, allowed a few nails for our carpentry. For chairs we were content to use tree stumps or round blocks; two blocks with a plank laid over made a table; pegs served instead of cupboards.

At one angle of the pen a gate was erected and outside the gate stood the guard-house. Two American sentinels were constantly posted here and no one could go out unless he had a pass from the officer of the guard; but this was a privilege in which few were indulged, except for the felling and transport of timber. Other sentinels stood at convenient distances around the pen, armed with loaded weapons. Our provisions were rice and salt pork, delivered with a scanty hand, nor could we obtain any drink but water, unless we paid a high price to the guards. The favourite liquor in these parts was cider.

American agents were very active in attempting to procure our desertion; but little attention was paid to them except by the worst soldiers. It will not be found surprising when I relate that Brooks the Dipper was seduced from his duty. He was tempted to sell himself as substitute for a hatter of Danbury, but soon deserted the Connecticut militia regiment to which he was posted and escaped back into the

State of Massachusetts, where he was safe from apprehension, and there went to live as servant with a private family. Corporal Buchanan also left us, never to return. He had been appointed sergeant to fill a vacancy that had occurred and given money by his officer to provide shoes for the company; for he had been a cobbler before his enlistment. His pass took him as far as Worcester, where leather was to be bought, and there he bundled with a young woman at an inn, and was tempted to carnal intercourse with her. She agreed not to cry out 'rape!' only when he undertook to give her all the shoe-money. Apprehensive of punishment if he returned empty-handed, he went away to the town of Taunton, which lies about forty miles to the south of Boston; where he obtained employment at a shoemaker's and was set to do bespoke work, the customers bringing leather to the shop to be made into shoes. From his wages, and from the sale of children's shoes and whangs from the leather left over from the bespoke tasks, he contrived in six months to save a considerable sum of money. Thereupon he sent a letter to a man of the same trade as himself in the Fourteenth Regiment, urging him to desert and proposing that they should set up together in business on their own. But though Sergeant Buchanan painted the pleasures of freedom and employment in very lively colours, the man remained faithful.

In this pen we continued without employment or sufficient food, the Americans evidently intending to encourage our desertion by this means; but it was constantly impressed upon us by our officers that Congress would in the end be obliged, for the public honour of the nascent American Republic, to fulfil its obligations by our release. We therefore continued patient. Our sufferings were aggravated by a decision of General Sir Henry Clinton, who had superseded General Sir William Howe in the command of the Forces in America, no longer to send us our pay in specie. His view was that so much coin as was due to us should not be put in circulation among the Americans, who would use it for purchasing arms from France; and that this would be an inducement to them to detain us longer. Many persons from the Southern states, where Congress money was less regarded even than here, had journeyed up to our camp at Prospect Hill for the purpose of exchanging paper for coin. They had to act cautiously, for the transaction ranked as treason. Two German officers, about this time, very unkindly informed against a Virginia merchant who would not give them for their guineas as much paper as they demanded; and had him packed off to prison! Thus we suffered for the public good, and the paper money issued to us was so unwelcome to the Americans, because of its daily depreciation, that though they did not dare to refuse it, they informed us either that they had nothing to sell of what we needed, or that our money was counterfeit. It must here be observed that an immense quantity of well-counterfeited Congress notes had been printed in New York by American loyalists, and widely scattered in Revolutionary territory to undermine public faith in the genuine issue, already tottering. The paper that we tendered was therefore naturally suspect as being supplied to us by the Paymaster in New York.

We amused ourselves with boxing matches, leap-frog, races, and with card-playing so long as our worn packs held together; and also undertook theatrical performances of Shakespeare, for which I was frequently selected, as gifted with a good memory, to take principal parts. My greatest hit was as Edgar in the *Tragedy of King Lear* and I remember the hearty laugh that went up when it fell to me to complain of hunger in that character, being in one scene disguised as a ragged Tom o' Bedlam: how 'rats and mice and such small deer, Have been Tom's food for seven long year.' This touched a responsive chord, for we eked out our provisions with all manner of small birds and animals which we snared. And it was notorious that I had been badly bitten in my left hand, which festered, by a flying squirrel which I had tried to catch for the pot. And also: 'Hopdance cries in Tom's belly for two white herring. Croak not, black angel: I have no food for thee.' What would we not have given for a well-cured Dublin herring!

Jane Crumer was a popular actress and once played Desdemona to my Othello. She was, besides, the object of universal admiration and pity for the constancy which she showed to her husband. This poor fellow had indeed recovered bodily health after the head-wound he received in the fighting at Freeman's Farm, but though still a fine-looking man and a Hercules in strength was by that blow left for the remainder of his life a poor puzzle-witted innocent, unfit for any but the simplest field labour. Mrs. Jane was better off for money than most of us. To reward her services at Saratoga in fetching water from the river, the wounded officers who had benefited from her gallantry had thrown money into her lap to the amount of no less than twenty guineas.

In the course of this summer we became very familiar with the beautiful birds of the country, which we encouraged to visit us by scattering crumbs: the cardinal bird, the feathers of which were as scarlet as a new uniform coat; the blue bird, a sort of small jay, which united in its plumage all the various shades of blue from the pale-blue of early dawn to mazarine and the Royal blue of silken facings; the fire-bird which was of pure flame colour; and the hanging bird whose plumage of orange was variegated with black. Jane Crumer was given by a sentinel a nest of the hanging-bird, which resembled a hornet's nest and was suspended by hemp stalks from the extremity of a bough. The young ones proved very tractable and she taught them a variety of tricks. They would take crumbs from her lip, chirp in unison, cease at a signal, and even 'die for their country'. There was also a bird which the Americans called a robin on account of his rufous breast, but which was three times the true robin's size, and songless. These birds were greatly inferior in song to those of Ireland: we heard no twittering exultant lark, no plaintive nightingale, no melodious thrush. As for the bird which they called a blackbird and which was of the size of our blackbird, but with a collar about his neck of iridescent blueish feathers, I took a great dislike to the species. These birds had no sweet fluting song but made a harsh disagreeable noise which caused them in some parts of the country to be named 'grackles'; they were great thieves, and tyrants to lesser birds, besides being disgracefully lecherous.

A pair of grackles had a nest in a tree on the other side of the pen when we first came, and a sentinel one day shot the cock-bird for sport. This we at first thought wanton, but the widowed hen, by some means which we could not determine, called a new cock-bird to her but a few hours later, who entered into all the duties and privileges of the conjugal state. The sentinel thereupon shot this cock too, and lo, the next morning the undisconsolate widow had found a third mate. Seven cock-birds this same sentinel shot and each time the hen-bird mysteriously summoned a new one from the skies. 'Last of all the woman died also,' remarked this waggish New Englander, quoting from the Gospels, and this time discharged his small shot at the hen herself. He killed her, but the body hung suspended upside down by the claws to the bough where she was sitting. Even in death she did not lose her attraction for the opposite sex; but two days later, when her body was already decaying, a new cock appeared and began to puff out his feathers and strut and go 'grackle-grackle' at her, in the manner which we had observed in the previous courtships of this very promiscuous bird.

Being distant from any township, we saw no fruit trees in blossom, which was the great beauty of Massachusetts in the Spring, but hard by the gate there grew a beautiful dogwood tree, a sort of white rose-bush, having at first more flowers than leaves, and highly ornamental. The wood of this bush or tree was very hard and fibrous; we used it for tooth-brushes. Branches of dogwood were tied about the necks of cattle in the summer, for a virtue it possessed of reviving them if they were exhausted by the heat of the sun. The flowers lacked the odour that might be expected of their beauty. Indeed, as the birds were in general without song, so the flowers were in general without smell. Once the orchard blossoms had gone, there was no more to expect in the flowery way. Summer in New England had no shepherd's rose or honeysuckle, just as Spring came and went without primroses, cowslips, bluebells, daffodils or daisies.

However, in the woods about us there were chestnut, walnut, cedar, beech, oak, pine, and the graceful tulip-tree with its curious leaves and tulip-shaped green flowers which it bore for a fortnight together; the sassafras, the flowers of which were employed by the Americans as an agreeable substitute for that bane of their country, tea, and also as a fast yellow dye for woollens; and the red-tasselled sumach, the leaves of which the Indians smoked, and likewise used as a vulnerary, as I have related in my former volume.

The nights were very noisy in this camp on account of a colony of frogs in a marsh near by, which made a noise like a crowd at an Irish cattle fair, with numerous different tones and voices intermixed. There were also whooping owls and a night-hawk named 'whip-poor-will', from this phrase which his repeated cry suggested; he was also called The Pope from the word 'pope' which he ejaculated when he alighted upon a bough or fence-rail.

Summer passed languidly, and still we remained shut in the pen. Our officers were allowed to lodge in the farmhouses of the neighbour-hood and come in amongst us for the purpose of roll-call and other matters of regularity. But they complained of frequent ill-treatment from the inhabitants, and Mr. Bowen, who was now appointed the regular surgeon to The Ninth (so that I was returned to my ordi-nary duty) was one day set upon with a whip by a Select-man who accused him of trespassing on his estate. When he resented the insult with a blow, Mr. Bowen and two officers who accompanied him, but had taken no part in the scuffle, were haled away to the common guard-room of the camp. Here they were kept for some days and obliged at night to sleep upon the floor, where the guards squirted tobacco-juice upon them for amusement and jested profanely at their expense. It seemed that Mr. Bowen would be a long while away from us, being later confined by the civil power to the town jail of Worcester. I was therefore again appointed temporary surgeon and allowed a pass, as at Prospect Hill: much to my pleasure (though I sighed on Mr. Bowen's account), since the confinement of the pen was heavily oppressing my spirit. However, Mr. Bowen and his com-panions succeeded after a few weeks in enlarging themselves. They briefed a lawyer of Worcester who undertook (for a considerable fee) to prove a flaw in the charge against them. He did, in effect, con-vince the Assize Court that the charge was unproved: for it specified a crime against the United States, when it was evident that the breach of peace (which he did not deny on his clients' behalf) could only affect the single state of Massachusetts!

In August I was given the full rank of sergeant, to supply the vacancy caused by Buchanan's desertion. Hitherto I had done the duties of a sergeant and borne the title without drawing the pay of the rank or enjoying its privileges. It was rare for a man without interest to be advanced to sergeant's rank in so little as eight years' soldiering, and I was not a little proud of myself.

In September we heard that Sir Henry Clinton had once again applied to Congress in behalf of our army. In a letter addressed to the President of Congress, and dated New York, September 19th 1778, he had acquainted Congress that His Majesty had given him positive injunctions to repeat his demand, namely that the stipulations of the Convention of Saratoga be fulfilled, and to require permission for our embarkation at the port of Boston in transports which would be sent thither.

Congress sent the following answer, which the Earl of Carlisle (one of the Commissioners for Peace then at New York) described very justly as 'uncouth and profligate':

SIR,

Your letter of the 19th was laid before Congress and I am directed to inform you that the Congress make no answer to insolent letters.

Signed, CHARLES THOMPSON, *Sec.*

This news caused a despair among our people, and many who had seemed most loyal made no secret of their intention to desert, now that there was no honour or advantage to be gained by remaining steadfast. Even Mad Johnny Maguire took the decision to abscond. He came and shook me by the hand and, said he, 'Gerry boy, I'm off now. Now don't you look vexed at me. For while I am here kept prisoner by the Americans I am no longer in the King's Service—now, isn't that so? And if you tell me that it is any sort of desertion to leave a service that I am no longer in, then by the Holy, you're a liar! Since I may not serve my King with arms in my hand, then I scorn to eat idle bread at his expense, however poorly. So, my darling Gerry, I'm off. I shall labour on my brother Corny's farm, as he has asked me, until times change. For I'm losing my robustness and my love of living, and that's a great sorrow to me.'

I could not find it in my heart to be vexed with Mad Johnny Maguire. I pressed his hand, avowing the sincere hope that we should meet again when the war was over. But in saying this, I was well aware that the war might yet be prolonged for months and perhaps years, now that the fainting American cause had been revived by French aid. I feared too that the Spanish and Dutch would also lend a hand, when they perceived how hard set upon we were; and these fears were not long afterwards proved to be well founded.

In October I was provided with a pass to visit the town of Brook-field, a long day's march to the southward. It was a melancholy duty with which I was charged by my officers, namely to visit Sergeant Buchanan and Private Brooks in their last hours, they being both deservedly sentenced by the Assize judge to death by hanging for the crime of murder. The first news that we received of this sentence was contained in a letter to Lieutenant-Colonel Hill from Sergeant Buchanan, which ran in terms something like these:

To Lieutenant-Colonel John Hill, Cmdg The Ninth Regiment in the Convention Army at Rutland

HONOURED SIR,

It is with great grief and true contrition that I lay before you my present case. You will be aware that in the month of May last I was commissioned by my company officer to provide boots for the company, and that I was supplied with the sum of one hundred and fifty dollars in Continental paper to purchase leather, thread, lapstone, awls &c for the making of them. This money was stole from me at an inn and getting no satisfaction for the loss, but being ashamed to return without, I repaired to the town of Taunton, where I worked at my trade in order to make good my account. Having saved so much, I bent my way back to Rutland in

July, hoping for forgiveness from your Honour; when I fell in with Private Thompson, who had run off from the Grenadier Company and who informed me that I had been posted as a deserter and Sergeant Roger Lamb appointed in my place. I thereupon resolved to escape to Montreal, where I had left behind me my wife and infant child, in the hope of obtaining pardon by means of General Sir Guy Carleton, to whom I would report for duty.

On my route to Canada, I passed through this town of Brookfield where I was noticed by a Mrs. Spooner, daughter to the well-known General Ruggles, who was remarkable for her attachment to the Royal Cause and offered to assist me with every means in her power to run safe through to Canada. Unfortunately for her, Mr. Spooner her husband was very hot in the Rebel cause, and this occasioned domestic disagreement and a murderous odium in her heart against him. The common bond of attachment to His Majesty's cause drew Mrs. Spooner and myself together, so that I became greatly enamoured of her, though unaware that the reciprocal warmth which she professed for me was only a sham. For her object (I am now aware), was to make me her Cat's Paw, and to be rid of her husband in order to marry her hired man. On Mr. Spooner's going for a journey to Boston, she disclosed to me a plot she had arranged for removing him by poison as he dined at a wayside inn; overcoming my scruples by observing that he was an officer in the Rebel Army and therefore to slay him in time of war was 'killing no murder'.

This plot miscarrying, on account (she said) of his drinking so heartily at the inn that he vomited up the poison, he returned unexpectedly to his residence and discovered me sitting in the parlour, at which he expressed much displeasure and, using many profanities, which I will not Detail here, ordered me to begone. Mrs. Spooner found me another lodging, and secretly communicated with me there, by means of the hired man, her paramour. She assured me that if I assisted her to rid the world of this Monster, she would confer considerable property upon me in goods and land and accompany me in the quality of my wife wherever I wished. I replied that I shrank from perpetrating any deed of violence and that I owed a duty to my wife and infant child; to which she replied that I was a soldier and would be failing in my duty if I hesitated to do away with so violent an enemy of my Sovereign. If I consented, she would safeguard me as far as the Canadian border (where her husband possessed property which would be hers at his death), describing me as her man-servant if I would not consent to be called husband; and there let me run across to freedom.

At this juncture, Private Brooks of my Company happened to pass through Brookfield while 'whipping the cat', which is a cant term in use hereabouts for obtaining casual employment at farm-houses during a vagabond life. In a foolish hour I took Brooks into a partnership of the intended violent transaction, promising him half the hard money that Mrs. Spooner had undertaken to give me. Mr. Spooner having ridden some distance from home in the day, we determined to dispatch him on his return at night. Brooks was chosen to be the executioner, for I shrank from embruing my hands in the blood of an unarmed man; and of Brooks' former desperate character your Honour will not be ignorant.

That evening Brooks, armed with a heavy log of walnut wood, waited in a convenient corner near the door of the Spooner mansion and fractured the skull of this ill-fated gentleman as he made his entrance. We threw the body down a deep draw-well and Mrs. Spooner then provided us with a quantity of money and advised us to keep out of the way until Mr. Spooner's disappearance should be accounted for by her in some credible manner. She could not, however, prevail upon the hired man to remain with her. He went off in our company, saying that a woman who could exult as she did over the battered body of her husband was no wife for him. His defection caused Mrs. Spooner much distress and she was rash enough to inform her neighbours that a party of British deserters had robbed her house and, after murdering her husband, had carried off his body. The hue and cry was therefore raised and we were apprehended at the town of Linn, where I was working in a shoe manufactory. Thus our common guilt was discovered, and the body drawn out from the well.

It was not until the hand of the Law was laid upon my shoulder that I became fully aware of the horrid nature of the crime to which I had been accessory; and when sentenced to death by the Assize Judge I became in a manner resigned to my fate. For I was advised by the Congregational minister who visited me in prison that, were I to be truly penitent and make complete confession of my scarlet wickedness, he would inform me how to enter into eternity with a calm mind, trusting in the extraordinary mercy of God vouchsafed to sinners. My heart was touched and imme- diately I knelt down to pray with him. After wrestling in prayer for some hours, I saw the light and knew in my heart that I was pardoned by God! My comrade in wickedness, Private Brooks, has also undergone a total change of heart since we were confined, and awaits with impatience the stroke of death which will set his soul free from its erring body and admit it into everlasting mansions.

May it please your Honour to forgive both of us in your heart for the disgrace that we have brought upon the Regiment, and of your well-known generosity of mind to send one of our former comrades to us here to be present at the hour of our execution, so that we may not die wholly encompassed by strangers upon this alien soil. We would esteem it a great favour were Sergeant R. Lamb to be selected for this service, as being a suitable repository for our last wishes and farewells, and a person whose forgiveness for past offences we both hope to hear from his own lips.

I am, Sir,

your greatly obliged and truly penitent Servant, the Sinner

J. BUCHANAN

(formerly Sergeant)

BROOKFIELD TOWN JAIL
Oct. 15th 1778

During my expedition to Brookfield, which I accomplished in a single day, I refreshed myself at a wayside inn and was there given by the landlord, a judicious person, an account of the recent prog- ress of the war, which disproved or clarified many wild rumours that had been current in our camp. He informed me that peace proposals had been made to Congress by the British Parliament, and Commissioners sent to implement these, soon after the news of the French alliance had been published. These proposals included an abnegation of the right to tax America, as of every other sovereign claim which might stand in the way of the free development of the American people, and an amnesty for all rebels—if only the link which joined the two countries, a common fealty to the Crown, might not be dissolved. But so much hatred against Great Britain had now been stirred up, and the people of America hoped for so great an extension of their trade by the French alliance, that Congress shortly rebuffed the Commissioners. This decision grieved a great many Americans who still considered themselves English; but they were powerless against the clamorous voices of the Patriots, who considered England a nation doomed to well-merited destruction.

Our main army under General Clinton had at the end of June quitted the city of Philadelphia (where General Benedict Arnold was now appointed military governor), and, falling back across New Jersey, had checked General Washington's Army in the stubborn rear-guard action of Monmouth, and come safe back to New York. General Washington had moved to Hudson's River, which he crossed; he then encamped at White Plains, on the Highlands, threatening New York and making his principal stronghold on the river the fortress of West Point, about half-way upstream to Albany. Our forces at New York had then carried out one or two very energetic and successful forays on either side of Hudson's River, and against towns and islands of the New England coast. Great booty was taken and much shipping of a privateering sort destroyed.

As for the French, they had hitherto disappointed the American hopes, though a fleet of theirs greatly outnumbering our own squadron had arrived in American waters and attempted, in conjunction with General Sullivan and a large force of New England militia, to cut off and capture the British garrison of Newport, Rhode Island. A common disgust soon arising between these precarious allies, the French had taken offence and sailed away. Moreover, a party of amorous French sailors in Boston so offended against the morals of this saintly place that a French officer was killed in the streets by the citizens. The alliance would have been ended there and then, had not the Massachusetts Council, fearful of the consequences of this act of popular folly, hastily voted a monument to the murdered Frenchman. The crime was politically charged against captured British sailors and ourselves, the wretched Convention Army! Many of General Sullivan's men had meanwhile deserted to our forces and, his siege of Newport becoming dangerous, it was raised. In fine, the war was not going so disadvantageously for our cause, after all; though against our successes must be set the capture by American privateers of near a thousand British merchantmen of a gross value of £2,000,000.

The same landlord also gave me news of a very bloody raid by American Loyalists and Indians of the Six Nations on a frontier district of Pennsylvania: one whole valley, that of the Wyoming river, was completely devastated, and many prisoners burned at the stake. I said, I sincerely hoped that this account of Indian savagery was no less exaggerated than previous ones.

He showed no animosity to me as a soldier in the British service, but only a sort of pity, which I resented as strongly. He told me that he had visited Dublin some years previously, and asked in a very sincere way, how I could reconcile my duty with my good sense? Though I evidently did not regard myself as a slave, and had a pride in my loyal subordination, did I not consider the free soil of America as in every way preferable to that of Ireland? He said that, for his part, he had seen so many unpleasant sights amidst the grandeur and pageantry of the rich in Dublin City that the total impression was one of pain and horror. Such hosts of street beggars, such troops of poverty-stricken children, such a mass of degraded poor people! How the labourers of Ireland, and of England herself, he said, contrived to live with such low wages and such high prices for the staple commodities, was above his comprehension. Yet with all this poverty and woe, taxation was laid upon the public with merciless severity, to fatten the minions of royalty and provide pensions and sinecures for the idle gentry. He showed me a newspaper where the present miserable condition of Ireland was set forth, and where it was reported (without much exaggeration, as my readers will be aware) that my country was then nearly ruined. The rupture with the colonies had closed the chief market of the linen trade, the provision trade was annihilated by a Royal proclamation, the price of black cattle and wool had sunk, thousands of manufacturers were forced to lock up their works. In Dublin bread had risen to famine prices and hungry crowds paraded the Liberties, carrying a black fleece in token of their distress; while in the country 'the wretches that remained had scarcely the appearance of human creatures'.

I felt it difficult to restrain my tears, as I perused this journal, for thinking of the want to which my own parents and sisters would necessarily be reduced and of my present impotence in affording them any help; yet the landlord's questions did not have the effect upon me that he intended. I informed him that, though he might consider it a depravity in me, I would in all events remain loyal to the King to whom I had sworn allegiance; and that the present distresses of Ireland and England were largely caused by the Americans' repudiation of this same allegiance, which had caused enormous suffering and expense in all three countries.

He remarked: 'You are an unusual sort of Irishman, I guess. Is it not true, pray, that the native character and political propensities of your people have ever been toward rebellion—that the Irish have ever been uniformly intolerant of the rule of the English Kings?'

'That, Sir,' I replied, 'is a calumny which has become hereditary to historians. The reverse is the case: during a matter of twenty reigns that have succeeded the first submission of the Irish princes, the fidelity of Ireland to the Kings of England has been very seldom interrupted. Irish soldiers have often been brought over to England to protect their sovereigns against the insurrections of British rebels. During the same period above thirty civil wars, greater or less, raged within the larger island—four British monarchs were dethroned, three murdered.'

He changed his tack: 'Well, if you are right and I have been misinformed, then on the contrary I am astonished that the unrelenting cruelties and misrule of the British governors have not goaded you into disaffection: for my part, I would never live upon any but free American soil.'

I replied, as to this, that I suspected the political well-being of a country that cast out its Tories, equally with that of a country that hanged its Whigs. But I contented him by saying that there were many customs and inclinations in America that pleased me, and that might with profit be transplanted into Ireland: for example, the hospitality and mutual assistance afforded to one another by the back-country people, and the high value set upon education. Yet I swore I would never turn my back upon the land of my birth, and would labour on my return to do all in my power to better its condition in the light of my novel experiences—as a loyal subject of the King.

It was not until some months later that I received news that my father had deceased in Dublin almost on the very day of this conversation, in poverty and debt, and in great grief at a report that had reached him of my death in the fighting at Saratoga. He died, however, at a time when Irish affairs were beginning at last to right themselves. It will be remembered how, at the close of this same year, King George was graciously pleased to consider the demands of my fellow-countrymen, to which on the 4th of November (Dutch William's birthday) they called his attention with loyal if extraordinary manifestations. On that day forty thousand Irish Volunteers, who had been enrolled to repel the raids on our coasts threatened by the American privateer captain, Paul Jones, paraded before King William's statue on College Green in Dublin City; firing volleys into the air, waving flags and trailing cannon to which were tied placards inscribed, 'Free Trade or This!' The display had immediate effect. In December, Resolutions were adopted in the Parliament at Westminster, granting to us Irish the free export of our products and manufactures, and privileges in trading with British colonies equal to those enjoyed by the merchants of England and Scotland.

At Brookfield I procured admission to the jail with little difficulty, by telling the turnkey that the Methodist minister who was Chaplain to the prisoners would know that I was expected to arrive. The Chaplain was fetched and brought me to the cell, where I was greeted by Buchanan and Brooks in such sanctified phrases that I was perfectly astonished. Both implored my pardon, which I readily gave, for the frauds, deceits and cruelties that they had practised upon me—some of which I had no knowledge of, while others I had forgotten—and attempted forthwith to convert me to their own religious ecstasy. Brooks before his confinement had not only been notoriously profane but almost illiterate; yet since his confinement he had attended so much to a devout perusal of the Holy Scriptures that he could now read them with facility, explain them to his unhappy cell-mates in an edifying manner and even select the chapters most appropriate to their sad condition.

The day of execution, which was that following my arrival, was a severe trial for me. I wished to humour the poor fellows by letting them suppose that they had affected my conversion; but honesty forbade. It was not that I was a disbeliever, or that I was addicted to evil courses—for I now lived, of necessity almost, a regular and decent life—but that to profess a change of heart would mean abandoning all hope of resuming my connexion with Kate Harlowe and our child. For this still remained with me the sweetest dream of all and altogether ineradicable from my fancy.

Mrs. Spooner, the murderess, was to die on the same day, but indulged loud hopes of escaping condign punishment. She pleaded pregnancy as an argument for being respited, and seemed impenitent a good deal. Her Tory opinions, however, fastened the noose tightly about her throat, and sealed the fate of her unborn child. The gallows were fixed at a distance of two miles from the jail and a holiday crowd of sightseers attended; who were punished for their idle curiosity by a great storm of thunder, followed with copious rain, that all of a sudden broke upon them from a fine and serene sky and drenched them to the bone. Mrs. Spooner met her end with hysterical screaming and fierce vituperations; but Buchanan and Brooks remained true to their new-found convictions and died with the name of Jesus upon their lips.

I must add one last note to my account of this ignominious catastrophe. Buchanan's widow, known as 'Terrible Annie', who had been Mortal Harry's widow before, and that of a drummer in the Thirty-Third even before that, was not sorry when the news of his death reached her at Montreal. She was a woman with the same mysterious power as the American hen-blackbird, or grackle, of attracting new mates to console her in her frequent widowhood. Her fourth husband was a quartermaster-sergeant of the Forty-Seventh Regiment, and passed for the greatest rogue in the whole Service.

CHAPTER IV

EARLY IN November 1778, when we had already, by considerable labour and thought, improved our slight huts so as to make them snug enough to shelter us through another severe New English winter, we were given our route for the back country of Virginia. Our destination was said to be Charlotteville, which lay near eight hundred miles away. The object was that the Southern States should bear their share of the expense of maintaining us, especially now that we were without pay from our own authorities; also, that we should be moved beyond reach of rescue. We were in great distress for want of money to undertake this march, and our commanding officers met to consult upon a means of procuring some. General Burgoyne had returned to England on parole, and General Phillips, who now commanded, spoke very warmly on the subject of our want of cash, protesting his inability to effect anything: 'Good God, my lords and gentlemen, what would you have me do? I cannot make money. I wish to Heaven you could slit me into paper dollars—I would cheerfully submit for the good of the troops.' However, the Paymaster somehow succeeded in obtaining enough currency to enable us to march, something less than two hundred pounds sterling in value but an enormous mass of paper; and this was distributed to the regiments. Our chief remaining distress was the raggedness of our jackets and breeches. Unfortunately, a ship that arrived at Boston under a flag of truce, with the uniform clothing long overdue to us, came just too late for its distribution to us. The march could not be postponed. However, we obtained some shoes, linen and blankets and on November 10th said good-bye to the pen. We resented having been tricked into clearing so many acres of forest-land and building enough good huts to accommodate several American families; for this would add greatly to the wealth of the proprietor without any benefit accruing to ourselves. However, we did not in revenge burn down our barracks, lest the route be countermanded.

From Rutland we marched south-east at about twenty-five miles every day, under guard of a regiment of Pennsylvanian Germans, and passed the Connecticut River at Endfield. This stage of the journey had little novelty for us, since we had made our way across the same part of Massachusetts, though a little to the north, a year before during our journey into captivity. Yet it was interesting to me to note the different degrees of civilization and prosperity attained in this region or that through which we passed. These were announced by the several sorts of fences that enclosed, first, the cleared land, where all was level; next, the half-cleared, where tree-stumps remained among the corn-stubble; and lastly, the uncleared, where the oaks and other hard timber were as yet only girdled and left to the wind for felling. The rudest sort of fence was a tangle of the light branches of trees; the next rudest was the Virginian fence, made by trunks of trees laid one upon the other at an obtuse angle, in a zigzag manner—a drunken man hereabouts was said to 'make Virginian fences' when he tacked to and fro along a road; then came the post and rail fence; and when a farmer had achieved so settled a dominion that he could go to the trouble of clearing his land of stones, he piled them up to form a wall with a ramp of earth, into which he drove palings of split timber—but this was very rare to see.

We were on the whole extremely fortunate in the weather, which was temperate and clear, though the frosts were severe during the nights when we bivouacked in the dismal fir woods, seeking shelter in the crevices of the rocks; and the rutted roads crackled with ice every morning. 'I swear God has turned Tory,' a surly old dame cried, looking angrily up at the blue skies as we marched past her door. General Washington had been considerate enough to supply wagons for our women and children, of whom there were about two hundred with us.

Our route now lay through the northern borders of Connecticut, but most of the so-called townships (as Endfield, Suffield and Sunbury, which we passed in this order) were not regular towns: each consisted of one or two hundred scattered farms belonging to a single corporation that sent a member to the State Assembly. A meeting-house or church, with perhaps an inn and one or two houses, marked the centre of this township, but often the church stood singly. We observed that the interior of many houses that we passed was only half finished. The man who cleared the land and constructed the house from the felled trees had usually completed only one half of it and left the other a mere shell (though with roof and glazed windows complete) to be boarded and furnished within by his son when he took a wife. We were pleased by the swarms of healthy children who rushed out of every house on our route, and by the handsomeness of the women who passed us on the road, often riding alone on horse-back or driving their own carriages. The weather continuing fine, they were dressed in white aprons, calico gowns and elegant hats. We learned that though every man was a farmer, most men also plied some mechanical trade, as tanner, sawyer, whitesmith, blacksmith, physician or tooth-drawer. Besides, every woman was mistress of so many domestic arts, including spinning, weaving of woollens and linsey-woollens, broom and basket-making—in which labours she was assisted by her children—that the country was in a manner inde-pendent of the industry of cities.

We marched through a fertile river-valley at New Hartford, where were abundance of geese and turkey-birds, and hogs of a prodigious size wearing around their necks triangular wooden collars which prevented them from breaking the fences of the cultivated fields. Horses and cattle wore a similar contrivance. There was a scent of cider-making in the air, or perhaps they were distilling cider into apple-jack spirits.

At the small town of Sharon some of us were allowed by a woman to inspect an exceedingly ingenious mill invented by one Joel Harvey, for which he was awarded twenty pounds by the American Society of Arts and Sciences. One water-wheel set a whole compli-cated machinery in motion for threshing, winnowing, grinding and bolting wheat; and for simultaneously beating and dressing hemp and flax. But the two branches could be disconnected if necessary, and only one operation maintained.

Now we had reached the confines of the State of Connecticut and were approaching Hudson's River in the State of New York. The time had therefore arrived for putting into effect a daring resolution that I had formed so soon as news reached us of our proposed transplantation to Virginia: I would quit the column of march and make an escapade to General Clinton's army in New York! In this venture the river itself would be my guide to safety, nor would I need to follow it more than seventy miles downstream from the point where our army was intended to cross over. I concluded that it would be much more agreeable, and indeed less dangerous, to have companions in my flight and therefore considered which of them I should approach.

I naturally first sounded Terry Reeves, as the most courageous and resourceful man in the Regiment, but he would not hear of the attempt. He asked, was I unaware that our officers (fearful of the regiments' being, at our eventual return to Europe, reduced to mere skeletons) had issued orders that any soldier absent from his corps for more than four-and-twenty hours should be returned as a deserter, and if brought back again by the American civil or military power, should be flogged without mercy? I replied that I was not unaware of this, but that the hope of striking another blow for my King and Country weighed more with me than any such orders. I could not convince Terry, and went away sadly. Smutchy Steel, however, now an excellent soldier, showed himself eager to accompany me. He said that, much as he loved Terry, he could not be sorry that he was not to be one of us: for Terry brought bad luck on himself and his companions in any venture, and never seemed to escape some injury—which was true enough. He recommended as our third companion Richard Harlowe, who had that very morning expressed a wish to 'make a run for it'. Smutchy reminded me that Harlowe was acquainted with the French and German languages, which would perhaps be of great service to us—especially the German, when it came to outwitting our guards. There were few companions whom I would have selected with less eagerness than Harlowe, but what Smutchy had observed about the usefulness to us of foreign languages struck me as very true; nor was anyone else of our acquaintance so gifted. 'Very well,' I said to Smutchy, 'let it be Harlowe, for beggars cannot be choosers. But do you speak to him yourself on my behalf. I have no wish to approach him directly.'

Smutchy presently reported that Richard Harlowe was ready to join our company. We were then at a place named Nine Partners, about forty miles to the north-west of the place where we now learned we were to cross. Smutchy obtained from Jane Crumer, who borrowed it from one of the soldiers' wives, an almanack for the current year 'being the second after Leap Year and second of American Independence, calculated for the meridian of Boston by Daniel George.' He handed me the book, saying with satisfaction: 'There is good news for us here.'

I opened at random and, to cod him, began to read a passage upon how to rear turkeys successfully: 'Plunge the chick into a vessel of water, the very hour if possible, at least the very day it is hatched, forcing it to swallow one whole peppercorn, after which return it to the mother, &c.'

'No, not that,' he protested.

I read again: 'The Foreign Vintage rival'd by the Gardens of America: Or, a Receipt to make WINE as good as most that is imported, and much cheaper. To a Gallon of Water, add a Gallon of Currants—'

'No, no,' he protested again rather testily.

I read further: 'The highest price is given at the Printing Office in Newbury Port, for all sorts of Linen and Cotton RAGS—the smallest pieces are (in proportion to their bigness) as serviceable as large. Good WRITING-PAPER will be given in exchange, at a very low price, if wanted'—'why, Smutchy, have you a mind to sell your old shirt for a sheet of foolscap?'

He tore the book from my hands. 'Now, don't be so provoking, Sergeant Gerry,' he said. 'Read here where the page is turned down. There's a new moon in two days' time, November 18th, at ten o'clock at night; and there the coming weather is forecasted also.'

Indeed, for all my jesting, it was a matter of awful concern to us both what aspect the Heavens would wear for our flight. So at last

I consented to read the prophecy for the next five days: *flying clouds and strong south winds which bear down all before them, and perhaps some rain or snow. MORE FOUL WEATHER.* 'Now, I wonder,' says I, laughing, 'is that the truth or just another smart Yankee trick to overreach us?'

'Neighbour Daniel George wouldn't dare deceive his public with regard to the moon,' was Smutchy's surmise, 'and I expect he knows the usual run of the weather in these parts. Well, then, the moon will not trouble us, being too young. As for the rain or snow, let it be rain and the more rain the better, for the sake of the powder in the rebels' priming-pans, and of the darkness. Faith, let it be as dark as the inside of a poacher's dog, I don't care. As for the strong south wind, that same will blow in our faces and bring us news of danger the sooner. God save Great Daniel George, I say.'

The country between Nine Partners and the river was well cultivated, and the inhabitants were for the most part Dutch. All this country had formerly belonged to the Dutch Republic which, I believe, exchanged it with the King of England for the spice-lands of Surinam. A few of our officers were well bitten by the Dutch landlord where they lodged at Opel, or Hopewell, our next stage. He and his family behaved very civilly and attentively to them and would scarcely permit them to pay for what they had consumed. The officers, thereby concluding that the household were Loyalists, opened their hearts and observed that it was a great shame that British officers should be put to such expense, which ought to fall upon Congress. The landlord then ran from the room and made out an enormous bill, which he insisted upon being paid. The officers, declaring it to be exorbitant in every particular and three times what had been agreed, this Dutchman said: 'Yes, gentlemen, but I had thought that Congress were to defray all your expenses, and did not wish to be severe upon them. Now that I know that it will fall upon you, I can't take a farthing less than this bill.' They were compelled to discharge it.

It was on November 17th, from our bivouacs in a wood a few miles beyond Hopewell (a name of good omen) that we made our attempt to regain our freedom, at breakfast-time on the morning of our departure. The Army was to cross Hudson's River that afternoon; and General Washington himself would be present to see it go by. Richard Harlowe had cultivated the acquaintance of a German corporal of the guard and now obtained permission from him to go to a house a hundred yards beyond the line of sentries, in order, he said, to buy a few eggs. He promised two eggs to the Corporal. After being gone for about three minutes, he came back (as I had suggested to him) as if to reassure the German that he contemplated no desertion. His account was that the farmer was sawing wood and would not give his wife the key of the hen-house, which he kept locked against the depredations of the soldiery, until he had finished his daily stent. This task would take him a good hour, which was longer than we could afford to wait; but it could be shortened if two or three British soldiers could be found to help him with it. The Corporal believed this story, because the sound of a saw could be heard proceeding from the farm; and Harlowe, with his consent, then called upon us to bear a hand. We agreed with feigned unwillingness.

We walked slowly through the trees to the farm, in order to allay the Corporal's suspicions; but immediately we were fairly out of sight began running away through the woods, avoiding any beaten track, and within a few minutes had put a mile at least between us and the line of sentries.

'Now,' said I, as we paused for breath on the banks of a rivulet, 'who's for pushing on, and who's for lying hid?'

Harlowe and Smutchy were for pushing on, but I argued that it was better to lurk close to the camp. In the first place, the searchers would expect us to go off as far as possible; in the second, if unluckily we were apprehended, it would be better that this should happen before the twenty-four hours had elapsed that would make us deserters. If we pushed on and were caught at a distance we might be sent back too late to benefit by the grace.

Harlowe held that the farther we ran, the less likely were we to be caught and brought back; but against this I argued that the farther we ran the more people we were likely to meet who might inform upon us.

'How do you expect to get to New York then, you sot?' he asked.

I patiently explained that, though our prime intention was to get safe through, we must reckon with the danger of apprehension. In the latter event, our hope lay in being caught either soon or so much later that our guards would by then have given up the search—which they would shorten doubtless in order not to miss their sight of General Washington, whom they looked upon as a national hero—and would have crossed the river. I believed that the Dutchmen, if they caught us, would not trouble to row us across the river under guard; for desertions in general were encouraged. Our greatest peril would be in the last stage of our flight, when we attempted to rejoin the British Army.

Smutchy then came over to my opinion, so that we were in a majority against Harlowe. We crossed the rivulet and soon perceived a small hut on the verge of a wood. Smutchy went forward to reconnoitre, and after a while motioned to us that all was well. We came up, knocked, entered and there found a poor woman, with two young children, in the act of filling their maple-wood bowls with 'soupaun' or maize porridge, as they sat at table.

The woman proved to be a Mrs. Eder, a New York woman, widow to a Dutchman who had been lately killed by a falling tree. The family was in very poor circumstances, as we could learn from the poverty of the kitchen furniture, and the pinched faces of the children. The little boy was sadly crying as we came in: 'No more 'lasses, Mama? No more 'lasses!' And she answered as sadly: 'No, my little one, no molasses and no milk neither, for the cow's gone dry!'

I apologized to Mrs. Eder for our early visit and entreated her to hide us in her house for a few hours. I told her that our German guards would soon miss us and make search for us, adding: 'I do not know what your politics are, Madam, and shall not enquire; but I can see that your little ones would do well this winter on a little butter and milk and molasses, which this money will purchase for them.' Here I showed her three Spanish silver dollars, and could see at once that I had come to the right market with them. The widow, who was young but had lost all title to beauty through the hard life she had evidently led, living alone in this wilderness, eagerly agreed to all that I asked. She even undertook to observe the movements of the guards, and if necessary mislead them by giving them false information.

'Where will you hide us?' I asked. 'Is there perhaps a hollow tree that you know in the woods, or a cave?'

She shook her head. 'The best place for you,' she said, 'is right here in this house. I will go out and lock up, and you may be sure that if any guard comes he will not be at pains to break down the door, unless he has previous information that you are here.'

When Harlowe asked her, how did he know she was not a double-dealer, she replied that she would leave her youngest child in our care as a pledge of her sincerity.

I said: 'Madam, we do not doubt your sincerity, but we accept your offer gladly. The little lass is a sweet child and will be good company to us. Can you give us some provisions into the bargain, for we have not yet breakfasted?'

She gave us what little remained of the soupaun, a few sour apples and a pickled pig's tail, which was all that she had in the house to offer. Presently she went off with her little boy, after locking us all into a small, clean apartment; where the little girl amused us with her prattle, of which we could understand hardly a word, being lisping English of the backwoods, mixed with Dutch.

We spent our time compiling our geographical knowledge of Hudson's River and reckoning on our chances of successful evasion. There were some Dutch books in a case, but they treated of law and theology, with not an Atlas among them. We knew that we were now about a day's march above the fortress of West Point, but upon the opposite bank, and that General Washington's Continental army lay squarely between us and safety, posted on the Eastern Highlands. Smutchy was of opinion that we must, if possible (using this woman as a first link in the chain), obtain recommendations from stage to stage that would persuade persons well disposed to our cause to help us through to safety, and travel only by night. I believed him to be right and Harlowe did not disagree.

About ten o'clock in the morning we heard voices: a German talking in halting English to an American. The German said in a deep voice: 'We must make search inside this hut, brother.'

'No, Hans,' drawled the American, 'Cannot you see, the key hangs on the nail outside? You can save yourself the pains. If the prisoners were there, I calculate the door would be locked from the inside.'

'Dumbhead,' returned the German, 'the people of the hut, perhaps they have locked the Englanders in from outside, not so?'

The American retorted: 'You are a dumbhead yourself. If the people of the hut wished to shelter deserters against us, I reckon, they would not have left the key hanging up where we could find it; unless perhaps they were dumbheads, too. It an't reasonable.'

The German insisted: 'Perhaps they have forgotten it in their haste. I go to see.'

'You're a mighty thorough man, damn you!' was the reply.

'At least I will look in at the window,' the obstinate Hans said.

We had been unaware that Mrs. Eder had left the key hanging on the door, and quaked inwardly when we heard the German approaching the hut with a heavy tread. He went first to peer in at the kitchen window, where he reported that nobody was at home.

Then he came to our window. We shuffled and lay close against the wall under the sill, to put ourselves below the angle of his vision as he looked through the glass. The child was lying in her cradle, sucking a stick of coarse sugar that I had found in my pocket and given her as a means of pacification. The German must have made some ludicrous grimaces at the child, for she set up a howl.

He told her playfully that she was a naughty child and must not fear a poor honest German. Then we heard him depart.

He shouted back to the American: 'Excuse me, I was wrong. There is one pretty child in that apartment who eats candy. The mother, she go away and lock it in there, so that it shall not fall in the fire, and do it a mischief, yes? Pardon! Let us go, brother!'

We could then hear them searching in the barns and sheds contiguous, and the attic over our heads, reached by a ladder from without; but they never entered the house. However, the American, standing close to our window, reported to an officer who had come up that they had investigated the whole place and found nothing.

Then the voices died away in the distance. The danger having passed, I said to Smutchy Steel: 'Now, faith, only a woman could have contrived that trick of hanging the key so invitingly on the nail! And I swear no man but a German would have been industrious enough even to peep in at the windows.'

'Ay, just like a woman,' asserted Smutchy.

'She nearly ruined us by over-shrewdness,' said the contrary Harlowe. 'And that is just like a woman, too.'

There were no further disturbances, and at nightfall the woman returned and, finding us still where she had left us, evinced great relief. She picked up her little girl and hugged her close. 'O I declare,' she cried, between tears and laughter, 'you have mussed your nice dress with a candy stick! What a pickle you are in, you greedy little wretch.'

Then she turned to us: 'You see, my friends, that I have been faithful to you. Your comrades have by now all crossed the River with most of their guards. There were very few American soldiers to be seen when I came away.'

To the three promised dollars I added a fourth from our store, believing that the outlay would justify itself. Then we told her that we intended to make our escape into New York, which we had not yet disclosed to her.

'You have set yourselves a very hard task, my friends,' she said. 'Now, sweet Pieterkin, run off and play with your little sister, for I wish to think in peace.' She pressed her knuckles hard against her temples. We did not interrupt her cogitations, which presently bore fruit. She gave us very minute directions to the house of her husband's sister. This woman was married to a Rhode Islander who was very lukewarm in his loyalty to the revolutionary cause. We must pass through a pine forest, around a naked hill and over a considerable stream. She herself had not been that way since the heavy flood of a month before, and feared that we might find the bridge carried away. Thereafter our route lay through cornfields and cleared ground for another two miles; and on the northern skirts of the next forest we would find the house we required, which lay remote from any others and was to be recognized by a ring of clipped red cedars which enclosed a duck-pond. The husband's name was Captain Webber.

We took affectionate leave of our faithful hostess and her children. I gave the little boy the crystal prism I had obtained from Diamond Island on Lake George in the previous year; which greatly delighted him. I told him to set it in the window when the sun was up next morning, for it would throw 'jackies' (or rainbows) upon the ceiling.

We followed our directions with care and picked up each consequent landmark until we hit the stream, which had the same name, Fishkill Creek, as that which watered General Schuyler's domain at Saratoga. The current was rapid, and I could not plumb the depth with a long stick; nor was there any sign of a bridge where our track ended. Neither Harlowe nor Smutchy knew how to swim, but I proposed to go across myself, taking one of them at a time with me. I assured them that if they would faithfully and courageously do as I said, namely gently lay their hands on my loins, striking out with their feet at the same time, I would soon ferry them over. However, they both declined my offer, as too hazardous an attempt in the dark, and proposed to trace the creek upwards in order to discover a fording place.

We were in luck; for we had not gone more than two hundred yards upstream before we found a tall tree that had been felled to lie across the river at a narrow place; and so went over dry-shod, after all. Such conveniences for crossing rivers are very common in America.

We considered now that we were well on our way, and must henceforth get along in good earnest.

CHAPTER V

AT LENGTH we arrived at Captain Webber's substantial house, to which we had been directed, and recognized it by the ring of cedars. There was no light showing in any of the windows, which was not surprising, for it had passed midnight. We went up to the door and rapped loudly.

A man's voice called to us: 'Who's there?'

I replied: 'Three friends of your sister-in-law, the widow Eder.'

'What friends?' the same man enquired, in some alarm.

Smutchy was bold enough to reply: 'Three British soldiers.'

A woman's voice then cried: 'Begone, soldiers. We want no Britainers here, and my brother Yan's sister should be ashamed to foist any such upon us. She was ever a troublemaker in the family.'

The man here evidently remonstrated with his wife, for upon our continuing to plead for admittance he came downstairs in his shirt, carrying a lantern, and unbolted the door for us. He was a tall, large man and wore a night-cap. 'Now, gentlemen,' he said, 'what is your business? My wife is greatly alarmed by your appearance at this hour and asks you to hasten your explanations. Besides, it is very cold.'

We went into the kitchen, which had a brick floor and was tolerably well furnished with papered walls, pewter platters on the shelves, and furniture in the heavy Dutch style. A tremendous ducking gun was suspended above the chimney shelf and a tall brass-faced clock ticked in a corner. I also observed a stuffed Bengalese parrot in a glass case.

'Put this about your legs, Sir,' said Richard Harlowe, taking from his haversack a new English blanket, one of those that had been issued to us just before we began our march, 'and you will feel warmer.'

'This is good wool,' he said, admiring it. 'We have but two thin blankets left to us: the rest were taken from us for the use of the militia, though I am a captain myself.'

'It is yours, and another as good besides, if you can conduct us safely to New York,' Smutchy assured him.

'It is mighty good wool,' he said again. 'But I should require a deal of money from you, if I were to consent. It is a dangerous piece of work, very dangerous, that you propose.'

'Take us to the British outposts,' I said, 'and you shall have all the hard money in our possession, which amounts in gold and silver to twenty dollars, besides the two blankets as advance payment. Moreover, the Commander-in-Chief, Sir Henry Clinton, will give you a further reward, a bounty of three guineas a man. That will cock you up for a whole winter, Captain Webber.'

But Mrs. Webber, who was gaunt and grey-haired, was by now standing in the doorway of the parlour where we were discoursing, and overheard what I had said. 'William,' she cried fiercely, 'you shall not go. As your devoted wife and the mother of your three fine boys, I will not permit you to go—no, though I have to offer you violence to prevent it.'

'Why, wife,' he said, attempting to conciliate her, 'times are hard, you know, and I confess the fee they offer is very advantageous, if I could be sure of that bounty. It would buy you a new dress and stockings and shoes for all the boys, besides the sheep of which we spoke to-day.'

She burst into tears, whether real or feigned I cannot pretend to judge. 'What!' said she, dramatically: 'Do you mean to break my heart, by running into the jaws of death? Would you deprive me of a husband, like my poor sister-in-law Eder, and orphan our boys? You know well that there are several camps and garrisons on the East Highlands between this and New York. You would not be able to go ten miles before you would be taken, and then you would be hung up like a dog.'

Her rude reasonings operated with all the power of simple nature upon Captain Webber. He changed his mind in a moment.

'Gentlemen,' said he, 'as I told you before, this is a very dangerous piece of work. All that my wife has said is true. Our people have very strong outposts all along the river as far as King's Bridge; and if I were taken in the act of bringing you into the British lines, I could obtain no mercy. Yet, unless I went with you to your journey's end, I should miss the bounty.'

All our arguments after this could not prevail with him, though we promised to add twelve dollars to the English blankets as an advance payment. However, he at last, for a single silver dollar, agreed to conduct us to another friend, a poor man known simply as Old Joe, who lived two miles further on our journey and who might probably go with us. Captain Webber assured us that he only consented to help us thus far from his not wishing to disoblige Mrs. Eder.

We set off at about one o'clock in the morning and arrived after an hour at the poor man's hut, which was situated on the top of a high mountain. A light was burning, and we found Old Joe and a young woman, a niece, attending his wife who was ill of a swamp-fever. The light was supplied by a green wax-candle, made from the berries of the tallow shrub, which burned with an agreeable odour. True tallow candles were seldom seen in the Northern States during the war, since all the fat cattle were taken for the supply of the armies. We explained our circumstances and I informed Old Joe, who seemed in a condition of great anxiety on account of his wife, that I had some medical knowledge. I recommended for his wife a decoction of the bark of a sort of willow which the Indians used against the disorder, and he appeared greatly relieved to have a physician in the house. For a dollar he agreed to bring us six miles further on our journey to a German settler whom there was every probability we might obtain for a guide, for this German had lost nearly all his sheep in the late floods and was in great want of money. We set off immediately and after making our way for near six hours, through a trackless desert, full of swamps, we found ourselves at the fringe of a wood, and at fifty yards' distance, an American barracks. Soldiers in buff and blue were carrying buckets of water and bundles of forage across a parade ground under the direction of a sergeant, whose back was fortunately turned to us. We shrank into the trees and Old Joe, being much terrified, fled from us with the greatest precipitation.

Harlowe ran after and caught him by the collar, asking him what he meant by this desertion of us. He confessed that he had missed his path and only now knew our whereabouts. We were in the midst of our enemies. The place was called Red Mills, close to Lake Mahopac and about six miles from Goolden's Bridge over the Croton River. As a last act of attention, Old Joe told us of a footpath which led to this bridge beyond the American camp. He advised us to cast a compass about the camp through the woods until we hit it. This path would pass by the hut of friends, who lay under an obligation to him; he described the hut but omitted to name the inhabitants. We thanked him and took his advice. The track appeared before long and we continued cautiously in the woods that fringed it, until we came to the hut about noon.

These were good people, Loyalist by inclination and, I believe, tenants of the Colden family who were landed proprietors thereabouts. When I asked the woman her name, she replied after a little hesitation that she was Hannah Sniffen, wife to James Sniffen. The husband was not at home, but only the wife, a grown daughter, and two boys. They were astonished by our appearance but evidently pleased with our company, the names of Captain Webber and Old Joe carrying weight with them. They inquired after the health of these families. When I told of the sickness of Old Joe's wife and what I had prescribed for her cure, Mrs. Sniffen, a bustling and red-cheeked woman, seemed interested and asked whether I were a tooth-drawer as well as surgeon and physician. She could, she said, not sleep of nights for a toothache, nor could she trust her husband with the pincers, lest he snap off the crown of the tooth, which was rotten, and thus make matters worse.

I replied that, in exchange for a good meal, I would cleanly draw every tooth in her head and welcome; for it happened to be in the range of my powers, given a small pair of steel pincers. So the bargain was concluded.

She gave us a cold roast of pork and boiled potatoes, together with a tart conserve of quince, and to each of us a great pewter tankard of spruce beer. Apart from the soupaun and apples at Mrs. Eder's—for we had not gnawed at the pig's tail there offered us—we had eaten nothing since our dinner at Nine Partners two days previously; this repast therefore, I need not add, proved highly acceptable to us. When it was done I felt sleep stealing across my eyes, so that I could scarcely keep them open. But I was bound first to conclude my bargain, by drawing her tooth, and had the good fortune to fetch it out whole, though its roots were very crooked, without injuring the gum. This feat excited admiration in the family and cries of 'Well, I declare now!' and 'Wasn't that a dandy pull?' The two boys also offered to submit themselves to my professional skill. But I refused them, as being greatly fatigued by my journey, and said that I proposed, with Mrs. Sniffen's permission, to lie down and take a nap on my blanket in the corner. My comrades were already preparing to do the same.

This intention, however, she warmly opposed, though her daughter sighed: 'They have earned a nap, the poor fellows, let 'em lie there, they won't be in the way of our feet, surely.'

'Don't be a fool, Mary,' cried the mother. 'Don't you know that our own soldiers often straggle here from White Plains? Some of them are as likely as not to come in upon us while these red-coats sleep. Then what will we not suffer for the crime of harbouring! I declare now I hear footsteps—run off, soldiers, run quick, I say, and hide in the garret!' She bustled us out.

It was only her husband, however, a little pale-faced, irresolute man. Looking at him, I could well understand his wife's hesitation in entrusting the pincers and her tooth to his care. He seemed glad to see us. We revealed to him our intention of escaping into New York; but he repeated the words of our other directors, as to the number of American posts, particularly on the River. He added: 'Boys, I swear now it will be an hundred chances to one, if you are not taken up.'

We promised to reward him liberally if he would conduct us. After a while he said: 'A young man lives several miles off from this spot, over to Pine's Bridge: van Wart is his name. He's a mighty smart boy and has friends both with the Cowboys and the Skinners. I reckon he will undertake the task. If he should, I have no objection to come too, for he knows the lie of the land. But I well know the dangers which we shall be exposed to, and will not go myself without a second guide.'

I asked, who were these Cowboys and Skinners. Mrs. Sniffen told me that they were the plague of Westchester County, into the northern confines of which we had just entered. The principal land-owners of the county, who had been very prosperous, favoured the British cause but were soon forced to take refuge in the City of New York. Their tenant farmers and other persons of substance had suffered enormous losses from the foragers of both armies; while such of the labourers and common people who remained had agreed to form robber bands as pretended auxiliaries of one army or the other. Those who belonged to the 'upper party', that is, to the Loyalists, called themselves 'Cowboys' from their habit of driving off the cattle of the revolutionaries; but cattle were not their only prey. Those who belonged to the 'lower party', the revolutionary, were known as 'Skinners', for they had harder hearts yet and would strip a victim of everything that he or she had in the world, down to the merest trifle, not scrupling to remove even stockings and under-linen. These Cowboys and Skinners ranged about in the neuter ground between the two lines of outposts, and while pretending to pillage only from opposing partisans were in reality perfectly indifferent whose throat or purse they cut. There was a close understanding, Mrs. Sniffen assured us, between these sworn foes who, after a mock-skirmish to satisfy the regular troops that they were in the way of their duty, would meet secretly as friends in some ruined farmhouse, there jocosely intermingling the strains of *Yankee Doodle* with the *Grenadiers' March* and *Hot Stuff.* The object of these encounters was the bartering of cattle and goods stolen on the one hand by the Cowboys from their fellow-Loyalists, and on the other by the Skinners from their fellow-revolutionaries. These goods being dangerous to dispose of in home territory could be exchanged with the enemy, and what each side got was made to appear as rightful booty taken in a pretended fight. Each side always claimed to have inflicted crushing losses on its foes and to have left many of them lying dead. When the celebrated Aaron Burr commanded the American advanced lines in this neuter land, and became aware of the depredations and cruelties practised by the Skinners, he is said to have exclaimed in indignation: 'I could gibbet half a dozen *good Whigs* with all the venom of an inveterate Tory!' For a party of these wretches, seeking to screw from an aged Quaker more money than he possessed, had roasted him naked in hot ashes as one would a potato, until the skin rose in blisters on his flesh. Then they thrice hanged him up to a rafter for a spell, and as often cut him down; and in the end left him for dead upon the ground.

Isaac van Wart was summoned, and arrived a few hours later, by which time we were refreshed by sleeping in the woods, where we had concealed ourselves in a drift of fallen leaves. He was, he avowed, a Cowboy in politics; but we could see at once that his courage was not equal to his profession. He was a wild-looking rogue and could neither read nor write. He boasted a great deal of his successes and stratagems in neuter ground, and how often the 'balls had sung like bees about his head'; but we were convinced that Mr. Sniffen entertained too high an opinion of his smartness. He agreed at first to undertake any desperate work, but on one pretext or another continually postponed the hour of our departure; nor would Mr. Sniffen consent to go forward without him.

It was two days before van Wart 'allowed that he would come', being constantly taunted by Miss Mary Sniffen with cowardice; and then only when we had presented him with five Spanish silver dollars on account and one of the two English blankets. Mr. Sniffen accepted the same fee and remarked on the unusual goodness of the dollars as coin; meaning that they had not been carved or clipped. An immense number of gold and silver pieces in Spanish, Portuguese and English currency had found its way into America since the war began; where they circulated in a variety of mutilated forms. The blame for the clipping of the coins was by the Americans uniformly fastened upon Lieutenant-General Archibald Robertson, a Scottish Engineer and Deputy-Quartermaster-General to our Army; so that the diminished coins were known as 'Robertsons'. However, each individual, on either side, would cut up any coin into halves, quarters, or eighth parts, for the sake of small change, and naturally many an eighth was in reality a ninth or a tenth. These frauds, known as 'sharp-skinned money', were nevertheless highly preferred to paper.

We set out at six o'clock in the evening on the fourth day of our adventure and travelled all night through deep swamp, thick woods and over difficult mountains, until three hours before dawn. Isaac van Wart then stopped suddenly and, said he: 'This is a dangerous, troublesome piece of work, I vow. I heartily wish I had never engaged myself in it; but your daughter, friend Sniffen, prevailed by her beauty over my prudent inclinations. Well, she is ten hours' journey away from us now, and the force of her fascination over me has spent itself. We are now perhaps four miles from Tarry Town and an equal distance from White Plains. There is an American encampment of a thousand men within a mile of us. I was there a few days ago and know where all the sentries are posted. There is one at the corner of that coppice yonder. If I should be taken, I would lose my life, for they already have cause to suspect me as a driver of Whig cows.'

He seemed to be under great terror and fear, which did not abate when Smutchy said roughly: 'We are not afraid of one or two sentries. Only conduct us the best way you can. If we unavoidably fall in with any of them, you may leave the matter to us and fly for your life.'

All that we could say had no effect upon him, and although we offered him on the spot twelve more dollars in hard money he would not advance one step further. To our surprise, Mr. James Sniffen, who had made no claims to courage and had insisted that he would not proceed without this van Wart, now changed colour. He undertook, of his own impulse, to carry us forward to our destination if van Wart only advised him how to avoid these sentries. This van Wart did.

Mr. Sniffen said, when van Wart had hurried off: 'It was but to reassure my wife that I showed such caution. I am greatly devoted to King George and if I prove the means of restoring three good soldiers to His Majesty's service, I shall count myself a good subject. Be damned to the rebels! Now, forward with good courage!'

It had been raining very hard during the whole night and was very dark, even when the moon rose, and therefore though we expected every moment to fall in with the line of sentries, we went through them unchallenged. Mr. Sniffen even led us in safety past a block-house which was full of sleeping troops, and remarked very coolly as we struck off into the woods to avoid it: 'Gentlemen, these block-houses are of remarkable construction, being made for lack of nails with jointed timber throughout. I reckon that in your country it would be difficult to find a barrack composed wholly of wood without a pennyworth of iron in the whole building, barring only the pot-hook and chain that hangs in the chimney?'

We agreed that America was a very remarkable country and the inhabitants ingenious beyond the ordinary; which seemed to please him very much.

We then climbed up precipices and waded through swamps and not long before dawn arrived at the house of some friends of Mr. Sniffen's, midway between Tarry Town and White Plains; and he rapped them up. We remained hidden outside until he gave us the signal that all was well and we might enter. We never learned the name of these people, who withheld it from us in case, being taken up, we might inform against them. They gave us refreshment of cold beef-steaks with lettuce, and cider, with hickory nuts as a side dish; but begged us not to remain in the house, which would be highly dangerous to us and them, as the American soldiery were scattered over almost the whole face of the country and were constant visitors.

We held a consultation: what was to be done? Mr. Sniffen pro-posed that we should hide ourselves in the hay-stack which stood near the house, until he could explore the country and find out the safest way for our escape. He told us that we should be as snug there as fleas in a sheepskin. We agreed unanimously and, just as dawn was breaking through the heavy rain, we climbed up into the hay-stack, which was unthatched, and each buried himself up to the chin in the hay. The downpour continued all day. At about noon, during a lull, someone rode up on a horse which he hitched to a rail close by. Presently he brought out our host to view the stack. We heard him saying in the Connecticut accent: 'Yes, Mister, that's a right elegant bit of hay and it will come in handy for our beasts. They consume a terrible amount of fodder. I expect I'll send a party along in about two hours' time to fetch it off to the camp. You'll be allowing us the use of your wagon, no doubt.'

'I declare that you are very hard on us, Captain,' expostulated the poor farmer. 'I'm sure I don't know how I'm to keep my beasts alive this winter if you now seize what remains of my fodder. They be'nt in too good a case already.'

'Well, I expect what you can't feed you must kill, and we'll pay you a fair price for your beef, be sure. The men must eat, the same as the cattle, and a good sight of them have right busy guts.'

'And my hen-roost regularly robbed by the soldiery and all my fences broke down! It is a hard life indeed for a family in the neigh-bourhood of a military camp,' continued the farmer.

'Ay, the boys will have their fun and cut their pranks,' returned the other lightly. 'But war is war, and you know, you can count yourself lucky that you an't situated on the other side of King's Bridge. The Commissaries there are pretty considerable harder than officers like myself.'

'I an't just capable to say as to that, Captain,' replied our host, 'but I hear at least that they pay in money that jingles and rings.'

'Well, I reckon you may say that,' commiserated the commissary. 'But war is war, and I'll trouble you to leave that stack where it stands till we come to fetch it off this afternoon.'

We were greatly alarmed at the prospect of our hay-stack being removed from about us; but, the Commissary riding away, our host stayed to reassure us that more rain was due to fall, and no party would come for the fodder. If they did, he would descry them at some distance and would warn us in time to run off and hide else-where.

Smutchy remarked: 'A thousand blessings fall upon the prophet Daniel George and upon his seed for ever.'

'Amen to that,' I responded.

We remained all that day in the wet hay-stack, snatching a little sleep in turns, one of us always acting as watchman. At six o'clock in the evening our host provided us with very good ham, for the curing of which this county was noted, and a glass apiece of cherry-rum. We emerged from the hay-stack and stretched our legs, but were still not permitted to enter the house. The rain coming down hard again, we returned to the stack and stayed there all night. Richard Harlowe spoke as few words as possible to me, though a sort of truce existed between us because of our common interest and danger. He now sullenly acknowledged my leadership and, if a dispute arose as to the course to be adopted, was always forced to yield to my way of thinking; for Smutchy regarded me as infallible and Harlowe lacked the resolution to part company with us. At this place Smutchy, who was helping Harlowe to descend the hay-stack, muttered: 'Hallo, what's here?' and then to me: 'Sergeant Gerry, come now, feel what I have discovered!' He pulled my fingers towards him and I felt a row of coins sewn in the seam of Harlowe's breeches.

This ran against the articles upon which we had agreed before we set out: which was to share, and share alike, all the money and other property in our possession, with Smutchy acting as our treasurer. Harlowe had only admitted to three dollars, and here was a further store which he had not declared. We took five guineas from him. He tried to save his character by saying carelessly that he had forgotten that they were there. However, Smutchy searched him more thoroughly and found another guinea, a Portuguese half-joe, a coin worth thirty-five shillings in English currency, and three badly clipped Spanish moidores concealed under the arm of his jacket. Smutchy then said hotly: 'I remember, Sergeant Gerry, a stroll that we three once took in company, when we were recruits together. When I laughed at this Gentleman Harlowe for his airs, you resented it on his behalf, did you not? What have you to say for his gentleman-like behaviour now, eh?'

I reproved Smutchy. 'This is no time for recrimination, for God's sake. Harlowe says that he forgot to put the guineas into the common stock. We have them now, at all events, and so much the better for the whole party.'

No more was said on the subject. We began to grow uneasy as this night advanced, lest James Sniffen also had forsaken us and left us to shift for ourselves; however, our kind host, when he visited us a little before dawn, bringing us breakfast, assured us that James Sniffen was a thorough man and a man of his word. His long absence was a proof that he had been vigilant in picking up all the intelligence he could with regard to the disposition of the camps and posts through which we must pass. Richard Harlowe would not believe this, and was for continuing without a guide; but we dissuaded him. Fortunately for us, the storm continued all day, blowing from the South; and the hay-stack, with ourselves in it, was not fetched away. Smutchy again loudly blessed Daniel George of Newbury-Port on this second day, and swore he should be kidnapped and appointed Astronomer-General to our Forces. Time passed for us very slowly.

At last, James Sniffen returned. He told us in a low voice from below that all was well; we must be prepared to follow him when darkness fell. We had twenty miles still to travel, but we might with determination reach King's Bridge that same night.

That evening at dark, when we had passed near thirty-six hours in the hay-stack, we said good-bye to those who had harboured us (and who would accept no recompense for all their kindness) and set off in high spirits on this final stage of our attempt. I could not say exactly what route we followed, but we crossed and recrossed the Bronx stream by fords and passed over several steep heights; the storm meanwhile not abating its violence and the darkness shrouding us so completely that it was difficult to believe that our guide knew his whereabouts. We had agreed not to ply him with any talk or questions, in order to give him no excuse for missing his direction. But never once did he seem at a loss. At last he told us with relief: 'We stand now on the forward slopes of the Heights of Fordham, and must proceed with the greatest caution, for there are American advanced troops hereabouts of whose stations I am ignorant. We are but three miles distant from King's Bridge. A mile further down this slope is Musholu Brook which leads directly to the bridge. I will come this last stage with you if you desire, but I think now that I can leave it to yourselves; for I am sure you would spare me the hazard of passing and repassing these outposts, being sensible of what risks I have already run in your service.'

Harlowe asked: 'But what of the Commander-in-Chief's bounty? Surely you will be coming to New York to draw the bounty?'

'No, Sir,' he replied. 'What I already have received, and what you have undertaken to pay in addition, will be sufficient to my needs, I expect.'

We soldiers consulted together and subsequently told him: 'If we come safe through, it will be due chiefly to your skill and vigilance. We believe that we have arrived where you say, and are prepared to proceed by ourselves. Here are the twenty dollars, which we promised to you and van Wart together, and here are three more guineas as a thank-offering. For if we get through, very well—our freedom is worth ten times that sum; but if we are caught and hanged it is better that you and your family should benefit than our captors. Go off now and all good luck go with you and yours, Friend Sniffen.'

Nevertheless he came a little further, from a sense of gratitude, and showed us the head of the Musholu Brook, where he clasped our hands in affectionate farewell and told us that we were now safe. This was no-man's-land and lay under the fire of the British batteries at Fort Charles, which commanded King's Bridge. We never saw our excellent guide again, but I trust that he got safe home.

We next came to a small hut beside a cabbage-patch, where a sudden doubt seized Harlowe but that our guide had betrayed us into the American lines. He was of opinion that we should instantly confirm the truth of Mr. Sniffen's story by questioning the people of the house. I myself had the fullest confidence in Sniffen. Since therefore he had assured us that we were now in neuter ground, with nothing to fear, I did not oppose Harlowe's resolution. He went up and boldly rapped at the door. The inhabitants, an old negro and his wife, were much terrified by our approach. Their fears increased when we ordered them to light a candle and kindle the fire in order to dry our drenched clothing. The old negro, falling on his knees, implored us not to insist on this service, for if the least light were seen at that hour, the whole habitation would soon be tumbled about our ears by shells from Fort Charles.

Then we knew for sure that all was well; and were not irked to remain in the dark and cold for the few hours that remained of this seventh night of our journey: we knew that to approach the bridge in the dark would be highly dangerous.

The rain ceased, the skies cleared, and soon a slow red dawn began to spread across the hills to our leftward. A rosy light glinted upon the waters of Harlem Creek which separates Manhattan Island, upon which New York stands, from the township of Westchester. With joyful hearts we went forward to the bridge.

'Halt, who goes there?' came in ringing accents from the out-sentry.

Such a moment must be imagined, it cannot be described. 'A sergeant and two men of The Ninth. We have made good our escape,' I answered.

'Advance and be recognized,' was the order, and, to the scandal of the sergeant of the Guard who had been summoned, the out-sentry grounded his firelock, tossed his hat in the air and rushed forward to hug us in delight. It was Mad Johnny Maguire!

'Och Gerry and Smutchy, my darlings,' he yelled, 'is it really your-selves now? And Gentleman Harlowe too!' (Here he gave us an arch look.) 'Oh, on my soul, what sad company you are keeping these days, Gerry, my jewel!'

I was almost as much astonished as Mad Johnny Maguire him-self by this encounter. 'Yes, indeed it is ourselves, Johnny—deserting backwards again, the three of us!'

Smutchy said: 'Give that Tower musket into my hand, dear Johnny. Let me feel its weight. I have been a sick man these thirteen months without my old musket, Johnny—a sick man and a slave.'

The Guard through whom we passed were Royal Welch Fusiliers, and showed a very soldier-like appearance, or all but poor Johnny himself. He was now, very properly I own, ordered to be confined, on account of his unsentry-like behaviour towards us. For private feelings should not relax discipline.

CHAPTER VI

I ASKED permission from the sergeant of the Guard to converse with Mad Johnny Maguire before he was confined; which was granted. Maguire then related how he came to be in New York. He had gone to join his brother Cornelius, who was farming near Norwalk, in the southern part of Connecticut, which lies across the Sound from Long Island. Reaching this place without adventure, he had been instructed by Cornelius in the care of the cattle, trees, crops and poultry. When Cornelius was satisfied that Mad Johnny could be trusted, with the help of the family, to manage the three hundred acres of his property, he eyed his ducking-gun where it hung on the nail and announced that he was about to rejoin General Washington on the East Highlands. Johnny thereupon refused to remain in the house if Corny went off soldiering, pointing out very rightly that this would amount to treason: freeing a soldier for service against the King was a crime equal to thus serving himself. So they came to loggerheads, in the literal sense of the phrase. Each seized up one of the heavy iron loggerheads, which they used red-hot in this part of the country for scorching their flip (a nasty mixture of ale, rum and molasses, but good against the cold), and began whacking at each other with intent to maim or kill. Johnny stretched his brother out the whole length of the kitchen with a blow on the crown, and then took to his heels and ran for New York; which was about two days' march away.

'Had you no guide, Johnny?' I asked.

'The Devil a one,' he said.

'Did you travel by night?' I asked.

'What would I be doing, travelling by night? The sun's good enough for me,' he said.

'Then how in the world did you come safe through?' I asked in bewilderment. 'Weren't you wearing scarlet?'

He winked at me and said very simply: 'Well, there was only one of me, you know, and I had the Irish way of speaking, so they thought me a deserter—why, faith, so I was—and naturally inclined to disaffection. It seems that there's a Doctor Ben Franklin, who has been addressing very persuasive letters of late to the Old Country, saying that rebellion is the whole duty and salvation of the Irishman. I walked towards New York along the Eastchester road, and whenever I saw a man approaching, I sat me down by the roadside and nursed my foot as if I were kibed, and let him come up. Then I would eagerly ask him, how far was it to the place I had just left; and I'd tell him that I was Johnny Maguire, a deserter from the army of New York, who was running off, with a sore heel, to join my brother Cornelius Maguire at Norwalk. I would limp a few paces with him, and then sit down again and nurse my foot. When he had passed out of sight, I would start up again and continue my journey.'

'That must have been an inconvenient method of travel when there were many people on the road,' I observed.

'Yes,' he agreed solemnly. 'On some days I gained two miles and lost three. But I got along better as the rain cleared the roads of travellers. Well, the nearer I came, the greater joy I feigned of having broken the chains of British slavery and run out into the free air of patriot America. Many a good meal that sentiment won me, and more drink than I could well hold, for with all their great cleverness they are very easily deceived. But I codded them with too much success, by Jesus God! One kind fellow invited me to ride in his fine yellow carriage and would not take "no". He fetched me half-way back to Norwalk and it was with difficulty that I gave him the slip. Well, in the end I came within three miles of this place, and now whenever I met anyone I made as if desperate of escape from my pursuers, and my heel troubled me more and more. At last a pretended friend betrayed me, in hope of a reward: he peached on me to a British sentinel who came and fetched me safely in! So now there's deserting backwards for you—cap that tale, Sergeant Gerry Lamb!'

We were now entertained at the guard-house to British victuals and British ale. The men were exceedingly hearty and the officers most obliging. When this repast was finished, though I would fain have slept all day, we were conducted forward to New York City, a distance of about fifteen miles, in order to report to General Headquarters. We were the first party to have escaped from the Convention Army since September.

The sergeant who accompanied us, by name Collins, a native of London, was to prove a good friend of mine. Unlike most of the other non-commissioned officers in this regiment he was very talkative; however, most of his discourse was both informative and amusing. He told me: 'You'll be up before Major André, the Deputy-Adjutant-General—now there's the best brain and the kindest heart in the whole British Army. General Clinton thinks the world of him. Naturally, some of the officers consider him a thought too French-ified—he is romantical, they say, and over-interested in millinery and the theatrical stage. Indeed, he designed all the costumes to be worn at our stage-plays at the Theatre in Philadelphia, took leading parts, wrote the prologues, painted the scenery, and all. The great Mischianza, General Howe's farewell celebration—now that was a prodigious fine show, and Major André, he invented and produced it all. Knights of the Burning Mountain, Knights of the Blended Rose, a regatta, a tournament, queens of beauty, maids of honour, ornamental fireworks—by God, there was a beautiful, sweet phantasy, a written romance come true before our awed gaze! It made a mock of the desolations of war that spread about us—and breathed defiance at the French King, who had just declared against us.'

Our travel-worn appearance excited compassion among the soldiers whom we met on the road, and two or three times we were called aside into a tavern and persuaded to tell our adventures. We passed under the strong works of Fort Washington and through McGowans Pass, a place close to the village of Harlem, so strong that a few companies posted there might well keep an army at bay. About noon we arrived in New York itself, which lay at the extremity of this island, and was even then a considerable city of ten thousand native inhabitants, though by the half below its present magnitude and importance. It was greatly overcrowded by the influx of the military and of very large numbers of Loyalists from all parts of the country, who more than repaired the loss of so many families 'on the other side of the question'. This congestion was made worse by the loss of eleven hundred houses—more than one-fourth of the city—burned by the Americans when they evacuated the city. The ruins of these houses lay to the east of Broadway (the fine street, seventy feet in width, that passed along a ridge in the centre of the city) and to the south of Wall Street, the abode of the well-to-do. Hovels of planking and old sail-cloth had been put up around the chimneys and walls that still stood, and the poor, tattered wretches who inhabited these dens gave the city a very squalid air. They were in part the usual refuse of humanity that is littered about the gates of any garrison town the world over, but in part also the most pitiable victims of this fratricidal war—landed proprietors and their families, descended from the first settlers, whom mob-law and rapine had driven from their estates and reduced to beggary. Of the houses that remained, some were built with good effect in the English style, very strong and neat and several storeys high; but the most were sharp-roofed, sloping Dutch buildings, with the gable ends projecting towards the street. The Dutch spirit, I was to find, still governed the city: the custom of the Dutch, who practically engrossed the markets and shops, was to give little and ask much, to conceal gains and to live for themselves alone. Dutchmen could be recognized by their comical custom of smoking 'cigars', leaves of tobacco rolled in the form of a tube six inches long, the smoke of which was drunk without the aid of any instrument. They were now, Sergeant Collins informed me, making enormous gains by the renting of apartments and the sale of provisions. The prices that he mentioned were four or five times greater than those that had ruled in Dublin when I was stationed there.

Other sights that surprised me on this first visit to the city were a long procession of negro slaves carrying bales of merchandise on their heads—near one-fourth of the inhabitants of New York were negroes or mulattoes—and three mistresses of officers, each in an elegant conveyance and wearing a coat of military cut with the regimental facings of her protector. The main streets were paved and clean and lined with trees. There were some very good shops in the streets about Broadway, a few of them as luxurious as any in Dame Street or Parliament Street in my native city, which may be justly pronounced two of the first trading streets in Europe. The contrast between these affluent surroundings and the frightful country from which I had escaped that very morning struck me very forcibly.

Before one of these shops, where were sold enamelled snuff-boxes and comfit cases, a handsome young fop in a sky-blue silk coat and flowered waistcoat stood in a negligent attitude, sucking the top of his malacca cane; which, when he pensively removed it from his mouth, proved to be of clouded amber. He also wore a Spanish military cloak, of Canary yellow silk with a pure white lining, and a sword with crystal pommel and Toledo scabbard. He so closely resembled a wax-figure or the paragon of a fashion plate that I had the fancy to make him talk, in order to see what language would break out of those cupid's lips. I asked him the time.

He stared at me in a vacant way; but when I repeated my question in a louder but still civil tone, he thought it wiser to answer me, as being supported by three other soldiers. Leisurely taking a jewelled gold watch from his right-hand fob-pocket, he regarded it for a few moments and then pronounced: 'Honest red-coat, I will tell you: it wants but three minutes of noon.' He so vividly recalled the motley fool in Shakespeare's Arden that I dared to quote:

'Thus we may see, quoth he, how the world wags.'

At this sally, he was good enough to laugh. '*Touché*,' he lisped and continued:

'And so, from hour to hour we ripe and ripe,
And then from hour to hour we rot and rot,
And thereby hangs a tale.'

I was for thanking him and proceeding on my way, having satisfied my curiosity and wit; but he called me back. 'Not so fast, my sun-burned Jaques,' he said. 'We have so far consulted only one chronological oracle. Stand by me while we approach the other.' From the fob on the left-hand side of his pearly white breeches he drew out another costly time-piece, and then the first again, attempting evidently to strike a mean between them in calculation. However, before he could arrive at any answer, the noon gun was fired from the Battery commanding the entrance of the North and East Rivers, and the noon chimes rang out from several sacred edifices.

'It is now noon,' he then said confidently.

'I am greatly your debtor, Sir,' I replied with a slight bow, which he was gentleman enough to return, saying, very truly: 'No, Sir, I protest—it was nothing.'

So we continued towards the fine brick edifice at the very end of Broadway which, by the guard of honour posted at the gate and the Royal Standard surmounting it, we could see was the General Head-quarters. But Richard Harlowe hung back and signalled to us to wait a short spell while he also addressed our friend the fop. We did not hear what was said, but the two spoke earnestly together for half a minute; whereupon Harlowe rejoined us.

Smutchy jested: 'Why, Gentleman Harlowe, was that pretty pet your young brother? And did he agree to buy your discharge?'

Harlowe shot a keen look at him and then replied in some con-fusion: 'No, he is only an Irish cousin.' We all laughed very heartily, though not yet sure where the joke lay.

At Headquarters we were instantly admitted by the Officer of the Guard who told us: 'The Deputy-Adjutant-General, Major André, has heard of your escape and is desirous of seeing you immediately.'

We were presented to Major André, who welcomed us all together, complimenting us upon our escape. He then asked me: 'Are you not Sergeant Lamb, who was in charge of this expedition?'

When I said that I was that person, the Major invited me into the parlour, first giving orders to his clerk to take my comrades and the escort to the buttery for entertainment. He then poured out a glass of Madeira for me with his own hand.

'Proceed, Sergeant Lamb!' he said simply.

I smiled: 'Where am I to begin, your Honour? You know it is a dangerous thing to ask an Irishman for his story.'

He broke into a very musical laughter. 'Well, you can tell me first, if you wish, how came you to join the Army.'

I replied: 'I think that it was because I was tired of being a clerk in the counting-house and longed for glory.'

He clapped me on the shoulder and cried: 'Why now, that was the very same reason that brought me into the service. But—I was lucky in a rich father who could purchase me a commission. What is your age?'

I told him: 'Twenty-three.'

'Well, it is more credit to be a sergeant at twenty-three than a colonel at twenty,' he observed very frankly. 'For, Heaven be blessed, it is rarely that purse or privilege have a say in the appointment of our non-commissioned officers—the mainstay of the Line.'

I have never before or since been spoken to by an officer in so easy and familiar a style, or by one to whom my heart immediately warmed with such spontaneous affection. His face, though of dark complexion, was mild, open and animated. He had a long and beautiful head of hair which, agreeably to the fashion of the day, was wound with a black ribband and hung down his back; the lace at his throat and cuffs was of Mechlin, exquisitely laundered; and the facings of his well-cut scarlet coat were of a rich green. In short, he was the handsomest man that ever I saw. Nor was there anything of the coxcomb in his manner, and when he came to business and asked me for particulars of my captivity and flight, I knew at once that Sergeant Collins had not erred in rating his intelligence so highly. It was characteristic of the Major, by the way, that he never referred to our American enemy by such terms as 'the Rebels' or 'the Yankees' or 'the Mohairs', but always very politely as 'the Colonists'.

First he enquired what I knew about the discipline, composition, arms and disposition of the Colonists' forces, the capacity and spirit of their officers, from experience or hearsay, and the present mood of the militia, the regular troops and the peasantry. He rapidly noted down my answers and, nodding, compared them with entries in a calf-bound ledger which he had by him.

'Did you ever see General Benedict Arnold?' he asked suddenly.

'Yes, your Honour,' I replied, 'I saw him galloping between the lines in the engagement at Freeman's Farm—a man without fear. It is a great pity that so judicious and gallant an officer should be major-general in the American service.'

Entre nous, many Continental Congressmen seem to think the same,' he laughed. 'I regret that I am not personally acquainted with him. But I know the young lady to whom he has now given his heart; she is sentimental and good. I wish her joy of him. Her father was most agreeable to me when I was in Philadelphia. On this account I fear that, despite her having the Military Governor for a swain, poor Peggy Shippen will be suspected as a Tory by the jealous Whig ladies there, and pronounced "contraband" at social gatherings. As for the General himself, my intelligencers report him to be living highly beyond his income in that city—a very expensive place, you know. I fear that will get him into more trouble with his enemies. But come, to the matter of your flight. I'll fetch a map and we may trace out your wanderings together. Here we are now, at five miles south-west from Hopewell, was it not? Where shall we mark the Widow Eder's hut?'

We lightly traced out the route in lead pencil on the map, and I marked the block-houses and camps to the best of my ability; also the bridges over the creeks and other matters of military interest. When I told him the name of our guide and described his house, wife and person, he laughed: 'So he called himself James Sniffen, did he? That was not his name. He borrowed it from a Whig farmer of White Plains—no, I know your man, and could name him if I would. Well, I'll keep his secret from you since he withheld it him-self; and I'll see that an adequate reward is paid him by my agents, as an encouragement to further works of mercy. He is a very bold man and has done a deal of work for our side.'

When I had given Major André all the information that I could, he expressed much satisfaction. 'Now, Sergeant Lamb,' he said, 'as a non-commissioned officer of The Ninth, you enjoy a privilege not accorded to private soldiers, which is to choose whether you will sail by the next packet to England, and there be posted to the Details of the Regiment; or whether you will continue to serve in America. I may say that I sincerely hope you will choose the latter course. We have need here of experienced soldiers.'

When I hesitated a moment before answering, he divined the reason. 'Let me assure you before you speak, that you will not be sent to any corps in which to serve would be distasteful to you—I know well how greatly regiments vary in quality. No, no, Sergeant Lamb, Sir Henry Clinton, the Commander-in-Chief, has authorized me to offer you your choice of entering in what regiment you please now serving in America.'

'That is easily answered then,' I said, 'I shall stay and serve. My choice is the Royal Welch Fusiliers. May I ask a favour, which is that Private Alexander Steel, who came with me, be posted to the same corps, but Private Richard Harlowe to another?'

'I will undertake that,' he said. 'And I will inform Colonel Balfour of the Royal Welch that you are a man of energy and education, and will desire him to retain you in your rank. Meanwhile, I thank you for your information and for your loyal decision. Good luck to you!' He warmly clasped my hand and then summoning his orderly sent me to Colonel Handfield (the present Commissary-General of Ireland) who was appointed to pay the men who escaped from captivity. I was given a bounty of three guineas in addition to the money that, according to the account I gave him, we were out of pocket by bribing our guides. I am inclined to think that much of this bounty that my comrades and I received was the result of Sir Henry's secret benevolence. Colonel Handfield used the term 'honourable desertion' for my quitting the Convention Army. This was the distinction that General Burgoyne himself made, when addressing the House of Parliament, between those soldiers who through every difficulty rejoined His Majesty's forces, and those who left their regiments for the purpose of settling among the Americans.

I caught a sight of Sir Henry before we left. He was a low man, stout and full-blooded with a lordly nose and an air of honesty and courage, though his reserve was not easily broken through nor was he so familiar with the troops as General Burgoyne had been.

We lay that night in the guard-room at Headquarters and the next morning, after viewing the sights of the Town, marched back to King's Bridge. Sergeant Collins complained much to me of the present expensiveness of New York, but expressed the hope that before long we should be 'launched on a new campaign that will push the tottering forces of the rebels into the abyss'. He said that he had been engaged that summer against the French in a sea-battle, three companies of the Regiment having volunteered to act as marines under Admiral Richard Howe. He had been in the fifty-gun ship *Isis,* Captain Raynor, when she engaged with the French seventy-four *Caesar,* which was so mauled that she put before the wind and sailed for the shelter of Boston harbour. 'But,' said he, 'the chief war hereabouts is not against rebellion—it is against the Treasury of Great Britain. It makes me hot with indignation to witness the scandalous jobbery and peculation that persists here, under the shield of the military Government.'

I asked him for particulars to support this general indictment. 'Oh,' he replied, 'every sight you see has a moral. Observe those cattle being driven to the slaughter-house. Whence do they come, do you suppose?'

'Rebel cattle driven by the Cowboys from Westchester county, or bought by them from the Skinners? Or perhaps sequestered from Whigs on Long Island or Staten Island?'

'I see that you know a thing or two. Well, whatever their origin, at least they have since been taken over by the Commissaries of Cattle at perhaps two guineas a beast, and sold as beef to the Army at two shillings sterling the pound weight, the hides and tallow remaining as the Commissaries' perquisites. There's a profit, now! And what do you see yonder? That is King's College, which was the university of this place, with faculties of Arts and Physic. There are now troops quartered in it. The Barrack-Masters charge an extravagant rent to the Crown for the use of these buildings, as also for churches, Quaker meeting-houses, breweries and the like. Do you suppose that one copper halfpenny is returned to the owners by these jobbers? No, no. And observe the wood smoke issuing from that row of chimneys?

That tells a tale too. The same Barrack-Masters fetch the wood from the forests of Long Island or Staten Island; they pay the Tory proprietors fifteen shillings a cord for it, and the Whigs nothing at all. Transport costs them less than nothing; the Treasurer is overcharged for that item. Yet at what price do they sell the fuel? At eighty shillings a cord!'

I doubted many of these tales as fabrications, but was later convinced of their truth. It was not only the lesser officials who benefited, either. In these years four successive Quartermasters-General of the Army in America retired to England, each reputedly worth not less than a quarter of a million pounds sterling. Two Deputy-Quartermasters-General, however, Archibald Robertson and Henry Bruen, being called upon at New York in 1782 to testify before a Board of General officers (where I happened to be employed as a clerk) to explain the prodigious expenses incurred by their department, insisted that the system of private contracts was preferable to that of direct purchase by the military government. They remarked in evidence: 'There is no man conversant in business, or that is capable of judging of human nature, who can suppose that a contract held by the public can or will be executed with that economy, care and attention as when the interests of individuals are immediately concerned. Nor could it, almost, be possible for the Head of any department, let his zeal and attention be ever so great, to see that strict justice was done in the purchasing of such a variety of articles as the land and water carriage of an army require, especially in this country.'

Sergeant Collins continued: 'Nevertheless New York is a pleasant and healthy station, compared with others in America. There are cooling breezes in summer, and a more temperate air in winter. I mean, rather, the part on the North River yonder where the well-to-do live; phoo, the trading part down by the East River stinks in the summer like the sick bay of a transport. September is very pleasant, with the apple-trees bearing fruit and blossom at the same time. But let me tell you: one of the most serious inconveniences is the want of good water, there being but few wells hereabouts. The city is supplied mostly from a spring almost a mile distant; the water is distributed to the people at the reservoir at the head of Queen Street which I will show you. That, and the high price of soap, accounts for prodigious charges for laundering. See here, my latest bill—seven shillings and sixpence for a mere dozen pieces!' Yes, there are many worse stations than New York in peace-time. We were here in 1773, two years before the troubles. Those were the days. Good beef was then at 3½d. a pound, very pretty mutton at the same; chickens at ninepence a couple, instead of the present four shillings for a single small bird. Those cursed Dutch shopkeepers, they are as trickish as Jews! Turtle-meat sevenpence a pound—we never see it now. Pineapples as large as a quart mug, for sixpence each—they are gone too. Still, there's one advantage in this prodigious rise of prices—the men can't get drunk so readily. In those days New English kill-devil sold at threepence the pint-measure; and a worse poison for the guts I never drank. In those days King George's fine statue still proudly rode his horse at Bowling Green; the damned rebels pulled him down and chopped him up and ran the pieces into bullet-moulds. Over forty thousand bullets he was made to yield, to be fired into the breasts of his loyal subjects—oh, the shame of the dogs!'

At King's Bridge I reported to Lieutenant-Colonel Balfour, to whose kind attention I must ever feel myself much indebted. The Colonel of the Regiment was General Howe; but naturally he did not command it in the field. Lieutenant-Colonel Balfour provided me with clothing and necessaries that same day and appointed me sergeant at the first vacancy.

The Twenty-Third, or Royal Welch Fusiliers, were then, as now, one of the proudest regiments in the Service and preserved a number of remarkable customs, most of them recording some glorious episode in history or preserving the titular connexion of the Regiment with Wales—a country, however, of which few of its men or officers were natives. We bore very fine devices on our colours and appointments. In the centre of the Colour the Prince of Wales' Feathers issuing out of a Coronet, and in three corners, the badges of Edward the Black Prince, namely: the Rising Sun, the Red Dragon and the Three Feathers with the motto *Ich Dien*. On our grenadier caps were the same Feathers and the White Horse of Hanover with the motto *Nec Aspera Terrent*—'Difficulties daunt us not'. The Feathers and the motto *Ich Dien* were painted upon our drums and bells of arms. Our Colours and appointments also bore the honour 'MINDEN'. One privileged honour enjoyed by us was that of passing in review preceded by our fine regimental he-goat, with horns gilded and adorned with ringlets of flowers. We valued ourselves much on the ancientness of the custom.

Martial finery can be an encouragement to formal discipline and clean drill, and I must confess that it did my heart good to be included in a parade of this regiment: it took out of my mouth the taste of drills perfunctorily performed in captivity, with sticks instead of muskets, and the memory of the awkward squads who had been set as guards over us prisoners at Prospect Hill and Rutland.

In the next few months we had our camp in different parts of Manhattan Island, and once near the village of Harlem, contiguous to which was the remarkable Strait of Hell Gate, always attended with whirlpools and a roaring of the waters. The tremendous eddy was due to the narrowness and crookedness of the passage, where the waves were tossed on a bed of rock extending across it. On one side were sunken rocks named The Hog's Back, and on the other a point of similar danger, The Devil's Frying Pan, where the water hissed as if poured upon red-hot iron. In the midst, the whirl of the current caused a vast boiling motion, known as The Pot. This place had been famous for its enormous and excellent lobsters, which in peacetime had sold for only three halfpence a pound; but the tremendous cannonading in the battle of Long Island disturbed them from their retreat and they went away, not to return. More recently Sir James Wallace, pursued by the French fleet, had taken the *Experiment,* of fifty guns, safely into New York through this perilous passage; to the great astonishment of Admiral Howe. The principal credit, however, rightly went to the negro pilot. At the moment of the greatest danger Sir James gave some orders on the quarterdeck, which in the pilot's opinion interfered with the duties of his own office. Advancing therefore to Sir James and gently tapping him on the shoulder, this mungo said: 'Massa, you no speak here!' Sir James, feeling the full force of the brave fellow's remonstrance, was silent; and afterwards, in thankful recognition of his extraordinary feat of navigation, settled on him an annuity of £50 for life. The phrase 'Massa, you no speak here' became proverbial in the Regiment, and once I had the hardihood to employ it in addressing a young officer, who joined us about this time, when he attempted to interrupt some instruction I was giving my company in the practise of wood-fighting. He accepted the reproof in good part, as became a true gentleman. This second-lieutenant (as they are peculiarly called in the Regiment, rather than 'ensigns'), young Harry Calvert Esq. is now risen to be Lieutenant-General, and Adjutant-General of the British forces: it was he whose kind condescension lately won me my out-pension of a shilling a day from the Royal Hospital at Chelsea.

I was able on one or two occasions to visit the New Theatre, opened at John Street in the New Year, where the Surgeon-General to the Forces was manager and the chief parts were taken by officers of the Staff. I delighted especially in the acting of Major André, who spoke his words with great naturalness and feeling; and the performances I attended of *Macbeth* and *Richard III* made me ashamed of my self-satisfaction as a stage-player in the Rutland pen. The female parts were taken either by the mistresses of officers or, failing these, by boy-ensigns of the garrison.

The regimental celebrations of St. David's Day, which fall on March 1st, were as usual the occasion of much good humour and drunkenness among the Royal Welch Fusiliers. The officers together, and the sergeants together, celebrated it in the customary banquet with set toasts. To every toast that is drunk in either mess, the name of St. David is habitually added, which adds a ludicrous solemnity to proceedings. The first toast is always to 'His Royal Highness the Prince of Wales—and St. David', the band playing the melody of *The Noble Race of Jenkin* while a handsome drum-boy, elegantly dressed and mounted upon the goat, which is richly caparisoned with the Regimental devices, is led thrice around the mess table by the drum-major. It had happened at Boston four years previously that the goat sprang suddenly from the floor, spilling the drum-boy upon the table among the glasses and flagons and, bounding over the heads of some officers, ran off to the barracks. Other toasts, to 'Toby Purcell's Spurs*—and St. David', 'Jenkin ap Morgan, the first gentleman of Wales—and St. David', 'The Ladies—and St. David—God bless 'em!', 'The Glorious Roses of Minden—Comrades—and St. David', keep the merriment in progress all night. All officers or sergeants who have not previously performed the service of 'eating the leek', in the manner immortalized by Shakespeare's Fluellen are now obliged to do so in St. David's honour, standing upon a chair with one foot resting on the table while the drums play a continuous double-flam until the nauseous raw vegetable is wholly consumed—after which they are consoled with a large bumper and acknowledged as honorary Welshmen. This duty I was obliged by my fellow-sergeants to perform; and Colonel Balfour, who had but recently joined the Regiment from the King's Own, did likewise in the Officers' Mess. Thus I became a person of triple nationality: Irish by birth, Mohawk Indian and Welsh by initiation and adoption. I hope that I never disgraced any of these three nations in my quality as a warrior!

Though our service at New York was broken by four warlike expeditions and several forays, the Regiment conducted itself throughout just as if all were 'peace, parade and St. James's Park'; I mean, as to the formality and regularity of our behaviour and the exquisite care that each soldier was made to take of his personal appearance. Many hours every day were spent upon the pipe-claying of cross-belts and breeches—which, however, dried far more quickly here than in the humid air of Ireland—upon the shining of shoes, the polishing of buttons and buckles, and, above all, upon the correct adornment of the hair. I recalled how, upon the disembarkation of The Ninth at Three Rivers in Canada, Major Bolton had informed company-

---

* These spurs, worn by Major Toby Purcell, who was with the Regiment at the Victory of the Boyne, are kept in the possession of his successor, the senior major of the Regiment, and displayed every year at the Feast of St. David. R. L. [They were destroyed in a fire at Montreal when the Regiment was stationed there in 1842; but the toast is still drunk at the St. David's Day dinner. R. G.]

officers that the tallow provided for us would now be better daubed upon our shoes, to preserve them from the damps, than upon our hair, to hold the flour with which we powdered it—and that this flour likewise would be of more service to us in the edible form of loaves. Few even of the officers had thereafter attempted to keep themselves spick and span. But the Royal Welch Fusiliers were no rough and ready regiment: the comb, flour-dredge and pomatum box were as prime necessaries with us as cartouche box, powder-flask and ramrod, and no slightest deviation from correct soldierly behaviour in barracks was ever allowed to pass, nor any gross conduct or unsoldier-like lounging in the streets. We were often sneered at for macaronis; but we let that pass as a compliment, for we also took correspondingly greater care of our arms than other regiments. For example, I was very pleased to find that the company-officers, being persons of substance and with a pride in their profession, had at their own charges provided their men with the fine black flints which gentlemen use in their sporting guns. These remained sharp even after fifty discharges, whereas the ordinary Army issue of dull brown pebble was never good for more than fifteen, and often less. What was still more to the point, when we were at Harlem and a part of the Regiment quartered upon a wharf, figures of men as large as life made of thin boards were anchored at a proper distance from the end of the wharf; at these the platoons fired as a practice in marksmanship. Floating objects such as glass bottles, bobbing up and down with the tide, were also pointed out to them as targets, and premiums given to the best shots. No other regiment to my knowledge practised this sort of musketry, the colonels being content merely with simultaneity of the volleys, and letting aim go hang.

I have always had a great love of the regular, the orderly and the neat; and as a sergeant in this corps I was able to indulge it to the full. My sergeant's wig, which was paid for by the Colonel, and fitted for me by the Regimental perruquier, was of the finest hair; and I kept it always in irreproachable trim. Smutchy Steel took kindly to this mode of life, but it can be imagined that Mad Johnny Maguire found it difficult to alter his old slovenly habits. He was always in trouble.

Richard Harlowe was drafted to The Thirty-Third. It then proved that, by one of these extraordinary accidents that occur frequently on extraordinary occasions, Smutchy Steel had hit upon the exact truth. The Shakespearean fop was indeed a close relative of Harlowe's and rather than again risk the indignity of being accosted in the street by a common soldier who could call him cousin—or it may well have been brother—had undertaken to purchase his discharge: on condition that a substitute were found, which among the destitute Loyalists was not a difficult task. So this bad soldier was lost to the Army.

CHAPTER VII

OF THE expeditions which we made from our base of New York in 1779 I need not write in detail. The first was undertaken on May 30th, when we were sent up Hudson's River in boats against Stoney Point and Verplanck's Neck, some forty miles beyond New York, where the Americans had forts. These forts were placed at King's Ferry, a narrowing of the river, which was the way that the revolutionary forces habitually took when crossing from the middle provinces into New England, or contrariwise. If this passage were seized they must make a circuit of sixty miles through the mountains. To me the chief interest of the expedition was that I beheld for the first time the beautiful scenery on the lower reaches of Hudson's River, here about two miles in breadth, which surpassed description. The western bank showed at first a continuous dark wall of rock which by its vertical fissures suggested Palisades, and bore that name. It was occasionally broken by a watercourse and everywhere fringed and chequered with the bright foliage of early summer. The eastern shore—which I regarded with interest as the country which I had traversed as a fugitive in the previous winter—gradually assumed a wild and heroic character, with woods, pastures, towering cliffs. All the noblest combinations of forest and water, light and shade, were now here seen in the greatest perfection, and by the pleasure in Nature which I discovered, I knew that I was myself again, emerged from the slough of disgust and disinterest into which captivity had for awhile sunken me. Yet the American houses, sheds, sawmills and forts, that I beheld, all of undressed wood and many in ruins on account of the war, had for me a dishevelled and melancholy appearance when I contrasted them in memory with the neat whitewashed houses and handsome churches with glittering tin spires that had lined the St. Lawrence River in Canada. Considering the matter in my mind, I decided: 'No, no, a modest and decent prosperity will always outweigh for me the most romantic prospect of peak, chasm and tangled forest.'

The division that we were in landed a little before noon at a point seven miles below King's Ferry. Another continued up the river, and before night had, with the loss of one man wounded, seized Stoney Point. This was a place of great natural strength but the works being not yet completed by the enemy were abandoned by them in haste. We meanwhile, advancing over rugged and difficult country, invested the fort on our side of the river, named Fort Lafayette, and bivouacked within musket-shot of it. By five in the morning our people on the other bank had hauled cannon and mortars from the fleet up to Stoney Point and bombarded Fort Lafayette from across the water. This proved to be a small but complete work with palisades, a double ditch, trees felled with branches outward, *chevaux-de-frise,* and a bomb-proof block-house in the middle. The seventy Americans in it soon beat a *chamade,* or demand for a parley, and Major André was sent in under a flag of truce by General Clinton to receive their surrender. The sole condition made by the Americans was that we should promise them good usage. Having garrisoned these two forts, we soon dropped down the river again.

On July 4th, the Regiment was sent in an expedition against the coast of Connecticut, a province which abounded with men as well as provisions and was a principal support to the American armies. Since the Connecticut people had long boasted that we feared to attack them because of their martial prowess, Sir Henry Clinton decided to undeceive them. By doing as much destruction as possible to public arsenals, stores, barracks and the like, he hoped to tempt General Washington into quitting the Highlands. If he took the bait, well and good—for his troops, though then being exercised by Baron von Steuben, a Prussian drillmaster, were no match for ours; or if he stayed behind, better still—he would earn a reputation, among the people of Connecticut, either of not caring at all what losses they might suffer or of not daring to come to their aid. The reason that Connecticut had been so long spared was that most inhabitants of the coastal districts were of the Episcopalian faith, and loyal by inclination, though kept in awe by the dissenting and revolutionary minority; it had been thought unwise to destroy the wheat with the tares. However, since these Loyalists were so slow to come out in their true colours, Sir Henry now gave them the chance to declare themselves—let them treat us either as foes or liberators, however they wished.

To be brief: our small expedition, of regulars and American Provincials intermixed, disembarked on either side of the Connecticut fort of New Haven, which lay about eighty miles up the coast from New York, and seized the fort which protected it. The vessels in the harbour and all artillery, ammunition, public stores ashore were either taken or destroyed; yet the town, which was a pleasant and substantial place, was not burned. However, as was to be expected, the presence of Colonel Fanning's Provincials among our forces caused some irregularities. They could not at first be restrained from the plunder of private houses; and the inhabitants, being thus provoked, fired from windows at the sentinels placed as guards to prevent any further damage. The people of New Haven were, by the bye, universally known in New England as Pumpkin-heads, because of an ancient law in Connecticut which enjoined every male to have his hair cut round his cap every Saturday; the hard shell of a pumpkin being often used instead of a cap. The intention was, it seems, to prevent those who had lost their ears for heresy from concealing their misfortune under long tresses. After a proclamation had been made to persuade these Pumpkin-heads to renewed allegiance the fort was dismantled and we re-embarked.

The expedition next proceeded to Fairfield, a town about twenty miles nearer to New York, and a little inland. Fairfield, and Norwalk its neighbour, had been spared from destruction two years previously during an expedition made by Governor Tryon of New York, who was now again in command, against the arsenal of Danbury. The Americans, therefore, trusting that the same indulgence would once more be shown to the place, used private houses as ambuscades against our people, when we advanced to the seizure of the public stores. We lost a number of men killed or wounded. Governor Tryon, remarking that the Americans must be taught to use private houses only for private purposes, or else accept the consequences, ordered the little town to be burned to the ground. This would have been a very painful sight to all our eyes, had not the resentment that we felt for the loss of our comrades mitigated our mercy. Yet I for one was grieved to see the English church go up in flames, among the secular buildings; and a poor woman with an infant in her arms who came running to my platoon, calling upon us wildly to stay our hands, was the wife of the incumbent, the Reverend John Sayre. He had been very badly treated by the Whigs for the four years foregoing, his wife babblingly told us, and reduced to reading on a Sunday, to his congregation, no more than the Bible and the Homilies; for the Liturgy was forbidden him. Yet how had his forbearance and saintliness been served, she cried, even by those for whose victory he offered his private prayers to God nightly! His fine church was in ashes and his snug parsonage too, the Communion plate destroyed, and she and he, with eight children, were now left destitute of provisions, home and raiment. Our company commander offered her safe conduct back to New York, but she refused it. She had been separated from her husband, in the bustle, and from two of her children, and would not budge unless the whole flock were assembled. So we left her there raving distractedly.

Norwalk and Greenfield, places taken immediately afterward, suffered a similar fate, since the opposition of the militia, called out in great numbers, was of a nature that no regular army could patiently endure. Governor Tryon's name was productive of such hatred among the population, who regarded him as the main influence for the continuance of the war on our side (as we regarded King Hancock and the Adamses as the chief agitators on theirs), that every shed or barn became a fortress against our advance and, before we had done, our loss in killed, wounded and missing amounted to one hundred and fifty.

In the neighbourhood of Norwalk, Mad Johnny Maguire asked permission from our officer to leave the column for ten minutes while we halted in a field. The officer enquiring the reason, Maguire replied that he owed a native of the place a debt of four shillings and threepence and wished to discharge it. The officer, acceding to this curious request, sent a sergeant and two men with Maguire to observe what he did. I was the sergeant selected.

We passed up a wagon-track to a group of farm buildings through an orchard of cherry-trees, bearing a fine crop of the common black cherries which they used hereabouts for their cherry rum, and little red honey cherries which were good for eating. Maguire, leading confidently, said to me: 'This is the farm of my brother Cornelius the rebel; and yonder is my nephew and namesake Johnny. Come here, halloo, come here, Johnny, my fine rogue and greet your uncle!' But the little fellow hung back, and ran screaming to his mother at the sight of armed red-coats. She was gathering cherries in a tree, standing on a ladder; and being a little deaf had not heard our approach. When we came up, she screamed too, though with the presence of mind not to overset her basket. Descending the ladder precipitately, she fell at my feet and begged us to spare her life and that of the family.

'I think I have the pleasure of addressing Mrs. Cornelius Maguire,' I said politely. 'Your brother-in-law has just come to the house to pay your husband a small debt.'

'Oh, it is but that rascal and thief of a Johnny?' she cried, fear giving way to an impetuous indignation. 'He that near killed my poor inno-cent husband, who was so good to him, cracking his head open with a cruel stroke of a loggerhead? Oh, by the Angels, I'll be equal with him.' She caught little Johnny by the hand and rushed towards the farm, picking up a hatchet from the wood-pile as she went.

We hurried after her and were spectators of a curious scene—a family tussle between Maguire and a swarm of his half-grown nephews and nieces, who had been at work on various household tasks in the kitchen, for the possession of Cornelius' ponderous fire-lock. Cornelius himself directed the operations of his family from where he lay, his head bound with a cloth, on a straw pallet in the corner of the kitchen. He was feebly calling: 'Trip him up, boys, fly at his eyes, girls, the black rapparee! Were it not for these cursed mumps I would be up myself, and oh, then wouldn't I knock him edgewise into Glory?'

Upon Mrs. Maguire entering the fray with her hatchet, we interposed and disarmed her, and I received the captured firelock from Maguire. 'Now,' said I, 'what do you say, Private John Maguire'—for in our new regiment sergeants were required to distance themselves from the men and it was never 'Johnny' and 'Gerry' between us now, unless we were alone together—'what do you say, are we to make a prisoner of your brother?'

Mrs. Maguire began to sob and weep and to speak of the ingratitude of her brother-in-law, who thus returned evil for good, and how she would 'never see her darling Corny again, and him so bad with the mumps and all, so that his poor vitals were swelled to punkin-size'.

I did not wish to cause more hardship than could be prevented; and it seemed unjust that Johnny, whose only thought in visiting his brother had been to pay a debt of honour, should deprive this hardworking family of its 'king-post', as Mrs. Maguire described him. However, that Cornelius Maguire was suffering from an infectious disease which also prevented him from walking was sufficient excuse for not taking him with us, especially as he was neither armed nor in military uniform. Yet we knew perfectly well that, the moment he was recovered of his complaint, he would return to his militia regiment. Johnny Maguire, nearly in tears himself because of the predicament into which his generous impulse had thrown us all equally, was struck by a helpful thought. 'Sergeant Lamb,' he cried, 'I have a notion where our duty lies. The greatest lack of General Washington's army is clothing and arms, but especially clothing. Now, listen, suppose we sequestrate this rogue's coat, gaiters, shoes, breeches, musket, powder flask and all—the same being private property to be returned to him after the war is won—that will be a deal better than either killing him or taking him off. For we shall deprive the enemy of a soldier without depriving this poor, decent family of a father.'

To this I acceded, and in spite of the screamed remonstrances of Mrs. Maguire, we rendered her sullenly groaning husband an 'invalid';

which was the usual term for those many soldiers of the revolutionary forces who were unable to parade owing to mere nakedness. However, she had her revenge. As Johnny said good-bye to her and offered to kiss little Johnny, into whose palm he pressed a shilling, she seized a great handful of the black cherries from the basket by the door and, calling to her children to do likewise, began crushing them against his uniform and accoutrements. 'Pipe-clay that off, you thief, you villain, you wretch! You would strip your poor sick brother naked, would you, O fie, you blood-thirsty ogre! Now, what will your officers say, eh, Johnny, tell me that—won't they put you among the Invalids, the same as my poor Corny, that you won't disgrace them?'

This remarkable family then burst into a great cackle of laughter, in which Johnny Maguire himself joined as heartily as anyone.

Mrs. Maguire was right about the disgrace. When we returned to the company, our officer put Maguire under arrest and returned him to the transport, such a poor spotted figure he cut amongst us. What is more, he took the mumps—which were very prevalent in the American army—from the contagion of the children with whom he struggled, and was very sick as a result.

The seaport town of Greenfield was next fired by Governor Tryon's order—I do not know upon what provocation; and we were proceeding to New London, the chief centre of the privateering trade in Connecticut, when news that the Americans were gathering in great force led us to postpone the attack until reinforcements could be fetched. We did not number three thousand men. In nine days we had caused the people of Connecticut such prodigious losses that Sir Henry Clinton was informed by his secret agents in this province that there was a movement on foot to make a separate peace with us, the inhabitants despairing of help from General Washington. However, New London was not attempted, since General Washington moved suddenly against Stoney Point and Fort Lafayette and dispossessed us of both forts by a charge-bayonet executed at night. Our forces were therefore drawn off to recover these important points; which was done.

It should be fairly said that General Washington could have

effected no more than he did against us. He was starved of troops by Congress, who now evidently expected the active work of expelling us from their country to be accomplished chiefly by the French: as in previous wars the expulsion of the French had been left chiefly to us. General Washington himself expressed the fear that virtue and patriotism were extinct in America, and that, instead, 'speculation, peculation and an insatiable thirst for money' had got the better of almost every order of his fellow countrymen. This was written in despair; but the anxiety of rich and poor alike at the increasing depreciation of the paper currency and the great want of coin, must have spurred everyone to provide himself with some form of wealth that would still have value when Congress declared a bankruptcy. And so they not long afterwards did, by repudiating their paper, to the tune of nineteen shillings and sixpence in the pound.

The simple and impartial narrative of this Connecticut expedition, which I have just given, may be profitably set against the accounts given by the American writers Ramsay and Belsham. These have endeavoured with all the artifice of wilful misrepresentation so to colour the facts as to make the British name odious to humanity. In expeditions of this sort scenes naturally occur at which the feeling heart revolts; but in war the humane soldier can do no more than alleviate its horrors—he cannot prevent them entirely, especially if those whose residence unfortunately becomes the seat of war do not govern themselves prudently. Mr. Ramsay strangely asserts: 'At New Haven the inhabitants were stripped of their household furniture and other moveable property. The harbour and waterside were covered with feathers discharged from open beds.' It is true that New Englanders and, indeed, all Americans, so far south-ward as the Carolinas, have an over-fondness for large feather beds, which the British find stifling and uneasy couches, yet no revenge was taken upon them for this peculiarity. Strange indeed that soldiers weighed down with arms, ammunition and provisions, should carry feather beds so far, merely in order to destroy them! And as for the household furniture, what were we to do with it? There was no space in our tents for wardrobes and clock-cases and the like, even had we exerted ourselves to remove them from the houses of the enemy. Such slanderous improbabilities refute themselves. I never saw anything of the kind.

Further, Mr. Ramsay has the hardihood to write: 'An aged citizen, who laboured under a natural inability of speech, had his tongue cut out by one of the Royal army.' And again: 'A sucking infant was plundered of part of its clothing, while a bayonet was presented to the breast of its mother.' It is impossible for one who has been in America during a great part of the war, and actually taken part in much of the fighting, to read such gross falsehoods without being balanced between indignation and laughter. Any such wanton action as the former, proved on a British soldier, would have been punished by his officers with the greatest severity; as for the latter, the little cotton shirt that suffices an American infant in the heats of summer would be a curious booty for any but a madman.

Mr. Belsham, though somewhat more cautious than Mr. Ramsay, is equally off the mark. His assertion that 'all the buildings and farm-houses for two miles in extent round the town were laid in ashes', I can take upon me to contradict as a most cruel slander; and grieve that such misrepresentations can be transmitted under the pompous name of history to generations yet unborn.

Let me add that our cause was ill-served by Members of Parliament who sought to justify the burning of the towns not by a plain state-ment of the provocation that made such sad acts necessary, but by reference to the tomes of Puffendorf and Grotius. These two learned legal authorities had, it seems, long before declared that the burning of unfortified towns, which were the nurseries of soldiers, was conso-nant with the accepted rules of war. Mr. Burke, for the Opposition, however, protested that our acts had exceeded all that the rights of warfare could sanction, in annihilating humanity from the face of the earth! The Prime Minister and the Attorney-General successively rose to rebuke Mr. Burke for this exaggeration and falsification of fact, but Mr. George Johnstone, who had been a rapacious Governor of the Floridas in the year 1763, and, more lately, a Commissioner of Peace, in company with the Earl of Carlisle, impetuously agreed with Mr. Burke that a war of destruction was indeed being waged against the American people. 'No quarter should be shown to the American Congress, and if the Infernals could be let loose upon them I, for one, Mr. Speaker, would approve the measure.' Governor Johnstone's foolish warmth was due to his resentment against Congress for repudiating the Saratoga Convention, and for treating him and his fellow-Commissioners with studied coolness.

On September 23rd, we were embarked at Sandy Hook, close to New York, four thousand of us, under the command of Lieutenant-General the Earl of Cornwallis, whom I have mentioned in my previous volume as the exemplary Colonel of The Thirty-third when I was at Dublin learning the new light-infantry movements. We were told that we were bound for the West Indies, for Jamaica was threatened by the French fleet. After succouring our garrison there we would seize all the French Sugar Islands, and the Spanish possessions too, for the Spaniards had by now entered the war against us. We were glad to learn of this expedition, as providing at least a change of climate. A new draft of recruits from England had brought the fever with them, which soon swept through the city and the island, so that within six weeks six thousand men of the garrison were unfit for duty. Our officers, who always took good care of our health, saw that we disinfected our tents frequently and also supplied us with Bark; nevertheless we had many men on the sick list and a few deaths. New York was extremely subject to such fevers, chiefly on account of the dirtiness and narrowness of the streets on the East Side of the town, where houses were set as closely as possible and the riverside crowded with confused heaps of wooden stores, built upon wharfs projecting one beyond the other in every direction. Companies of negro slaves employed by the City Council used to carry through the streets, balanced on their heads, stinking buckets of night soil from the privies of the well-to-do, and empty them upon the mud of the water-fronts, where noxious vapours were bred. The hovels of the poor destitute Tories in the burned-out part of the city were also centres of infection.

Our voyage to Jamaica was cancelled when we had been but two days at sea (in very foul weather), since it had been reported that the

French fleet had left the West Indies and were making again for the mainland of America. We returned on September 29th, and had two months to wait before we were re-embarked for the South.

News came that greatly grieved me. The American General Sullivan had been ordered with four thousand men to attack those settlements of the Six Nations through which I had passed two winters before, in the company of my friend Thayendanegea; the Indians, supported by some Loyalist troops, had met the General in battle at Chemung by the Susquehanna River and been entirely defeated. He had thereupon burned all their villages and towns, some of which consisted of sixty, eighty and even one hundred houses, and visited upon them a far severer destruction than we upon the settlements of Connecticut. For his men destroyed the crops of the Indians with the greatest thoroughness, even pulling up the vegetables and currant-bushes in the gardens, and killed every orchard of cherry, apple and peach, by girdling the trees. In my later travels in the back country of America I fell in with a soldier who had served in this campaign and happened to be a man of finer feelings. Said he: 'When we burned down the Indian huts, that was well enough. It seemed a just vengeance for what had been done to our own houses in the Wyoming valley. We laughed at the crackling flames. But when we came, according to orders, to cut down the corn-patches, then, I swear, my soul revolted. Who could see without tears the stalks that stood so stately with broad green leaves and gaily tasselled shooks—filled with sweet milky fluid, and flour—who could see these sacred plants bowing under our knives, to wither and rot untasted in the fields?'

The Indians, who were commanded by Thayendanegea, got safely away, but were forced that winter to move up into Canada and there rely upon General Carleton's charity. The news, as it first reached us, described the massacre by the Americans of the whole population of the Six Nations, and it may be imagined what gloomy thoughts oppressed me. From the moment that I had bidden farewell to Thayendanegea in the woods near Saratoga before the capitulation I had never for a day ceased to think of Kate Harlowe and our child, and still played with the fancy that some accident of war or the eventual signature

of peace would happily reunite us. In planning my escape from the
Convention Army I had even first considered whether or no I should
run, not downstream to New York, but upstream past Albany—with
a view to making my way through the American frontier settlements,
following up the Mohawk River, and attaching myself to the Rangers
under Colonel Guy Johnson, who were operating in company with
the Six Nations. For I believed that Kate would still be living in the
Indian town of Genesee, where Thayendanegea had reported her to be.
Kate was a magnet that I had found it exceedingly hard to pull against.

The grief that the false news of the massacre engendered did
not have the expected effect upon me, of driving me to drink and
debauch: I was now too old a soldier to take that foolish course.
On the contrary, I bent all my energies upon improving my military knowledge by the reading of books borrowed from my officers
and upon making myself worthy of the regiment in which I was
now fortunately enrolled, by a strict attention to my duty. Though
winter here did not usually set in until the New Year, snow fell in the
middle of November, with premature frosts; and very hard weather
was predicted by the behaviour of the birds and beasts. It proved
to be the hardest winter of two centuries; when such common wild
game as deer, turkeys, squirrels and partridges were almost exterminated throughout the Northern colonies, when every privet hedge
in Pennsylvania was destroyed by the frost, and when Hudson's
River froze over as far down as New York City, and afforded a solid
causeway of salt-water ice from shore to shore, a distance of above
a mile. However, we escaped it. On the day after Christmas, 1779,
the Commander-in-Chief, having received orders from Lord George
Germaine in London to carry the war into the Southern provinces,
sailed with us and a great part of the army to recapture Charleston,
the capital city of South Carolina, which was then in the hands of the
American General Lincoln. There was already a great deal of ice in
New York Harbour when we sailed.

We expected to arrive at our destination by Ladies' Christmas, as
we call Twelfth Night in my country, but soon were made to under-

stand that we could not expect a continuance of the fair weather with which we set out. On December 28th, it blew a very hard gale of wind dead on the shore, from which we were distant thirty miles; we had to lie to until the next morning. The troops in our transport were very sick and in the morning the seas were still high and the fleet was scattered: one transport in the night had lost two masts. On the next day, fine weather; on the New Year's Eve, an extraordinary fog on the surface of the water—the north wind blowing, and the sea boiling under a sort of steam which never rose more than a few feet from the surface. New Year's day fine, as an augury for the year, but then suddenly another storm which blew from the north-west for no less than a week, forcing us to take down all our sail and lie to the whole while.

Our sick men grew very weak from this continual buffeting and, the hatches being battened down because of the huge seas, we could not ventilate the part where we were quartered, so that the air grew very foul. Salt pork and biscuit were never the proper medicine for sea-sickness, yet no other food was procurable. The water was cured with alum, which prevented it from rotting but was very disagreeable to the palate.

Sergeant Collins was the most active of us. When asked by what means he avoided this perpetual retching and vomiting, he gave us the old naval remedy, in rather a shamefast way: which was, to swallow a lump of greasy pork and as often as the stomach refused it, to swallow it again. At the fourth attempt the stomach being dominated, he said, by this expression of the throat's firm will, the pork was no longer bandied about between them, but decently passed on to the guts. However, not one of us cared to try this receipt, though it were as old as Noah's ark itself. I had brought two pounds of Souchong tea with me, and this was a great comfort to the sufferers while it lasted, as I laced it with rum.

There was one day's abatement of the gale on the 9th, and then it blew continuously from the west for six days more, during which we again lay to. The green water poured continually over us and carried everything away that was on deck. Many men were hurt by being flung against oak or iron by the rolling and pitching of our craft. We shipped a deal of salt water, and our supply of fresh water began to get very low in the scuttle-butts. I believe that it was in this gale that the ship foundered which carried the heavy guns of the expedition, and three or four other ships. The *Russia Merchant,* a transport carrying artillerymen, their wives and children, settled down slowly within sight of us, having sprung her timbers beyond hope of caulking. She was an old, crank vessel and should never have been commissioned for so important a service. We were unable to render any help, being pooped ourselves by the heavy sea, and all our boats and the mizzen-mast carried away. However, in spite of the tremendous seas, the *Lady Dunmore,* a privateer sloop of ours, went alongside and took off the crew and passengers. We gave her three hearty cheers for this bold action. The last boat had hardly got away when the *Russian Merchant* turned on her side and went down in a great boiling of water.

Our scattered fleet was crossed a few days later by an American fleet of twenty-six sail, come from the Dutch island of Eustacia, the greatest depôt for smugglers in the Indies—the Dutch not yet having openly joined the alliance against us. The sea was then calm. The Americans took a few of our ships which had become separated from our escorting fleet and plundered others. In return, a vessel of the Royal Navy captured a schooner of theirs which had lost its rudder. The transport that we were in, the name of which I disremember, being a difficult Dutch one, was hard put to it to escape from an American schooner; but we caught a wind which they missed and so drew out of range of her guns. This was most extraordinary, for she was gaining on us, and was within a mile and a half, when suddenly she lay becalmed. Our breeze then failed too, but a new one sprang up from another quarter which we caught while she continued to be 'held in irons'. We had rigged up a jury mizzen-mast.

These trials continued until the first week of February, when having overshot South Carolina, we arrived at Tybee in Georgia, a port at the mouth of the River Savannah which separates the two provinces. Our company behaved throughout with the greatest discipline and fortitude; so that it was easy for me too to laugh in the face of danger and to appear indifferent whether we sank or swam. Much pity was expressed for the horses which we had on board, that starved for lack of forage; we were obliged to shoot six of them and the remainder did not live out the voyage. Indeed, of all the two hundred horses that we had with us, for the cavalry and artillery, not one came safe ashore.

Ours was among the last of the transports to reach Tybee, with hardly time to get water and fresh fruit aboard, especially oranges and lemons of which we stood greatly in need for the cleansing of our blood, before we sailed again. We arrived back again in the summer season, and I saw for the first time palm-trees and aloes, with other trees and plants which I knew only from the Scriptures. A heavy and delicious perfume mingled strangely with the stench of the harbour; for Georgia lies some fourteen hundred miles to the southward of Quebec, nine hundred from New York, and in the same degree of latitude as Jerusalem and the Delta of the Nile. The prodigious extent of North America is hardly realized in Europe: it equals that of the whole North Atlantic Ocean.

I should greatly have enjoyed a visit to Savannah, the principal town in Georgia, which lay a few miles up the river of the same name, but it was not to be. The small garrison of Savannah, a few weeks before, had successfully repulsed the first combined assault of a French fleet and an American army. Following the failure, there had been recriminations, as before, between these ill-assorted allies. The French fleet had then sailed away, part to Europe, part to the West Indies; and General Lincoln, the American commander, was now wintering his troops at the polite city of Charleston, a hundred miles up the coast. We meant to catch him there, and accordingly sailed from Tybee on February 10th, to a place called North Edisto, which lay thirty miles short of the city; arriving there without further misadventure. We took part of the garrison of Savannah with us, who had suffered greatly of late from the yellow fever.

CHAPTER VIII

CHARLESTON, our object, was situated near the Ocean on a tongue of land formed by the confluence of Cooper River on the north side and Ashley River on the south: their united stream met the ocean below Sullivan's Island, where the Americans had a fort provided with heavy batteries. Between the city and the island was a harbour commodious for ships. The swelling tides of these rivers, together with pleasant sea-breezes, made Charleston more healthy than the neighbouring low country, so that invalids from the West India islands frequently came there to recuperate from fevers. However, the drinking water was frequently putrid and the sultry climate had reduced all the white people thereabouts to a bilious suet-colour and so diminished their energies that any sustained physical effort seemed impossible to them. Every white man of consequence kept a number of slaves and none would think to demean himself by performing the least action that could be performed as well by dusky hands, whether it were loading his sporting gun, combing his hair, or cutting up the meat on his trencher preparatory to eating it. Even the schoolboy going to his lessons had a little slave to carry his satchel, and the young miss who let a fan fall from her relaxed fingers to the carpet would scream for a slave rather than stoop to recover it herself. Contempt or pity was expressed by these people for the 'poor whites' who, for lack of money to buy and support a slave or two, were obliged to do menial tasks themselves.

The institution of slavery being the most striking aspect of the Southern States, I shall be excused for enlarging upon it in the course of this account. Its familiarity prevented the inhabitants of Charleston from looking upon it as in any way shameful or odious, though they professed, as American citizens, to cherish civil liberty and to assert the freedom and honour of human nature. The Charlestonians were indeed known throughout America for their hospitality, urbanity and enlightened minds; and it should be mentioned in their praise that throughout the war they continued to import books and all the new improvements of the arts from England and other countries of the old world. Charleston was the centre, especially, of the musical art in America and almost every man could scrape on a fiddle, toot on a flute, or perform pleasantly on some other instrument; and every woman sang.

On the coast this side of Ashley River were a number of low-lying islands which we must successively occupy: Edisto Island, St. John's Island, St. James Island. On our arrival at the village of North Edisto, the day after leaving Tybee, we landed unopposed and took possession of St. John's Island, the further shores of which were bounded by Stono Creek. From this creek a winding canal called Wappo Cut led into Ashley River, directly opposite Charleston, with St. James Island lying on the right hand of it. I mention these particulars because on the day after our arrival at St. John's Island I was selected to go with a detachment under Major Moncrieff, our Chief Engineer, to take soundings of Stono Creek. He wished to determine whether provision boats could be taken up to our camp from the sea. This was my first adventure in the Southern States and though little of military importance happened during it, I recall the whole itinerary with a vividness of first impressions that survive untarnished when many more notable later circumstances fade altogether away.

Major Moncrieff, a talented Scotsman, when we had almost finished our task, felt the heat in our boat highly oppressive and called for a halt and refreshment. We were passing a swampy field in which a number of negro slaves, both men and women, clad only in loincloths, were dabbling about. They were attending to the cultivation of the young rice. Rice was the staple of this province and required very much labour. We pulled to the bank and Lieutenant Sutherland of the Engineers, who was with us, beckoned to a young negro, who came towards us. To my surprise the unfortunate creature hardly knew three words of English but jargoned in an incomprehensible gibberish—no doubt the native language of the Congo jungle from which he was stolen to be a slave.

However, a woman wearing a ragged cotton shift came to his aid and addressed Lieutenant Sutherland: 'Good day, Massa Cunnel. You want him, darra driber? Him driber sleep ober dere, under darra tree.'

'Then go wake the Driver, my good woman,' said the Lieutenant, not ill-pleased to be addressed as Colonel—'Tell him that the Chief Engineer to the British Forces wishes to speak to his master.'

'Hilloo now, darra's a mighty hard word, Massa Cunnel, my honey, darra ole Chief Ingy-what-you-say! I tell him "British Cunnel him come: wake up, or massa vexed."'

So off she bounded and soon a young mulatto overseer, or driver, came walking his horse slowly across the rice-field. He appeared annoyed at having his noon-time sleep interrupted, but durst not show it for fear of punishment.

'Take me to your master,' Major Moncrieff ordered.

The Driver objected: 'Massa mebbe sleep. Him good massa but mighty angry man, him bery fierce be waked up.'

'I'll take the consequences,' said the Major. 'I understand that the gentlemen in these parts are most civil to strangers.'

When the Driver saw that we were determined on our visit he changed his tone: 'No, me lie to you. Massa not sleep, him right glad to welcome you, nobody neber so glad, nothing can be like.' He spoke to the slaves, threatening them with dire punishments if they idled in his absence, and then showed us where to tie up the boat and disembark. He led the way to the planter's house, which stood behind a grove of palmetto-trees, with a large barn beside it and two or three stacks of rice-straw. Before we reached it, we passed a row of tumbledown huts, about thirty of them, thatched with palmetto leaves, from which a fetid animal smell issued. Two old naked hags of negresses, with white wool on their heads, and shrivelled bosoms, peered out as we passed. They uttered cries of astonishment and admiration at our weapons and clothes.

'Dem's de meat-houses,' said the Driver, pointing. 'Massa's a consid'able warm man. Own one hun'ed good working niggers. All de urras but ole grand-mammy and ole grand-daddy, dey work in de rice swamp.'

He rode ahead to warn his master of our approach. This gentleman was named Captain Gale—every person throughout the South held a military rank of some sort, even though he had never spent but a single day with the provincial militia—and was the complete Master Planter. He appeared to us in undress—cambric shirt, canvas breeches, and a night-cap, his feet stockingless, a riding-whip in his left hand (for the correction of his slaves) which was always at the waggle. He came forward with the right hand outstretched to welcome the officers. He was neither drunk nor sober, but in a state of confused exhilaration. 'Egad, gentlemen, I am right down glad to welcome you! Upon my soul, it does my eyes good to feast them upon British regimentals again. This is a prelude, damme, to a fine show. You Britons will soon settle the hash of the damned rebels across to Charleston. Why, since they nested there I have been quite cut off from society, but for the Bennets and Mottes and M'Cordes, my neighbours. Huzza, now! What do you say to twigging a tickler of old peach to His Majesty King George's health? Heigh, Cudjo, *Cudjo,* CUDJO, you plaguey black dog, must I ever split my throat bawling to you? Bring us the old peach and three peachers instantly!'

A startled voice came from a room behind: 'Hi, Massa! Sure Cudjo always answer when he hear Massa halloa!'

Cudjo, another young mulatto, then came running up with the guilty air of one who has been caught napping. He brought with him a bottle of peach-brandy and three glasses on a tray. Captain Gale playfully cracked his whip at the fellow and called him a cursed, lazy Jack.

His Majesty's health was then duly drunk on the verandah, while I posted sentinels about the grounds; having done so, I reported to Major Moncrieff for orders. He was good enough to suggest to his host that I would be the better off for a tickler too, remarking that I was a non-commissioned officer who had already seen considerable service in the war and been rewarded with a bounty by Sir Henry Clinton for bringing a party of escaped prisoners safely through General Washington's lines.

Captain Gale was at once all affability towards me and sent Cudjo flying for another glass. 'Well, my fine hero,' he cried, 'so you outwitted that old Virginian Fabius, did you, like a Hannibal and breached his fence? That's right, that's right! And now you'd be revenged on those damned Yankee pedlars for what they did to you? O the rogues! That's right! There's a great sight of 'em within Charleston. Show them no quarter, but give it to them handsomely! Break their backs like dogs! Cut them over the face and eyes like cats! Bang them like asses! Huzza! Britons, lay on! Were it not for my cursed loins which trouble me, I'd be with you too, I swear, staving at full butt against the sons of bitches.'

I respectfully drank the King's health in the 'old peach', which was very good liquor but with a powerful effect upon an empty belly.

Major Moncrieff spoke a few words in praise of the plantation, which Captain Gale heard with complacence; and Lieutenant Sutherland remarked that a planter's life must be pleasant enough.

'God's mercy, I have nothing to rail against, but only this damned war. It has swept the country clear of yellow boys and shining silver Carols and landed us with bushel-loads of Continental prock which crackle insult and treachery at a man the instant he takes them into his fist. Thank God, that you gentlemen have come to our rescue at last, for things were getting mighty difficult for honest men.'

He boasted about his 'black cattle', by which it seems he intended the negroes. He had six house-boys and wenches, all of them mulattoes, as best for domestic work. 'I breed 'em myself,' he said jovially, 'for, egad, then I have nobody to blame but myself for their weak points. Cudjo's mother, she was a strapping fine Gold Coast lass, a virgin, and I got her for nothing: that is, I won her from an old dried-up Frenchman of Tradd Street in Charleston, after an all-night sitting of cards. A pretty long heat that was before I wore the old Frog down, point by point, and at last the prize was mine. Cudjo favours me a little, I think—see the big nose on him and my lumpish thighs—and I had another son by the same wench, who's my groom, and a pretty smart creature too, though I do boast of him. The Driver I had by another Coaster whom I used as cook wench: she was the devil and all, for she grew jealous of Cudjo's mother and poisoned her—well, I forgave her that, ha-ha, jealousy is no bad fault in a woman—but then, damme, she got lined by a big black buck who came over with a musical pasty from Bennet's. So I lost patience with the jolter-headed bitch and returned her to the hoeing team. What do you think of that now, Major?'

Major Moncrieff replied, for he was accustomed to this sort of gentry, that it was an ill trick the wench played him.

'Ah, but that's not the half of it,' Captain Gale proceeded. 'She cast her brat at three months, as if to spite me, and fearing she would play me some such wry trick again, I traded her for a Virginia mare in foal to old Bennet. However, she proved a good breeder after all, and my mare lost her foal, so old Bennet had the laugh on me. Oh, to be sure, they're difficult cattle, these female blackamoors.'

'They must indeed keep you busy, night and day,' said the Lieutenant very drily.

'We dine at two o'clock, gentlemen,' Captain Gale continued, 'and I insist you'll honour us with your company, and there's good feeding for your men too—a trencher of fat pork with sweet potatoes and hearth-cakes, if that's to their taste. How say you, Sergeant?'

I replied: 'That would be very welcome, your Honour, I'm sure.'

'As for ourselves, gentlemen,' he proceeded, 'I know what our fare will be.' Here he leered archly and poked both the officers in the belly with his forefinger. 'A green goose with currant jelly and a bottle of old Madeira to wash it down, do you see? Something *nice* for you, do you see, Major Moncrieff, my noble son of thunder!'

I remained listening with attention to the extraordinary talk of this planter, and soon was privileged to see his white wife and daughter appear to greet the British officers. Both wore very handsome French dresses in a new fashion, and enormous poke-bonnets of blue gauze of the sort that all the better class of women affected thereabouts; they were made with a caul fitting close on the back part of the head. The front, stiffened with small pieces of cane, projected two feet or more forward above the face and was adorned with cherry-coloured ribbands.

Major Moncrieff paid the lady, and Lieutenant Sutherland paid the daughter, a few compliments in the New York style, which they swallowed as avidly as sugar-candy, simpering and casting such looks at the officers as were perfectly surprising to me. I noted that Miss Arabella, who had been born in this mansion, had contracted a negroish kind of accent and dialect. For it was the custom in the Carolinas to deliver a white child, as soon as it was born, to a negro foster-mother, so that it never tasted a drop of its mother's milk; and by constant association with negro servants a planter's daughter would carry their accent and vitiated manners with her through life.

The company now disappeared into the house and I took my leave, in order to look after the men. As I went, I thought to myself: 'These are people whom I shall never understand.' Nor was my perplexity eased when, upon discreet enquiry from one of the Motte family, a week later, I found that Captain Gale, though reputedly a 'jack of both sides', that is to say a trimmer between the loyal and revolutionary causes, was a man very well spoken of in St. John's Island. He was a considerate master to his slaves—as one might say that a drover was considerate of his cattle in not over-driving them or over-whacking them or stinting them in drink or forage; and they repaid him with a dog-like loyalty, which was very touching when I caught a glint of it in Cudjo's eyes. To his wife he was affectionate, never 'taking the timber to her' even when egregiously drunk; his breeding of mulatto bastards she accepted very calmly as a part of the rustic economy, and did not think it a nasty act. To his daughter he was an indulgent father, and winked at her amours while they did not bring him into disgrace. He had a son whom he had sent to an English college.

The Captain's manner of life, like that of most of his fellow-planters, seems to have been as follows. He would rise about eight o'clock, drink off a morning sling of strong apply-brandy and water, sweetened with sugar, and then mount his blood-horse and ride round his plantation to view his stock of human and beef cattle, returning about ten to breakfast on ham, fried maize cakes, toast and cider. He then sauntered about the house, playing on a flute or throwing dice, left hand against right. About noon he drank his midday draught of old peach and water to give him an appetite for dinner and pleasantly teased his servants and the little dark children sprawling about on the verandah.

At two he dined and thereafter slept for three hours. Lastly, after sipping a little tea with Mrs. Gale and Miss Arabella, he began his serious work of the day, that of tippling himself into stupefaction with apple-brandy; which achieved, his mulatto house-boys would convey him to bed for the night. This routine he interrupted about once a week, to attend a horse-race, a cock-fight or an auction of slaves or cattle; and on court-days to visit the neighbouring Court House in his capacity as magistrate. On the first of every month he took his wife and daughter into Charleston for a taste of society, where they stayed three days, and from whence he returned in a state of insensibility laid out on the bottom of his carriage.

Major André, as Adjutant-General, came to visit us on February 20th, where we bivouacked at Stono Ferry. He remarked to our commanding officer, Lieutenant-Colonel Balfour, in my hearing: 'We must be very careful not to flush General Lincoln's army from cover by any hasty show of force until we can cut off his retreat. The Commander-in-Chief is very positive on this point. He is glad now of our delay in reaching this place, since it has given General Lincoln courage to muster all his militia and set them to work at improving his fortifications. I wish to Heaven we could be sure that he will not make a bolt for it.' Colonel Balfour expressed as his opinion that: 'General Lincoln would be most unwise if he did not retreat, when informed that more than seven thousand trained troops are come against his five thousand half-trained, and under officers skilled in siege warfare. Five thousand are hardly sufficient, I believe, to man such extensive works. Yet he may perhaps be tempted to stand a siege, if what our people did at Savannah last summer, against much greater odds, touches and challenges his pride as an American.'

'Pray Heaven that he has such a pride,' said Major André.

'Well,' said Colonel Balfour, 'Sir Henry's pride is touched too. For he failed against Charleston four years ago, though that was owing to no fault of his own.'

Colonel Balfour then excusing himself and going away, I had the hardihood to address Major André and ask permission to inform him of something. He was sitting, hand at hip, on a handsome grey charger which was cropping the grass under a flowering Judas—a strange crooked tree whose red flowers burst directly from the bark and suggested the blood which poured from the traitor Judas at his hanging. He appeared deep in anxious thought. He started at the sound of my voice, but was good enough to recognize me; and encouraged me to say whatever was on my mind. I then begged pardon for interfering in matters which did not concern me, but continued: 'Your Honour may rest assured that General Clinton will hold his ground. For I heard positively from my guards at Rutland that he had been very hot against Generals Schuyler and St. Clair for their abandonment of Ticonderoga Fortress when we invested it—he swore that any American who would not defend to the last shot a city entrusted to his defence deserved to be hanged without mercy. General Arnold disputing the point with him, and applauding General St. Clair's decision, I am told they nearly came to blows. I overlooked to mention this item to you when you were condescending enough to call me into your parlour last September.'

He struck his brow with his knuckles. 'Why now, Sergeant Lamb, call me a fool not to have thought of that before! Ay, it's true enough, I heard of it too at the time. I am indeed infinitely obliged to you, my friend, for recalling the matter to my recollection. Now I can set Sir Henry Clinton's mind at rest. Oh, we'll bag that bold fox, I warrant.'

St. David's Day led in March with the usual regimental jollity: in which we Fusiliers invited all our neighbours to join. Major André sang in our officers' mess a comical parody he had written, *Yankee Doodle's Expedition to Rhode Island*, of which I can recollect only the verse:

> In dread array their tattered crew
>   Advanced with colours spread, Sir;
> Their fifes played Yankee-doodle-doo,
>   King Hancock at their head, Sir.

He was loudly applauded. On being called upon for a speech he made a remarkable statement: 'My Lords and gentlemen,' he said, 'this has been a long war, but *it will be won this year.* Do not, I pray, press me for an explanation when I tell you that an American sheep-dog will soon come secretly into our fold, bringing the whole flock with him.' This obscure promise was bandied from mouth to mouth, and by some held to mean that General Washington was privately treating with General Clinton for terms. Others thought that General Charles Lee was going to 'play General Monk', and head a loyal counter-revolution. But Major André spoke with such conviction that all believed him as to the approaching end of hostilities.

Then came Easter, a prime festival season in Virginia and the Carolinas; and notwithstanding the war the inhabitants of the country about Charleston abated little of their customary ceremonies of drinking, wrestling, quarter-racing and egg-rolling. This last practice being something of a novelty I shall take the liberty of describing it. They boiled hens' eggs in log-wood, which dyed the shell a fine crimson. This colour would not rub off, yet one might with a pin scratch on the shells any figure or amatory device that struck the fancy. The favourite devices were true lovers' knots, Cupids, flowers, and pierced hearts; and the adorned egg, marked with the name of the Valentine (for Easter here had much of the fourteenth of February about it) was a sentimental gift between young people in love. The little children, being also provided by their parents with these gaudy eggs, rolled them towards one another down into a grassy hollow, so that they struck together at the bottom; and the egg whose shell was dinted became the property of him whose egg remained whole. The ultimate winner of these childish lists was named 'King Easter'. However, this Easter jollity was turned to disgust by news that Congress had repudiated their paper-money. It was recalled that in the previous September Congress had proclaimed: 'A bankrupt faithless republic would be a novelty in the political world, and would appear among respectable nations like a common prostitute among chaste matrons.' Now the rouge-pot was unblushingly applied by this chaste matron to her own cheeks. There had been gross abuse of the exchange all over the Continent: instead of creditor pursuing debtor, the position was reversed. The debtor came running with a sack-load of paper, purchased for a very little hard money, to pay off a loan or a mortgage; and the creditor could not refuse it. Many orphans and minors were similarly cheated by their guardians and trustees.

Wappo Cut was bridged and a large division of our army, crossing over it from St. James Island, marched twelve miles up Ashley River. They were then ferried over to the root of that tongue of land, the tip of which was the city of Charleston. By then it was already the end of March, for Sir Henry was proceeding with great caution and careful method, making sure of his communications and supplies, seizing and fortifying all places of military importance, and building bridges over rivers and causeways over swamps. General Lincoln meanwhile had not only held his ground but even sent north for reinforcements. News of this caused general satisfaction in our ranks. We never for a moment had any doubt as to the happy issue of a general engagement, or an attempt at storm.

None the less, General Lincoln might well hope to wear down our patience, if he could keep his twenty thousand mouths well fed: for the entrenchments that he had raised since our fleet was first sighted were strong enough. They extended in the rear of the city from Ashley River across the whole tongue of land to Cooper River, a distance of one mile and a half. The first obstruction presented to our people was a broad canal filled with water; this terminated at either end in a morass, commanded by a fort with a clear field of fire along the canal. Next came *abattis*—trees buried slant-wise in the earth, their sharply lopped branches pointed outward—then a dry ditch with two rows of palisades, and lastly a chain of redoubts connected by trenches. There was also a big horn-work made of masonry in the centre of the line, which formed a sort of advanced citadel. Such were their defences against our sole approach by land; and on the waterfronts numerous strong batteries forbade the approach of ships, while stakes and other obstructions discouraged a landing from boats. Our fleet lay outside the harbour, below Sullivan's Island, but came no nearer because of the fort there, which was provided with heavy guns to dispute the passage.

A part of the army was busy as bees in a tar-barrel on the night of All Fool's Day when Sir Henry, or rather Major Moncrieff who conducted the siege as Chief Engineer, set two thousand men digging siege-works within half a mile of the American lines. Our regiment now lay at a place named Linning's, on the further bank of Ashley River immediately opposite these works, and our task was to carry over tools, wooden frames and other engineers' stores in small boats. During the night the working parties threw up two strong redoubts, each enclosing about a quarter of an acre of ground, which were not discovered by the enemy until daybreak. On the next night, they added a third redoubt sited between the two others, and for a whole week every night continued digging like beavers in the wet soil and constructing emplacements for our artillery.

On April 9th, in the early afternoon, we heard very heavy gun-fire from beyond the town and presently learned that the fleet had courageously forced the river passage, with only trifling loss, and become masters of the harbour. However, General Lincoln had sunk a number of vessels across Cooper River from Charleston, which made an impassable boom against our fleet; he also held the opposing bank of the river with three regiments of cavalry. The Americans were thus able to convey a regular supply of provisions across Cooper River into the city; and on April 10th seven hundred good Virginian troops came down the stream in small craft and joined the garrison unopposed. 'So much the better,' we thought. 'The more fish in the seine, the greater will be our haul.' We were now ourselves reinforced by three thousand troops from New York.

That same day a white flag was sent to General Lincoln summoning him to surrender his army as prisoners of war, with a promise of protection to the inhabitants' persons and property; for Sir Henry had not yet bombarded the city and did not wish to do so without fair warning. General Lincoln replied shortly that he would have quitted the city two months before had he intended to avoid battle.

So the siege was on, and our ten-inch mortars soon began dropping carcasses, or incendiary metal, into the city; which fired five or six houses and greatly alarmed the inhabitants. Besides that, we had three eight-inch howitzers at work and seventeen twenty-four-pounders, with Coehorns, Royals and other guns. They made a deal of noise. Through a spy-glass I saw a shell break against the tower of St. Michael's church where the enemy had an observation-post. The fleet also assisted in this bombardment.

Another week, and our people across Ashley River had sapped forward and completed another parallel of trenches a quarter of a mile nearer the enemy. Meanwhile our cavalry, having found horses to replace those lost, by a forced sale from the planters of Port Royal near Savannah, had crossed Cooper River thirty miles upstream and cut to pieces the whole American cavalry division posted there. Infantry followed them, securing all the posts on the further banks, so that now the net was closed. Charleston was invested from every side.

On April 21st, General Lincoln sent a white flag to our lines and called for a truce. He proposed to march out with his garrison, drums playing and colours flying, and to take all his arms and ammunition too. Sir Henry must undertake not to pursue this column for ten days, and the few American ships anchored under cover of the batteries must be allowed to put out to sea equally unmolested. This offer was of course refused, as based upon a comical misreading of the true situation.

On with the siege again! A third parallel was now advanced close to the enemy's moat, which was bled at the northern, or Cooper River end, by a ditch driven forward into it. The moat was dry in two days: and a company of German Jaegers, or sharpshooters, used it for cover to gall with close rifle-fire the American sentinels in the trenches. Our losses by enemy fire were now about seven or eight a day. On May 8th, some batteries of guns being advanced within a hundred yards of the garrison, Sir Henry, from motives of humanity, offered the same terms as before. But General Lincoln still played his hand as if it were richer in tricks than we knew it to be. He returned a haughty answer and there was a great deal of defiant huzzaing heard and a violent cannonade from every gun that they could fire, seemingly in a drunken frenzy, but without any loss to us. It was true that when the hot weather came our army might well lose many thousands of men from fever; and that the French might be expected soon to attempt to raise the siege. But Sir Henry was aware that no more than one week's supply of fresh provisions remained in the city, and that the daily ration of maize was reduced to six ounces for every person. He knew too, by spies in Congress, that no plans of combined operations between the French expedition and General Washington's armies were to be concerted until the former arrived in American waters. He therefore ordered the cannonade to continue.

The first shot sent was a shell filled not with explosive powder but with rice and molasses, as an indication that we were aware of their shortage of food. This shell was returned half an hour later with a message chalked upon it: 'Intended for the 71st Regiment and their brother Scots.' It then contained sulphur and hog's lard. This laborious joke referred no doubt to the famous Scottish itch, caused by the overheating of Caledonian blood with too simple a diet of oatmeal. The lard was for external use as an emollient and the sulphur as an internal purificant. The Scots were among the most loyal subjects of King George, and those settled in the Carolinas had not budged from their principles either. After this raillery the earnest shot and shell began to fly again.

Our people sapped closer still and preparations for a general assault were made. Yet, after all, it did not come to a storm, for citizens and militia very soon forced General Lincoln to surrender; the original terms being still generously held out to them. The capitulation took place on May 12th. The garrison were allowed some of the honours of war: for example, all officers were to keep their swords and pistols, and their baggage was to remain unsearched. The troops in general were to march out of the town, their arms clubbed, not at the shoulder, and abandon them by the canal. Their drums were not given the honour of beating a British or German march—though they might play *Yankee Doodle* if they pleased—nor might their colours be unfurled from the casings. The regular troops and seamen were then to become prisoners of war; the militia to disperse to their homes on parole and, while they kept the same, to continue safe in their lives and properties; other able-bodied citizens to be treated in the same manner.

Out they all came at two o'clock in the afternoon of the 12th, to be disarmed: five thousand, six hundred of them, with seven generals, two hundred other officers, and a thousand seamen. The Americans never pile up their arms, but lay them upon wooden racks, or, more generally, ground them; which was now done. We were also yielded four hundred guns, quantities of ammunition, five stout warships and a vast amount of public stores. The regular troops who took over the city (the Loyalists not being trusted to enter, lest they should rob and insult their fellow-countrymen) behaved very discreetly and without exultation. There was satisfaction among us all to know that, with this surrender of the whole American Southern army, at a cost to ourselves of only two hundred and fifty killed and wounded, about the same as theirs, an enormous extent of country had been restored to the Crown. It had been hoped among the rank and file that the order for storm would be given, which would have meant the wild intoxication of battle and, by ancient usage, liberty to plunder when the city was taken. But I, for one, was glad that it had not come to this. I had seen enough of blood and detested the notion of plunder, which evokes from the breast of man all that is most brutal and odious.

This, by the bye, was the first instance in which the Americans had ventured to defend a town against regular troops; and the result demonstrated General Washington's wisdom in advising against such an attempt. It is, however, just to remark that Charleston was the only considerable city in the Southern part of the Confederacy, and worth preserving by every possible exertion; and that near ten thousand Americans were fast marching to its relief. Some turned back upon hearing news of the capitulation; others were caught and routed by our cavalry. A large French fleet, convoying six thousand soldiers in transports, was also on the way; but, hearing the news at Bermuda, sailed instead against our Northern forces.

CHAPTER IX

SIR HENRY CLINTON returned to New York with most of the army, the French fleet being soon expected in Northern waters. He left behind four thousand men under the Earl of Cornwallis; among whom were the Royal Welch Fusiliers, then numbering about five hundred men. Before he sailed, he issued a proclamation, freeing from their parole all prisoners except regular soldiers; but declared at the same time that any person who refused allegiance to King George would be considered a rebel. He promised the Carolinians reinstatement in their ancient rights and immunities, and exemption from all taxes except those imposed by their own provincial government. Lord Cornwallis was instructed to keep his hold on the province at all events, and to encourage or oblige its able-bodied men to form a militia to assist him in this task.

South Carolina was inhabited by a great variety of peoples. Since its foundation a hundred years before by a small number of English settlers, it had successively received French, Swiss, Germans, Dutch, Scottish and Irish immigrants, all of the Protestant faith. To them had recently been added fortune-seekers from Pennsylvania and Virginia. These races did not readily mix, but formed separate settlements on the several broad rivers, or their numerous tributaries, which watered the country. Each race had its own political convictions. There were seven main classes of opinion: viz. staunch Whigs, timid Whigs, Whigs, jacks of both sides, Tories, moderate Tories, and furious Tories.

The hot climate of the South encouraged the passions, so that crimes of violence were extraordinarily frequent, by comparison with the settled parts of the Northern States. In the North, in time of peace at least, no man ever troubled to take a gun with him on any excursion except in hope of game; and did not even bar his door at night. In the South, robberies on the road, burglaries by night, and perpetual family feuds were the general rule. A man who went even to his place of worship without a loaded pistol in his belt would be considered a fool. Drunkenness was universal and the morning slings and midday draughts of strong grog were rightly admitted by the people themselves as the chief curse of their country; though the great sultry heat was advanced as sufficient excuse for the error. It can therefore readily be understood why the merciless, cruel deeds that the rival partisans of King and Congress did to one another were in this torrid zone often beyond description in print.

On the whole, the white people of the Carolinas, and of the South in general, formed two classes: the rich and the poor. The poor were not (as is usual in other climes) supported by the rich, since the rich owned slaves whose labour was cheaper and whose black and oily skins fitted them better to withstand the climate than did that of the poor whites. The rich engrossing all the land and all the trade, the poor whites grew still poorer and more low-spirited. Enough food to live upon was easily come by in the South, where sixpence would buy rice for a month, fruit abounded and every creek was populous with fish—why, that noblest fish of all, the sturgeon, who in England is accounted royal and whenever caught must be rendered to the King's household as a right, him the negroes and poor whites captured easily and often, for their own use, as he took his midday sleep in the muddy waters of the great rivers. This 'white trash', as the poor whites were called, seldom got money and what little they did get they laid out in apple or peach brandy. A more indolent, vicious and uncivilized race of men I never met, yet they would boast themselves as the Lords of Creation when speaking of the negroes. It was a great misfortune that so many of them attached themselves to our forces, in hopes of plunder, and with their cries of 'God Save the King' as they robbed, burned and ravished, disgraced our own good name.

The Royal Welch Fusiliers were ordered to Camden. This small township lay one hundred miles inland from Charleston, but not two hundred feet above the level of the ocean, and in a very hot, damp situation near the banks of the Catawba River which ran between swamps. These swamps abounded with juniper and cypress; live oaks, bearded with lichen; and a long rich grass which fattened the cattle driven into it. Parts of these swamps were absolutely impervious to travellers because of close tangled thickets, the chosen lurking-places of foxes and racoons. Other parts were quaking bog or mere morass filled with strange creatures, horny or slimy, and gave off a sickly, putrescent smell, which breathed of fever.

Our men were warned by the Surgeon to avoid water that was not cleansed with a small addition of spirits. Nor should they eat any fruit, such as the luscious pineapple, or the golden persimmon that puckered the mouth, if it were still warm with the sun; else these would surely give the eater colic. We were also warned against eating fresh pork in these hot months, and some who disobeyed died of poisoning. Moses was a wise law-giver in forbidding pork to the Jews in sultry Palestine. We acquired a taste for the great green water-melon with its pink flesh and black seed. We used, overnight, to pour a gill of rum into a hole bored at one end, which became absorbed and deliciously incorporated in the fruit by breakfast time.

Life in tents was excessively hot and it was not until the summer was well advanced that materials were brought us for making huts. Our drills we performed in the early morning and we were often taken for route-marches at night; partly in order to accustom us to finding our way through difficult country in the dark, but partly to shake the heavy humours out of our blood. In spite of every such precaution against fever, and the constant taking of Bark, we lost a number of men, though not so many as the other regiments. If any continuous labour was required of us by day, we sweated so pro-fusely that we became quite faint. For this we found a remedy in adding a little salt to our drink, which restored what had been lost by sweating. The cattle and hogs of the Dutch plantation near us used the same remedy. They would come out from the swamp and down to the quay where our barrels of salted provisions were landed; crowding around them to lick off the brine. By their greediness they made it very difficult for us to roll the barrels up to the encampment. Their need of salt was so great that I once saw a great old hog come up to a sweating mare, tied to a post by an officer's marquee, and rearing up on his hind legs greedily lick her neck, flanks and legs.

A good deal of maize was grown hereabouts. The slaves who tended the crops of this plantation went stark naked and seemed a most discontented cattle, compared with Captain Gale's property. I heard that in the West India Islands there was a descending gradation in the humanity severally shown by the different European races, and that the same rule generally applied on the American continent. The most indulgent were the Spaniards; the next most indulgent were the French; the English were not so kind; but the most severe and merciless of all were the Dutch. It was strange that this was the same order into which the political governments then fell, in descending gradation of absoluteness—from the sacred autocracy of Spain to the obstinate republicanism of the Dutch. But that 'Republicans are always the worst masters' is an old saying, and a good argument (if any were needed) in favour of Royalty.

The poor negroes here were over-worked and under-fed in a manner that would have been considered shameful had they been horned cattle. They were called up at daybreak, and herded out immediately into the corn field. There they laboured without any intermission until noon, when half an hour was allowed them for their meal, which invariably consisted of maize-flour made into coarse cakes and baked on their working hoes. To this was added a little brine washed from the salted herrings which the Dutch household ate. At dusk they returned, after labouring all the remaining hours of daylight, and to keep them out of mischief were given a large quantity of Indian corn to husk. If they did not complete their allotted task, they were tied up in the morning and ruthlessly lashed by their drivers. The hours for sleep were seven, nor was the least rest or refreshment allowed them on Sundays or holidays. They slept on the bare ground. If any negro tried to escape into the swamp he was flogged nearly to death when apprehended; and after, if it was his second attempt, he was hanged in sight of his fellows. A negro who dared to raise his hand against a white man, even in defence against barbarity and outrage, was sentenced by the Law to have the whole limb lopped off. However, this was seldom done, because it was more profitable merely to give the fellow as many lashes as his constitution would stand, and then sell him to another master. Our proximity to this barbarous plantation was very disagreeable to us, and a party of sergeants privately warned the driver that if he did not at once mitigate his severity towards 'the cattle', his own back would be scarred.

The situation of these poor wretches was very different from that of the swarm of slaves, the property of revolutionaries, who had joined themselves to us during our march from Charleston. On our approach they had thought themselves absolved from all respect to their masters, and quit of their servitude. The pity that we felt for them, and also the great use to which we could put them as labourers, prevented us from undeceiving them: they might live upon the scraps that fell from our tables, and welcome. They made very good servants and I employed one myself, by name Jonah, who had been 'raised' in Virginia and was very expert at fishing and at racoon-hunting in the swamps. These emancipated slaves at first lived a luxurious life with us in the matter of high feeding and short hours. Afterwards they were industriously employed, when orders came to build a magazine near our camp and to unload, from the boats that came up from Charleston, large stores of rum, ammunition, salt provisions, &c. They soon learned to swear—a luxury denied to negroes in servitude—to gamble with dice, and to sing Dr. Watts' hymns in chorus, which they performed with surprising tunefulness and devotion, though knowing nothing of the Christian religion.

Our retention of these negroes, who became greatly attached to us, was characterized by the settlers of the Catawba as sheer robbery; they said that we also encouraged desertion and neglect of work among their own slaves. Many thousands of negroes, indeed, were now camp-followers of the various detachments of the Royal army. In order therefore to conciliate the inhabitants, all slaves whose owners were not in arms against us were, if claimed, sent back to their bonds. Thus I soon lost my Jonah, whose freedom unfortunately I could not afford to purchase at the eighty guineas which was his declared value. He was in a lamentable state of mind when informed that he must return to his master, who, he said, was a drunken old wretch and would flog him nearly to death. However, upon my interceding with some of my officers and describing Jonah's excellent qualities, they agreed to purchase him jointly as a servant for their Mess. When I informed Jonah that he was promoted, from a mere sergeant's orderly, to being the slave of two captains and three lieutenants, he first fell at my feet and nearly overset me with his embraces; and then capered about, shouting in an ecstasy all the oaths and hymns that he knew, like a poll-parrot before visitors.

Despite the continual oppressive heat, which seldom broke in a thunderstorm, I was greatly interested in the curiosities of the country. Early in the summer, enormous quantities of fireflies danced about the Camp and its environs, from dusk to dawn at a height of a few feet above the earth. I had seen them before in the North, but never to such entrancing effect. A dozen of them enclosed in a small phial would provide enough light to read even small print by; and a hundred thousand of them, all darting and dipping at once give out an illumination which was perfectly surprising and outshone any artificial fireworks that I have ever witnessed. The hissing rise and fall of the towering rocket was missing to this display, but the perfect silence of the interlacing glints was both beautiful and awesome. The light emitted by any single insect was continuous, but shut off at will from swoop to swoop. As with the glow-worm, the light of the firefly is used for purposes of courtship: it shines no more as the summer advances. Fireflies could be very annoying to sentries and travellers by night, dazzling and distracting their gaze.

I also saw the humming-bird, the smallest and most beautiful bird in all Creation. It appeared to be jewelled rather than feathered, and fed only on honey. This it extracted from flowers with its long beak, hovering over them like a humble-bee, which in size it did not exceed. The smallest gun-shot would blow the humming-bird to bits; so those who would satisfy their curiosity with a sight of his corpse must put a bladder of water into their musket, which knocked him dead without injury to the feathers. When the honey season was over he hibernated, but whether his lurking-place was earth, wood or water nobody could inform me. I recollect also a Southern thrush, of twice the size of our European bird, that sang at night very finely; and a carrion-bird called the turkey-buzzard whom the natives shot for the sake of his feet—these when dissolved into an oil were very salutary in the sciatica and for easing rheumatic aches and pains.

There were noble fish in the Catawba River, and excellent eels in the smaller creeks. In the swamp crept the terrapin, a small sort of turtle which makes the best-tasting soup in the world—unless that were the oyster soup which we enjoyed at Harlem near New York from the fine oyster-beds contiguous. But I must mention two very troublesome insects to set against these other beautiful and beneficial creatures: viz. the wood-tick and the seed-tick. The wood-tick was a sort of bug which infested the bushes of the swamp. He drank blood through his proboscis like a vampire and swelled to a huge size before dropping off. He fastened especially upon the cattle. The seed-tick, also called the chigger, was much worse; he lurked in the long grass and attacked the feet and ankles. He was small enough to creep into the pores of the skin, where he would throw up blisters constantly for days on end. To rub the affected part was very dangerous, because the inflammation sometimes mortified. I myself had three such blisters, very painful, on my right ankle, which I got from going out injudiciously in grass one early morning without my cloth gaiters. I was advised to avoid duty for a day or two and meanwhile to cure my foot in tobacco smoke, like a herring in a chimney, in order to fumigate the pores and kill the vermin. This had the desired effect.

The continuance of the war had become most tedious; and its unpopularity in the army in America, as well as among the merchants and manufacturers at home, was reflected in the price of officers' commissions which had descended to less than one quarter of their peace-time value. In the officers' mess the toast was no longer drunk: 'A glorious war and a long one.' It was now: 'A speedy accommodation of our present unnatural differences.' There was much talk of a truce—the Empress Catherine of Russia was offering to act in the capacity of mediatrix. It was considered evident that the whole of America could not be conquered while Britain had also to face, single-handed, the united navies and armies of France and Spain; and the Ministry was therefore willing to compound, if King George would consent, by granting the Northern States their independence while we retained our conquests in the South. The Americans feared that they would be forced to accept these terms if we continued to hold Charleston: for present possession in all legal disputes, private or public, is a title very difficult to shake. The Revolution was now languishing for lack of money, and of soldiers willing to engage themselves for long periods; and the news of Charleston had made a very sharp impression on the common people. It was therefore resolved by Congress to restore public confidence by a daring use of their fast-dwindling forces. A pretended invasion of Canada would be undertaken, in order to draw off our New York troops, and then an expedition would strike southward at our small army with as much speed as was commensurate with safety.

General Washington recommended Major-General Nathaniel Greene, the American Quartermaster-General, to command this expedition; but General Horatio Gates, whose laurels were still green from Saratoga, impressed upon Congress that only himself was fit for the command, and that his popularity with the troops was such that they would mutiny were any other leader appointed. General Washington's recommendation was overruled and in July of that year, 1780, General Gates came marching towards us with as many regular troops as General Washington could spare from his small army, and whatever militia he could pick up by the way.

It will be remembered that Captain Gale had sneered at General Washington as an 'old Fabius', Fabius being the name of a Roman general who by avoiding an engagement with the Carthaginian invaders had restored the broken fortunes of Rome. General Washington's Fabian policy was equally derided by General Gates who, as it was expressed, had lately 'been brought forward on the military turf by his backers in Congress and run for the generalissimoship'.

It is reported that, on his way from Philadelphia, General Gates passed through Frederick Town in Maryland, where he fell in with his fellow-General, Charles Lee.

'Where are you going?' asked Lee.

'Why, to take Cornwallis,' replied Gates.

'I am afraid,' said Lee, 'that you will find him a tough steak to chew.'

'Tough, sir!' cried Gates. 'Tough, is it? Then, by Heavens, I'll tender him. I'll make *piloo* of him, Sir, and eat him alive.'

General Lee bawled after Gates as he rode off: 'Take care, General Horatio Gates! Take care, lest your Northern laurels degenerate into Southern willows.'

The army that Gates now commanded had been assembled for some weeks at Hillsborough in North Carolina. The regulars were regiments from the States of Maryland and Delaware; the militia had been recruited in North Carolina, and the army by the later addition of a Virginian regiment was brought up to about four thousand. After issuing a proclamation inviting the patriots of Carolina to 'vindicate the rights of America', and holding out an amnesty to all those who had been forced 'by the ruffian hand of conquest' to give their paroles, he hastened against us.

This was our position. South Carolina, though apparently pacified, was in a state of extreme unrest. Besides the matter I have mentioned, of the negroes who had run off to follow the drum, there was great dissatisfaction caused by the pressing of the planters' horses, for the use of our cavalry and transport: they feared that they would not be paid sufficient compensation, if any. Moreover, enormous stocks of rice, indigo, tobacco and other riches of the province were seized from the houses of absentee Whigs and sold to Loyalists at below the market price. The submission made by the people was therefore only nominal, and when a levy was raised among the young unmarried men, who alone were required to serve, it soon appeared that they had no notion of taking up arms in support of their King; nor could they be persuaded by any means to become good soldiers. To hold the vast territories of South Carolina and Georgia we had no more than four thousand dependable troops, of whom near a thousand were now sick of fever.

Thus, because of the detachments that had to be left to garrison Charleston and other places of importance, and to guard our lines of communication, we could only bring against the Americans about seven hundred regular troops, and twelve hundred volunteers and militia. Lord Cornwallis, when he came up from Charleston to command us in person, found our striking forces concentrated in the neighbourhood of Camden. He might have retired behind the Charleston lines, but this course did not commend itself to him. We had sick at Camden in the hospital, and the magazine contained powder and provisions that we could not afford to abandon. A retreat also would encourage the South Carolina militia to renounce their new allegiance and to be revenged for their surrender at Charleston. Indeed, two regiments had already mutinied and carried some of our sick away into North Carolina.

Upon arriving at the borders of North Carolina, General Gates was advised that the longer of the two possible routes which he could take in his advance against us was the better: this was a westerly circuit by Charlotte and Salisbury through fertile country inhabited by revolutionaries. He chose instead to come direct at us through a country of sandy hills and what were called pine-barrens, interspersed with swamps.

A prisoner from his army later told me: 'It was a country poor enough to have starved a forlorn-hope of caterpillars. Hearts alive, what hope had we at this August season when the old corn-crop was gone and the new not yet in? Especially in a miserable piney-wood Tory desert, where even in peace-time many a family must starve, unless they can hit lucky—knock down a squirrel from the pines or pick up a terrapin from the swamp! We chewed the corn still green, stripped from the thin patches that we came across, and sinned against our bellies with unripe peaches. A few half-starved Tory cattle, met in the woods, we butchered; and one day my mess made a soup of an old bitch fox and the powder we kept for our queues. On the night before we came against you we were still very hungry; and, for want of rum, General Gates ladled us out molasses. That may be good enough fare for a Yankee, but it turns any honest Southern stomach inside out; by jing, many of us were mighty sick that night and fell out along the road by companies!'

On August 13th, the American army reached Rugeley's Mills, about fifteen miles to our north. This was a place that the Royal Welch Fusiliers knew very well; for we had been sent forward there a few days previously, but soon withdrawn to Camden lest we be over-whelmed. On August 15th, at ten o'clock at night the order was given us to march against General Gates and surprise him at dawn in his encampment, if he were still there—for Lord Cornwallis had infor-mation that at this very hour General Gates was to march against Camden and surprise us at dawn in our own encampment. We set off in the most profound silence, with orders not to sing, whistle or raise our voices above a whisper. But the loud undisciplined noises of night birds and insects from the swamps would have made the most animated discourse inaudible at twenty paces. At midnight we came to a river called Saunders' Creek, and this occasioned some delay, the front of the column waiting for the rear to catch up. There was a scouting party ahead, of Tarleton's Greens, a volunteer force of mixed cavalry and infantry, very bold and bloodthirsty men. Their uniforms were light-green, they wore waistcoats without skirts, and black cuffs and capes, and were armed with one sabre and one pistol apiece. The spare pistol-holsters were receptacles for their bread and cheese. Behind them came a half-battalion of regular light infantry, then ourselves, then The Thirty-Third (Lord Cornwallis' own reg-iment) and then the rest of the army. About two in the morning, when we had made some nine miles, halting every now and then to await reports from our scouts, we heard a brisk sound of firing ahead of us. We were soon informed by a Green, who galloped back, that his scouting party had met enemy cavalry, and had instantly charged them. The enemy were in greater force, however, than the Greens had bargained for, and an officer being wounded they broke off the skirmish.

We were now ordered to shake out from our column and form a line across the road; which we did, though it was very dark, with no moon that I remember. Soon we perceived the dim forms of the enemy advancing, also in line, and opened platoon fire. For about a quarter of an hour there was a brisk exchange of volleys; but since neither side knew what was in opposition, or would venture to charge until the main body of its own army could form up in support, this fire soon ceased. General Cornwallis was delighted to find that the position in which we now found ourselves was most favourable, being narrowed by swamps on either hand, which prevented us from being outflanked by the superior numbers of the enemy. Had we started our march but an hour later, General Gates would have been able to seize a most advantageous position near Saunders' Creek; but we had forestalled him.

We rested on our arms all night. The ground was sandy, with scrub and a few very straggling trees. The nearest human dwelling was a wretched farm about a mile away.

I was the youngest sergeant in the Regiment and the proud honour therefore devolved upon me of carrying one standard of the Regimental Colours. The Goat did not come with us into action, for he had been bled so badly by the wood-ticks that he could hardly stand, much less march fifteen miles. My position was in the middle of the right wing, which consisted of ourselves, the Light Infantry, and The Thirty-Third. In the centre were our artillery—but only light pieces, two six-pounders and two three-pounders. The left wing, commanded by young Lord Rawdon (accounted as at once the ugliest man in Europe and the bravest), consisted of the infantry of the Greens; five hundred undependable American Loyalists; and The Volunteers of Ireland, a regiment which had been raised at Philadelphia during our occupation. These compatriots of mine were almost all deserters from the American army. Many of them, Dublin men, had been customers at my father's shop and knew me as a child. Colonel Ferguson, their commander, was troubled one day that a volunteer had been caught in the act of deserting back to the enemy; he did not wish to order a flogging and therefore left the man's fate to be adjudged by his comrades—they tucked him up at once from the nearest tree. In reserve stood the Seventy-First Highlanders and the cavalry of the Greens, with two more six-pounders.

Colonel Balfour, by the bye, was not with us, being now Governor of Charleston, and the Regiment was therefore commanded by Captain Forbes Champagné, our senior captain. Being the eldest regiment we held the right of the line, according to tradition.

As soon as daylight appeared we saw the enemy drawn up in two lines, very close to us. There was a dead calm, with a little haziness in the air. Opposite us were the Virginian militia who had joined the enemy only the day before; with the North Carolina militia posted next to them, facing The Thirty-Third who were on our left. We recognized these corps by their facings. Only a few random shots had been exchanged when General Gates, dissatisfied with the position of the militia, ordered them to re-form on a more extensive front. This movement was intended to prelude an assault, but Lord Cornwallis, observing what General Gates was about, decided 'to catch him on one foot', as a boxer would say, and desired Lieutenant-Colonel Webster of The Thirty-Third, who led the right wing, to advance forthwith. The order was sung out: 'Make ready, present, fire!' and the whole line crashed out in a volley which filled the air with acrid smoke. The enemy replied in a ragged manner; then came 'Charge bayonets!' and all around me, slap! every Fusilier's hand came smartly against the sling of his musket as if it were a parade for the King's birthday. The officers, pale and resolute, drew their hangers and with a huzza we went forward at a run in perfect alignment. There was not enough air to shake out the silken folds of the standard in display of Rising Sun, Red Dragon, White Horse and Three Feathers, but I wagged the staff as I ran. The heaviness of the air also prevented the smoke from rising; and, the action becoming general all along the line, so thick a darkness overspread the field that it was impossible to see the effect of the fire on either side. The Virginian militia, uncertain whether to continue the extending movement which had been ordered them, or whether to stand their ground, or whether to advance immediately against us, were thrown into total confusion. First some, and then all, ran back to the protection of their second line; but the North Carolina militiamen, who were posted there, caught contagion and ran too. Another North Carolina regiment, however, opposed to The Thirty-Third, behaved very well and fought to their last cartridge; for they had an excellent commanding officer, a General Gregory. Men of all races, I believe, are equally brave in battle if led by dependable and beloved officers.

The smoke became so dense that we could not see what we were about, but the British huzza and the 'Southern yell' of the Americans—which they had adopted, I think, from their neighbours, the Cherokee Indians—gave us an indication of who was friend and who foe. We did not pause to pursue the militia, but wheeled sharply to the left and with charge-bayonet and volley engaged the flank of the Maryland regiment as it came up from the rear.

The action continued for three-quarters of an hour, being very obstinate in the centre, where The Thirty-Third and The Volunteers of Ireland lost heavily from artillery and small-arms fire. At last the cavalry of Tarleton's Greens came around under cover of the smoke and charged with their sabres. I had never before witnessed a cavalry charge and its excitement intoxicated me, as I saw through the smoke the green uniforms sweep down, with sabres slashing and hacking, on the buff and blue ranks of the Continentals. Only remarkably well-trained and well-posted infantry can accept a cavalry charge; these were resolute enough men, but not cavalry-proof. They began to break.

Soon it was all over, though their right wing, unaware that the game was already lost, were making a brave push against the Loyalist corps opposed to them. The American commander here was Major-General Baron de Kalb, a German in the French service, whose ruddy youthful looks made him seem twenty years younger than the sixty-three which were his true age. He fell with eleven bayonet wounds in him, after having killed one or two of our people with his sword; and Lord Cornwallis afterwards buried him, very properly, with all the honours of war.

About one hundred Americans escaped in a compact body by wading through a swamp on our left, and got clear away. The remainder fled indiscriminately down the Rugeley road, and were pursued about twenty miles by the cavalry of The Greens; the road was covered with abandoned arms and baggage. Almost all the officers overtaken had lost their commands. One thousand Americans surrendered, six hundred lay dead, three hundred severely wounded were conveyed to our hospital at Camden. They lost the whole of their artillery (eight brass field-pieces), all their ammunition, all their baggage, all their two hundred wagons; and seventy officers, killed, wounded or prisoners.

The Regiment's losses were not heavy, being only six killed and seventeen wounded, of the two hundred and ninety to which sickness and skirmishing had now reduced our five hundred. Captain Drury, a valuable officer of ours, who was lying under a tree wounded in the leg, was hotly reproached by a party of twenty prisoners, two of them sergeants, because he ordered them back to the rear under the command of the slave Jonah. They told him that it was a monstrous indignity for white men to be left to the tender mercies of 'a rascal blackamoor', who threatened, if they attempted to escape, to 'blow them through'. Said the Captain, pretty testily, for his wound irked him: 'My good fellows, I cannot spare soldiers for the service. And let me tell you: your Massachusetts allies boast in their newspapers that my friend, Major Pitcairne of the Marines, was shot dead at Bunker's Hill by a negro, Peter Salem. If negroes are qualified to shoot British officers, God damn it, they are equally capable to act as escort to American rank and file. If you prefer, however, to be shot out of hand, that can be arranged too, by Heaven!' However, on the whole, the prisoners behaved with politeness and gave no trouble.

Jonah was very scornful of the defeated Americans. He said: 'It am high time for dem damned rebels to turn deir bayonets into pitchforks, den dey go foddering de beeves.' For this sentiment I severely reproved him.

It was nearly three years since Mad Johnny Maguire and I had fought side by side against General Gates' men. Maguire came up to me after the fight, his face and regimental well grimed with gunpowder, as ours all were. With that relaxation of decorum allowed, among the Fusiliers, only after a conspicuous victory or on St. David's Night, he cried: 'By my soul, Gerry my jewel, we are at last revenged for Saratoga. Now I wonder what in the holy name of God has become of that spectacled scoundrel Gates? I was looking for him

in the smoke with my bayonet, like Diogenes with his lantern, who-
ever that same busy Diogenes may have been. But the Devil a sight
of him did I get.'

Says I: 'Well, Johnny, you know I could never forgive General
Gates for charging our officers and ourselves, after we were in his
power, with depredations that never existed but in his own imagination. Ay, where is he? I haven't heard that he's been taken, or his body
found among the slain.'

General Gates had attempted, as he afterwards explained to
Congress, to rally the flying militiamen. Indeed, he was heard to
vociferate: 'I will bring the rascals back into line.' He was then 'swept
away by the torrent of fugitives'. However, he soon shook himself free
of them. He was mounted on a race-horse of some reputation, which
took him sixty miles before it foundered. It is said that he killed two
more horses of lesser value before he reached Hillsborough in North
Carolina, from whence he had started. An old letter, by the bye, was
lately published, written from General Gates to General Lee, which
he concluded with the following emphatic and patriotic lines:

> 'On this condition would I build my fame,
> And emulate the Greek and Roman name;
> Think Freedom's rights bought cheaply with my blood,
> And die with pleasure for my Country's good!'

Congress never trusted General Gates with an army again, and
presently noticed him officially to resign his command. He was
greatly chagrined that, for one little defeat, his victory at Saratoga
trumpeted across the whole of America, and indeed the world, had
been blotted from the page of glory and made as if it had never been.
He turned away to his private affairs, in disgust with political and
party distractions. But now his former admirers and well-wishers
suddenly struck their heads in surprise, and 'Heigh!' they cried,
'why did we never think of it?—in that whole Northern campaign
he contrived never once to come under fire. And did he not shirk
taking part in the famous battle of Trenton when invited to do so by

General Washington?' General Benedict Arnold, now commanding the chief fortress in America, West Point on Hudson's River, was at last remembered by these feather-headed critics as the true victor of Saratoga. Yet their praise came too late, and was soon stifled; as will appear.

I was kept very busy for some days after this battle, being appointed temporary surgeon to the Regiment; a duty for the performance of which I earned my officers' thanks.

CHAPTER X

OUR VICTORY at Camden opened the way for a British invasion of North Carolina; and in September 1780, so soon as sufficient provisions arrived, we were marched up the Catawba River to Charlotte, which lies in that province. Movement was the best cure, Lord Cornwallis thought, for the increasing sickness of the army, which had reduced its strength to an alarming extent. Charlotte, which yielded after a slight skirmish, was a place of importance to us on account of its many flour-mills and several large, well-cultivated farms, rich in cattle. The town itself consisted of but two streets, dominated at their intersection by a large brick building, Court House above and market-house below.

While we were there, we were well enough fed: at one mill alone, Colonel Polk's, twenty-five tons of flour were seized and a quantity of wheat. Fresh beef there was in plenty, for the woods abounded with grass both in summer and winter and black cattle ran wild in them; but the grass being coarse they were exceedingly lean. These cattle were in ordinary times sold to drovers from Pennsylvania at a low price; who took them back to fatten on the rich pastures of the Delaware. The oxen being in general mere hide and bones, unfit to kill, we found it our unpleasant necessity to kill milch-cows, and even cows in calf. We butchered upon an average one hundred head a day. This slaughter caused great indignation among the inhabitants, who were among the most revolutionary people in the whole Southern States. Several messengers with despatches for the Commander-in-Chief were murdered on the road, and our foraging parties were frequently fired upon by marksmen lurking behind trees.

The country about was covered with close, thick woods. The roads were narrow and crossed in every direction; and the outlying plantations small and ill-cultivated. There may have been a few Loyalists in this district, but the vigilance and animosity of the revolutionaries checked them, and we could not rely upon any information that came to us of the movements of the enemy. For though their field force had been destroyed, the war was by no means at an end. Three bold and intelligent partisan leaders, Sumpter, Marion and Horry, with a few score of active horsemen, armed with sabres hammered from mill-saws and well mounted, kept the flame of rebellion alight. These harried our communications, struck at our isolated posts; they had no base or garrison town against which we could strike, but seemed to be both nowhere and everywhere. They were brave men and lived very frugally upon hoe-cake and sweet-potatoes baked in the embers. Colonel Tarleton with his Greens was always on their track, but the country people in general, to whom these guerrillas seemed heroes, gave them the assistance that they denied our people. A party of them even dared to attack Polk's Mill, where my company happened to be on piquet duty under Lieutenant Guyon. Our sentinels were vigilant. We drove them off with fire from a loopholed building near by.

In the baggage captured at Camden was found correspondence proving thirty substantial citizens of Charleston to have been our secret enemies, in correspondence with the revolutionaries; and several prisoners taken in the same battle were found to hold certificates of allegiance to King George in their pockets. The former persons, except some who escaped, from being warned in time, were arrested and confined to the hulks; the latter were executed. This strong action inflamed the feeling of the province against us to a still greater degree.

Towards the end of September I fell sick of a dangerous fever and my comrades despaired of my life. It was a month before I was fit for duty again, and I remained very listless and feeble for some time after. I owed my life to the faithfulness of poor Jonah, who played truant from the Mess on my account. He sat by me all night, where I lay in the Camden market-house which had been converted into a hospital. He prevented me by main force from flinging off my clothes in my delirium and rushing down to swim in the river, which I persisted in naming the Liffey; and he was always ready with hot or cold drinks as I needed them. The febrifuge he supplied was salts of wormwood, mixed with lemon-juice, sugar and water. When I could fancy no meat, or heavy diet, this poor mungo caught fish and made me broth, and treated me in short with a solicitous affection that I have never before or since enjoyed at the hand of any man, and seldom from a woman's.

Sergeant Collins often came to visit me in my sickness. When I was able to converse intelligently with him he said: 'How now, Gerry Lamb! You seemed to recognize me in the height of your delirium. Do you recollect what you told me?'

'I remember nothing,' I assured him. 'My mind is like a lake over which a storm has raged. It reflects only the blue sky and forgets the thunder and lightning.'

'Well,' he said laughing. 'You were in terrible concern about Major André, the Deputy-Adjutant-General, and declared that he was about to be hanged upon a Judas-tree at Linning's. You begged me to plead with General Washington for his life. Soon it was not a Judas-tree, it seems, but a gallows. You gave me a very pitiful account of how the Major comported himself during the execution, exactly as if you were a witness of it. "Oh, that villain of a hangman with his black face and his impudent leer," you shouted. "Is Major André to suffer at the hands of a slouch like him?" Then you muttered: "Look, look, who is the chaplain! Who else would it be but the Reverend John Martin? He was at Pretty Jimmy's wake, you know. He's the Devil himself, so he is. And look who stands beside him! It's Isaac van Wart, the Skinner, with thirty Robertson dollars jingling in his pockets. Thirty Robertson dollars and a Judas-tree—there's a charming concurrence!"'

I began sweating at Sergeant Collins' recital, and asked for a drink of grog, which he found for me. 'Tell me more,' said I.

'Why,' said Sergeant Collins, 'it was only the delirium. Would you really hear more?'

'Ay, tell me everything,' I said.

'It was really most singular,' he continued. 'You described how the Major stood rolling a pebble under the ball of his foot, and how his little dwarf servant burst out weeping and was reproved by him. Then how, with courage and disgust blended, the Major leapt into the cart under an immense gibbet, snatching the halter from the hangman and setting it with dignity about his own neck, with the knot under his right ear; and how he bound his eyes with his own handkerchief. Then, not in your own Irish brogue, but in a gentle English accent, you cried: "All that I request of you, gentlemen, is that you will bear witness to the world that I die like a brave man!" And again a whisper: "It will but be a momentary pang." You spoke no more after this, though the flesh crawled upon your face, and a few instants later, a violent shock seemed to pass through you and you fell back upon the pallet as if dead.'

'I remember nothing of that,' I said aghast. 'You are not codding me?'

He continued: 'Jonah set up a howl, thinking you had gone from us; and indeed you had every appearance of a dead man. I could not feel the least tremor in your pulse. But the faithful creature flung himself upon you, breathing into your lungs and slapping your cheeks and hands; and you at last gave a slight groan and returned to life. From that instant your fever abated and you were in a fair way to health.'

It was not for three or four weeks that we heard a report that struck us with stupefaction. The first article was that General Benedict Arnold had deserted to our army at New York, and the second that Major André had been captured by a party of Skinners in neuter ground on the eastern bank of Hudson's River and was now threatened with death as a spy! Sergeant Collins brought me the news, white to the lips, and 'I misdoubt,' said he, 'that he is already hanged. October 2nd was the day upon which you recounted the particulars of his execution.'

Alas, he was right! The bare report that reached us concealed a most extraordinary story; and before long we knew what the Major had meant when he hopefully assured our officers at the St. David's Day banquet that an American sheep-dog was soon to lead his flock into our fold, and so end the war.

The history is as follows. Major André had written in a private manner to his friend, Miss Margaret Shippen (whose name he had mentioned to me when I waited upon him in New York), now wife to General Arnold; offering her his services in procuring such slight millinery for her as cap-wire, needles and gauze, which were unobtainable in Philadelphia because of the war. This letter he intended her to show to her husband, whom he believed to be the secret correspondent 'Gustavus' who had lately been sending General Clinton most valuable information about the American army. It seems that when she innocently replied, General Arnold, unknown to her, added a note to hers, confirming his identity, and arranging for a safe channel of correspondence between André and himself.

General Arnold, by his own account, had originally taken arms against King George because a redress of American grievances could then only be obtained by force. This reason was, he said, later removed when decent redress was offered by the King's Commissioners; and when the French alliance was ratified by Congress all his ideas of the justice and policy of the war were changed—he became a secret Loyalist. This does not seem unlikely; and add to this that Congress had from the first goaded him into disaffection by slighting his merits and delaying his promotion. As Governor of Philadelphia, in 1779, he was treated in the same shabby style. The Executive Council of the city laid before Congress a packet of complaints from citizens against his 'imperious and crooked way of conducting public business'; and Congress was highly pleased to order a court-martial. Then, despite General Arnold's plea for a speedy trial, his accusers kept the matter suspended over his head for nine months, during which he fretted without cease. After a long investigation he was, indeed, fully acquitted of all charges that touched his honour; but was sentenced to be reprimanded for his 'imprudence' in having employed certain public wagons, then lying idle, for removing private property from the reach of our foragers, and for having once given a pass to a trading vessel on the Delaware River without mentioning the matter to General Washington!

This reprimand General Washington conveyed, as delicately as he could, to General Arnold; but later showed his disapproval of Congress by bestowing upon him the command of the fortress of West Point.

West Point, which commanded Hudson's River a few miles above the fortress of Stoney Point, was the Gibraltar of America. Rocky ridges, ascending one behind the other, protected it against investment by any force less than twenty thousand strong. It was the magazine of immense quantities of stores, and also kept open for the Americans the passage between New England and the middle provinces. Half a million pounds sterling, and immense labour, had been spent in its construction and three thousand men formed its garrison. It was this place that General Arnold now proposed to hand over to King George—a blow that, Sir Henry Clinton thought, would end the war at a stroke. General Arnold asked in return for his gift not a million pounds or so—which would have fallen far short of the real value, since the war, directly or indirectly, was costing us millions every month: he desired only that he should be given a rank in the British Army equal to his rank in the American service, and compensation for the loss of his private property, which he modestly estimated at £6,000. Major André obtained permission from Sir Henry Clinton to attend a private meeting with General Arnold and arrange details for the admission of the British Army into the fortress.

To be brief, in September 1780, Major André secretly met General Arnold near Fort Lafayette, and there arranged and settled every-thing; but by some accident was prevented from returning to the ship that had brought him up the river under a flag of truce. He therefore returned on horseback by a roundabout way, with a safe conduct from General Arnold made out in the feigned name of 'John Anderson'. He had the plans of West Point, and a Detail of the state of the forces there, hid in his stockings. He passed safely over Pine's Bridge, the same that I had passed in my escape to New York two years before; but, near Tarrytown, came upon a party of eight men gambling under a tulip-tree by the road-side. One of them was dressed in stolen British uniform and Major André concluded that he was among friends; for he had passed over the Croton River, then considered the boundary between the British and American sides of the Debateable Ground. He acknowledged that he was a British officer on important business and asked them to assist him safely to

King's Bridge. But they proved to be American Skinners, nominally members of the Westchester militia. They were here awaiting the return of some friends who had gone to sell stolen cattle to the Cowboys. When they declared themselves, he altered his tone and told them that he also was in the American service, but had pretended to be British as a ruse to get him through; he then produced General Arnold's pass. 'Damn Arnold's pass,' they said. The truth was that they wanted money and his first introduction of himself as British afforded them an excuse for 'skinning' him. They proceeded to rob him of his two watches (silver and gold), and a few guineas; and then stripped him of his riding boots, which were a very valuable commodity in the revolutionary lines. They thus accidentally came across the papers hid in the stockings, and pulled them out, believing them to be paper-currency. Their leader, the only one of them who could read, cried out: 'A spy, by God!' Major André then grew alarmed and offered them a thousand guineas between the party if they would bring him safe to King's Bridge. They debated whether to do so: but either they distrusted his ability to provide so great a sum at short notice, or feared that, once in safety, he would go back on the bargain. They therefore concluded to bring him back into their own lines, in the hope of being rewarded for the capture of a spy; but were equally unaware of the worth of their prize as innocent of any true patriotic spirit—being Skinners, not regular soldiers.

Major André, pretending indignation at his detention, desired the American officer before whom he was brought to inform General Arnold that John Anderson had been arrested with General Arnold's own pass; which was granted. General Arnold, on receipt of this report, abandoned everything. He leapt upon a horse and was soon at the river, where his own barge was waiting with its crew; in this he hurried downstream, with a white flag, to the British ship which was waiting for Major André, and so came safe away.

'Whom can we trust now?' cried General Washington in despair when the news reached him, and the shock was very great; for it seems that he himself was to have inspected West Point about the time of its proposed abandonment to our forces and would therefore have been seized. Moreover, he had shown such favour to General Arnold, notwithstanding all that had been whispered against that strange man by his enemies in Congress, that he now stood suspect of being himself concerned in the treason.

The unfortunate Major André had been persuaded by General Arnold to discard his regimentals for the purpose of his ride; and, being under an assumed name, was therefore in the character of a spy. A court-martial by American and French generals sentenced him to death. They hoped thereby to oblige Sir Henry Clinton to give up General Arnold to their country's vengeance, in exchange for Major André. But to do so was plainly not consistent with British honour. Sir Henry offered to barter the Major against six American colonels; but this was refused. General Arnold then himself proposed to Sir Henry that he might be permitted to ride out and surrender himself to General Washington in exchange for the man whom he had involuntarily betrayed to his death. Sir Henry replied: 'Your proposal, Sir, does you great honour; but were Major André my own brother, I could not consent to such a transaction.'

Every possible argument was tried upon General Washington to persuade him to save the Major's life—appeals to his humanity, to his honour, to justice; rich promises; threats of retaliation against the Charleston traitors then in our hands. But nothing availed. The American people demanded a victim and, since General Arnold had escaped, this must be Major André. General Washington could not save the Major, even had he wished, nor even substitute an honourable fusillade for the disgrace of the gibbet. Unless he displayed the same ruthless fury as the rest of his countrymen, his own position would be knocked from under him; and he knew that there was none capable of replacing him as Commander-in-Chief. Moreover, General Greene, the Marquis de La Fayette and others, whether from private rancour against Arnold or a desire to appear as single-minded partisans of the cause of Liberty, were so insistent upon the disgraceful sentence being carried out that they seemed to be literally thirsting for Major André's blood. General Washington therefore signed the death-warrant; and, to the extraordinary grief and horror of the whole British Army, the execution was carried out. It took place in the same manner exactly that I had described in my delirious vision, and at the very hour. No doubt the profound affection with which the Major had inspired me contributed to my vision, nor was I the only one so favoured. His sister and several other persons were warned in dreams of his melancholy fate. The officers and sergeants of the Royal Welch Fusiliers went into mourning for him, and so did several other regiments.

As for the eight Skinners: they were rewarded by being each given a farm and a yearly pension of two hundred dollars for life. Three of them, one of whom was my faithless guide Isaac van Wart, were awarded silver Congressional medals inscribed *Fidelity* and (in Latin) *Patriotism Triumphs.* There is a popular stanza that runs something in this style:

> Treason doth never prosper: what's the reason?
> If treason prospers, 'tis no longer treason.

But for a succession of trivial accidents, Major André would have come safely back into the British lines; West Point would have been yielded up; and Benedict Arnold, playing the General Monk, might well have restored the Colonies, for a time at least, to their former allegiance and won the thanks of posterity. But it happened otherwise, and the cause of Liberty was revived by that excess of indignation which discovered treason excites in the breasts of luke-warm patriots. General Arnold was burned in effigy in towns and villages, often with obscene and disgusting circumstance; and every man who happened to bear the same surname as he, whether related to him or not, was obliged to change it, in order to quit himself of the odium that it now conveyed.

About this time, we in the Carolinas suffered a great setback. We were waiting at Charlotte for the order to advance further into North Caro-lina and strike at Hillsborough, when news came that an unsuccessful attack by the enemy had been made on a post in Georgia, far to the south. Major Ferguson, with eleven hundred Loyalist militia and volunteers, was detached to intercept the enemy on their return. But he was himself intercepted by enemy forces of whose existence Lord Cornwallis was unaware—an army of three thousand backwoodsmen from across the Blue Mountains. Their anger had been stirred by the news that the Cherokee Indians, their bitterest enemies, were now on the war-path as King George's allies. They had also been promised pay for their service in the unusual currency of human flesh—so many negroes, taken from the Tories, for each man according to his rank! At King's Mountain a swarm of these rough, uncivilized men, armed with Deckard rifles, surrounded Major Ferguson's people and shot them to pieces from behind trees and boulders; the Major himself was mortally wounded, and nearly half his force were either wounded or killed before the remainder clubbed their firelocks in surrender. The mountainy men hanged up a score of prisoners, and then returned home.

This Major Ferguson was, after Major André, the most beloved officer in the Army and had the greatest power of any to enlist Loyalists in our service. He was also the most remarkable marksman then living.

A curious instance, by the bye, of the disparity of British and American ideas of honour and policy in warfare, is afforded by contrasting Colonel Daniel Morgan's order for the concerted attempt upon General Fraser's life, near Saratoga (which was carried out), with Major Ferguson's adventure at the time of the Brandywine fighting in 1777. According to his own account, he was out scouting when he observed an American officer, remarkable for Hussar dress, pass slowly within a hundred yards of him, followed by another dressed in dark green with a large cocked hat and mounted on a bay. Major Ferguson ordered three good shots to steal near and fire at the horsemen; but 'the idea disgusted me; I recalled the order'. Major Ferguson's account continues: 'In returning, the Hussar made a wide circuit, but the other passed within a hundred yards of us; upon which I advanced from the woods towards him. On my calling, he stopped, but after looking at me, he proceeded. I again drew his attention, but he slowly continued on his way and I was within that distance at which, in the quickest firing, I could have lodged half a dozen balls in or about him before he was out of my reach. I had only to determine; but it was not pleasant to fire at the back of an unoffending individual, who was acquitting himself very coolly at his duties; so I let him alone.'

It was afterwards proved that the gentleman in the cocked hat was General Washington himself, the Hussar being a French aide-de-camp!

Major Ferguson's defeat at King's Mountain obliged us to defer our hopes of conquest and retire back into South Carolina. It was as miserable a march as I remember, for retirement is never agreeable even in fine weather, and it now rained for several days without intermission. Lord Cornwallis was sick of a fever and the command devolved on Lord Rawdon. We had no tents with us, and at night, when we encamped, it was in the wet and stinking woods; nor for several days had we any rum but only water as thick as puddle. The roads were over our shoes in mud and water. Sometimes we had bread but no beef, sometimes beef but no bread; seldom both together. On two occasions we were without food for fully forty-eight hours. For another five days we lived upon unground Indian corn, two and a half heads being a man's daily ration. At first we merely parched it before a fire; but soon we discovered a better way of treating this hearty but difficult grain. Two men of every mess converted their canteens into rasps by punching holes in them with a bayonet. The ear was then scraped against the rasp and the flour that resulted was made into hoe-cakes, baked on our entrenching tools. We were in a very weak state, I can assure my readers. When we came to a river called Sugar Creek, swollen with a rapid flood, and the steep clay banks as slippery as ice, we could not get the wagons over except by using as draught-animals the Loyalist militia that remained to us. They were our chief reliance in this retreat, as knowing the country and not only protecting us from treachery and surprise but acting as foragers. They also had the difficult art of driving black cattle into the open from the recesses of swamps.

Up to our breasts in yellow water, we forded the Catawba River which at that spot was nearly half a mile over. Fortunately our crossing was not opposed by hidden riflemen. So, after a journey of a fortnight, in which I am proud to say that the men never even murmured against the hardships they underwent, we came to the small town of Wynnsborough, which lies between the Catawba and Congaree Rivers; and there remained for the rest of the year 1780.

CHAPTER XI

HOW DID the war go for our arms at the close of 1780? The French alliance was so far of no assistance to the Americans, and the six thousand white-uniformed Frenchmen who had failed to relieve Charleston were landed at Newport, Rhode Island, and there blockaded by the British Atlantic fleet. A second division of Frenchmen, who were to have followed, were locked up in Brest by the British Channel fleet. General Washington's troops found Congress a cruel stepmother in the matter of pay and supplies; they were ragged and half-starved and lived from hand to mouth. Lately their condition had become worse, for General Nathaniel Greene was intrigued against by Samuel Adams and other Congressmen and forced to resign his post as Quartermaster-General. General Greene wrote to General Washington that he had 'lost all confidence in the justice and rectitude of Congress. Honest intentions and faithful service are but a poor shield against men without principles, honesty or modesty.' The troops had not been paid for one whole year even in Continental currency, and those whose time had expired were refused discharge. In the New Year there was a serious mutiny at Morristown in Pennsylvania: thirteen hundred Pennsylvania Ulstermen marching towards Philadelphia, under the command of three sergeants, with the resolve to force Congress to pay them. Before they set out, they had been ridden against by their officers armed with swords, and had killed one of them, a captain. They were met half-way with promises of redress and persuaded to return to duty. Another mutiny, of New Jersey men, was put down by shooting, and General Washington presently asked leave from Congress to raise the amount of lashes that might be awarded for such ill-behaviour to five hundred. Who were now the Bloody Backs?

On the other hand, the war was bearing very heavily upon the spirits and pockets of the British people. Towards the end of August 1780 came exceedingly grave news. Our outward-bound East India and West India merchant fleets, sailing in company, had been convoyed by the Channel Fleet as far south as the north-western promontory of Spain. There the Admiral in command, obeying the explicit orders of the Earl of Sandwich, from Admiralty House, turned homewards; leaving the protection of this glittering prize to a single line-of-battle ship and two or three frigates. On the 9th of August, the convoy was intercepted by a combined Spanish and French fleet of great strength. The commodore of the escort being forbidden to engage an enemy that so greatly exceeded him in strength, abandoned the convoy to the enemy. Thus were lost forty-seven West India merchantmen and transports, with cargoes valued at £600,000; five large East Indiamen with coin, bullion and other valuables aboard to the amount of £1,000,000; also two thousand sailors, eight hundred passengers, twelve hundred soldiers, eighty thousand muskets; and an immense quantity of naval stores destined for Madras as a means of re-equipping our squadron in those waters that had been mauled in battle with the French. In the memory of the oldest man, the Royal Exchange at London had never presented so dull and melancholy an aspect as on the Tuesday afternoon when the notice of this double loss was issued by the Admiralty. No instance had ever been known in the mercantile annals of England where so many ships had been captured at once, nor where loss was recorded of above one-fourth the sum of this. In the same month news reached London that an unescorted Quebec fleet of fifteen ships had been met off the Banks of Newfoundland by an American frigate and two brigantine privateers. Only three of our ships escaped. This came as a very serious blow to the garrison and people of Quebec. I may here append that in the course of this war against the combined fleets of France, Spain, Holland and the United States we lost three thousand merchant ships captured or sunk, besides other naval damage.

The fault for these calamities did not lie with our sailors or their captains. The Earl of Sandwich, alias 'Jeremy Twitcher', it has already been noted, had wickedly thrown away our command of the seas.

He had starved the dockyards, lied to the House of Lords about the number of warships in commission, bullied and betrayed his admirals; and condemned the few lonely frigates still afloat to choose, in their encounters with the magnificent fleets of our enemies, between fighting against dismal odds or running for safety. Often enough they chose the former alternative, and sometimes snatched an unhoped-for victory. The names of Howe, Rodney, Hyde Parker and Keppel need no recommendation from my humble pen! Yet I must not omit mention of Sir George Collier's feat at Penobscot Bay; for this glorious action (which by the spite of Lord Sandwich was acknowledged by no ringing of bells or other public acclamation— Sir George, indeed, being superseded in his American command and on his return left unemployed and unpromoted) struck directly against the Americans in their own waters.

Penobscot is a harbour on the wild northern coast of Massachusetts, lying in what is now known as the State of Maine. In the summer of 1779 a settlement of distressed Loyalists was there planted; and the erection of a fort begun by a few companies of the Eighty-Second and Seventy-Fourth Regiments. No sooner did the people of Boston receive news of this work than they determined to mar it. Twenty-four transports, containing three thousand troops, and nineteen warships, manned by two thousand sailors and mounting 324 guns—the whole constructed at a cost of near £2,000,000— were despatched to Penobscot. Yet our small garrison, posted behind slight works held off the Bostonians for near three weeks. Sir George Collier then sailed to the rescue with a squadron mounting no more than two hundred guns. The American ships formed a line of battle, but broke at the first attack and were driven up the Penobscot River. I have seen a copy of a letter written by the American military commander, General Solomon Lovell, to the following effect: 'To give a description of this terrible day is out of my power—to see four British ships pursuing seventeen sail of our armed vessels, nineteen of which were stout ships; transports on fire, men of war blowing up, and as much confusion as can possibly be conceived.' To be brief, none of all the American ships escaped capture or destruction, and those of the Bostonians who escaped to the shore found themselves a hundred miles from any base, and without a morsel of food. A grand argument then ensued between the sailors and soldiers, the latter accusing the former of cowardice, the former returning the insult, and, weapons being snatched up, sixty men fell in fratricidal battle. Hundreds more perished of famine or exhaustion on their march back through the wilderness to the settled parts of the province.

This disaster dulled the martial ardour of 'the Saints' for the remainder of the war; yet we were not greatly benefited by it. The British troops in America were insufficient for its conquest and more could not be spared from our Islands. The contesting nations resembled two boxers, badly battered, struggling in a clench, hardly able to stand, each unable to raise raw knuckles and deal a deciding blow to the other's jaw. General Arnold believed that he knew how victory could be achieved. 'Money will go farther than arms in America,' he wrote to Lord George Germaine. 'Offer the Continental troops all the arrears of pay owing to them, equal to about £400,000, half-pay for seven years, two hundred acres for every private soldier, and proportionately more for every officer, together with a bounty of twenty guineas hard money on their coming over. Thus you shall draw two or three thousand of the best soldiers in America to the King's Service.' He believed that this force would be sufficient to take West Point and cut off the Northern States from the rest. General Washington would then be obliged either to fight on our ground or disband his army; for his supplies of meat were on the East side, and his supplies of bread-stuffs on the West. If this operation were deemed too hazardous, another plan offered, which was to leave but a small garrison in New York and concentrate the whole army to seize Baltimore, at the head of the Chesapeak Bay which divides the State of Maryland; and, after overawing Maryland, Delaware and Virginia, which lie contiguous, proceed against Philadelphia from the south. Natural obstacles, such as mountains, swamps, forests, rivers were few in this quarter. However, General Arnold was not heeded; and is likely to have been in error at least about the expected desertion of so many American soldiers. When, in fact, the mutinous

Ulstermen of Morristown were approached by British emissaries, with offers to receive them in the Royal camp, they turned these tempters over to the hangman.

It is, however, to be remarked that Joseph Galloway, the Congressman from Pennsylvania who came over to our side from disgust with the Adamses and with the French alliance, declared that not one soldier in four of General Washington's army was a native-born American, one half being Irishmen and the remainder British, with some German deserters and a sprinkling of Northern negroes; and, if his testimony is to be doubted, we have General Greene's word for it that he fought us towards the close of the war largely with British soldiers. The American has ever been impatient of discipline and long engagements to the degree that he loves independence, and General Washington's regular army was trained in the European style. Few native-born Americans were therefore inclined to enlist in it, but preferred the easy and insubordinate militia life, where the ranks ruled the officers, not the officers the men, and all fought in Indian fashion, shooting from ambush and avoiding the onset.

The Commander-in-Chief, Sir Henry Clinton, was for commencing no further military operations on a grand scale, but conserving his gains and 'breaking windows' until the Revolution collapsed from exhaustion. Perhaps his way was wisest; though it depended for its success upon British supremacy at sea, which by the Earl of Sandwich's criminal neglect of our fleet and dockyards we had now forfeited to the French, Spanish and Americans. Yet Sir Henry did not have the last word, for Lord George Germaine was still bent upon conducting the war from Downing Street in his own remarkable fashion.

In South Carolina, Major Ferguson's defeat had encouraged the revolutionary cause to a dangerous degree. Our rear and flanks were threatened, our provisions cut off, our posts attacked.

Colonel Tarleton, with his Greens, returned blow for blow, but the guerrilla bands could not be exterminated and now overran the whole province. General Washington appointed General Greene to replace General Gates in North Carolina, to oppose our expected invasion of North Carolina, and in December he arrived at Charlotte, where he collected two thousand men—insufficient to attack us, but enough to do us mischief if used in detachment. The Earl of Cornwallis immediately broke camp and marched us up the right bank of the Catawba against him. General Greene then divided his army into two columns, one of which, under General Daniel Morgan, was ordered to work around our front and harass our posts in Georgia. This column contained the famous Virginian riflemen, and some good regular troops, cavalry and infantry, of the Continental Line. Lord Cornwallis made a similar division of his forces; sending Colonel Tarleton with a strong column in pursuit of General Morgan, who decisively defeated him at The Cowpens, fifty miles north of Wynnsborough and half that distance from the camp that we had reached on our advance up the river.

At The Cowpens, Colonel Tarleton lost eight hundred men, including the whole of our Light Infantry, two guns, the Colours of the Seventh Regiment, and the confidence of all the remaining Loyalists in the province. He had overmarched his men—an imprudence characteristic of cavalry-commanders—and besides, General Morgan's riflemen were the best light troops in the whole American Army. As usual, they concentrated their fire upon our officers, and disposed of a great number at the first onset. General Morgan also had a stroke of luck, for which he was honest enough not to claim credit: the left wing of his second line at a late stage of the fighting decided to retire two hundred paces, in order to conform with a manoeuvre of the right. This increased the distance of the charge that our people, already out of breath from hustling back the first line of militiamen, were called upon to make; and coming on in a broken crowd were halted and confused by a very cool volley. They broke under the counter-attack. Colonel Tarleton escaped, with most of his cavalry; but the news of the disaster shook us greatly, especially as General Morgan's force had been rather the weaker in numbers and suffered almost no loss in the fighting.

Yet even so Lord Cornwallis could not bring himself to abandon once more his proposed invasion of North Carolina. Valuable reinforcements had arrived from New York, including the Brigade of Footguards; and these (until the disaster of The Cowpens) had brought our numbers up to the total of four thousand men. The reinforcements were intended by Sir Henry Clinton for defensive rather than offensive use, but Lord Cornwallis, who had obtained from Lord George Germaine the right to communicate directly with him rather than at second hand through Sir Henry Clinton, now felt himself at liberty to behave as though his army were an independent command. He should have been warned by the fate of General Burgoyne, who had similarly embarked upon an independent invasion, trusting to the same broken reed to concert the movements of the New York Army with his own. His Lordship had even so disobeyed General Clinton's instructions, about securing South Carolina at all costs, that he had dismantled the fortifications of Charleston—to prevent Loyalists from seizing and holding it, I suppose, while we were away. He had now assembled enough arms, guns and provisions for a regular campaign and it seemed a pity not to use them. At least, he must do his utmost to cut off General Morgan's retreat and prevent him from rejoining General Greene.

Since we had lost our light troops, Lord Cornwallis determined that the whole Army should, for the sake of speed, travel as light as possible. He therefore ordered the destruction of all our superfluous baggage; no wagons were kept except those that carried ammunition, salt, and hospital stores, and four empty ones for the conveyance of the sick and wounded. He set an example to his officers, whose coffers were crammed with a superfluity of hats, clothes and footwear, novels, plays, wine, condiments, perfumery, silver, glass and bed-linen, by first reducing the size and quantity of his own possessions. There was no objection raised by either officers or men to this sacrifice, even though it deprived us of all future prospect of spirituous liquors. It was a sorry sight to see so many hogsheads of good rum staved in; and a great novelty for the quarters of a British General, and an Earl at that, to be incapable of affording even a glass of wine to visitors, and for his table to be as destitute of comforts as a common soldier's.

Lord Rawdon remained behind with a small force at Camden, which had now been well fortified.

The first difficulty that faced us on our march was the re-crossing of the upper Catawba River, the opposing banks of which were strongly held by the enemy. This our main army was to accomplish at a point well across the North Carolina frontier, by a private ford, M'Gowan's, while a diversion was made six miles lower down by another of our columns. M'Gowan's Ford, which was about half a mile over, lay within a short distance of the Blue Mountains, now covered with snow; and the crossing was made just before dawn on February 1st, 1781, on a dark and rainy morning.

I will not trouble my readers with a close geographical account of our three-hundred-mile pursuit of General Greene's divisions, which succeeded in re-uniting in the second week of February. We were endeavouring to cut him off from Virginia, the next province to the north, whence he received his supplies. Suffice it to tell that we marched through North Carolina, at the average rate of nearly twenty miles a day, by way of Salibury and the pine-clad, clayey foot-hills of the Blue Mountains; gaining every day upon our adversaries and unmolested by their rear-guard. The air was invigorating and the sunshine on fine days delightful. But it rained very heavily, with intervals of snow and sleet, fully half the time, and we were greatly fatigued by our exertions. General Greene was making for the Dan River, across which lay Virginia and safety. We should have caught him and compelled to give battle, had Lord Cornwallis not been deceived by pretended Loyalists who told him that the lower fords of this river were impassable, which they were not, and persuaded him to use the upper ones. General Greene by forced marches reached the lower fords, and finding a sufficiency of boats got his last stragglers across on February 15th, just as our vanguard arrived. But a great part of his militia had already deserted and dispersed to their homes. His line troops were in a very bad case, having but one blanket for every three men and very few boots; so that we might have followed them by the trail of blood the poor fellows left, like wounded animals. Like us, they had no tents.

Since General Greene had escaped us, we were marched slowly back to Hillsborough which, though the chief town of upper North

Carolina, did not boast a hundred houses. There Lord Cornwallis erected the Royal Standard and issued a proclamation calling upon the province to return to its allegiance. We were greeted upon our arrival with the news that General Benedict Arnold, now fighting upon our side, had taken a force of American Loyalists up the James River into Lower Virginia, and for three weeks 'broken windows' to some purpose. He had captured several ships in cargo, blown up an iron-foundry where cannon were manufactured and burned a vast quantity of public and private stores. The fragrant smoke of tobacco rolled in clouds over the country, not diffused through clay pipes, calumets or cigars, but issuing from the roofs of burning warehouses at Richmond and Norfolk. General Arnold returned without loss to his base at Portsmouth, at the mouth of the river.

I cannot omit to mention a most foul transaction that took place not far from Hillsborough on February 25th. The Loyalists to our immediate south having risen in numbers in answer to the Proclamation, Colonel Tarleton was sent forward to assist their organization; but Colonel Harry Lee of the American Light Horse was there beforehand and the three hundred Loyalists mistaking Lee's column, whom they met in a narrow lane, for Colonel Tarleton's, approached them with friendly shouts. They were at once surrounded; though they begged for quarter, the relentless Americans refused it, and they were all butchered in cold blood. Had twenty revolutionary Americans thus fallen to British arms, how would the pages of Ramsay, Belsham and the rest have foamed with the charges of murder, massacre, blood and malice! But very bloody deeds were done between partisans throughout the campaign; even some of Colonel Tarleton's Greens were guilty of rape, murder and indiscriminate hanging. A troop of British dragoons attached to the Greens were so disgusted with these proceedings that they refused to 'wear the Green', and remained in their scarlet.

The inhabitants of the hilly upper parts of North and South Carolina differed very greatly from those of the swampy lower parts, both in vigour and complexion. They were a fine, strong, ruddy people, combining hospitality with savagery to a remarkable degree and greatly addicted to drink. Hardly a man but was six foot tall and broad in proportion; hardly a two-roomed cabin but had its still for the brewing of peach-brandy. The women were erect and beautiful; not drunkards, but reputedly of relaxed morals. There was a custom here in vogue of 'swapping wives' which they took to a remarkable pitch of wantonness: one man who thought his daughter-in-law more handsome than his wife, proposed an exchange to his son, who consented on the condition that his father gave, with the mother, two cows and two horses. The women concerned, so far from being the victims, were said to have been the instigators of this unnatural transaction.

Most of our officers had brought dogs with them, and at Hillsborough enjoyed great sport in quail-shooting and rabbit-hunting. The American rabbits disdained to burrow in the ground, so that we had no use for ferrets; after a good chase they would go to earth (if I may so express myself) by running up a hollow tree. The slave Jonah, who acted as our huntsman, showed us the 'Virginia ferret'. He cut us a hickory pole, and split it at the top, which was to be poked up the tree and twisted in the animal's fur, to haul him down kicking. This proved very practical. On one occasion when I assisted at such a hunt an oppossum was caught, which is a sort of rat with a long, bushy, prehensile tail. It was seen suspended by this tail to the extremity of a branch and knocked down with the hickory pole. Where it fell it lay perfectly motionless, feigning death; and the officers' spaniels, though they barked at it and worried it so that I heard the bones crack, yet would not eat it up, from the natural horror that almost every animal, but the jackal and hyaena, feels of devouring what he has not himself slain. Lieutenant Guyon, my officer, out of humanity took up the poor creature, which lay limp in his hands, and brought it back to the house where he lodged. There he laid it upon the window-ledge in the sun, sitting still at the further end of the room and watching it attentively. After a while it furtively opened one eye, twisted its head slowly about to see whether it was observed, then suddenly sprang up and out of the window and disappeared. Jonah remarked very sagely: 'Him like rebel Whig in Ca'lina. Pertend him good dead rebel, den up he jump, do murrer mischief to dem poor Tories.'

No sooner were we halted at this place than we began to remedy our uncouth appearance, by washing our soiled linen and brushing our muddy regimental clothing. But the several yellow and reddish streams that we had forded made mock of our most industrious efforts. Pipe-clay we had none, and though we dressed our hair as we should, and polished buttons and buckles, our appearance suggested a debtors' prison where decayed gentlemen with more pride than luck barely subsist upon fourpence a day. Provisions were also exceedingly scarce, since the country was in any case but sparsely settled, and the American army stationed here before us had eaten up the surplus stocks of corn and beef. When we had gleaned after their reaping, the country was swept bare; and though Lord Cornwallis had promised that the draught-oxen, the only cattle that survived in the neighbourhood, should not be slaughtered except in case of necessity, that necessity arose, and even the Loyalists complained loudly of the hardships they incurred because of it. The Commissary of Supplies was obliged, as a most unpleasant duty, to go from house to house in the town with a file of men, commanding the citizens to yield up their provisions: for in time of war an army is never allowed to starve while the citizens whom it is defending still have grain in their bins.

We retired southward about thirty miles to the upper tributaries of the Cape Fear River. (This river meets the ocean at Wilmington, two hundred miles to the south-east, where we had a detachment.) Here we were obliged by General Greene with the offer of battle. His army had been augmented to five thousand men and, crossing again into North Carolina, he took position at Guildford Court House, where Lord Cornwallis hurried to attack him.

We lay at this time twelve miles southward from Guildford Court House, with our headquarters at a Quakers' meeting-house of New Garden, in the forks of Deep River. I remember that being sent on detachment with the Commissary, Mr. Stedman, to command provisions from the plantations in the neighbourhood, a venerable Quaker from whom we obtained a considerable quantity of corn made some very sensible remarks.

'How is the general spirit of the Province hereabouts?' asked Mr. Stedman.

'The greater part wish to be united to Britain, Friend,' he replied.

'Then why do they not join us?' Mr. Stedman asked. 'Or if they join us, why do they quit the Colours so soon?'

'Alas, Friend, canst thou ask this? Art thou ignorant of the resentment of the revolutioners against those who wish thy cause well? And of the many times that these well-wishers have been deceived in hopes of support, or abandoned to their enemies when thy army has relinquished its posts? And of the revenge that these bloody-minded men take upon the families of those who serve King George?'

'Pray inform me upon this point, Sir,' said Mr. Stedman.

'Friend, fear of injury works upon men's hearts more powerfully than hope of reward for honest or loyal dealings. The Tories of North Carolina live in terror of the Whigs. There are some who have dwelt like hunted beasts in the wilderness for two and even three years, not daring to return to their homes, and are secretly supported by their families, or faithful slaves, with hoe-cakes and jerked meat hid now and then in the recesses of the wood for them to find. Others, promised safety by their neighbours, have been shot at from behind a tree as they worked in their corn-patch; or tied to a tree and flogged until insensible. Not far from here a suspected Loyalist was shot dead in the early morning as he lay in bed with his wife.'

'These circumstances are indeed abominable,' cried Mr. Stedman. 'But do these poor people expect to live so happily or so undisturbed under any rule but that of the British King?'

'No, Friend,' the Quaker replied. 'Nor does that come in question. The people have experienced such distress between the ebb and flow of revolution and loyalism that they would submit to any government in the world, Christian, Jew or Turk in order only to obtain peace. And so great are the odds against which thy nation is contending and so foolish are thy Ministers (forgive my boldness) that they despair of victory for you. They tend to the side of Congress. Yet be assured of this much—as soldiers in the rebel militia they are of small comfort to General Greene.'

CHAPTER XII

GENERAL GREENE was unlucky to have lost the services of General Daniel Morgan who after his resounding victory at The Cowpens had retired from the service, pleading the ague and rheumatic pains. These ailments, though painful, would not have been sufficient to keep so courageous and patriotic a soldier from battle had General Morgan felt that he was estimated by Congress at his just worth; but he had too often been disappointed by deferred promotion and given cold thanks for his extraordinary services, nor did he agree very well in policy with General Greene. He retired to his farm and never served against us again. General Greene was what they termed in the South a 'judgmatical' man, that is, a man of careful judgment. His military knowledge was wholly derived from reading, not from experience in the field, but his dispositions on this occasion were pretty well. The ground he chose was certainly most favourable for defence.

The whitewashed Court House stood on a gentle slope at the skirt of an irregular clearing of about one hundred and twenty acres. The only other buildings in this clearing were two small farmhouses and three barns. The Court House had been, I suppose, sited here as lying at a road-junction and at a point nearly equidistant from several scattered plantations which formed the township of Guildford. Our approach to it from the south was by a narrow defile with thick woods on either hand. On emerging from the defile, we would first come upon a smaller clearing of about fifty acres, with the road running between. General Greene's advanced line of defence, consisting of North Carolina militiamen, was posted behind a rail fence on the further edge of the smaller clearing, where the woods began again. Two guns were mounted ahead of this line to distress us as we debouched from the defile; also companies of picked riflemen were thrown forward on either flank, and two squadrons of cavalry were ready to charge if we showed panic. The North Carolina men were to be discouraged from breaking, by a few veteran troops posted immediately in their rear with orders to shoot any man who flinched. This wood extended for half a mile until our road reached the larger clearing at the back of which the Court House stood; in the middle of the wood, behind a stout breastwork, General Greene had placed a second line, of better militia, including the famous riflemen trained by General Morgan. The last line, posted on the slopes about the Court House consisted of the regular and veteran troops. Three-quarters of a mile separated the leading militia from the veterans in reserve.

It may well be wondered why General Greene had placed his lines at so great a distance from one another. The fact was: he knew that General Morgan's victory at The Cowpens had been gained by defending his position with successive lines of infantry, each strongly posted, so that when one line was dislodged our charge would spend its force before it reached the second position; and he trusted that after we were staggered by the first skirmish the density of the woods would make us break our alignment and come against his best troops in exhaustion and disorder. Had General Morgan been present he would have approved General Greene's dispositions in principle, but criticized the detail. It is a good thing to separate one's lines in such a way that the defence is in depth, and the enemy is exhausted in attempting to pierce it; but a bad thing to separate these lines by too great a distance. The front companies will feel lonely, and suspect that they have been devoted to destruction for the benefit of those behind. Unless they are seasoned troops they will not hold their ground for long.

The full circumstances of the battle, which took place on March 15th, 1781, are so complicated and have been so ably presented by Mr. Stedman in his History that it would be an impertinence on my part to attempt to improve upon him. I will therefore content myself with giving my own experiences in the battle, recommending my readers to study Mr. Stedman for a more general account.

The Royal Welch Fusiliers went into action about two hundred and twenty officers and men strong; some eighty having been lost by sickness and skirmishing since the Camden battle. We were marched off at dawn from New Garden, without having eaten our breakfast—and not from our officers' neglect, but only because there was no breakfast to eat. We had been on very short rations for a week and now possessed no food at all. After a frosty night, the sun shone benignantly and warmed our stiff bodies; while the croaking of frogs and the twittering of birds pleasantly reminded us that the Spring was now well advanced. Life without a daily issue of grog was uncomfortable, I own, for the old soldiers especially. Even Saint David had been cheated of his customary bumpers: the amount of peach-brandy that Captain Champagné had contrived to collect for that pious purpose on March 1st did not amount to more than half a gill for each mess.

At about noon, our cavalry scouts brushed with theirs about four miles from Guildford Court House, and Lord Cornwallis, unable to get any information from prisoners or natives as to the enemy dispositions, was forced to fight blind. We Fusiliers were in the centre of the advancing army, and heard confused artillery and musket fire ahead of us. Presently a rider came down the column with orders to Lieutenant-Colonel Webster of The Thirty-Third, who commanded our division, to hurry forward and deploy to the left so soon as we reached the first clearing. At about half-past one o'clock in the afternoon, we found ourselves advancing across the wet, red clay of a ploughed field, with The Thirty-Third on our left and The Seventy-First on our right. Music of fife and drum was not lacking; but, the regimental drummers being now employed as musket-men, we used young American boys who had joined the Colours at Camden. Our chief fifer was the negro Jonah, who played the *Grenadiers' March* and *The Noble Race of Jenkin* with great spirit.

We were the leading troops, and first came under rifle-fire at about a hundred and fifty paces from the wood towards which we were hurrying. Since our Tower muskets were, as usual, greatly out-ranged by the American rifles, we were obliged to hold our volley and continue our advance, despite great losses. The marksmen on the flanks especially galled us. Here fell Mad Johnny Maguire with a bullet through the heart; but I did not know of my poor friend's fate until the next day when he was found by Smutchy Steel lying in a furrow upon his back, his rugged features bent in the pleasant smile which in life had seldom left them.

At sixty paces we halted to fire a volley; then Colonel Webster gave the word 'Charge!' But The Thirty-Third, who had suffered heavily, not yet being up in line with us on the left, we paused for a moment, at forty paces from the enemy, to allow them to come up. Colonel Webster, misunderstanding our hesitation, cried out in more than his usual commanding voice, which was well known to our Brigade: *'Come on, my brave Fusiliers!'* The North Carolina militia were massed with arms presented behind the railfence and taking aim with the nicest precision. We went forward at a smart run, and they would not meet our bayonets. Despite the guards set over them to prevent this very thing, five hundred fled away to the flanks and thence dispersed to their homes: 'to kiss their wives and sweethearts', as General Greene afterwards amiably expressed it.

Next we came against the Virginians in the middle of the wood, who fired very sharply at us from behind their breastworks of brushwood. We could not get at them because of the trees that they had felled in our path, and must change direction, working round to our left.

I happened to run ahead with a party of about ten men, Smutchy Steel among them. As we gained the end of the breastwork, which had cost us many valuable lives, and went in among the Virginians with the bayonet, I observed an American officer attempting to fly across our front. I immediately left my comrades, whom I put under Smutchy's orders, and darted after him. He saw my intention to capture him and fled with the utmost speed. I pursued—I do not know how far—to where the trees were less dense, but the underwood high and tangled. He fell once or twice, and was slow in rising, and I was gaining on him when suddenly he turned about and threw up his hands. Like a dream is a battle, when the spirit is so highly inflamed that the soldier hopes not, fears not, repines not, but proceeds without astonishment or reflexion from one remarkable or terrible circumstance to the next. It appeared natural enough to me that the American officer should be my former comrade Richard Harlowe—though how he came to be in the enemy's service I knew not and do not know to this day—and that I should deny him quarter, as I did, shooting him through the head with my fusil in summary conviction of his traitorous dealing. His sword I drew from the scabbard in detestation, and with an effort snapped it across my knee.

I was now aware of a confused noise upon my left, where I saw several bodies of riflemen drawn up behind brushwood, the cast of a crust from me. A vigorous contest had evidently been in progress here between the Second Battalion of Guards and these people: for several dead Guardsmen and Americans lay about me. I stopped by a dead Guardsman, and stooping down, replenished my pouch with the cartridges remaining in his. Then I reloaded my fusil in a very deliberate manner, as one who walks in his sleep, careless of danger; they shouted and fired several shots at me, but not one took effect. Glancing my eye the other way, I saw a company of Guards advancing to the attack, and was glad to observe that they had been belied by popular rumour: so far from being effeminated by the luxuries of the Metropolis or enervated by idleness, they fought with vigour and majesty. I would have joined them now, but to do so I should have had to run the gauntlet of the Americans who lay between. How to act I knew not. I wished to join in the fight, but could effect nothing. I fell back a few paces.

On the instant, however, another remarkable vision seemed to swim up before me: the Earl of Cornwallis himself, riding towards me across the clear part of the wood, unaccompanied by any aide. He was mounted on a common dragoon's horse, his own charger having been shot. The saddle-bags were under the creature's belly, which much retarded his progress, because of the underwood that caught against it. I immediately ran forward and snatched at the bridle, turning the horse's head. 'Your Lordship,' I cried, 'another few yards and you will be surrounded by the enemy. This way, I beg of you.'

He thanked me, mentioned that he was unconscious of the danger, and observing the White Horse on my cap, asked where the

Royal Welch Fusiliers were. I told him that I had become detached from them by the pursuit of an officer, but believed, by the shouting and cheering of a few minutes before, that they had now broken the second line. Still keeping the bridle in my hand I ran alongside of the horse in the direction from which the shouts had proceeded, until we came upon the Royal Welch Fusiliers. They were re-formed in the skirt of the wood just short of the farm-land behind which the Court House stood. To their left ran a road and on their right was a small hill. His Lordship noted this hill at once as commanding the Court House, and the very place to post our batteries, which were now coming up the road.

'General Greene should not have overlooked this place,' he said in my hearing, as one who mildly reproaches an opponent in a game of chess for a neglected opportunity. The guns were hauled up the hill and unlimbered, and at once opened fire upon the American third line. There was heavy fighting already in that quarter, where Lieutenant-Colonel Webster, who had become separated from us, had led The Thirty-Third and other troops. Presently we heard distant huzzas, and then these drowned by a tremendous Southern yell; and we saw a sight which surprised and dismayed us. The Second Guards, caught in the rear by Colonel Lee's sabres and in the flank by the bayonets of the First Maryland Regiment, were fairly on the run across an open field. Lord Cornwallis did not hesitate: he ordered Lieutenant Macleod of the gunners to fire grape-shot point-blank into the mêlée! This in a moment broke the American pursuit, by making the horses unmanageable, but it was at great cost to our own people. 'A necessary evil,' said his Lordship, returning very pale to where we were formed. 'So a man would do right to shoot off his own finger where a rattlesnake bit him, lest the poison lose him his whole arm and life itself.' The Marylanders then returned to their original post in the neighbourhood of the Court House.

Ourselves and The Seventy-First formed a solid line to which five regiments now rallied, including the survivors of the Guards. It was now about three o'clock and the crisis of the battle. But Colonel

Tarleton with a cavalry charge broke the enemy militia on our right, where fighting was in progress about a mile distant from us; our re-formed line then swept forward across the farm-land, which was deeply seamed with gullies, and the Americans went off in haste.

The Royal Welch Fusiliers had the luck to capture two of the four brass six-pounders close to the Court House, which General Greene abandoned with their ammunition. A few prisoners were taken. Ourselves and The Seventy-First as the troops least exhausted were ordered to pursue the enemy as they fell back to our left towards a river called Troublesome Creek: but we were near fainting from hunger and our long exertions and could do little against them.

In this desperate battle, we lost in killed and wounded above five hundred men, near one-third of our whole army. Among the mortally wounded was Lieutenant-Colonel Webster, whose death a few days later struck Lord Cornwallis with such pungent sorrow that he exclaimed: 'I have lost my scabbard.' The Royal Welch Fusiliers were reduced by sixty-eight officers and men to a total strength of but one hundred and fifty. The Americans left between two and three hundred dead on the battlefield; by which we could estimate their losses in killed and wounded at twice as many as ours. Well, it was a victory, but such a victory as my old commander General Phillips said, when he heard the news, as 'the sort of victory that ruins an army.' (General Phillips had lately been exchanged against an American prisoner of equal rank and was now with General Arnold at Portsmouth in Virginia. While in captivity he had caused great resentment among the Americans by his downright manner of speech and by telling his officers 'not to heed the Americans more than a flock of cackling geese'. Many of our veteran officers and men, I confess, made troublesome prisoners.)

We camped that night upon the field of battle. It was a very black night, and the battle had been scattered over so wild and difficult a country that darkness fell before we had brought in our own and the American wounded. The Court House, with the meagre farm-buildings and sheds, was insufficient to shelter even those whom we found. It rained in torrents all night and the cries of the wounded and dying, for whom no shelter could be found, exceeded all description for painfulness. We had no food, no drink, no shelter. So complicated a scene of horror and distress rarely occurs even in military life; yet I had experienced as bad or worse in the Saratoga fighting, where the gloomy necessity of constant retreat had weighed upon our hearts like lead. To-day at least we had won a resounding victory against a courageous and well-fed enemy, advantageously posted, whose numbers exceeded us by nearly three to one. As for myself, I admit that my heart was strangely elated in spite of all. The death of so many good comrades, especially of Mad Johnny Maguire, should have stilled it to sobriety. But one consideration now dominated every other: Richard Harlowe (or Pearce) was killed, and I was now free to marry the woman whom I had widowed with my own fusil, and who was the mother of my child. For I was convinced by a strong intuition not only that she still lived, but that I would meet her once more, and before many months had passed. I should dearly have loved to seek out Richard Harlowe's corpse and search it to find his commission or some other proof of his death; but I could not be spared from duty.

Smutchy Steel was promoted to Corporal as a reward for his soldier-like services that day, and I was glad to be able once more to discourse with him on equal and familiar terms, we being now both of non-commissioned rank. Though originally of a low and vicious disposition, he had been insensibly improved by the exacting round of duty and discipline: so much so that he was entirely changed in mind and character into an honourable and moral person, whom I was proud to call my friend. Such cases in the Army are as frequent as they are surprising, and constitute a strong argument for the military life; if the officers be worthy of their trust.

The morning after the battle we buried the dead, from whom we took such shoes as were in better condition than our own, and marched back to the New Garden Meeting House. There we left seventy of our most severely wounded under the charge of the good Quakers, with a flag of truce and a petition to the Americans to relieve their distresses. That same afternoon we were fed for the first time for forty-eight hours, the ration being a quarter of a pound of maize flour and the same amount of very lean beef. The nearest place whence we could hope for regular provisions was Wilmington on the North Carolina coast, above two hundred miles away, following the bank of the Cape Fear River. So off we marched, by short stages. General Greene then turned to pursue us; but our rear-guard fought only slight skirmishes with his van, and he did not follow us above forty miles. We were very hungry and for bread we were one day served with liver, and another day with turnips, which roots have small nourishment in them.

A settlement of Highland Loyalists at Cross Creek lay on our route, but even there we could not find four days' forage within twenty miles, and could not therefore halt for refreshment. These Highlanders, notwithstanding the cruel persecution that they had constantly endured from the Revolutionaries, had shown great affection and zeal towards us, collecting and conveying to us all the flour and spirits in the neighbourhood. Their attention saved the lives of a number of our wounded, worn out by traversing this barren desert; none the less, we lost a great many on the road. The enemy militia did not appear in arms against us, but contented themselves with driving the cattle out of our reach, carrying off supplies of corn and breaking down bridges over the numerous creeks which we must pass.

The only commerce of which this remote country was capable was in horses. They multiplied very fast in the swamps and were sold in the Spring to drovers from Pennsylvania who grazed them upon the road on their return. Agriculture here was patriarchal, that is to say, only enough crops were raised for the consumption of the growers. Each plantation raised and dressed its own wool and leather, and the chief lack appeared to be nails and salt. Yet so skilful were the settlers with axe and hatchet that at a pinch they could construct and roof huts without a single nail—a most tedious business.

The day before we reached Cross Creek an incident occurred which went far to prove that the Quaker of New Garden had been telling the truth. An extraordinary-looking person came to join our Colours, who looked (so someone truly remarked) as if he had escaped from the collection of natural monstrosities exhibited at Surgeons' Hall in London. He was bent with rheumatic pains, and shaken with ague; his hair was white as snow, his body utterly emaciated. He was but thirty-eight years old, he said, but for three years had lived the life of a beast in the swamps, having scooped a den for himself in the bank of a river and provided it with a concealed entrance. Nobody of his kin or acquaintance remained to supply him with necessaries, except some cousins who lived at a great distance and once or twice in a year ventured to visit him. He had often been pursued and shot at by his rancorous enemies, but always escaped. His meat was terrapin, fish and small animals, generally eaten raw; and his bread was acorns, which from long use had become quite agreeable to him. His clothing was composed entirely of skins, jobbed together with sinews. On his head was a racoon-skin cap. But for having no umbrella, no musket and no Man Friday, he would have well served for a cut in illustration of Mr. De Foe's *Robinson Crusoe*. He was now enlisted in the Provincial Forces. By living so much alone, this poor fellow had contracted the habit of talking to himself in a debate of two voices, and his wits were almost turned; but he proved a valuable scout and had not lost his skill with a rifle. When Mr. Brice, who distributed the rations of the Provincial Forces, gave him his share, the new recruit let great tears fall into the pannikin of flour and exclaimed: 'At last, Sir, I know myself for a human being again, by the token of beef and flour.'

Of this very disagreeable march, there are two more incidents worthy of the reader's attention. The first happened at Ramsay's Crossing, about March 22nd. That evening I was called upon to mount guard upon the American officer-prisoners, which was a duty given to regular sergeants, though the guards themselves were American militia. The Provost-Marshal of the Army, instructing me in my duties, warned me that a certain cavalry officer was a very dangerous person and would do all in his power to escape: since conscious that he had not only violated his oath of allegiance but acted with great cruelty against the inhabitants of the Carolinas. He feared the gibbet were he sent to trial at Charleston, of which he was a native. I desired to have the officer pointed out to me, and the Provost-Marshal did so. 'I know the gentleman,' said I, 'I have even eaten and drunk at his expense. He is Captain Gale, is he not, of Wappo Creek? He was a Furious Tory when I last heard him declaim. Well, your Honour, I shall take all precautions to keep him with us.'

'Do so, Sergeant,' said the Provost-Marshal, 'for if he escapes, I fear he will prove unlucky to the river-people who have assisted us in our march.'

He went off, and not being able to lock the prisoners into any hut, none being available for that purpose, I bound Captain Gale's wrists and ankles with a cord, one end of which I fastened to my own wrist as I slept. Towards morning I awoke, at some slight noise, but jerking the cord found it still attached, as I thought, to the captive, and resumed my sleep. To my astonishment and alarm, when dawn came, I discovered that the Captain was gone, and the other end of the cord was tied to a little bush. I questioned the sentinel who had been on guard, but he professed to know nothing. I instantly confined him, raised the alarm and reported my loss to the Provost-Marshal, who sent out cavalry in pursuit; but to no purpose. We never caught Captain Gale.

Lord Cornwallis was highly displeased when the circumstance was made known to him, and commanded the Sergeant of the Guard to be brought before him; threatening to 'break him for so gross a dereliction of duty'. I was thereupon summoned to Headquarters and felt very bad as I approached his Lordship's presence; but to my great relief his stern frown changed into a smile when he recognized me. He said to his aide-de-camp: 'Why 'tis the sergeant of whom I told you—he who proved a good fairy to me in the wood during the battle. This case is over before it has begun. The sentinel was bribed, that's clear. Put him on trial for his life: the Sergeant may return to his regiment and will act as witness.'

I may add that Lord Cornwallis frequently addressed a 'good morning' or a few kind words to me afterwards when we met; and I was often employed by him to copy out the duplicates of his despatches. The latter circumstance accounts for the knowledge that I acquired, from casual talk and the confidence of his military family, of the direction of the war by Lord George Germaine and Sir Henry Clinton.

The second interesting circumstance of the march happened when we were at Grange's plantation, but two days' march from Wilmington, on April 5th. It was then that I first witnessed at close range one of the great wonders of nature for which the American Continent is famous. It was an unusually sultry day, provocative of petulant tempers, and bred no less than three duels (one fatal) among the Hessian officers of Bose's Regiment. Hot streams of air now were felt and sudden gusts from different points of the compass. One gust twitched off my cap and wig as I was passing across the yard of the plantation where we were about to be quartered. They were cleverly caught before they fell by two little negro boys, who laughed merrily at me as I restored the honours of my head. All at once a great cloud of darkness rose in the north, and from the distance I heard a great roaring, grinding noise gradually approaching, like the noise of crunched sugar prodigiously magnified. I knew it at once for a tornado. I was for taking shelter in the great red barn opposite; but thought better of it and remained where I was in the open yard.

Now with a resounding clap the tornado struck. It carried with it a great cloud of green leaves, torn branches, dust, hay and rotten wood, and cut a twisted path a hundred yards across in which barns, trees, houses were alike levelled with the ground. I turned, clutching at my cap with both hands and was thrown flat on my face as the whirlwind passed over me. All the breath was sucked out of my lungs and I nearly choked. Down went the great barn, collapsing inwards by some atmospheric trick, and the 'meat-houses', or negro cabins, beyond, were blown clean away. As I raised myself on my elbows, and looked up, I saw a most remarkable sight: a great empty butt (of the sort in which the stinking mash is kept when they make their peach-brandy) sailing through the air as if it had been fired from a mortar. It crashed squelch against a stable wall, which went down like a house of balanced playing-cards. Stones, planks and bricks were now flying about me, as hot as under a cannonade, and this continued for three minutes during the whole of which I found it very difficult to breathe.

A slight lull followed and then came a storm of thunder and lightning and drenching cold rain which lasted for another hour. A tall tulip-tree that had escaped the whirlwind, from standing a little outside its track, was struck before my eyes and scathed the whole length of its smooth grey trunk. Two of the wounded and a number of negroes were killed. That storm proved very annoying to me, for it carried away, with my other poor baggage, the journal that I had kept posted every day throughout the campaign; my memory, being none of the best, has played many tricks with me in attempting, so many years since, to reconstruct the sequence of my adventures.

CHAPTER XIII

WE WERE fast approaching the end of the War, which had now been six years in progress, and Guildford Court House proved the last pitched battle in which I took part. I had fought in six. Yet I was by no means yet at the end of my fighting, still less of my wide wanderings, and I may affirm without boasting or fear of contradiction that, before I had done, the track of my feet upon the American Continent marked a longer and more distant route than that of any other soldier in the Royal armies.

Wilmington was a poor place and though we found stores awaiting us there which were very grateful, especially rum and a few hundred pairs of shoes, our necessities could not yet be wholly supplied. We had eighteen days' rest, which together with sea-baths restored most of the convalescents to duty.

It was here that Captain Champagné, who was an assiduous fox-hunter, called for volunteers among us to learn the equestrian art; for he said that this was cavalry country and horses' legs could save our own on innumerable occasions, especially in scouting and for-aging. About half the regiment came forward, Smutchy Steel and myself among them, and Colonel Tarleton, who was an old friend of the Captain's, obliged him with a number of horses. So I became a recruit again, in a manner of speaking, though with this advantage over most of the other rank and file that as a boy in Ireland I had learned the rudiments of horsemanship from my patron, young Mr. Howard. The other marching regiments flocked as spectators to our riding-school, in order to laugh at our ungainly seats and awkward tumbles. But we knew that they secretly envied us, and we persevered. A sergeant of the Seventeenth Dragoons acted as our instructor, and taught us the proper care of our horses, besides. He said to me one day in a condescending manner: 'Upon my word,

Sergeant Lamb, I don't wonder that as men of honour you are bent on learning our profession. For my part, I cannot comprehend how any man can enlist, without mortification, in any other arm of the service but the cavalry! I believe I would as lief be a churchwarden as a sergeant in the Line.'

'Why,' said I, disguising my resentment with a smile, 'it is not all psalms and long faces in our poor foot-swinging congregation. I assure you that we have very lively meetings in the vestry on occasion.'

'Ay, no doubt,' he said magnificently. 'But the cavalry rules the battle.'

'At least it did not rule at Minden,' said I, growing more nettled, 'when six British regiments, mine among them, tumbled the whole French cavalry to ruin; and when the British cavalry never entered the action at all. And what is more, when shells and grape-shot are flying, I am thankful that I chose the Line. For I can answer for my own legs that they will not play the coward or prove unmanageable: as the boldest cavalryman cannot answer for the legs of his mount. You forget, Sergeant Haws, that an infantryman has his own proper pride.'

He was a stupid man, but presently concluded that he had come near to a positive insult; and soon he begged my pardon, which I was glad to give, and we had a long drink together. Yet we never became close friends. The cavalryman in general regards the infantryman no more than a Jew does a pig; being raised three feet above him, he absurdly seeks to translate this superiority of altitude into a moral superiority. But it is generally accepted that, as a rule, mounted infantry fall less short of their duty in action than do dismounted cavalry.

Sergeant Haws had a continuous complaint against the horses of Virginia, which he owned were fine animals, that they were marred for riding by the false gaits taught them by their lazy masters. For to a Southern planter a trot was odious, as unsettling to his liver; and a fair gallop he found most fatiguing. The horse was therefore taught those unnatural modes of progression, the pace and the wrack. In the first the animal moves his two legs on one side together alternately with the other two, and, being therefore unable to spring from the ground as in a trot, proceeds with a sort of shuffling motion. The

Virginian planter habitually sat with his toes just beneath his horse's nose, the stirrups being extremely long and the saddle put about three or four inches forward on the mane. English ladies, monks, priests and lawyers once favoured the pace, under the name of the amble, but it disappeared from the manège about the time of the first George. A passage in Chambers' *Cyclopedia,* I find, contradicts Sergeant Haws as to the unnaturalness of this gait, declaring that the pace or amble is usually the first natural step of young colts. In the wrack the horse gallops with his fore-feet and trots with those behind. This is a gait that looks very odd to the European, and greatly fatigues the horse; but the gentlemen of Virginia found it conducive to their ease, which was all that they considered. It was also judged to be a safer motion for a sleepy man, or a man far gone in liquor, than a trot or a gallop. The pace and the wrack were taught to the horses, when foals, by hoppling them—in the first case with two bands, one linking the two off legs, the other the near legs; in the second case with a single band for the hind legs.

General Greene's defeat had gained him as much as a victory. Our lack of stores and our great train of sick and wounded, had forced us to come so far away from our base in South Carolina, that he was now at liberty to enter that province himself with what remained of his army. I may note here that General Greene never won a battle in his whole career, yet always managed, as in this case, to obtain the fruits of victory. He wrote very frankly about himself that few generals had run faster and more lustily than he; but that he had taken care not to run too far and had commonly run as fast forward as backward. 'Our army,' he said, 'has frequently been beaten but, like the stockfish, grows the better for it.' Lord Cornwallis was indeed in a quandary when he had a clear and positive report that General Greene was pressing hard against Camden, where Lord Rawdon's garrison was pitifully small. We did not have sufficient stores for marching back across the five hundred miles of barren country which intervened, and several broad rivers must be crossed, from which the enemy would no doubt remove all boats as we approached. To return by sea to Charleston, his Lordship thought disgraceful. Besides, sea-voyages usually proved ruinous to cavalry horses; and some weeks would be wasted in waiting for transports, during which time our army, already reduced to a mere fourteen hundred men, would suffer severely from sickness in the heats of this unhealthy station. A third and bolder course, however, remained, which was to go forward into the rich province of Virginia. There we could join forces with General Phillips' army and perhaps do such widespread damage as to draw General Greene hurriedly away from South Carolina.

In the event, the courage and determination of Lord Rawdon checked General Greene for a time; yet South Carolina was lost, except only Charleston. Even this would have gone, and none of our frontier garrisons have been brought away safe but for an accident—the arrival of three British regiments from Ireland. These had been intended by Lord George Germaine to reinforce Lord Cornwallis in South Carolina for his campaign against General Gates; but when the news of our victory at Camden arrived, Lord George had assumed that the province was finally reduced and sent a packet in pursuit of the transports with orders for them to sail to New York instead. An American privateer fortunately intercepted this despatch, and the troops continued to Charleston, where they arrived in the nick of time. General Greene remained encamped on the Neck near the city. Do what he might, he could not prevent the Whigs of South Carolina from attempting to extirpate the Tories, nor the Tories from retaliating in kind upon the Whigs. Thousands of men were hanged by grapevines from trees, or by cords from the poles of fodder stacks, in the very sight of their children and women-folk. A civil war is always more cruel and vengeful than a foreign war; but here the angry climate was chiefly to blame.

Sir Henry Clinton was grieved when he heard that Lord Cornwallis had abandoned the Carolinas to their fate. He also trembled for his own safety at New York, were he the object of a combined attack of French and Americans. It lies outside the scope of this work to attempt to disentangle the web of cross-purposes that was then woven between Sir Henry Clinton and Lord Cornwallis. Each had his own different plan of campaign and carried it out as best he could according to the limited knowledge that he had of the other's situation and his own; both were equally hampered by orders and counter-orders from Lord George Germaine (whose plan of campaign differed from that of either) and by their ignorance of what help they could count upon from Lord George in Downing Street, and from the Earl of Sandwich at Admiralty House. None of the despatches that each wrote the other cleared up the mist of misunderstanding but only increased it. The Earl of Cornwallis was in the worse case, as being expected to serve two masters, Sir Henry and Lord George, who contradicted each other and each continually countermanded his own successive plans as he became aware of altered circumstances; moreover, most of these despatches reached their destination either too late or not at all. Lord Cornwallis must therefore incur no blame for acting upon his own judgment, even if that proved at fault. He confessed himself greatly disappointed with the Loyalists of the Carolinas; the hope of their rising in large numbers, as expressed by Lord George Germaine, being totally disappointed. Many hundreds of them at different times had ridden into camp to shake hands with him and congratulate him upon his victory; but not two companies could be persuaded to remain with our Standard. His Lordship told an officer too, in my hearing, that he was quite tired of marching about the great American Continent as it were in search of adventures.

There were no memorable occurrences in our forward march from Wilmington on April 25th, 1781. Since many rivers and creeks intervened between the Cape Fear River and the James River in Virginia, including the considerable floods of Nuse, Tar and Roanoke, two boats mounted on wagons were drawn along with the army. We had sufficient rum, salt and flour for a three-weeks' journey, and set off in good heart. The country was as barren as it had been described to us, but we were not molested in our march. Colonel Tarleton went ahead with his Greens and sixty mounted Royal Welch Fusiliers. Whenever he reached a settlement he was at pains greatly to magnify the size and power of our forces. I remained behind with the rest of the regiment, but was mounted and did some scouting and foraging.

It was not until we came to Tar River after a crooked journey of two hundred miles that, the country becoming more populous, we were able to supplement the stores carried upon the wagons; but at the same time met with some opposition at the river crossings. The militia of Halifax on the Roanoke River turned out in force, but our advanced troops bustled them away; and on May 20th, we joined forces on the borders of Virginia with General Phillips' army.

I was much grieved to hear that General Phillips himself was dead, only the week before, of a fever. He was a man equally beloved and respected for his virtues and his military talents. The Marquis de La Fayette, who had led down a small army with the prime object of capturing and hanging General Arnold, was not far off, but broke camp as soon as he was aware of our arrival. It seems that the young Marquis had lost his boasted French *politesse* since his arrival in America, for when a flag was sent to him across the river to inform him that General Phillips lay dying in a certain house, and request him to drop no more shells about it, he disregarded this embassy, and the cannonade continued. One ball passed through the room next to the death chamber. General Phillips' last words were: 'Now why in the world cannot that vainglorious boy let me die in peace? 'Tis very cruel.'

The junction of the armies was at Petersburgh, a town of about three hundred houses on a tributary of the James River, which runs into Chesapeak Bay. There were fine falls at the upper end of the town and some of the best flour-mills in the country. The houses were of wood roofed with shingles: the better sort were white-plastered, with brick chimneys and glazed windows; the poorer sort were left rough outside, with wooden chimneys clay-lined and only shutters to the windows. This was an important centre of the tobacco trade and also contained a number of general stores which used to supply the back country. Now trade was at a standstill, the merchants being unable to export their tobacco, for fear of British men-of-war and privateers, and thus to replenish their shelves.

The great warehouses and the mills of Petersburgh belonged to a Mrs. Bowling, whose mansion General Phillips, and now Lord Cornwallis, used as their headquarters. This fine mansion was situated on a vast grassy platform on a considerable slope above the town. I was quartered in the stables there, at his Lordship's request, in order to be at hand for copying out his despatches. I remember how, early one Sunday morning, I paused entranced in the garden and thought to myself: 'Ah, what a sweet green oasis in the desert of War!' In my nostrils was the scent of clove pinks, of which a long border stretched down the garden path on either hand, and my eye feasted on the ripe apricots and nectarines hanging upon the well-pruned trees, the swelling green peas trained upon their sticks, and strawberries of enormous size netted against the depredations of birds. At the same time a mocking-bird was singing very finely from a plum-tree above my head, hopping incessantly from branch to branch; he was about the size of a thrush, but more slender. The mocking-bird would imitate the note of every other bird, but with increased strength and sweetness—to the discomfiture of the bird he mocked, who would fall silent and fly off. He imitated for me on this occasion the cardinal and the painted plover, and then (as if to raise a laugh) the wail and whimper of a black piccaninny! I clapped my hands and called out 'bravo!'; whereupon he flew off.

The interior of the mansion, one wing of which, by Virginian custom, was wholly dedicated to guests, appeared solidly but not exquisitely furnished, and rather for good cheer than for the cultivation of the polite arts; with much massive silver but no books or albums; several comfortable sofas but no cabinets of curios, and so forth.

The people of Virginia felt sentimentally about their great magnolia bushes with the broad leaves and heavily perfumed flowers; and about a very sweet white flower of smaller size called the 'bubby-flower' because it was presented by gallant young men to their sweethearts to place between their breasts. In New England, contrariwise, flowers and music were alike considered luxurious and 'a sign of slavery'. Virginia was the most mature and agreeable province in America that I had yet visited, and the nearest to my own country in manners. Fox-hunting with hounds, unknown in New England (where the chase was only for the sake of the pot), and cock-fighting (which the Yankees held un-Christian and barbarous), were with drinking and horse-racing the chief amusements of the Virginians. The fortune of the province, I must add, was founded upon tobacco, as firmly as that of the Northern provinces upon the cod-fish.

In our passage by the James River and other streams we observed to our surprise a great deal of derelict land in what seemed to us advantageous situations. The fact was that tobacco is a crop that soon exhausts the soil, and the settlers, when they had sucked all the richness out of a piece of land did not trouble to put it into good heart again but, with the money it had fetched, bought fresh land in the interior and settled there until that in turn was worn out. The exhausted land soon threw up a spontaneous growth of pine and cedar, but did not recover its fertility for about twenty years.

This was the season when the young plants of tobacco had just been removed from the seed-beds and transplanted into fields, where they were set out in hillocks at about a yard's interval, each from each; as hops are planted in Great Britain. Now the slaves, who were in general less brutish, since more humanely treated then those of the Carolinas or Georgia, were constantly tending the plants, picking off a large black fly of the beetle kind and all manner of other greedy insects, and removing weeds and worms with their hoes. When the plants attained about a foot in height the slaves would break off the tops, the suckers and the coarse lower leaves, in order to encourage the fine upper leaves. The plants would reach maturity in August and then be cut down for removal to the drying-houses, where they would be smoked, damped, sweated and smoked again. This work required the most delicate judgment, lest the leaves should crumble or rot. When sufficiently dry they were then stripped from the stems, sorted, and packed by means of strong presses into hogsheads of a thousand-pound capacity. The hogsheads were sent for inspection to a State warehouse—trundled along by a couple of strong pins at either end, by way of axles—and certificates given in exchange for them; which certificates passed as currency in the province, and a man generally reckoned the value of a horse, a watch or a silver dish not in coin but in so many hogsheads of tobacco. However, much of this paper, the only American currency that had not hitherto depreciated in value, was now worthless from the raids made by General Arnold upon the tobacco warehouses.

When we arrived at Petersburgh we found a bitter dispute in progress between General Arnold and the Royal Navy, each side claiming the tobacco stored in Mrs. Bowling's warehouse as its own prize. Lord Cornwallis settled the dispute, in Indian fashion, by burning the whole stock, amounting to four thousand hogsheads. However, from consideration for his hostess, Mrs. Bowling, he first had it removed from the warehouses. It was a pleasure to us to learn that this tobacco, with what had been destroyed at Richmond and other places, was the property of the French Government and amounted to almost the whole of their annual remittance. We were surprised that with such discouragement the planters continued the manufacture of tobacco; but they must keep their slaves employed, and I suppose they hoped for better times. The Virginians, by the way, unlike the Carolinians, neither took snuff nor chewed tobacco, and few of them smoked—out of consideration for their women-folk, whose nostrils were easily offended.

The province now raised a deal of cotton, a shrub which flourished better on inferior land, or on land that had already had its first richness taken from it by tobacco; on virgin soil it produced more wood than cotton. This substance was contained in the swollen pistil of the flower, which burst open when ripe. The flocks intermixed with the seeds were then gathered by negroes; and the seeds later removed by means of a gin, a contrivance of two smooth rollers moving in contrary directions. The plant, which was set in regular walks, was kept down by cropping to a height of four feet. Though previously all cotton had been sent for manufacture to England, since the war the provincials had of necessity carded, spun and woven their own cotton-cloth, but little inferior to Manchester goods; the labour employed being that of female slaves. Much of this cloth here dyed blue with indigo, also of native growth.

Reinforcements now arrived from New York. They had been sent by Sir Henry before he knew of Lord Cornwallis' intention to come into this country, and they brought up the combined armies, of which his Lordship now took command, to above five thousand men. This made us greatly superior to the American forces in Virginia, and he determined to chase the Marquis out of the province. We crossed the James River without opposition at a place called Westover where the river was two miles broad. The Marquis decamped from his position at the tobacco town of Richmond and retreated north up the York River, ourselves in pursuit. However, he went too fast for us and Lord Cornwallis contented himself with ordering the destruction of tobacco and other public stores wherever they were found. General Arnold was not with us: he was recalled by Sir Henry to New York, whence he undertook a very successful raid against New London, in his own State of Connecticut, and did frightful damage. Congress would have done well to treat him with more decency and gratitude when his outstanding powers were exerted in the American cause.

We were near a place called Hanover in early June when orders came from Lord Cornwallis that greatly interested the Royal Welch Fusiliers. All the seventy horsemen among us were to be mounted upon blood-horses, numbers of which had been seized from the plantations of revolutionary officers, and sent upon a very enterprising jaunt under Colonel Tarleton, in company with one hundred and eighty Greens. The Virginia General Assembly were shortly to assemble at Charlotteville, in the foot-hills of the mountains seventy miles from us, where were the head-waters of the Rivanna, a tributary of the James River. They would meet under guard, for the purpose of voting taxes, drafting the militia and making an addition to the regular forces of the State. Their president was the famous Mr. Thomas Jefferson, a citizen of Charlotteville, and the chief author (or rather compiler) of the Declaration of Independence. To break up this meeting was the object confided to us.

At dawn on June 4th, we set out, making our way between the North and South Anna Rivers. Our horses went unshod, as is customary in the South during the summer. It was an exceedingly hot day, but to have one's back unencumbered by the great luggage of a marching soldier, and even to be provided with pistols in place of a heavy musket, was delightful to us. The country was wooded and uncultivated and for several miles we did not pass a single human habitation or meet with a single person. We halted at midday to refresh ourselves, but pressed on again after two hours, and by eleven o'clock at night had reached Louisa after about forty miles' ride. Whenever we passed over a bridge we first blanketed it to prevent the drumming of our horses' hooves from giving the signal of our approach. At Louisa we were regaled with hearth-cake, bacon and peach-brandy by a Loyalist planter. At two o'clock we were in the saddle again and before the dawn of June 5th, struck the great road which ran along the skirt of the mountains and communicated between Maryland and the Southern States.

Here we were in luck. The rumble of wheels was heard in the distance, the crack of whips and the shouting of drivers to sleepy horses: it was twelve heavy wagons under a slight escort coming down the road from Alexandria. These we seized, taking the escort prisoner. They were found to be laden with clothing and French arms for General Greene's forces. We could not waste time or men in conveying these goods back to our army, and therefore burned them. This was a great disservice for the enemy, for long before this, according to General Greene's own account, more than two-thirds of his men were entirely naked but for a breech-cloth, and never came out of their tents; and the rest were as ragged as wolves, and shoeless. Soon after daybreak, at Dr. Walker's plantation and in its neighbourhood, the Greens took from their beds a number of the principal gentlemen of Virginia, who had fled to this mountain border for safety. We had with us two Loyalist gentlemen who knew the records and characters of these persons, one of whom was a member of Congress. Some they recommended for mercy, some for capture, and a third sort for immediate slaughter. However, Colonel Tarleton was careful to do nothing violent: a month before, Lord Cornwallis had read the Greens a lecture on their brutal rapacity and, two of them, being picked out of a parade by country people as the authors of rape and murder, he had executed as an example to the rest. His Lordship had likewise forbidden all acts of terror and revenge. The more active enemies of King George were therefore secured and put under guard, the remainder paroled and allowed to remain with their families. We now halted for half an hour, having come seventy miles in twenty-four hours. We were very saddle-sore, those of us who were but horsemen for the occasion.

Precautions were taken to secure every person going in the direction of Charlotteville, which lay seven miles ahead of us, so that our arrival there might come as a surprise. Among those we seized was a great plump negro, driving a gaudy yellow cart, who acted as the Charlotteville postrider. In his mail bags several important letters were discovered. Negroes in Virginia were forbidden by law to bear the consequential dignity of post-rider, but this one was, by a fiction, deputy to a four-year-old white boy who rode in the cart with him. It was the child who wore the laced hat of office and had taken the oath before a magistrate, 'by the Almighty God', to carry the mail safely through. His childish lips were not, however, equal to a blast upon the post-horn, nor his fingers to the management of a pistol; and even the shrill cries of alarm raised by his black deputy failed to disturb his slumbers when we surrounded the cart and impounded the bags.

Various were the accounts given by this negro and other persons on the road as to the force assembled in Charlotteville: some trying to dissuade us from our adventure by magnifying the State Guard, others encouraging us by denying that any soldiers whatever were there. But we must strike at once or not at all. We were therefore ordered to urge our horses forward with all possible expedition. Captain Champagné begged as a favour from Colonel Tarleton that, should a charge be made into the town, our people might be given the honour of leading it. This was granted.

It was about breakfast time when, despite the warning of our scouts that the ford of the Rivanna was guarded by a company of Americans, we swept down the banks and across the water in a head-long gallop, losing but three men wounded, and pistolled the flying guards. The town was erected on the opposite bank: it was but a small place, consisting of about a dozen gentlemen's houses, with their negro-cabins and tobacco-houses, one 'ordinary' (or tavern), a Court House, and some barracks. We were immediately directed to charge up the street, which we did. So animated was my spirit that to the surprise of my comrades and the terror of my horse, who swerved, plunged and nearly threw me, I uttered a loud war-whoop in the Mohawk style. Some American officers now came running out from the houses, pistol in hand, to oppose us. They were shot down, and while one troop continued to the Court House, where the Assembly met, and another to the magazine, Captain Champagné led forty of us for some distance up a mountain in an attempt to catch Mr. Jefferson.

A good carriage road of about three miles brought us to a large mansion in the Italian style, with columned porticoes, which was Mr. Jefferson's residence, named Monticello. We were told by his servants, as soon as we arrived, that their master had heard the distant noise of shots and seen our red-coats coming up the hill. He had then provided for his personal liberty by a precipitate retreat: his horse was fresh and good and he was not to be overtaken by our exhausted ones. Captain Champagné entered the mansion, taking me with him, to make a close search; but Mr. Jefferson was indeed gone.

Monticello, which occupied about an acre and a half on the extreme summit of the mountain, was a place which greatly differed from the other plantations of Virginia. Mr. Jefferson was not a sportsman and no trophies of the chase adorned the house, of which he was himself the architect and to which he had given this Italian name. Instead, we found evidences of his philosophic studies, viz. terrestrial and celestial globes, a large telescope through which he had observed our approach, meteorological instruments and observations, and a sort of alchemist's den with phials, retorts and alembics. The centre of the mansion consisted of a large octagonal saloon, with glass folding doors opening upon a portico at either side. From one window there was an extensive prospect of the Blue Mountains rising for about three thousand feet, from the other, across a well-tended vineyard, we could see the wooded valley of the Rivanna. There was also a library upstairs with decorations in the antique Roman style, but not yet completed. The Captain apologized to the lady of the house (whom I suppose to have been Mrs. Jefferson), for our intrusion and after a short examination of the premises, from which he removed some papers of an official kind found in a chest, led us down the hill again.

Meanwhile at Charlotteville seven members of the Assembly had been captured, with a few officers and men; one thousand new fire-locks from the Fredericksburg manufactory had been broken; four hundred barrels of gunpowder, several hogsheads of tobacco and a store of Continental uniform clothing destroyed. We abstained from the plundering or destruction of private property, but spent all day in searching the district for what could be considered of public owner-ship or capable of hostile use against us.

We remained in the town for the night. Early the next day a party of twenty ragged men came into our piquets on the hill, huzzaing and singing. I was on duty not far away and strolled up with Smutchy Steel to see who they might be. The man who led them cried out at sight of me and came running to me with hand outstretched. I con-fess that I did not give a very cordial greeting to this savage, who had a great black beard, red moustachios and long matted hair, and was clad only in a pair of cotton trousers, with half one leg missing. But Smutchy had a sharper eye. 'Why, Terry Reeves,' he cried, 'is it not yourself?'

The meeting between the three of us was truly affecting—Cor-poral Reeves' companions were all members of the Army taken at Saratoga, chiefly men of the Twentieth and Fourteenth Regiments, but there were two others of The Ninth. They told of their long march from the pen at Rutland, during which they had suffered very great hardships. On their arrival they had been informed that they were not expected to arrive until the Spring, and thereupon led into a wood where were a few log huts in the course of construction, but unroofed and filled with snow. The provisions were very bad, with only a little maize-flour and no meat or rum: to keep them-selves warm the soldiers had drunk hot water in which red peppers had been steeped. They had lived a most miserable life for the last year and a half, the huts being made miserable by a plague of rats of enormous size. By sickness and desertion The Ninth, Terry said, was reduced to about sixty men; the inordinate drinking of cheap spirits had accounted for above a score. They had lately been ordered up to Little York in Pennsylvania. It was at the same time decided that their officers, in further violation of the Convention, were to be removed from them. When Terry Reeves heard this, he had asked permission of the American Colonel Cole, at whose plantation he had been working as a mechanic, to stay behind. A regiment without officers, Terry held, was no longer a regiment. Besides, the climate of Virginia was more agreeable to naked and hungry men than that of the Northern and Middle States; and Colonel Cole had behaved in a gentlemanly fashion. These other men had obtained the same permission from their masters. Terry told me that he was sorry now not to have joined Smutchy and myself in our escape from Hopewell; however, the war was not yet over and he hoped to strike another blow for his King and Country. He mentioned that the person who had done most for The Ninth in settling disputes, in organizing amusements and profitable labours, and in a thousand other ways, had been Jane Crumer, who still remained very faithful to her poor innocent husband and was called 'The Mother of the Regiment'.

Upon my warm recommendation of Terry Reeves to Captain Champagné, he was immediately taken upon the strength of the Regiment in his own rank. He had become a proficient horseman during his captivity and on our homeward journey that afternoon rode by my side, dressed in a captured Continental uniform and armed with two fine pistols taken from a dead officer. The other men were also incorporated in the Regiment, which with the sick and wounded now returned to duty, and a small draft, was brought up to the strength of about two hundred and fifty officers and men.

Our route was more southerly, down the valley of the Rivanna. Two of the captured Assembly-men rode close behind us, conversing with the Captain. They seemed relieved at the courteous treatment that they received and were very frank about the war. They said that the American cause was now at its last gasp, with the Congress armies unpaid, ill-fed and mutinous, the statesmen and officers of the North and South at odds, and the British raids upon the more prosperous parts of the country most crippling in their effect.

'It all turns now upon this,' said one of them, very earnestly, 'whether your people can prevent the intended co-operation between the French fleet and army and ours before the fall of the year. Hitherto the French have been a hindrance rather than a help, from raising hopes which they have always continually disappointed. They hold it against us that they have been disappointed in the shipments of tobacco, rice and indigo that they hoped from us in exchange for the muskets they sent. But that was no fault of ours. The vigilance of your fleet and the destructive raids of that traitor Arnold have prevented us from fulfilling our obligations. However, it is possible that they will respond to the pressing appeal now made to them, and then we shall see. But it is now crack and crack how matters turn; and let me tell you fairly, Sir, that if once more the French prove, like Egypt, a broken reed, then the jig is over. We Virginians at least will gladly dissolve our alliance with them and enter into honourable treaty with Great Britain. For, by God, we are now in a bad box.'

We came back safe, with no more adventure to myself than a rotten old pine suddenly crashing down in front of my horse, which, like myself, was sleepy from weariness and the hot sun. The woods hereabouts were full of such old rascals tottering with the slightest breeze.

CHAPTER XIV

NO OTHER event of remarkable interest took place during the whole of that summer. More public stores were taken and destroyed at various towns through which we passed, but Lord Cornwallis durst not lead us up into the Middle provinces without reinforcements. He hoped that Sir Henry Clinton would now evacuate New York and join him in Virginia, using Portsmouth or some other nearer seaport for a base. But Sir Henry was aware that the French had at last listened to the appeal of Congress—who were totally bankrupt and forced to obtain supplies by bills of impress, since nobody would accept their bills of credit—and were sending to their aid chests of coin, a fleet of overpowering size and a considerable army. General Washington called upon the country for one last effort to refill his depleted ranks, and now proposed with French help to drive Sir Henry out of New York, where were less than four thousand men. Sir Henry therefore ordered Lord Cornwallis to abandon his operations in Virginia and send every man he could spare to succour New York.

We had passed through the town of Richmond and were now encamped at Williamsburgh, an ancient place by American standards, lying in a plain between the James and York Rivers. It was a pretty place of three streets, with neat white houses surrounding a green, in the English style. Here was the University College of William and Mary, of which the Bishop of Virginia was president—a heavy building like a brick-kiln; and the former Capitol of Virginia, a spacious brick edifice, in the hall of which stood the statue of a former Regal Governor, the head and one arm knocked off by Revolutionaries. There was also a hospital here for lunatics, but it appeared ill-regulated.

On receiving these new orders, Lord Cornwallis, though he would have preferred to return to South Carolina to assist Lord Rawdon, left Williamsburgh and marched us down towards Portsmouth. The Marquis de La Fayette who finding himself unpursued when we halted at Hanover, had returned to harass us, now tried to cut off our rearguard during our crossing of the James River. Lord Cornwallis allowed our piquets to be driven in, to encourage the Marquis, and then with a counter-attack completely routed him and took two guns. This engagement, in which I had no part, took place near Jamestown, famous as the first settlement made by the English in Virginia. But no sooner had we crossed the river than another express arrived from Sir Henry, asking instead for three thousand troops to assist him in a raid through New Jersey on the enemy magazines at Philadelphia. We continued our march to Portsmouth. On our way we skirted the great Dismal Swamp, which extended southward into North Carolina and occupied about one hundred and fifty thousand acres. In the interior were large herds of wild cattle, the descendants of cattle lost on being turned into the swamp to feed, also indigenous bears, wolves, deer and, more remarkable, wild white men who were lost there as children and were perfect beasts. The swamp and its neighbourhood were remarkably healthy, and the water of a medicinal quality sovereign against fevers and bilious complaints: it was of the colour of brandy and tasted strongly of the juniper, a tree which abounded in it. Before the war, a very great quantity of barrel-staves had been cut and shaped on the swamp by negroes in the employment of The Dismal Swamp Company, but the work was carried on from Norfolk, close to Portsmouth, which was burned down in the second year of the war by order of the Regal Governor, and the enterprise abandoned. In that single burning £300,000 worth of damage was done; and even this was a very small part of the material loss incurred by the province because of the war. War was ever an expensive luxury to any nation but to such poor carnivores as the Huns and Vikings who had little to lose and much to gain.

When we arrived at Portsmouth, three thousand of us were duly embarked on transports for New York; but, just as we were putting out to sea, still another express arrived from Sir Henry to prevent our sailing. Lord Cornwallis was to keep the whole of his forces and return to Williamsburgh. There based, he was to fortify an adjacent harbour, where our larger ships could lie under cover of shore batteries, either at Old Point Comfort or Hampton Roads. Sir Henry's change of plan was due to a direct command from Lord George Germaine that not a single man was to be withdrawn from Virginia. Lord Cornwallis, disgusted with this continual chopping and changing, visited the two ports mentioned, taking his Engineer with him; but found that for geographical reasons they did not answer Sir Henry's purpose. We therefore were taken in the transports down the estuary of the James River and then by sea into the York River. Here, at a little distance from the mouth, where the stream suddenly narrowed to less than a mile across and ran five fathoms deep, were two ports, opposite to each other—Gloucester on the northern and York Town on the southern bank. These Lord Cornwallis believed, though they had faults, would correspond better with Sir Henry's requirements. He evacuated Portsmouth, an unhealthy and inconvenient station, at the end of August. A large number of Loyalists and their families, who had taken refuge in Portsmouth, could not be left behind there to the fury of the returning Revolutionaries; and were brought with us into Gloucester and York Town.

York Town, to which the Royal Welch Fusiliers went, contained about two hundred houses, a few taverns and stores, a jail and a church. The church was Episcopalian, the common religious persuasion in Virginia. Religion, however, had been totally interrupted by the war, the clergy being Loyalists, and the English bishops patriotically refusing to ordain Revolutionaries in their place. The churches, never well attended, had been allowed to fall into ruin. This did not greatly discommode the Virginians, I believe. Most of the gentry, including General Washington and Mr. Jefferson, were little better than Deists, and the lower orders quite pagan. The fact was that General Washington, on first assuming his command, had forbidden the clergy to offer prayers for their Sovereign and Royal Family. He had asseverated that he was 'disposed to indulge the professors of Christianity with that road to Heaven which to them shall seem the most direct, plainest, easiest and least liable to exception'; but to sanction prayers for the Monarchy to which he was so inveterate did not suit his humour. Of near a hundred incumbents in Virginia, no more than twenty-eight, being Whiggishly inclined, or trimmers, remained in their parishes throughout the war. It was the same story in all other provinces of America. I heard tell of one parson, the Rev. Jonathan Boucher, at Annapolis in Maryland, who while the Revolution was first brewing preached always with a brace of loaded pistols on the cushion before him, chastening 'all silly clowns and illiterate mechanics who take upon them to censure their Prince'. One day the mob set a brawny blacksmith to waylay and beat him. In the event, the priest of God struck down the priest of Vulcan with a single punch below the ear, which earned him the admiration even of his foes. Yet he took no pride in this victory, and when the day came when he could continue no more in his cure, he told the people of Annapolis: 'You shall see my face no more among you, brethren. For so long as I live I shall cry with Zadok the priest, and with Nathan the prophet—GOD SAVE THE KING!'

At York Town, swamps drained by creeks lay on either side of the town, which was built along a slight cliff above the river; between them was half a mile of firm ground. These swamps were covered with red cedars and pine-trees, and an important industry hereabouts had been burning them for tar. The felled trees were simply heaped in a shallow pit, and the tar, running out, was later gathered up, cleared of the charcoal mixed with it, and put into barrels. Most of the tar-makers, however, had quitted the country, and no labour was anywhere to be had for fortifying York Town. We soldiers must rely upon our own exertions. The task was rendered very disagreeable because of the sultry weather, and the ground being baked exceedingly hard. We had but four hundred tools for the work, half of which were unserviceable. Sir Henry Clinton indeed ordered a great quantity of picks and shovels to be sent to us from New York, but these had not arrived. In the whole neighbourhood no more were procurable; for the agricultural work hereabouts was done with hoes.

At the very end of August, in a fatal moment which may be said to have turned the wavering scale of fortune in favour of the Americans, the French Admiral, Count de Grasse, arrived in the Chesapeak Bay with twenty-eight ships of the line. The sight was mortifying and astonishing to us, for five days before our Admiral Hood had been in those waters with fourteen ships, but, not finding the Frenchmen there, had sailed off to join Admiral Thomas Graves at New York. Admiral Hood had been positive that de Grasse would not bring with him more than ten ships—yet here was the best part of the French fleet!

Count de Grasse surprised two British frigates anchored in the mouth of York River, taking one and driving the other upstream beyond us. Then four of his frigates sailed past us, convoying a large force of French soldiers to join the Marquis de La Fayette at Williamsburgh; they went by night and we could not stop them with fire from our batteries. A week later we heard a cannonade from the sea. It was Admiral Graves who had sailed from New York with eighteen ships in order to intercept another French fleet of eight ships and a convoy of military stores and heavy artillery, that had slipped out of Newport, Rhode Island, and was thought to be coming our way. Instead of these eight ships of war, he found Count de Grasse with four-and-twenty, and immediately attempted to engage him; but, from the wind and other circumstances, he could not force the enemy to a battle which he preferred to decline. Our ships suffered some damage and Admiral Graves returned to New York to refit and fetch assistance. In his absence the eight ships from Newport arrived with their important convoy.

Lord Cornwallis would now dearly have loved to go out against the Marquis de La Fayette and his five thousand men. But he considered it wiser to employ us in improving our position, since his orders were to provide a secure base for the British fleet: true, our united squadrons would be inferior to the enemy, but the British had often before fought at a great numerical disadvantage and gained the victory. We therefore continued at our work of entrenchment, but because of the same scarcity of tools we made slow progress. We were unable to do more than raise an inner line of defences with parapet and stockade, which were to be protected at some distance forward by three redoubts. Other posts covered the passages through the swamps, including the road to Williamsburgh, which followed the bank of the river. The soil, when we broke through the hard outer crust, was very light and more suitable for the growth of cotton than for the construction of ramparts; we eyed it with mistrust. The defences at Gloucester across the river were completed in a shorter time, the earth lending itself more agreeably to military purposes.

News now came that General Washington, who had so long been immobile with his army on the Highlands of Hudson's River, had moved at last. He was coming down against us with a large army, paid in hard money from the French military chest, to which was joined the French army from Rhode Island: in all eighteen thousand men, to swell La Fayette's five thousand. But we remembered the successful defence of Savannah against a similar combination of arms, and consequently feared nothing. On September 28th, York Town was invested by the enemy, who camped at a distance of two miles away, General Washington's men facing the open half-mile between the swamps. Unfortunately our three advanced redoubts were not yet completed. We marched out to meet the enemy and formed in open ground, between these poor works, but he would not give battle. The next day we were pleased to hear that a message had come for Lord Cornwallis from Sir Henry Clinton, who, finding that Washington had slipped away from Hudson's River, undertook to sail to our relief on October 5th, with twenty-six ships of war and five thousand men.

Since the unfinished redoubts were untenable against heavy artillery, Lord Cornwallis withdrew us to the inner line, which we continued industriously to improve. The enemy occupied the positions that we had left. Half of the Regiment had been sent out along the Williamsburgh road on the extreme right, where assisted by a force of forty Marines they held the star-shaped advance redoubt on the cliff beyond the creek. Opposed to them was a French division under the Count de St. Simon. These felt the defences of the redoubt but were driven off by a salvo of grape. Forty more of our mounted men skirmished across the York River under Colonel Tarleton against the French Hussars, or rather Lancers, of the Duke de Lanzun. The rest of us, myself included, were on fatigue duty in the town, which was excessively crowded. Over six thousand troops, and perhaps three thousand civilians, were cramped into a space about five hundred paces in breadth, by twelve hundred in length. Sickness soon broke out and raged through the camp, the sanitary conveniences of the town being very bad, and the weather continuing hot.

Orders came to my company on the morning of October 4th, to attend Lieutenant Sutherland, now the Chief Engineer, on the cliff above the river, where he set us to excavating a deep bomb-proof magazine. We worked at this task for a couple of days, and erected a wooden framework to support the roof. On the third afternoon the Earl of Cornwallis came himself to supervise the task, and criticized a few particulars. I overheard him instructing Lieutenant Sutherland, who came with him, how the window embrasure was to be cut overlooking the river, and how the stairway was to run. 'It is to be hung with green baize,' said his Lordship, 'which I will provide; and do you see that there is width on the stair for bringing down the bed, the *poudreuse* and the large *armoire.*' I cocked up my ears then; for this was clearly not to be a magazine for storing ammunition but a safe retreat for some lady. Two years before the Earl of Cornwallis had lost his beautiful wife, to whom he was greatly attached, and though at Charleston he had rejected the rather shameless advances of many Tory ladies, it was rumoured that at Portsmouth he had fallen in love with a beautiful Irishwoman, lately arrived from New York, and brought her here with him. However, his Lordship had been so discreet in this affair that nobody knew for certain who she might be.

Said Terry Reeves to me when I told him what I had heard: 'Good luck to his Lordship and the lass! It is unnatural for a man to live single, especially when he has so many cares upon his shoulders as has Lord Cornwallis.'

'He is a man whom I hold in great esteem,' I said.

'Ay, esteem,' said Terry, 'but for all that I wish another commanded us. A cross-eyed officer never brought an army good luck.'

This was October 6th, on the evening of which, in heavy rain, the enemy completed their first parallel of trenches at about six hundred yards from our parapet. Our cannon and mortars from the forward redoubts continually disturbed them at this work, which was done at night. They replied with occasional shots from their heavy artillery at a distance, which knocked up great clouds of dust, demolished houses and did much military damage.

Two days later I was sent for to Headquarters for my usual task of duplicating despatches—for which, by the bye, I was rewarded by his Lordship at the rate of one shilling a page—but by some error, when I arrived at Mr. Secretary Neilson's house, where Lord Cornwallis lodged, I was conducted by the negro servant to his private apartment and desired to wait.

I heard a female voice in the corridor singing a song from Mr. Gay's *Beggar's Opera,* which was very popular at the time, to the tune of 'Patie's Mill'.

> 'I, like the fox, shall grieve
>   Whose mate hath left her side'

and, as the door opened, it continued:

> 'Whom hounds from morn to eve
>   Chase o'er the country wide.
> Where can my lover hide,
>   Where cheat the wary pack?
> If love be not his guide,
>   He never will . . .'

Here it broke off suddenly, like a musical box demolished with a blow of a hammer; for seeing me, Kate Harlowe (who was dressed and coiffed in the finest French style) could only gasp and shudder. 'You, Gerry! O, it is not you, Gerry? I thought you dead—I heard it for certain. O, had I been so advised I should never have taken to this life!'

'You are his Lordship's mistress?' I asked in agitation.

She nodded in answer and began to weep. It was clear that she had altogether forgotten her resolve of coldness towards me.

'Where is our child? Does she live?' was my next question.

She wept still more and told me that she did not know. When General Sullivan's army had laid waste Genesee village, the child, who was being suckled by an Indian woman, had been among a small party of fugitives whom the Americans had cut off. Kate had done her utmost to obtain news of the child and even made a long solitary journey into American territory for that purpose; but could learn nothing. She had then made her way to New York, where an exchanged officer of The Ninth had informed her that I was killed. She had in despair become the mistress of an artillery captain, who brought her to Portsmouth; but there he grossly abused her, when in liquor, and Lord Cornwallis happening to pass the house and hear her cries, entered and gave the officer a severe beating. She then passed under his Lordship's protection, and he had since treated her with great affection and gentility.

'But, Gerry,' she cried. 'Even had I known you lived, how could we have continued together? I am married to Richard Harlowe; and be sure he is the sort of salamander who will never die of gunfire.'

'He is dead already,' said I. 'O, Kate, I killed him myself in battle in Carolina. He was fighting under General Greene.'

'You are telling the truth?' she demanded, her eyes now shining with joy.

'I never lied to you,' I replied. 'My dearest, I have dreamed of this meeting for so many years, and your image alone has sustained me in my long misery. Cannot you break your connexion with his Lordship and marry me?'

'When the siege is over, I will,' she said. 'But it would be most cruel to him at present, when he has such need of me—and ungrateful too.'

'Will you not give me a kiss?' I asked, seizing her hand, which was stone cold. 'One single loving salutation in token of this promise?'

'Until I pass from his Lordship's protection, I cannot,' she said. 'I am his mistress. To kiss another man meanwhile would be to wrong him and make a common prostitute of me. Go now, dear Gerry. Be patient, and I will be true to you with my heart, since not with my body. Forgive me; but I cannot come to you now.'

I retired from the room, my breast tormented with mingled feelings of joy and mortification, pride and shame. Hearing his Lordship below giving some instruction to an officer, I slipped into a closet to avoid encountering him as he ascended the stairs. Soon he came up, two steps at a time, and I heard him greeting Kate in his merry, manly voice, as he entered the parlour. My great esteem for him at once prevailed over my jealousy and baser feelings. He was saying: 'Your bower is very prettily furnished, my lovely girl. You will be as safe there from the rebel shot as if you were in the Town of London itself. I will escort you there to-night, I promise you.'

I then went below and, his aide giving me the despatches which I was to copy, I concentrated my mind upon the task; but my hand shook, and though I made no blots or errors, my penmanship was not what it should have been. I excused myself to the officer, alleging that I was overtaken by a return of an old fever—as was, figuratively at least, true enough.

That evening our company was sent up to Fusilier Redoubt, as the right-hand post across the creek was named, to relieve another company. The French were constructing a counter-work at a short distance from us, and there was a hot exchange of fire. Captain Apthorpe commanded us, a very officer-like gentleman, who rejoiced that at last we stood confronted by our natural enemies the French, who fought moreover in a way that we understood.

'I believe,' he said, addressing Lieutenant Guyon, 'that the Regiment of Touraine is in the Count de St. Simon's division. Our Regiment has already had the pleasure of engaging them more than once, when we fought under the Duke of Marlborough. And were they not also at Dettingen?'

Lieutenant Guyon replied: 'I believe you are right, Captain Apthorpe; and that we took them down handsomely.'

On October 9th, the enemy batteries opened upon the town from their first parallel, a distance of six hundred yards, making a very ominous noise. We sprang to arms, and soon the shells began flying about our own ears at Fusilier Redoubt, and in great numbers. This was by no means the first time that I had suffered a cannonade, but so well-nourished and violent a one did not lie in my experience. The whizz and roar was almost continuous, and the air was grey with the dust of our shattered parapet. Besides mortars and howitzers, they were pounding us with a battery of nine nine-pounders at only sixty paces distance. Our fraizing, that is to say the rows of palisades on the exterior of our parapet, was breached at several points and a number of men were killed and wounded. A shell broke directly over my head, so that I fell with my ears ringing and blood gushing from my nose and ears; and I imagined that I was mortally wounded. However, no metal had struck me and I staggered to my feet, prepared to continue with the fight.

Of what ensued I have no clear memory, on account of the dizziness of my head, but I was a veteran soldier by now, to whom battle was become second nature, and I gave my people their orders, I am told, in a very cool and sensible manner. At least, I remember tall French Grenadiers, in white uniforms with sky-blue facings, issuing from their works and advancing at a trot towards us; led on by officers who waved their swords and plumed hats and cried *En avant, mes enfants!* or some such encouragement. Our guns were trained point-blank on them, like infernal pointers at a dead set, and blew their leading files to ruin with grape-shot as they struggled through the obstacles of felled trees that intervened. On they came again in a great crowd with *Vive le Roi!* and *Vive St. Simon!* Our musketry halted them on the glacis, and then down we swarmed at them with charged bayonets and drove them back.

They re-formed out of range and came on again; but I cannot distinguish between the first onset and the second. They numbered three thousand in all, and were volunteers, not impressed men, the best to be had in France. This time, I am told, they gained the lip of the parapet and it was very bloody work before we could dislodge them. Lieutenant Guyon engaged their leader (who wore a brilliant order), sword against sword, and took him with the *point d'arrête* in the throat. I have a confused recollection of seeing Lieutenant Guyon killed with a bayonet thrust and of seizing his weapon from him as he fell, and reviving my old practice of small-sword fencing in a combat with a French officer. But some person intervened, and then the smoke of battle cleared and the French were gone.

A bullet struck my head, furrowing through my scalp, and what then occurred I can only relate *as it appeared to me,* for its actual occurrence can only appear an absurdity to a judicious mind. From the tangle of trees a man came strolling very calmly up the glacis, wearing the dress of a French chaplain, with a little purple cap and lace at his neck. He had in his hand what appeared to be a breviary, and stooping over the prostrate bodies of the French soldiers he gave them each in turn the valedictory sacrament. So far my account will pass muster, but then, as it appeared to me, he rose and came towards me with pointed forefinger, revealing the wet black lock and sallow features of the Reverend John Martin! He said to me in a cold, sneering voice: 'How now, friend Lamb, have we met again? And will you take the stick to me as you promised? But listen, for I have news for you: I shall never have the pleasure of joining your hand with Mrs. Kate's in holy matrimony. For she was killed this morning at about nine o'clock by a bomb-splinter at the entrance to her green-baized retreat.'

I ran at him with my sword. But my feet caught on a broken palisade and I fell, and seemed to continue falling and falling, for a thousand years into a bottomless pit, such as that which is said to be prepared for the reception of the damned souls at the second coming of the Saviour.

I came to my senses some hours later. I was still in the redoubt. Smutchy Steel was by me, and grinned with delight to see me recover. I asked him in a weak voice, that seemed to proceed from a great distance away, what had occurred.

'Oh,' he said, 'we beat 'em off, the third time, and that was the end. Your wits were a little turned, I think. You went rushing out with a sword against a poor harmless French priest—now I had thought better of you, Gerry—you always told me that you had no quarrel with the Papists. But here's sorrowful news for you and me. When you fell in a faint and were carried back, poor Terry Reeves was given your command. He is dead. A nine-pounder ball struck him.'

I fell to sobbing from mere weakness, but soon as I had rallied my forces I called the faithful Jonah to me. I told him that, when he went down that evening with the party to draw the rations, he should enquire whether the rumour was true that a lady had been killed at such and such a spot by the cliff, that morning at nine. When he returned, it was to tell me that it was true: a 'very beautiful young woman in a green sprigged dress', killed with a bomb-splinter through the throat. But nobody seemed to know her name.

For the next three days I rambled in my speech, so Smutchy told me after, wept frequently and said many ridiculous things, telling of sights that were mere mirage and invisible to other eyes. But I was kept at my duty, for I had no fever.

The enemy meanwhile had battered our unfinished defences on the left of the town, silenced the guns that we mounted on them and searched the whole line of houses at the cliff top. Mr. Secretary Nielson's house was holed in a number of places, but Mr. Nielson himself was so philosophical as not to quit until his negro servant was blown to pieces at his side. On October 11th, the enemy crept nearer, and established his second parallel at but three hundred yards from our parapet. Our people defended themselves with howitzers and coehorns (or light mortars of four and a half inches calibre), but the guns at our embrasures were dismounted as soon as shown. For the enemy worked sixty powerful breaching-guns and a number of heavy mortars. About this time a despatch from Sir Henry Clinton came up the river for Lord Cornwallis, informing him that the departure of the relieving fleet had been delayed by a complexity of mischances, and expressing great anxiety for his situation.

A desperate project was pressed upon Lord Cornwallis by Colonel Tarleton and others; which was to remove the greater part of the garrison by night and take it across the river for an attack upon the forces of the French General, Choisy, who was investing Gloucester. It was believed that we might easily break our way through; and by travelling very light and seizing all the horses of the Roanoke country, which was rich in provisions and fodder, we might force a passage through Maryland, Pennsylvania and the Jerseys and attain

New York. His Lordship seemed confused in his mind and unable to agree to this project. His vaccilation surprised his officers, for he had hitherto shown himself very collected and resolute. But I heard privately from his chief clerk, under whose direction I had worked and with whom I was intimate, who had it from his Lordship's own valet, that his Lordship on the morning of October 9th, had been 'struck with great horror and grief by the news of pretty Miss Kate's death'. He had since been drinking more than was his habit, and soliloquizing to himself as he paced about his parlour alone. The valet added that Lord Cornwallis had not shown himself so unmanned since news had reached him two years before of the death of his lovely Countess. I must decline to enlarge upon my own feelings of grief, not wishing to present them as it were in rivalry to those of Lord Cornwallis.

It was not until October 14th that his Lordship could be persuaded to agree to the plan of escape; by which time our palisades were all down and but one single shell remained for the remaining eight-inch mortar, and a few boxes of coehorn shells. Undismayed by a sortie from our lines, in which eleven of their guns had been spiked, the combined armies of the enemy were preparing for the assault. The spiking of these guns, it may be observed, was a botched task, the soldiers who took part in the sortie not being provided with spiking irons. They merely broke off the points of their bayonets in the touch-holes, and these were readily removed afterwards. By now our effective forces were reduced to four thousand men, two thousand being unfit for duty from sickness or wounds, but continued of undaunted spirit; and since we were seasoned troops, who could march and starve with the best, we had no doubt at all but that we would pull the chestnuts out of the fire.

On the evening of October 15th, therefore, the Light Infantry, the greater part of the Brigade of Guards, and seventy Royal Welch Fusiliers (Smutchy and myself among them) were embarked upon boats and taken across the river to Gloucester Point. We were to effect a landing there and with our fire cover the passage of the rest of the army. But hardly had we reached the other side, which was about midnight, when the weather, from being calm and moderate, changed to a most violent storm of wind and rain. Our boats were blown down the river nearly to the Ocean. The passage of the rest of the troops, who counted upon these same boats, now became impracticable, and though the storm abated and we managed to make our way back to York Town before morning, we were greatly harassed by fire from the banks and lost a number of men.

Thus expired the last hope of the British army. Our defences were tumbled to ruin and it was the opinion of the principal officers at a Council of War that it would be madness to maintain them. In the morning, at Lord Cornwallis' orders, a drummer mounted upon our parapet and beat a parley. The Duke de Lanzun then came forward alone, waving a white silk handkerchief; and was informed that Lord Cornwallis proposed a cessation of hostilities in order to settle terms for a capitulation.

To be short: this was granted by General Washington and terms adjusted for our surrender as prisoners of war on the following day. The capitulation was signed on October 19th—the very day that Sir Henry Clinton, after long delays, sailed to our relief from New York with seven thousand men.

The honours of war granted to us were much the same as General Lincoln had obtained at Charleston, and he himself, being now exchanged, received the surrender of Lord Cornwallis' sword; but at General O'Hara's hands, his Lordship being sick. We marched between a long lane, with well-groomed French troops on one side, ragged Americans on the other; and piled up our arms. We were forbidden, in revenge for the Savannah terms, to use either a French or an American march. Our musicians therefore very properly played *The World Turned Upside Down.* Our standards were cased, not flowing, and this enabled two of our officers—Captain Peter and, I believe, Lieutenant Julian—to remove the Colours from the staves and conceal them upon their persons. The field officers of the Count de St. Simon's Brigade sought out Captain Apthorpe and highly praised him upon our defence of the star-shaped Redoubt. They could hardly credit it when they learned that we had fought that day against odds of nearly twenty to one. They observed at the same time what a pleasure to them it was to converse thus agreeably with Englishmen of distinction and sensibility—glancing rather severely at their American allies as almost totally ignorant of the 'language of culture', namely French. At the same time the young Duke de Lanzun sought out Captain Champagné to congratulate him upon the fine bearing of his mounted Fusiliers in the skirmish near Gloucester. These compliments to some degree comforted our people for the disgrace of the surrender, which was the first (as I trust the last) occasion that the Royal Welch Fusiliers were ever forced to yield since their first enrolment in the year 1689. Our losses, of thirty-one officers and men, had left us the weakest corps in the whole army.

The usual jealous quarrels broke out between the officers in the victorious army. An Ensign Denny, of the Marquis de La Fayette's division, was in the act of planting the American flag on our broken parapet in sight of the three armies, when up galloped Major-General Baron Steuben, General Washington's Prussian drill-master, seized it from him and planted it himself. This raised great laughter among our people and great scandal and argument among theirs. An American colonel challenged the Baron to a duel. But General Washington hushed the matter up, for the old Baron was better acquainted with the laws of war than the Marquis de La Fayette. The Baron had commanded in the enemy trenches when the drum first beat the parley, and the honour of planting the flag was therefore his.

I had by now somewhat recovered my health of mind, and was naturally curious to gaze upon the person of General George Washington, for whose patience, uprightness and courage the British army in general had conceived a great respect; though there were many who could not abide him for his part in condemning poor Major André to the rope. I espied him in the company of a group of high French officers, with whom, however, he was unable to converse in their own language. He was as plainly clothed as he was well mounted. His body was tall, but not stout, his face much pockmarked and with the largest eye-sockets I ever saw in a man. The expression was severe, as of one who has struggled successfully for many years against malice and disloyalty in his associates, and against the sins of pride and anger in himself.

CHAPTER XV

THIS SURRENDER was to prove fatal to our cause in America, though we still had a quantity of troops stationed on that Continent, and though King George, who received the ill news with perfect composure, was for a continuance of the struggle at all events. Lord George Germaine resigned at last, which was something gained by the country he had so ill served, and was rewarded for his extraordinary services with a viscountcy. The universally detested Earl of Sandwich, alias Jemmy Twitcher, continued in office a few months longer. (His latter years were lonely, for two years before this he had lost his arrogant, greedy but devoted helpmeet, Miss Ray, whom a former lover of hers, the Reverend James Hackman, shot dead with a pistol at the door of Covent Garden Theatre.) The Ministry now declared that none but defensive operations could be conducted against the Americans, and in effect no engagement upon a grand scale was thereafter fought. The fact was, we were waging several important wars at the same time: with the Spaniards at Gibraltar and Minorca—with the massed hordes of India—with the Dutch in almost every sea and ocean of the world—with the French in the West India Islands and India, besides here in America. The poet William Cowper wrote truly and feelingly at this time:

> Poor England! Thou art a devoted deer,
> Beset with every ill but that of fear.
> Thee nations hunt. All mark thee for a prey.
> They swarm around thee, and thou standst at bay,
> Undaunted still.

Moreover, the Armed Neutrality of Europe, a league consisting of Russia, Prussia, the Scandinavian and Baltic nations, Portugal,

Turkey, and in fact nearly the whole of Europe, was opposed to us. These countries were banded together to resist by force the 'brigandage and cupidity' of our Navy, when we stopped and searched neutral vessels bringing munitions of war to our numerous foes.

The Opposition now howled for a complete withdrawal of all our forces from America, the better to preserve our own islands. Yes: and we might never have found ourselves in such a fix but for their leaders, who had put party interest before national honour. Careless of the lives of our poor fellows in America, they had secretly promoted the American cause by traitorous correspondence with Dr. Franklin and Mr. Silas Deane, as well as by false reports and libels printed in their scurrilous newspapers. Yet between politicians, who shall judge? Of the Tory leaders, most of those who were not merely idle and incompetent in their duties were downright evil. In Shakespeare's phrase one might cry: 'A plague on both your houses!'

It was truly grievous to perceive the style of exultation in which the party writers of the Opposition indulged on the capitulation of Lord Cornwallis. One of them, in direct terms, spoke of 'the pride of Lord Cornwallis'. What pride? The very reverse was his Lordship's true character. In this campaign (I declare these facts from my own knowledge) he fared like a common soldier. He assumed, he would admit of, no distinction, not even indulging himself in that of a tent. When a beloved officer is the object of viperous attack, it must rouse a resentment in the mind of every old soldier still living, *who knows the contrary to be fact,* which it is not very easy for military feeling to bear, or even for Christian forgiveness to pardon. Mr. Ramsay, too, has a very prettily manufactured tale on this occasion: 'The door-keeper of Congress, an aged man, died suddenly, immediately after hearing of the capture of Lord Cornwallis' army. His death was universally ascribed to a violent emotion of political joy.' Mr. Ramsay strongly reminds me of a celebrated Republican preacher, in England, who had the impiety to take for his text the words of good old Simeon, 'Lord now lettest thou thy servant depart in peace, for mine eyes have seen thy Salvation', when he preached a sermon to celebrate the French Revolution!

It is interesting to recall that the American Revolution was the means of introducing into France novel ideas of independency, which, gaining a hold among the common people, proved fatal to the established Government. The young French officers of the Newport army who travelled about America and were entertained by a vigorous, hospitable and self-sufficient peasantry, impatient of Government, returned to Europe and there, with great enthusiasm, propagated philanthropical notions. Indeed, they lighted a train of gunpowder that blew their own magazine sky-high. Europe would have been spared thirty years of bloodshed, had these red-heeled young philosophers stayed at Court. It is said that Queen Marie Antoinette's party had difficulty in forcing on the unfortunate King Louis XVI the treaty with America. Though not averse to depressing Britain, he regarded it as an unfair measure and, when asked to sanction it with his signature, threw away the pen. On repeated importunity, however, he relented and signed the instrument which was indirectly to prove the death-warrant for himself and his lovely young Queen. A large number of the high officers before whom we defiled (including the Duke de Lanzun) were before many years to die under the knife of Dr. Guillotine's humane instrument or languish for years in prison; and among the rank and file were numerous men destined to be their judges, jailers and executioners.

The Spanish monarchy was likewise ruined by the same contagion and so served out for the part that it took against us.

Let me here append, as a curiosity, an extract from a speech delivered in Congress, when the news of our surrender arrived, by the famous Dr. Witherspoon, President of Nassau College at Princeton, and the first Classical scholar of America. I must, let me make clear, take exception to his severe and ungrateful attack upon General Washington, as also to his censure upon Admiral Sir Thomas Graves (who afterwards fought very gallantly under Admiral Howe at the Glorious First of June). In the Chesapeak fighting Sir Thomas did all that could have been expected of him; but he was unlucky. However, Dr. Witherspoon's praise of Lord Cornwallis at least is not amiss, and

I trust that the speech will not prove uninteresting as showing the disunion and uncertainty of American opinion at this time.

It is incumbent on us to thank Heaven for the victory which we have just obtained, and though over a handful of troops, yet they were flushed with success, and led on by a General, whose valour is no less illustrious than his discretion; by a General not equalled in courage by the Macedonian madman, or, in wise and solemn deliberation, by the Roman Fabius; nor has his defeat tarnished his fame; for he was encompassed about with a mighty host of the picked troops of France and America, aided by a formidable navy; and, to sum up his difficulties, he was attacked by famine in his camp.

It would be criminal in me to be silent on this occasion, which has diffused such joy in every breast. To procure America freedom and happiness has ever been my study, ever since I arrived among you; for this I have encountered a variety of hardships, and suffered not a little in my private fortune and reputation.

Now, gentlemen, since victory irradiates our arms, let us snatch this opportunity of securing to ourselves advantageous terms of peace; so shall we reap a profitable benefit from the example of all the wise states so eminent in history.

Some may think it very censurable, and highly derogatory to the dignity of this mighty Commonwealth to crouch and offer terms of peace, when we have been gathering such blooming laurels; but when we duly weigh all the circumstances of our overrated victory, the reasonableness of my advice may more fully appear to every dispassionate man.

Lord Cornwallis's troops had boldly marched through the heart of our country, opposed not only by woods, rivers and swamps, but also by all the force we could send against him, which was greatly superior to him in numbers; his whole army, I would say his foraging party (for it does not deserve the name of army) did not exceed four thousand; and, small as it was, it had spread universal dismay; it had struck terror even into General Washington's camp, and wondrous to relate (!) brought that man of valour out of his lurking place (which it would seem he had taken a lease of) at the head of no less than thirteen thousand troops, whom he had been training to arms, and teaching to storm mock castles these three years, in a strong impregnable camp, where no enemy would ever think it worth while to disturb his slumbers, and so panic-struck was the American hero, that even with the great and formidable army under his command, would he not dare to attack an English foraging party; no, he must first be sure the French were before him with eight thousand of the gens d'armes, as a breastwork, to save his gallant troops, whose blood has ever been so precious to him. And to complete his safety, that thirty sail of the line-of-battle ships, manned with twenty-five thousand seamen (half of whom might act ashore) were within call of him. Heavens! Gentlemen, if every victory is to cost us so dear, if we must send into the field fifty thousand men before we can capture four thousand fatigued, half-starved English, we must view at a very remote distance, our so much wished for Independency: to bring this about if we go on as we have, for these long seven years, we ought to have more than all the wealth of all Mexico and Peru, and our women must bring forth four males at one birth. O dauntless spirit of immortal Cromwell, behold how enervated are thy descendants!

Gentlemen, trivial and contemptible as our success is, we got it by mere accident; we got it not by the vigilance of our allies, or the powers of our arms; we got it by the neglect or cowardice of the British Admiral, who would not, when he had the golden opportunity, take possession of the Chesapeak; and to this gross blunder alone are we to ascribe our fortune. But, gentlemen, although one commander has abandoned his post, and betrayed the best interests of his country, can we suppose that his guilt will not meet that severe and exemplary punishment it deserves? Can we hope that British vengeance will never wake, that it will always sleep? When that culpable Admiral is put to death, do you foolishly imagine his successor will not be alarmed for himself, and profit by his fate? Yes; he will exert himself, he will be master of the Chesa-peak, upon which you know our destiny hangs; for if that is once shut up, Virginia and Maryland, the springs of all our resources, the objects which enticed your good and great ally to aid you, are no more! Then a few British soldiers may harass our planters, lay waste their lands, set their tobacco in flames, destroy their docks, and block up such ships as they cannot burn or capture.

It is a painful task, gentlemen, for me to set before your eyes a true picture of your affairs, but it is the duty of a friend. He who flatters you at this awful period smiles in your face while he stabs you in the vitals; it is by exhibiting to you such a picture, that you will be convinced you ought to send Commissioners to treat with Britain for peace, without a moment's delay. Our enemies, I own, are surrounded with danger; a strong confederacy is in arms against them; yet although they possess but a speck of land, the fortitude of Britons, their exertions and supplies, have astonished the wondering world; they are by no means exhausted: they have hitherto asked for no alliance, they have singly and alone kept all their combined foes at bay. Britain has yet in store very tempting offers to hold out to any potentate whom she may court; she is mistress of our seaports; the large and fruitful colony of Canada is hers; her fleets have all arrived from Quebec, the Baltic, the West Indies and East Indies, without the loss of a ship; her arms in Asia have carried conquest before them; so long as they hold their dominions there, they will have a perennial source of riches. Such is the situation of our foe; but how much more terrible may she become, if she joins to her already resistless marine the fleet of another power!

Suffer me to use the words of the prophet Jeremiah, and ask you, 'If thou hast run with footmen, and they have wearied thee, how then canst thou contend with horses?' When your enemy has once made such an addition to her strength, she will rise in her terms upon you, and in the paroxysm of her fury insist upon your submission, your unconditional submission! In order that I may not displease some of you, who hold a man a traitor for telling you wholesome truths, I will suppose all I have said to be exaggerated; I will suppose Britain to be in a galloping consumption; then let me interrogate you. Do you increase in power and wealth? The very reverse is your case. Your maladies, I am sorry to tell you, are incurable. Where are your numerous fleets of merchant ships, which were wont to cover old Ocean? Have you so much as one to convoy your cargoes, or save them from capture? Have you any goods to export? Where are your luxuriant glebes and smiling meads? Alas! they are now an uncultivated waste. Your commerce is extinct; the premium of insurance on the very few ships which dare to peep out, never more to see their natal shore, so enormous, seamens' wages so high (for nothing but death or an English dungeon is before them!) that ruin and bankruptcy have overwhelmed all descriptions of men; hardly any possess the conveniences, none the luxuries of life but faithless secretaries, avaricious commissaries, and griping contractors. These, indeed, loll in their coaches, live in princely palaces, have a numerous train of vermin to attend them, and fare sumptuously every day. 'Curse on the wretch who owes his greatness to his country's ruin!'

Would to God I could here draw a veil over our calamities! but the zeal I have to serve you will not allow it. I must thunder in your ears that your trade is annihilated; your fisheries, that fertile nursery of seamen, that fountain of all we could ever boast, are no more! Our ploughshares beat into bayonets, our soldiers mutinying for want of pay; our planters beggared, and our farmers ruined! You are oppressed with taxes; not to emancipate you from bondage—no, with taxes to support the lazy; to pamper the proud; to exalt mean, cunning knaves and dissipated gamblers to the first offices of the State, to pay armies who have the figures of men, but the hearts of hares; they are, God knows, numerous enough; but of what use? Why do we call in soup-meagre* soldiers? Are our own cowards? Are they not disciplined after so many years dancing a jig to the fife and drum? Will they not look an enemy

---

* That is to say French soldiers who subsist upon thin soup.—R. L.

in the face when their religion, their liberty, is at stake; when their wives and children are butchered before their eyes?

O America! America! Thou art now ruined and past redemption, consigned to destruction! Curse on this French connexion! I see thee prostrate on the ground, imploring mercy at the feet of the Gallic monarch. If France conquers Britain (which, for your sakes, I pray God to prevent!) I tremble when I think of the accumulated miseries with which you will be loaded. The French have already cheated you out of Rhode Island from whence, as from a flaming volcano, will stream fire to burn your ships, and lay your seaports in smoking ruins. Methinks I see already the Canadians rush in upon your possessions in the North, and the French and Spaniards overrun your southern colonies! Like an impetuous torrent they sweep all before them! And even those of your own flesh and blood, whose lands you have confiscated, whose fathers and brothers you have murdered, join to lay you desolate! I see you turned into a desert, exposed to the ruthless elements, calling upon some hospitable roof to hide you from the storm! May Heaven save you from calamities, and dispose you to sue for peace! 'Now is the appointed time; now is the day of salvation!'

CHAPTER XVI

MY OFFICERS, made aware from my attention to the wounded after the battles of Camden and Guildford Court House that I was a surgeon of sorts, sent me over the river from York Town to the General Hospital at Gloucester, a town of not more than twenty houses, to supervise our wounded; for the Regimental Surgeon was sick. Captains Champagné and Apthorpe, as well as the junior officers, were very obliging when they bade me farewell; and professed their deep regret that sergeants could not, equally with themselves, be permitted to return to Europe on parole. The most affecting good-bye was spoken to me by the negro Jonah, whose condition as a slave inscribed him among the officers' baggage which the terms allowed them to retain. He was to sail to England with them, as steward to their mess, by the next packet. When he learned that we were to be parted, he fell at my feet and blubbered. Said he: 'Sarnt Lamb, massa, you be de best friend poor old black Jonah ebber hab. You done rescue me from de meat-house and make me mighty consequential military nigger. Jonah, him nebber forget darra good Sarnt Lamb, nebber find murrer like to him.'

Only Captain de Saumerez continued with the men of the Regiment, in order to protect them from abuses while in the quality of captives. They were now marched off with the rest of the troops to Winchester, in the backcountry of Virginia.

I remained behind in the hospital at Gloucester for five weeks, by which time my wounded comrades had either succumbed to their wounds or were in a fair way to recover. Being sent back across the river one day I went to muse at the grave of poor Kate. It lay close to the entrance of the bomb-proof boudoir, which still remained handsomely furnished for her pleasure and that of Lord Cornwallis, and attracted numerous sightseers. I wished that the Quaker Jonah were there to pray with me: my heart was still stunned and mute.

The only cure for melancholy being action, I resolved upon another escapade from the hands of my enemies. Rather than rot again in a prisoners' pen—as I would be bound to do as soon as the hospital was removed from this place—I would willingly face any conceivable hardship and danger, in the wilds of America, as a free man. With this object in view, I waited the next day, November 28th, upon the Surgeon-General, and resigned my situation in the General Hospital; acquainting him that I intended to follow the troops to Winchester. Having then received the balance of pay due to me for the hospital service, which was forty shillings, I relinquished my wig and epaulettes and put on the clothes of a private soldier who had that day died of a wound. I packed my knapsack with shirts, stockings and other necessaries; and also took about half a pound of flour, some dried beef and a small bottle of rum—but these were to be a reserve and only drawn upon in an extremity. My next consideration was how to elude the French and American sentinels who guarded the barriers on the road to the North. This was likely to prove a difficult task, but I was aware that both the French guard and the American were relieved at ten o'clock in the forenoon and I judged that the best time to elude them was when the relief was in progress and their attention therefore distracted.

I was right in this conclusion. I found the French guard, who were Soissonais and wore fine rose-coloured facings, more concerned with the ceremony and show of the guard-changing than with the chief object in hand, which was to prevent prisoners from escaping. I wrapped a blanket around my regimentals and appeared as an innocent sightseer, seating myself on the barrier. While the old guard were inspected by their officer before dismissal, and the new guard were being addressed by theirs—the sentinel of the old guard being already withdrawn, and that of the new guard not yet posted—I climbed down on the other side of the barrier and strolled along the Rappahannock road.

The American method of guard-changing was equally characteristic of the newer nation. At ten o'clock the old guard was due to be relieved and therefore merely walked off, trusting that a few minutes later the new guard would arrive. I found the post deserted and, passing the barrier, immediately struck right-handed into the tangled pine-woods that fringed the road.

I made a circuit of about a mile in order to avoid the piquet guard, which was thrown out at a convenient distance to protect the camp from possible attack, and then made for the road at a point a few miles beyond. Unfortunately, not knowing that the road took a sharp turn to the left after a few miles, I did not strike it again so soon as I had expected. I grew confused and alarmed and thus became aware how weak my health still was. To extricate myself from this wood seemed like a task set a dreamer in a nightmare. There were many ponds, which to a romantic eye would have seemed delightful but grossly offended mine. I climbed upon a slight hill above one of them just as the sun was setting, but could make out nothing save continued forest, nor keep my teeth from chattering in the sudden chill that ascended from the pond.

Before it was completely dark I came upon a rough track that led from a clearing where some trees had lately been burned for tar, and this fetched me to a collection of poor houses standing close to the road of my search.

I went to the nearest house and knocked. A rough man came to the door, swaying on his legs. He had but one eye and, as I descried in the blaze of a huge pine-wood fire that burned in the grate, very long nails.

'What do you want?' he asked in a ruffianly voice, his whole person reeking very strongly of apple-brandy.

'A lodging for the night, if you please,' I replied.

'Do you see these talons of mine?' he asked, displaying them in uncination. 'Now ain't they a pretty set? I suppose you wouldn't like to fight me, would you—nothing barred? Bite, bollock and gouge is my trade—in which I lost one eye, over to Hob's Hole, last quarter-races. Yet I would be happy to risk another peeper in a good cause. I warrant you're a red-coat son of a bitch, run off from Gloucester, heigh? Now I'm surprised you dare show your cursed face at my door: phoo, you lousy fellow! You red-coats ain't fighters: all that you are equal to is swaggering about at the grogshops and nanny-houses. Who turned you out of the Carolinas, tell me that? Little dried-up General Marion did, he and his patriot crew on their poor starved tackies, with grape-vine bridles and sheep-skin saddles: ay, they made you run all right, I'll warrant 'em. Well, say now, will you fight? Or shall I swing you back by the collar to Gloucester Point?'

A woman's voice came from the room within. 'Dear me now, Joe my honey, why will you ever be picking quarrels? Perhaps this trav-eller has a little hard money to pay his score. Hearts alive, in these times, we surely can't quarrel with hard money?'

I naturally did not own to the possession of coin, lest it be all stripped from me on some pretext or other. Instead I begged them to take me in as a charity.

'Charity, eh, a pretty story! I swear you're in the wrong furrow,' cried the woman warmly, coming forward; and I observed that she was very fat and had only one eye, like her husband, and that the flesh about it was bruised red, blue and yellow. Her face was blowsy, and scratched from cheek to chin. 'Charity indeed, you ugly jack? Those that have no money have no business to travel. Get you gone!'

Here her husband interposed, thrusting her aside: 'No, stay, you poor bastard,' he said. 'I'll fight you for the price of a night's lodging.'

I told him I could not oblige him, being unskilled in the manner of fighting in use thereabouts (compared with which an Irish boxing match is mere kiss-in-the-ring) and but lately recovered from a severe illness. He called me a white-livered gallow's fruit and rushed out from the door to kick at me with his hob-nailed shoes; but tripped over his spaniel in the half-light and measured his length in the mud.

The sight of this couple disgusted me. I had never witnessed a rough Virginia fight, but the mode had been described to me as resembling that of wild beasts. The practitioners, who were of course all men of the lower orders, prided themselves upon the dexterity with which they could gouge or scoop out an eye. To perform this horrid operation the combatant would twist his forefingers in his adversary's long side-locks and then apply his thumbs to the base of the orb. What was worse than all, these wretches would endeavour to the utmost to castrate each other.

I went away into the woods, my stomach sick, my heart low, and my head ringing again as when the shell had broken above me; so that I was scarcely able to determine what course to take. The weather turning very cold with a violent wind from the north, I made a desperate effort and brought myself to the door of a house a few hundred yards away. Through the chink of a window-shutter I saw a severe-looking woman of about thirty years old seated at a table surrounded by a number of children. She was ladling them out a meal of rice and boiled bacon, with a bowl of milk for each poured from a pitcher.

I knocked, and she bade me enter.

'What do you want?' she demanded.

'Please, madam, only the favour of a corner of your house to sleep in. I have lately been ill and have lost my way upon the road.'

She looked at me very sternly and asked: 'How can you expect such a favour from me, or any woman of Virginia, seeing you came from England with an intent to destroy our country?'

I replied very humbly: 'Indeed, madam, you are wrong. I was never in England in my life. I was first sent from Ireland to protect the homesteads of Canada from an unprovoked invasion by Americans.'

She startled at this. I continued: 'But you know how wars go, madam: one campaign leads to another. I have at least always refrained from plunder and private injury, and obeyed my officers, as a soldier is bound to do.'

A little girl slipped down from her stool and came up to me: 'I have a little red bird in a cage,' she said. 'It is very clever, you know. It eats the crumbs I give it. Come and see it, poor man.'

'Child, go back to your food, instantly,' the mother said scoldingly but not unpleased.

'Then I will show the poor man my bird afterwards,' said the child gravely.

'Your little maid has a sweet nature,' I remarked. 'She knows that I am unfortunate and wishes to do what she can to cheer me.'

The woman almost angrily ladled me out some of the rice, together with a small piece of the bacon, and drew up a chair for me. 'Eat,' she commanded. I ate.

She then drew me a pewter pot of cider. 'Drink,' she commanded. I drank.

The little girl said: 'My name is Henrietta. My brothers provoke me by calling me Etta. What is your name?'

I told her that it was Roger Lamb and she simply laughed. The other children were abashed and said nothing. The woman began asking me questions about Ireland, which I was at pains to answer as fully as I could. While we were talking, her husband came in, with a large bundle of faggots on his shoulder, which he threw on the floor. He was a large, heavy man with a humane countenance.

'Whom have we here?' he asked.

'A straggler from Lord Cornwallis' army,' I replied. 'A Cyclops and his wife refused me lodging further down the road, though I could hardly stand from faintness. But your good wife has been very kind to me.'

He considered for a moment. 'I served with Dan Morgan in Canada. But twenty-five men of our whole regiment saw home again. The sufferings that I experienced in that year are burned in my soul. Well, upon my word, it would be very hard indeed to turn you out of my door on such a severe evening as this. You may bide here this night. Wife, fetch a little straw from the barn, and shake it down here by the fire.'

She did so, and the husband and I talked amicably, as fellow-soldiers, upon the hardships and cruelties of war, and the wife interposed now and again, speaking very sharp against the French connexion. She said that at Alexandria on their way to these parts, the French officers had danced minuets with several handsome young American ladies, in the middle of the camp; and this was very well, though she did not hold with dancing herself. But the nasty French soldiers who watched the dance in a great circle had from the heat of the weather disengaged themselves from their clothes, and stood around dressed only in their shirts, which were neither long nor in good repair. 'Moreover,' she said, 'the officers themselves were very sly and lecherous. Each had brought a fashionable assortment of coloured ribbands from Paris, such as our ladies of Virginia tie in their poke-bonnets, with which they counted upon buying the honour of the best-bred girls in the dominion.'

The husband judiciously remarked: 'Indeed, wife, I hope that they found they had reckoned amiss. But, as you know, when such girls are confronted with officers of rank and title, there is "no wisdom below the girdle".'

'La, husband,' she cried indignantly. 'How coarse you talk, and before a stranger too!'

The good man, before I retired to rest, showed me two Cherokee Indian scalps, properly dressed and mounted on frames, that he had taken in revenge for the murder of his wife's brother. I slept soundly, and awoke greatly refreshed. I gave the children some trifling presents: to one a lump of chalk, to another a Fusilier's button, to little Henrietta a Virginia bill for (I believe) eighteenpence or some such small amount. It was printed upon the silver paper used by English hatters—a consignment of this paper having been seized by an American privateer, and made into money by the Virginian Assembly, as difficult to counterfeit. Tobacco money, Congress money and the earlier Assembly money were all now highly suspect, because of the reams of counterfeit circulated by loyal Americans. The children and their parents seemed much gratified by my gifts, and after a breakfast of milk and stirabout I left them with the warmest emotions of thankfulness.

Henrietta kissed me, before I went; and I reflected fondly as I marched along the high road that my lost daughter must, by now, be about the same age as this dear child, namely four years and a piece.

During this day, November 29th, I marched very hard on the main road, which was sandy, without meeting any interruption: for a party of convalescents had marched this way, two days before, from the hospital and it was supposed that I had not been able to keep up with them, and was trying to overtake them. I came to the Rancatank River at a place called Turk's Ferry, where a negro, who was conveying several fine hogs over the stream, allowed me a free passage in his scowl, or flat-bottomed boat, upon my agreeing to help him manage his unruly drove. Like the Prodigal Son of the Parable this worn-out mungo envied his swine. He told me: 'Him Bockarorra Gentleman'—meaning the white planter—'make de poor black man workee, make the hoss workee, make the ox workee, make ebberyting all workee togarrer, only de hog. Him, de hog, no workee: him eat, him drink, him saunter, him sleep at pleasure, him old hog libb like murrer gentleman.' By evening I reached the town of Urbanna on the Rappahannock River, above forty miles from Gloucester Point.

I entered the town boldly, keeping to the account of myself as a convalescent straggler, which the travellers I met had fastened upon me by their inquisitive guesses as to my condition and intention. I came to a large building which proved to be an 'ordinary', and a stout, florid gentleman in a gay waistcoat accosted me from his chair on the portico. 'Heigh, Soldier, there is plenty of room inside for such as you, and plenty of drink.'

I enquired: 'How for such as me?'

He laughed. 'Well, you look mighty innocent, but you can't deceive me. You are looking for a master, I'll be bound.'

'I do not understand you,' said I.

'Then I'll be plain,' he said. 'There are a great many of your men in my house, who are determined to remain in the country. They have hired themselves to different gentlemen. You had better join with them. You shall be well used and in a short time you may become a citizen of America.'

I thanked him, and thought it wise to go in, for I did not wish to offend him, lest my true character might appear.

On the porch hung a placard which read:

Four pence a night for a bed.
Six pence with supper.
No more than five to sleep in one bed.
No boots to be worn in bed.
No dogs allowed upstairs.

No drinking tolerated in the kitchen.
New England travellers to pay on the nail.

Inside I found about forty British soldiers, none of them of my
own regiment, but one of The Thirty-Third, who had hired themselves to different gentlemen about the country as mechanics, grooms,
overseers and such. Each plantation in Virginia resembled a small
village and now carried on various novel industries, by slave labour,
to supply the manufactured goods that had formerly been imported
from England. Experienced tailors, potters, weavers, whitesmiths
and the like who would initiate or superintend such labours were
therefore highly useful to the planters. I was strongly importuned by
these soldiers to follow their example, rather than be conveyed to a
prison pen in a barren country; but my mind revolted at the thought.

Towards midnight in came a shift-eyed person with a wide hat and
a silver-headed cane. He represented himself as a lawyer and a close
comrade of the famous Mr. Daniel Boone, of Bridnorth in Somer-
setshire, who had passed westward over the Alleghany Mountains in
the year 1759, and become an enthusiastic admirer of the territory
he found on the further side of the range, called Kentucke. This eloquent person, drawing me into a corner, enlarged upon the diversity
and glories of nature met with in that delightful clime of Kentucke:
her fruits and flowers so beautifully coloured, elegantly shaped and
charmingly flavoured, the great quantity of game, the fertile soil, the
enormous and dignified Ohio rolling through the plains in incon-
ceivable grandeur, the distant mountains penetrating the clouds
with their venerable brows. Just before the war, he informed me, Mr.
Boone had made his first settlement in this same favourite though
forlorn district; and there engaged the Indians in a conflict of great
savagery, losing two of his own sons and two brothers at their hands.
Now, however, 'peace crowned the sylvan shade', for Mr. Boone had
been reinforced by a great number of settlers, who had removed
across the mountains with their families in order to avoid the exac-
tions of Congress and the raids of King George's soldiers.

I observed that his account was interesting, and believed that much of reality and fact must belong to his description—which to some would appear greatly exaggerated. He appeared somewhat offended at my saying this and warmed up to a peroration recalling that of a recruiting sergeant in search of 'prime young fellows to exercise the profession of arms'. At the close he offered me, free and without charges, a debenture of three hundred acres, with a fine deep bottom, in a fertile location upon the Ohio—and now wasn't that a handsome offer, he asked.

I enquired, to what sort of a trap was this cheese set as the bait?

He solemnly assured me that there was no trap at all. Mr. Boone wanted brave and hardy men to strengthen the infant settlement, which would soon be a new State sending its own delegates to Congress, and therefore offered land free to likely settlers in order to increase the common wealth.

Here I had to affect the clown, and asked this recruiting sergeant whether it were not true that Indians carried off and roasted white men at a slow fire, then hacked them gradually in pieces, as one might snip slices off a prime Virginia ham?

He asked, was I then a coward?

For reply I chanted, in a close parody of a song from Mr. Bickerstaffe's comedy, *The Recruiting Sergeant:*

> Ay, ay, master Lawyer, I wish you good day,
> You have *no need* at present, I thank you, to stay:
> My stomach for Kentucke's gone from me, I trow.
> When it comes back again, I'll take care you shall know.

My companions set up a shout of laughter at this declamation; and the gentleman from Kentucke flew in a rage and rushed out of the room. I wished the soldiers good-night and soon fell fast asleep.

Early on the next morning their masters came with horses and took them all away. I retired out of the way to the privy, lest I be accosted with an offer of odious service.

When all had ridden off, I prepared to discharge my debt. But the landlord, who was a militia colonel, refused my coin with a wave of his hand. He said to me: 'Why, now, I swear I thought you had given me leg-bail! You are Sergeant Lamb of The Twenty-Third, are you not? An acquaintance of yours in The Thirty-Third gives you a high character. He says that you write a very good hand and understand accounts.'

'Yes,' I replied, 'I may own to those accomplishments. If there is some task in that way that you wish to put upon me, I shall be pleased to undertake it immediately. You have been very hospitable to me.'

'Well, now,' he said, 'I have a proposition to make. You are an Irishman, I am told. Then I will build a school-house for you and make you as comfortable as I can, and you shall stay here with us and instruct the children of Urbanna, who have run wild these three years and forgotten even their alphabet. You shall eat and drink at this house and earn ten dollars a month besides.'

I felt my whole frame agitated at the proposal: the more so because, though the proposal was dishonourable to a soldier, the man who made it, unlike the shifty Kentucke lawyer, was evidently of a liberal and philanthropic mind. Smothering my indignation, I stammered out as graceful excuses as I could find; then, though the weather was stormy and I felt very unwell, I immediately left his house. As we parted, I tried to insist upon payment, but he would not go back on his word, and shook his head at me for 'a most perverse, proud fellow who did not know what was good for him'.

The country beyond Urbanna wore but a poor aspect. The road, which was level and very sandy, ran through woods of black oak, pine and cedar for miles together: there were several bridges across creeks and causeways across swamps which abounded with snipe. After a few miles on the road I overtook a Sergeant Macleod of The Seventy-First, who was an acquaintance of mine, and a drummer of my own company, named Darby Kelly. They were in fact what I was by a fiction, namely stragglers from the convalescent party. Drummer Kelly suffered from a leg wound and Sergeant Macleod, a man of great hardiness and enterprise, had nearly died of the yellow fever. When the Sergeant asked me how I came to be on the road, I replied: 'I am escaping to New York. I did so once before after the Saratoga capitulation, together with two companions; and, please God, I shall do it again. Will you join me?'

Sergeant Macleod replied solemnly in his slow, thick Scottish way: 'You ken well, Sergeant Lamb, how entwined about the very heart of man is the love of liberty. But though 'tis easy enough to brag about pushing through a tract of land, of five or six hundred miles covered with enemies, I misdoubt how it can be realized in practice.'

'By a stout heart, and a trust in the humanity of the better sort of Americans,' I replied, '—especially of the women.'

When I recounted my former experiences, Sergeant Macleod was convinced that I was not 'just havering', as he expressed it; and both he and Kelly decided to throw in their lot with me. We lay that night in a fodder-stack near Hob's Hole, or Tappahannock, twenty-five miles beyond Urbanna. It was a sad-looking town of about a hundred houses. As dawn came and we resumed our march we came upon a mulatto fish-pedlar. He was calling tunefully as we met him:

Fishee, fishee!
Flounder and Blackfish! !
Shark-steaks—for dem darra likes 'em;
Swordfish—for dem darra fights 'em.
Fishee, fishee!

We bought shark-steaks from him, which was all the wares he had for sale. He informed us that the Rappahannock River, which ran three-quarters of a mile broad at this point, was full of sharks, which the negroes caught on strong hooks baited with shark-flesh and then despatched with spears. We roasted the steaks on sticks held over a fire of pine-branches, and they ate very well.

We addressed ourselves to our journey with confidence the next morning, but Drummer Kelly presently complained that we marched too hard for him. He said in great despondency, when we halted for awhile: 'It is impossible, you know well, ever to make good our escape. For my part, I will go no further with you towards the cold North. I will stay where I am and solace myself after all my hardships. Hob's Hole was no bad place. I shall find employment there, I do not doubt.'

We could not alter his determination by any arguments and therefore left him sitting by the roadside. Sergeant Macleod remarked, morosely, as we resumed our march: 'Ay, no trained drummer should ever lack employment in this sultry airt, where no son born to woman will willingly labour unless he be oft and scientifically flogged.'

I replied: 'Drummer Kelly could flog to a hair's breadth, and to watch him slowly slide the lash through his left hand before he laid on was the terror of all our criminals whose wounds still smarted. But, faith, it is strange that a man so lacking in compassion towards others should be so tender on his own behalf.'

The river now gradually narrowed. The same evening we reached a place called Port Royal, unremarkable except for the very noisome stench of its river front, and were now a day's march short of Fredericksburg, the tobacco town. Our night was passed in the drying-house of a derelict plantation. We had found in the mud on the road a heap of rice fallen from a wagon: we washed this and made a meal of it, with the crimson berries of the pokeplant and some shark-steak that we had saved.

On the following day, as we were coming out of Port Royal we overtook a fine wagon of the sort named Conestoga from a town in Pennsylvania where they were manufactured by the Dutch. The underbody was painted blue and the top part a bright red: there was a hooped tilt over it of tarred cotton cloth. The wagon was filled with sacks.

The wagoner rode one of the horses of his team—an old man with a smooth, very red face. We learned later that he was nicknamed Sops-in-Wine after an apple (called in Canada *pomme caille)* the flesh of which is red to the very core and of a remarkable sweetness. He hailed us with: 'Huzza, my hearties, how where might you be bound?'

We told him: 'To Winchester.'

He asked: 'You be'nt of that sort who sell themselves to the gentlemen hereabouts, I guess?'

'No,' said I, smiling. 'We are not for sale. Were you about to make a bid for us?'

For answer he pointed with his whip across the river and asked: 'Do you know how yonder land is named, hey?'

We said that we did not know.

'Well,' said he, ''Tis King George County, lying a matter of seven miles from here. *God bless King George,* I say; and those as hear me may believe, if they will, that I bless the township only.'

We understood by this speech that he was a Loyalist and therefore asked whether we might ride concealed in his wagon. He told us that we were welcome to come as far with him as we wished in the direction of Philadelphia, where his master Mr. Benezet the Quaker lived. He had come southward three months before in the wake of the French army, with a load of tinware, cutlery, cloth and other manufactured articles from New England. He was now returning with rice, indigo, lemons and tobacco, by way of Frederick Town in Maryland and Little York in Pennsylvania. Four other wagons of the same train were a mile ahead. His offer of protection was gladly received on our part, and we promised him two shillings a day in hard money for the conveyance, he undertaking to keep us in corn-bread and cold bacon.

After an hour or two we passed the party of British convalescents resting by the roadside, but thought it prudent not to hail them.

We travelled undetected for five days, hidden among the sacks in the rear of the wagon and without any view of the country through which we were passing. We kept our own company while Mr. Sops-in-Wine dined with the others of the train.

The wagon was a comfortable conveyance. I was surprised to learn that instead of axle-grease our protector used powdered soapstone— the same pale, greasy stone that was used by the Red Indians for their carved calumets and other ornamental instruments. We passed over the Rappahannock at Fredericksburg, being ferried across in a flat which our protector cursed as very dangerous and leaky.

We now passed through Colchester and crossed the Potomack River at Alexandria, where was a large glass manufactory and where the women dressed more luxuriously than in any city of America, especially in the matter of plumed bonnets. We were now in the Romish state of Maryland. On the fifth day the wagon was unfortunately hailed by an American Continental soldier who had been wounded in the foot at York Town and was hobbling along with the aid of a stick; his destination, he said, was Frederick Town. Ours happened to be the leading wagon of the train that day and the driver dared not refuse to take the man in. He was a talkative, knowing fellow and when we heard the manner in which he addressed Mr. Sops-in-Wine, we thought fit to come out from our concealment before he entered. I will not attempt to recall his precise manner of addressing us, but it was most opprobrious, and he told us that his people had given us a good whacking at York Town and who were the cowards now, hey, ourselves, or they? We told him that we had never accused the Americans of cowardice; but he wagged his finger at us and cried: 'So I dare say! So I dare say!'

Sergeant Macleod thought it best to inform this soldier that we had fallen sick and stayed behind on the road, being members of a party that left York Town for Frederick Town—whom we were now rejoining. But he replied only with a knowing leer: 'Ay, so I dare say, lobsters, so I dare say!'

This disconcerted our plan for the present. We were fast approaching Frederick Town, through which we could not pass concealed in the wagon on account of the American soldier. When therefore we were at about six miles' distance from the town we considered it both more prudent for our own sakes, and more honest dealing with Mr. Sops-in-Wine, to quit the wagon entirely and boldly go through the town on foot, trusting to the inspiration of the moment to satisfy any awkward questionings. This happened on December 10th, 1781. The good wagoner, before he left us, promised to wait a few miles on the other side of the town. But in the event he must have waited in vain. We crossed the Little Monocaccy Creek, by a ford where the stones were very loose, the current rapid, and the water rising to our breasts. Four miles more and we came to Frederick Town, which was a substantial town built chiefly of brick and stone, with several churches, and inhabited by near two thousand Germans. Soon as we entered, the American soldier gave the alarm from behind us. He had obliged the wagoner to whip up his team to keep up with us, for we were marching fast; and now he halloed to two guards posted at the entrance of the principal street: 'Heigh, brothers, there go two more birds for the cage! They thought to give me the slip, but I was too smart for the sons of bitches.'

We were seized and led through the town in triumph, two guards walking a little behind each of us, with one hand gripping a wrist and the other a shoulder. The Seventy-First, who had numbered 248 rank and file at the surrender, but were reduced by desertions and sickness to two hundred, were here imprisoned in barracks with some other regiments. We were put among them and found ourselves in a most deplorable situation: nearly fifty British soldiers huddled together in a room that had been built for the accommodation of eight Americans. It is true that we had an extensive parade to walk about during the day, but as the weather was already remarkably cold, very few men availed themselves of that privilege and the room, though warm, grew fetid to a nauseating degree.

Sergeant Macleod exclaimed to me: 'Faugh, Sergeant Lamb, you do not think to bide here many more days, I dare say?'

'No,' said I, 'I value the health of my lungs more than the society of my fellow-unfortunates.'

CHAPTER XVII

THE BARRACKS and parade at Frederick Town were surrounded by numerous sentinels, but before Sergeant Macleod and I attempted to find a weak link in this chain we would try another plan. We learned that small parties of prisoners, under a strong guard, were often ordered out to get wood for firing. We soon prevailed on the quartermaster-sergeant of The Seventy-First, who was in charge of the hut, to enrol us in the next wood-cutting party, which was set for December 12th. We then strove to persuade as many of the party as possible to venture an escapade with us. But only one other man, a private soldier also named Macleod, would consent.

When the day came, I waited with anxious suspense for the call which would summon us out to our task. First I emptied my knapsack, and distributed my superfluous necessaries among my comrades; but I put on three shirts, took my spare pair of shoes in my pocket, wrapped my blanket about my shoulders and carried my hatchet in my hand.

We arrived at the wood about half a mile from the place of confinement, at ten o'clock, and immediately set to the work of cutting. The two Macleods kept close to me, and we felled a pine together and chopped it up into logs. I then observed to one of our guards: 'Pine-wood burns bright, but is all consumed in a short space of time. Pray, will you let me and my companions fell that fine large maple that stands just beyond you?'

He consented, but with that rudeness which ever characterizes the low mind when in office, he grinningly detailed to us several disagreeable uses to which, for aught he cared, we might put the timber when we had reduced it to small pieces. We strolled together in a leisurely manner to the maple and, the better to colour our pretence, began loudly disputing as to the best manner of felling it; and then set about the work, keeping our eyes constantly fixed on the guard. At last, he turned himself about to watch the other prisoners.

We seized the opportunity and darted into the thickest part of the wood. Anxiety and hope, being pretty nearly balanced in our minds, were the twin wings which urged our flight. Our guards must have possessed the feet of deer before they could have overtaken us. We ran on through the woods, as near as I could conjecture for two hours, scarcely stopping to take breath. We steered due north. At last we considered it safe to walk, and continued for another three hours or more, alternately walking and running until we struck the Great Monocaccy just below Bennet's Creek. Here we paid our fare to a negligent old boatman and crossed without being examined—for the blankets wrapped about us disguised our regimentals and gave us rather the appearance of Indians than British soldiers.

Luck went against us once more. We were proceeding through a wood when we suddenly ran into an armed party of Americans who instantly surrounded us, and marched us back prisoners to Frederick Town, which happened to be their destination. They bantered us in a not unfriendly way upon our folly in 'not knowing our places'. But worse was to follow. Soon as we entered the town, very footsore, about evening, a man lounging on the *stoep,* or elevated porch, of a tavern, called out: 'Now, I'll be damned if it an't that indefatigable Sergeant Gerry Lamb again. He's the very devil and all for escaping. Why, he ran off from the Convention Army near Fishkill Creek, when I served in the Engineers, and won safe to New York. Last week I saw him brought prisoner into this town after escaping from the Gloucester Hospital. Take good care of him, soldiers, or he'll give you the slip again. He has quicksilver at his heels, has Gerry Lamb.'

This deserter was intoxicated, and perhaps intended me no injury, but my captors paid attention to what he said and passed me on with a bad character to the prison guard. Sergeant Macleod and the private soldier, his namesake, were then separated from me. They were turned in along with their regiment again, but I was sent a prisoner to the American guard-house.

The weather was extremely cold, and the guard-house was an

open block-house, through which the snow and frost made their way unopposed. With much trouble I prevailed on a guard, for sixpence, to bring me a little straw to lie upon, in one corner. But I soon found that my lodging would be a very hard one; for whenever the guard discovered that I had fallen asleep, they applied a firebrand to the straw, and as it blazed, they set up a yell like the Indians, rejoicing in my distress, and deriding my endeavours to extinguish the flames. When the relief used to be turned out, I sometimes took the liberty of drawing near the fire, to warm my half-frozen limbs; but this indulgence was of short duration, for when the sentinels were relieved they came pouring into the guard-house, and, if found near the fire, I was usually buffeted about from one to the other, and perhaps a dozen fixed bayonets at once placed at my breast. When I found that I could obtain no mercy from these savages, and that every day I was worse used than on the preceding, I wrote a letter to the American commanding officer. In this letter, which I handed to the Lieutenant who inspected the guard, I informed the commanding officer of the treatment that I daily received, and entreated him to have me rather confined to the Town Jail.

This request was granted three days before Christmas Day, but my condition was not bettered by it. My remaining money and possessions were taken from me and I was placed in the upper part of the prison, to which I had to climb by a long board, furnished with slats, which was almost perpendicular. In this dreary place, without any fire-place, I found twelve criminals chained to the walls. Some were deserters from the militia; some horse-thieves; two were pedlars confined for pursuing their trade without a licence; one had insulted a Congressman; one had tried to pass counterfeit money. Soon I was secured beside them, and gave them a civil greeting. After asking me a great variety of questions, which I answered carefully, they resumed their single and perpetual business, which was to argue on politics together. Not one man of them, by the bye, had a good word to say for Congress. For Generals Washington and Greene they professed considerable esteem, and were pleased that I judged this esteem as on the whole well founded. The poor fellows received a very small allowance of provisions, which was hoe-cake and a little rusty bacon, with water to wash it down; however, not a morsel was allotted me, as not being on the charge of the prison, but a military prisoner confined by my own request. However, these 'jail birds', though some of them may have lived very vicious lives—I know not—took compassion on me. The man who had insulted the Member of Congress and ruled the roast here, declared that it was 'kind of hard' that I should starve to death. At his suggestion they agreed each to set aside for my subsistence a twelfth portion of their pittance. Had it not been for their humanity this work would never have been written: I should have starved to death.

I must here fairly account for the bad usage that I received: the regiment of horse that was cut to pieces in August 1776, at Long Island, was composed very largely of young men from the Western confines of Maryland. This was a source of general inveteracy to all British prisoners, it being represented that the regiment was refused quarter and massacred; how true this may have been, I cannot say. I had also become an object of particular severity because it was believed that I still meditated my escape—as was indeed the case.

In this jail I remained for twelve days, until past the New Year of 1782, suffering the bitings of hunger by day, and shivering all night with the cold. The only remission from our fetters was when once a day we were fetched down to the necessary-house under guard of two men with muskets. Though it can hardly be imagined that aught was wanting to our sufferings, yet the case was indeed worse. We were continually annoyed with the yellings of an emancipated black woman, confined at the bottom of the jail for the murder of her child. She used to yell the whole night long, weeping and wailing for her 'poor honey lamb', her 'lill' peach blossom', who had 'done gone to be an Angel', as she hoped, 'in Hebben'.

I cudgelled my brains to devise some means of escape and in the end bargained with the negro who brought the victuals and water-jug that I would give him one of my three shirts (which I still had on) if he provided me with pen, ink and a sheet of paper and conveyed a letter for me to an officer whom I knew to be in the town. This was Major

Gordon of The Eighth, for whom I had undertaken the service of cleansing a small offensive wound that he suffered at York Town and of attending to the eleven wounded men his regiment left behind at Gloucester Point. He was a most generous gentleman: indeed he had voluntarily offered to take the place of Lieutenant-Colonel Lake, the field-officer appointed by Lord Cornwallis to command the captive army—and this only because he was a bachelor, whereas Colonel Lake had a wife and children at home.

The negro brought me the instruments I required and I wrote to the Major, acquainting him with my distressed condition and begging him to intercede with the American commander on my behalf. All I asked was to be liberated from jail and placed with other British soldiers.

The negro soon came back to tell me that he had delivered the letter, and therefore claimed the shirt. I did not know whether or no to believe him, but fulfilled my part of the bargain and waited anxiously for the event. On the morrow a soldier arrived at the foot of the board and bawled out: 'Is there a prisoner here named Robert Land?'

No one replying, the soldier was going away, when I had the inspiration to call out: 'Ay, pardon, here I am!' for I guessed that my name had been miswritten on a warrant of release, and I would in any case rather be enlarged for awhile as Robert Land than remain fast in my fetters as Roger Lamb.

He said to me, 'Come now, Land, look sharp and put your best foot forward. Do you love jail so much that you are thus slow to quit it?'

'You must first unfetter me,' said I.

'Now, isn't that a plaguey thing!' he cried. 'Heigh, turnkey, where are your cursed keys, you wretch? Now, quick, nip up that board and unfetter Mr. Land, the British soldier, or I'll blow you through with my blazing iron. I'm in a pretty considerable tearing hurry this forenoon.'

In a twinkling I was unconfined and, trembling for weakness, descended the awkward board. The soldier took compassion on me when he saw my pale and hollow cheeks, and permitted me, despite his haste, to recover my money from the prison officer; though this greedy personage would not return me my spare shoes, which I saw that he was wearing himself. I then entrusted five shillings to the negro, with an extra shilling for himself, to lay out on victuals for my companions in misery. I believe him to have been a humane and honest fellow and hope that he discharged this duty.

The soldier now told me: 'I have orders to take you to Captain Coote.' I feared that after all I might have been mistaken in answering to the appellation 'Land', but was comforted when, on being conducted through the town to the quarters of Captain Eyre Coote of the Thirty-Third Regiment, that gentleman greeted me in my right name. 'Why, Sergeant Lamb,' he cried, when we were alone, 'what have these rascals done to you? You look like a spectre!'

I related him my experiences in a few simple words and confessed my determination and hope still to effect my escape into New York.

The tears of sympathy filled his eyes. Said he: 'Ay, Sergeant, we are all unfortunate, but must keep up our courage still. Major Gordon wishes to convey his regards to you: he has laboured under a complication of disorders since he first came here. He is not unmindful of your case but has referred it to me. You will be glad when I tell you, I have obtained from the American commander an order for your release. You are now to come under my command.'

I hastily thanked Captain Coote (later to become Lieutenant-General Sir Eyre Coote) for his kindness, and took the liberty of congratulating him upon the news, that had but lately arrived in the country, of the victory of his uncle and namesake over an enormous horde of Indians under Hyder Ali at the battle of Porto Novo. 'Ay, Sergeant,' he said, heaving a sigh, 'but my poor uncle has yet a long course to run. The sick old man, with his handful of half-starved men, and the dice loaded against him by the treachery of the Madras Government, marching and countermarching in that pestilential climate—it grieves me to turn my thoughts thither, and towards those other brave commanders of ours distressed with terrible odds in distant parts of our Empire. In India, Goddard, Popham and Camac; and my friend Flint at Wandewash reduced, I hear, to constructing wooden mortars and grenades of fuller's earth! General Elliott besieged and bombarded these long months at Gibraltar, and poor Murray whose flag still flies—as I hope—at Port Mahon. Our comrades pent up in Charleston, and several other garrisons languishing in Pensacola and the West India Islands under constant threat of destruction by fever or the French and Spanish fleets. The Americans have but one war to fight, and a host of allies; we are fighting now alone and for our lives, like a bull set upon by three mastiffs in front, while a couple more sneak round to lay hold on his vitals. Would to Heaven I were free of my parole: I would attempt to escape in your company.'

While the faculties of my nature remain entire I shall never forget the affecting manner in which Captain Coote addressed me. Said I, 'Your Honour, my reasons for deserting were love of liberty and loyalty to my Sovereign. You have confirmed me in them and I will never rest until I find a chink in my prison door and break out again.'

Captain Coote then said: 'Hark 'ee now, Sergeant Lamb: I have already directed my sergeants to build you a hut in the pen and to take you into their mess. This they are glad to do, for they all esteem you. Here, will you accept this guinea from me as a tribute to your steadfastness? And when you have rested yourself somewhat and resumed your purpose, my hope and prayer is that you come safe through.'

I went off in triumph to join The Thirty-Third in their pen, and there found my hut nearly constructed; but hardly was I settled in some degree of ease and comfort with these excellent people, when an order came that, for regularity, all men who were quartered with regiments not their own should be returned where they belonged. I was to be sent under guard to the Royal Welch Fusiliers who were confined at Winchester, about eighty miles away to the westward.

This journey of five days, by way of the South Mountains and Harper's Ferry, was unremarkable. My two guards were silent and surly both with each other and with me. They guarded me very close by day and secured me by night with heavy fetters, which I must carry during the march. All the way along the Potomack River, the soil was rich and chiefly, it seemed, given up to wheat-growing. Beyond the gorge through the South Mountains lay a broad limestone valley, the water of which at first caused me severe gripings. In the middle of this valley, with the snow-covered Devil's Backbone behind it, lay Winchester, which I found to be an irregularly built town of about two hundred houses. The Royal Welch Fusiliers occupied a pen in a fort near by, which had been constructed during the previous war by General (then Colonel) Washington as a protection against the Red Indians.

Here I was welcomed by Captain de Saumarez, who commanded the Regiment in captivity and had heard of my hardships. He said: 'Sergeant Lamb, will you take a hint from me? I understand from the guards who brought you here that you are a marked man. The sergeant says that his comrades have been constantly employed in apprehending you and escorting you from one place to another. It is my notion that when in three days' time we march up to Little York in Pennsylvania, they will arrest you, as soon as you fall into the ranks, and confine you here in Winchester Jail; from whence you will not obtain release, except by death, until the war ends.'

I thanked the Captain for his warning; and on the morning of January 16th, when the Regiment, with all the others, marched up to Little York, I reported sick and remained behind at the hospital. The Surgeon, to whom I was known, very obligingly sent me to lie on a pallet in the death-hut, appropriated to the men whose lives were despaired of.

The two days that I spent here proved of some refreshment to me. When they had passed and the American guards had all moved away from the town in order to escort the army to Little York, it was not difficult to escape from the hut. It was left unguarded, because of the fatal purpose to which it was devoted. I must here say that I had confided to Smutchy Steel that I intended to follow behind the Regiment; and had asked him to do a service for me if he could. This was, to inform our old comrades of The Ninth, who were now quartered in the neighbourhood of Little York and there enjoyed a considerable degree of liberty, that I was on the way. I told him that I would represent myself as never having escaped from The Ninth at all, since their first surrender at Saratoga. My tale would be that I had stayed behind at Charlotteville working (like poor Terry Reeves) on Colonel Cole's plantation, when The Ninth removed from thence in the previous April; but now was rejoining them.

The road, I found, ran very straight for about a hundred miles, with seven rivers or large creeks to pass, and a ridge of hills. I set off early on the morning of January 18th. The weather was extremely cold, but I had Captain Coote's guinea, or rather its change in quarters, picayunes and coppers; as also my blanket and a few necessaries which I had obtained in the death-hut, from the effects of a Fusilier who died while I was there. In my knapsack were four pounds of flour, a gill bottle of rum and some dressed meat.

The severe treatment which I had received from the Americans seemed, in my mind, to excuse me from revealing the truth about myself. I was resolved only that I would not attempt to win the favour of any person whom I met by speaking with pretended disloyalty of my King and Country. This was one of my hardest marches, since it was made in the depth of winter and I was sick, alone and always in fear of being haled back to the jail. The wind was from the north-west and bitter beyond description. However, the very severity of the weather aided my purpose, since I met nobody upon the road who troubled to ask me questions, except one foolish old man who smelled like a pig-drover, though he had no hogs with him. He stopped me a few miles short of Spurgent, where I must recross the Potomack.

'Stop, Mister!' he cried. "Why, I guess now you be coming from Charlotteville by way of Wood Gap.'

'Nein,' said I, pretending to be German, for I could not abide the fellow. It was almost the one word in the German tongue which I knew at this time but 'ja', which is its opposite.

'Why, then, I guess as how you be coming from Kentucke?' he offered again.

'Nein,' said I again, dully.

'O, why then, pray now where might you be coming from?' he persisted.

To shake him off I reeled off some such unintelligible nonsense as: 'Twankydillo, lilliput, finicky blitzen, niminy-piminy buzz-buzz potsdam finicky-fanicky, ulallo hot-pot *Fredericksburg.*'

He caught at the last word and said, as if he understood every word that I had spoken: 'Why, then, you must have heard all the news. Pray now, Mister, what might the ruling price of bacon be in those parts?'

I pretended to grow angry: 'Kenn kein Englisch,' cried I, providentially recalling the words with which our German guards at Rutland pen had always put us off, did we ask them any slight favour.

This he understood. 'Ay, ay, Mister, I see now you be'nt one of us. Well, I must be going on my way. I have a long tack before me.'

'Ja, ja,' said I, leaving him and continuing my march to the Potomack, which I crossed without question, proffering my fare to the ferryman without a word and pretending to suffer very violently from the toothache. During this time I lived on my rations, sleeping by night in sheds or fodder stacks. Often the snow was up to my knees, and the rivers that I had to ford were full of floating ice. I nearly lost two toes from frostbite, in my passage of the South Mountains, but rubbed them well with snow before it was too late. I made about fifteen miles a day. I passed on my way four freshly made graves of the army that had gone ahead of me.

I was now in the Commonwealth of Pennsylvania and from the language which I heard spoken knew that I was in a German part. These Germans were industrious, quiet, sober people and alone of all Americans abstained from asking impertinent questions of travellers. They always made for the richest lands, where they settled down in orderly communities and both built and farmed as for a lifetime—there was none of that hasty, restless pioneering manner with which English-speaking Americans staked out a plot in the wilderness, felled trees, ran up a slight hut, ploughed between the stumps, took their toll of the soil, and after a few years sold their plot cheap and passed on again to new ground. These Germans, and the Dutch intermixed with them, built fine solid houses and great red barns, tilled the land lovingly, keeping it always in good heart by a rotation of crops, and employed themselves and their households in all manner of artistic industries.

About January 25th, as I was stumbling along the road, very sick now, about five miles from Little York, a woman called out merrily from behind a stone wall:

'How now, Spirit, whither wander you?'

My heart lifted with joy and I declaimed in reply:

'Over hill, over dale,
    Thorough bush, thorough brier,
Over park, over pale,
    Thorough flood, thorough fire
I do wander everywhere—

Why, dear Mrs. Jane, do you recall at Rutland what trouble we took with the Fairy, the little drum-boy who would not learn those very lines?'

'I have expected you to pass here these two days. Was the road so bad?' asked Mrs. Jane Crumer. 'You look very sick, Gerry Lamb. Come, my poor husband is down the road. He will give you a drink of peach-whiskey.'

Crumer's wits were still turned, I found. He said to me: 'Why, Sergeant Lamb, are you back so soon? Yesterday my Jane wept, when she told me that you had run away. See how she smiles now!' He had lost all sense of the passage of time, and thought himself still in the year 1779, when I had escaped to New York from Hopewell. That Jane Crumer had wept then, touched my heart—and that she smiled now.

The peach-whiskey warmed me and I went along the road with them very cheerfully. But the happiest surprise was to come: Smutchy had contrived to convey my message to the sergeants of The Ninth and they had already obtained, from the unsuspecting American officer set over them, a pass in my own name in which I was described as belonging to their regiment. This precious piece of paper was handed to me as I entered the town, for several of my old comrades besides Jane Crumer and her husband had kindly and attentively watched for my arrival.

I thus avoided being put into the pen which had been constructed for the Royal Welch Fusiliers, and was adopted as an inhabitant of Convention Village, that had been built about two hundred yards away from the pen by the small remains of General Burgoyne's army. The villagers were allowed very great liberties and regarded as almost citizens of America. I found that the pass gave me the privilege of ten miles of the neighbouring country, while I behaved well and orderly. I was conducted into the hut which my poor loving comrades had built for me here as soon as they heard of my approach. They had furnished it very comfortably with bed and blankets, chair and table, candles, liquor and even an iron stove.

CHAPTER XVIII

I REMAINED for six weeks at Convention Village, visiting my former companions from hut to hut. I was astonished by the spirit of industry which prevailed among them. Men and women were employed in a variety of mechanical trades which they had either driven before they followed the drum or had learned during their captivity. Even the children were impressed into usefulness. One of my former comrades had married a 'She-Kener' or gipsy, a tribe that had been brought to the country from Germany by Dutch slave-traders as 'redemptioners', but had soon bought their freedom and were now settled down in this part. This gipsy taught the women lace-making and basket-weaving. Some soldiers whittled wooden spoons and likewise learned the trade of cutting bowls, plates, skimmers, cups and saucers from dish-timber: that is to say, from the large knots that occurred in old sugar-maples, soft-maples, beech and ash. From a single such lump of dish-timber a whole nest of bowls could be scooped. A man who had been a brass-worker sent his fellows around the countryside with money from the common stock to buy up old candlesticks, lamps, kettles and other brass and copper, paying by weight, then hammered the metal out and re-worked it into buttons, knee-buckles and shoe-buckles. Some of the soldiers he took on as apprentices; others became pedlars and sold the articles about the country, adding lace, brooms, wooden ware (inclusive of carved butter-stamps) and baskets to their stock.

I was called upon by my comrades, almost as soon as arrived in the village, to take the part of Richard Plantagenet in a public performance of the *History of Henry the Sixth;* Jane Crumer playing that of Queen Margaret. A chief reason for the esteem and even affection in which the Villagers were held by the people of Little York was these regular dramatic entertainments. The Americans had hitherto been almost unacquainted with stage plays and the impression made upon them by their first hearing poetry spoken with feeling and intelligence was very remarkable; I believe that they have never since lost their taste for the works of Shakespeare. When later I mentioned the matter to Major Mackenzie of my regiment, he remarked: 'Why, now, what a lazy jade the Muse of History is—how she repeats herself! Two thousand years ago an expeditionary force sailed westward from the ancient maritime state of Athens against the vigorous Greek colonists of the New World of Sicily. The affair miscarried and a great number of Athenians were taken prisoners; but these mitigated the severity of their lot by performing the Comedies of the playwright Euripides, which greatly delighted their Syracusan captors.'

Jane Crumer was indeed the Mother of the Regiment: she even formed the workers into a guild or brotherhood and with the monthly contributions that they paid compiled a respectable sum of money which could be drawn upon by persons in ill-health or those desirous of borrowing money for the purchase of tools or materials. She administered this fund very wisely, but not knowing how to cast accounts in due form now took lessons from me in that art. She begged me to remain with them and act as schoolmaster to the children of the Village, of whom there were a great number, since the married men had in general not deserted their regiments; but when I informed her that I could not relinquish my intention of escaping, she desisted, with a sigh for my obstinacy.

So well had she tamed the 'rough and ready Ninth' by the gentle bonds of female discipline that when I strove by every argument to arouse that animation that ought to possess the breast of the soldier, I made no impression at all upon them. I offered to head any number of them and make a noble effort to escape into New York, but none of them would listen to me. They were very well off here, they said, and here they would continue at least until Peace were signed, and perhaps for the rest of their lives. The climate suited them, they liked the people of Pennsylvania, and they had had enough of war. Twenty or thirty of them had taken wives, German women for the most part.

Jane Crumer smiled at me when I told her of my ill-success,

assuring me that peace had its victories no less than war. She pointed across the parade at Long Winifried (the woman who had stolen the Town Bull at Boston and vanquished the Select-man) seated outside her hut, the familiar clay-pipe still between her teeth. She was transformed from a harpy of the camp into a very respectable basket-maker and the best of housewives, though her tongue was still tart. 'Gerry Lamb,' said Jane Crumer, 'you are but young. When you have overpassed the Fourth Age of Man, and ceased in Shakespeare's words to "seek the bubble, Reputation, even in the cannon's mouth" you will, I believe, enter upon the Fifth Age very decently. You will become a most judicious Justice—and I hope then to know you better.'

Said I: 'Now, Mrs. Jane, you must cease funning, I beg. You know that it is not glory that I seek, but we British are plunged up to our ears in war, and for my part, like poor Terry Reeves, I intend to "stand up for my King and Country till I die!"'

She begged my pardon and cried: 'No, no, Gerry Lamb, I did not mean to thwart your ways. I admire your steadfastness and I wish you every success. It is only that these poor remains of the Regiment are those who always lacked the resolution to escape, men of peace, not natural soldiers like yourself, and it is better that they remain here. The rest have all run off long ago and many came safe through, as you know. But the most part were apprehended and some shot, some hanged, some cast into prison. The news of their fate has discouraged the remainder.'

Accordingly, I sent a message to my comrades of the Royal Welch Fusiliers in the pen, wrapping a paper around a stone and tossing it over the palisade when the sentinel's back was turned. It was addressed to Sergeant Collins, and in it I wrote that I intended to head a party for escape to New York, upon St. David's Day. I considered that in all the British Army the seven men named in my letter could not be excelled for courage and intrepidity. They were three sergeants, viz.: Collins, Smutchy Steel and Robert Prout the transport-sergeant; and four private soldiers, Tyce, Penny, Evans and Owen. I mentioned that if they decided to come they were to meet me in my hut at midnight on the last day of February. At the same time I sought out Captain de Saumarez at his quarters in the town and told him of my intention, mentioning the names of the men. As my money was almost expended, I begged him to advance me as much as was convenient. He applauded both my intention and my choice of a day; and the same evening sent me no less than eight guineas, one for every man of the party.

Although my old comrades of The Ninth would none of them venture with us, they did all that lay in their power to further our escapade. Two of them even consented to hold the sentinel in play at the hour for which the evasion from the pen was planned, by pretending to be drunk and cutting capers in the vicinity of his box. The night fortunately was very dark, and at midnight the seven men duly entered my hut, having scaled the palisade unobserved. There they remained for the rest of the night. I took the precaution to bind them to certain Articles of War. The expedition that we were now undertaking must be conducted under military discipline, and being unanimously chosen their leader I demanded perfect obedience. Smutchy, who had been with me during my previous successful escapade, and now bought a cavalry pistol from one of the villagers, volunteered to execute the sentence of death upon any man who disobeyed my orders. In return, I undertook to hold a Council of War whenever I was myself in doubt as to the course to follow; but my own decisions must be obeyed as if they were those of Lord Cornwallis himself.

On March 1st, therefore, after drinking a few parting glasses in my hut to the success of our venture, 'and St. David', we set out westward in two parties towards the frozen Susquehannah River, which lay ten miles off. With the leading party went Jane Crumer, who was by now so well known in the country that it would be supposed that the men with her were members of the Convention army. The rear party I myself conducted, and my pass, which was good as far as the river, would no doubt cover the other four men, who would say that they had left theirs behind. We passed through the country without challenge and said our thanks and farewell to Jane as we came in sight of the river. Looking back, I observed that she walked away very disconsolately as if she would readily have come with us, but for the responsibilities that she had undertaken at the Village, and her poor disabled husband. She then turned herself about, and observed my backward looks. We both returned to the place where we had parted, moved by a common sympathy; our eyes filled with tears, I kissed her hand, but neither of us found words for this second good-bye.

The ice when we came to the river was rotten with thaw; for the weather had been mild during the day, and it was evident that we could not attempt to cross. However, a severe north wind now blew up and I judged that it was now freezing again. The Susquehannah at this point was about a mile over. We resolved to remain on its banks all night in the hope that by morning the ice would bear our weight. In a thicket some of us felled a few saplings and made a hut of hurdles to protect us against the wind, while others collected brushwood. I went along the bank to where I had noticed a man setting fishing-lines at a hole in the ice. I believed that he might have observed us, and wished to assure myself that he was of no danger to us. His face appeared familiar and I had no difficulty when I approached to put a name to him. 'Why, now, Happy Billy Broadribb,' I cried, 'how goes the fishing?'

This Broadribb was a Royal Welch Fusilier. He had received his nickname because of the gloom which was permanently settled upon his countenance; he had deserted us during our expedition against Fort Lafayette two years before. He had been very negligent of his hair and accoutrements on that occasion and had impertinently answered the Sergeant who reproved the fault, protesting that 'pipe-clay and pomatum will lose us the war' and that 'the Americans at least have a great deal more sense than to waste their time in such fribbling ways'. The Sergeant ordered him a lashing of twenty strokes, to be carried out the next morning; but he deserted rather than submit. 'Happy' Broadribb seemed very shy of me at first, as a sergeant in the regiment from which he had 'deserted in the face of the enemy'; but it occurred to me that he might be of assistance to us, and I therefore showed him every possible friendliness.

'Why, Happy Billy,' said I. 'Sergeant Farr who ordered you that lashing is dead, poor fellow, these eighteen months. He was a very severe officer. I believe that nobody blamed you in his heart for answering him back as you did. But were you not a friend of Harry Tyce? He is yonder in the bushes with a few others of the Regiment, and would, I am sure, be glad to shake your hand again.'

'Nay, I must be going,' said Broadribb, looking very ill at ease. 'I am sure I cannot look any Welch Fusilier in the face. Besides, it is very cold.'

'We have a gallon of peach-whiskey between us,' I said, 'and you shall warm yourself with a dram.'

He then consented to accompany me into the thicket. But first, I asked him: 'Well, pray, old Happy, how have you spent the last two years? Have the people of America fulfilled your expectations of them?'

He sighed and replied lugubriously: 'To tell you the truth, Sergeant Lamb, I have passed a most miserable existence since I left the Service. The Americans universally profess scorn for me as having deserted my King yet being averse from an engagement to fight for Congress. It is very hard. I have roved about Pennsylvania and New York and the Jerseys ever since, working most industriously for my livelihood; but have ever met with more kicks than halfpence.'

'What sort of work have you done?' I asked.

'Why, now, any and every sort of work—"whipping the stump", with an axe over my shoulder, peddling Notions, helping in a saw-mill, rowing at a ferry, hoeing turnips for a Dutch farmer, even "goose-herding", though I am a sad hand with the needle. I believe I know every inch of the country between here and the British lines. The Loyalists have been better friends to me than the Rebels, for I have made no bones about regretting my desertion.'

We went together into the thicket, and in a tone that I hoped my comrades would understand I cried out: 'Here comes a friend in need, Fusilier William Broadribb who once deserted the Regiment in a huff but has lived to regret it. I believe that he will now make amends for his single error by acting as our guide back to New York.

He knows the whole lie of the land as well as General Washington himself. Come, comrades, where is that peach? A deep swig of ben-booze for old Happy Billy Broadribb.'

Private Tyce, who was a Yorkshireman, took the cue well and slapped his old mess-mate on the back. 'I'm right glad to see you, Billy Broadribb. It will all be plain sailing. You will guide us by the paths you know, and when we win safe through to New York we will as one man intercede for your pardon with Sir Henry Clinton—how say you, Sergeant Lamb?'

'He will grant it,' I replied with assurance. 'There is no doubt whatever on that score. And what is more, when I ran over the same course three years ago, Sir Henry was most liberal in his reward of our guide, as Sergeant Steel here will testify.'

Here Sergeant Probert interposed in his excitable Welsh way: 'I care not what Sir Henry gives, but I do know this, by damn, that I my own self will reward Billy with a great deals of money, and with a great many drops of drink too.'

We made Broadribb happy indeed with repeated drams of peach-whiskey and encouragement of him as a misunderstood and ill-used person; and he finally consented to guide us throughout the journey. But, drunk though he was, I was pleased to observe that he did not on that account lose his judgment, but on the contrary gave us very valuable advice. He said that he knew the temper of the country very well, and that whereas two or three men might pass through it unmolested, nine in number were too many altogether. We must divide up, as soon as we had passed the river, for so great a body of British soldiers would soon spread an alarm through the country and cause immediate pursuit. He also strongly advised us to change our regimental clothes for 'coloured' ones at the first opportunity.

We told him that we would sleep on the proposal. We had a merry supper party upon the fish he had caught, which we roasted at the fire, also some slices of sour German bread and the peach-whiskey.

We took turns to keep watch and at dawn I went down to the river to test the condition of the ice. It cracked under my feet, yet bore me. I brought the good news back to the party, and we resolved to make the crossing without delay. Though the ice was exceedingly weak and broken up in many places, we ventured with the firmest resolution. It shivered and complained beneath us at every step we took. We proceeded in Indian file at a few paces' distance and had armed ourselves with long saplings so that if any man were engulphed the others might haul him to safety; but in the event we crossed without accident. Having gained the further bank, Sergeant Collins said to me: 'Well, now, Lamb, I believe that Broadribb is right. We must divide our forces if we are to succeed. How do you say?'

'I am very reluctant to do that,' I replied, 'but I can see no alternative. The Loyalists, who might be willing to assist two men or three, would most probably be fearful of entertaining so great a party as ours is now. I propose therefore that we break up into four and four. Broadribb can choose which party he would care to guide. Do you and I, Collins, each choose a man in turn; for since you are the senior sergeant you must command the other party.'

We made our choices. My first was Smutchy Steel, my second Sergeant Probert, my third was Private Jack Tyce. Sergeant Collins chose the other three private soldiers as being men of his own company. Happy Broadribb elected to accompany me, because of his friendship for Tyce and because he believed that I would have more influence than Sergeant Collins, should we succeed in our attempt, in the matter of obtaining his pardon from Sir Henry Clinton. Then I said: 'Very well, that is decided. Collins, my advice is to travel by night and hide by day, and to use a chain of friends, making certain of each next link as you go.'

'Why, for sure, that is what I shall do. But what of the first link? Happy, can you not direct me to a place from which to make a start?'

He undertook to do that and gave Sergeant Collins the name of a Loyalist widow living seven miles off, who would doubtless be friendly to them if they approached her discreetly. We then took leave of one another with aching hearts, while expressing full expectation of meeting all together at New York: we even considered what dishes and wines would grace our banquet of celebration. After some argument we compounded for beef-steaks, a fricassee of chicken, a prime leg of mutton, a boiled goose well stuffed, a sweet sauce of cranberries, copious Madeira, eggs and bacon, and a pineapple apiece—if such a fruit could be procured. Smutchy protested that for him no board was well spread without a steaming dish of 'Irish Roots' boiled in their jackets. We engaged to provide him with half a peck on his trencher, with salt and fresh butter to eat them with.

Sergeant Collins and his men continued towards the house proposed to them, but we hid all day among the trees on the snowy hill-side that formed the further bank of the river. In the morning our guide brought us to the house of one of the King's Friends, as Loyalists were here termed. He proved more useful to us than agreeable. His business was the collection and sorting of silk, linen and cotton rags for paper-making, and he was able to provide us from his stock with four suits of very bad coloured clothes, taking our regimentals in exchange. He was a grim, unsmiling man and would not permit us to enter his house, warning us that though we might use his shed, we must expect him to disown all knowledge of us if we were apprehended on his grounds. We asked him for a few cold potatoes or a little bread, but he had nothing to spare, he said. We did not see him again, nor did he wish us 'God speed'.

I put on my suit with disgust, for it had the rank musky smell of negro in it. Private Tyce, smiling a little to see the usually correct and formal Sergeant Lamb dressed in such a rig, I struck an attitude and declaimed in theatrical style, from my favourite character of Edgar in *King Lear*:

> No port is free; no place
> That guard and most unusual vigilance
> Does not attend my taking. Whiles I may scape
> I will preserve myself: and am bethought
> To take the basest and most poorest shape
> That ever penury, in contempt of man,
> Brought near to beast; my face I'll grime with filth,
> Blanket my loins, elf all my hair in knots,
> &c., &c., &c.

At eleven o'clock that night we began our march, making towards Lancaster, an industrious German town of eleven hundred houses; but we decided to avoid its streets and brought up our right shoulders a little, keeping always to the woods. To have passed to the south of the town would have been dangerous: it would have taken us into territory inhabited by the inveterate Presbyterians of Ulster, whose town of Londonderry was a chief focus of revolution as well as the seat of the young American linen industry. As Irishmen, Smutchy and I could expect no mercy did we fall into their hands. But the Germans were not, so Broadribb assured us, either inquisitive to travellers or cruel to the unfortunate.

At dawn we arrived at a village named Litiz. There was a house a little distant from the others with an ill-written sign to the effect that refreshment for man and horse was to be had there. Broadribb informed us that the warmth of the whiskey had died down in him and that he needed more of the same, and a good breakfast to settle it. We judged it necessary to humour him, and since we had no spirit to spare, it was natural to allow him a little money for a drink. Unfortunately, we had no smaller coin with us than a silver dollar, and I could not trust Broadribb in a tavern alone with such a sum. He would soon become intoxicated and might forget us altogether while we waited outside in the woods. So we must go in with him. We therefore rapped at the door, and I suppose that the landlord must have taken a peep at us from the window and thought us ill-looking customers; for he scrambled out of the back-door, bare-footed and half-dressed, buttoning himself as he went. We were apprehensive that he had run out to alarm the neighbours and therefore ourselves ran in the opposite direction and took shelter in a small wood.

Here we remained, almost perishing with hunger and cold until night, not daring either to light a fire or to resume our march until nightfall. Broadribb grew very gloomy and we were forced to give him our remaining peach-whiskey. He told us that we were heading towards the township of Caernarvon, where was a barn in which he had, not long before, rested himself all night. On that occasion, the farmer when he had passed through the barn in the morning had not discovered the presence of his visitor, even when a loud sneeze escaped him: he must have been either sunken in a brown study or, more likely, stone deaf. Broadribb led us without a fault across the Conestoga Creek by a footbridge and along a woodland trail until at dawn he halted us and 'there is the place', he said. It was a stone dwelling-house with a great red barn contiguous, as also a boarded maize-shed of the sort that broadens upward like a wheat-rick and has half an inch of interval between the boards to allow ventilation for the maize-heads stored in it. We deliberated whether or not to steal a few heads of maize where a broken board permitted, but we had no rasp to grate them into flour; so with one consent we went to repose our hungry and weary selves in the red barn. The door was open, we soon entered and, climbing up a long ladder, concealed ourselves under some sheaves of wheat which were in the loft. We rubbed a few ears in our hands in Galilean fashion and chewed the grain; but fell asleep still chewing. I kept a spy-hole open between the sheaves in case we were surprised.

We were cheated of our rest, for just as sleep was deliciously stealing over my senses, with many coloured images and confused dancing lights, a shrill whistling of *Yankee Doodle* spoilt all, and I awoke with a start to see a tousle-headed, lanky boy with a pitchfork coming up the ladder. It was clear that he was about to remove the wheat for thrashing.

I aroused the others and instantly disclosed myself. Says I: 'We arrived to see your master pretty late last night and took the liberty of spending the night in his barn.'

He stared at us and, evidently misliking our looks, backed down the ladder again, carrying his pitchfork at the charge, and then ran out of the barn. In my haste to forestall him with his master I jumped from the loft upon a heap of hay and ran after, entering the house almost as soon as he. The boy was shouting about us to the farmer, a big, blinking, grey-bearded German, who made a trumpet of one hand placed to his ear, and replied, 'Yes, yes, my child,' very indulgently.

We saluted him with politesse and he desired us to sit down. Though it appeared that he was a widower and childless, the place was spotlessly clean. There was a collection of curiosities ranged in well-made glass cabinets: such as Indian arrowheads of red, grey and black flint, tropical nuts, lumps of ore, fossils, a carved whale's-tooth and a wampum-belt. I happened to admire a gaily decorated fire-board (used to fill the fire-place in summer time) which was suspended from a nail on the wall. The intricate design of birds, trees and flowers had evidently been scratched into the soft wood, then filled in with colour and varnished over.

He smiled complacently. 'Mine own work,' he said in a thick German accent. He then pointed to a painted chest, decorated in the same style, with houses and people portrayed among birds and flowers. 'Mine own work,' he said again. We all expressed great admiration for the chest, and indeed it was most pleasingly painted, though the figures were crude and the flowers ill-sorted with them as to size. Then he showed us a work upon which he had been engaged as we came in: a sheet of illuminated handwriting, nearly complete, under a painting of the Whale spewing up the prophet Jonah. The writing was German verse and appeared to be a hymn. He had on the table beside him a colour-box containing quill pens, brushes (which he told us were of cat's hair), a small bottle of cherry-gum varnish, and others of coloured inks—red, green, blue, yellow and cuttle-fish brown.

I smote him upon the back, and uttered some resounding compliment. It was clear that, hungry and sleepless though we were, we could not hurry matters, but must cultivate the friendship of this artist by the easiest and most natural means—a regard for his work. After a while he said to me, in the mixed whispering and shouting characteristic of deaf people: 'Ha, can you do Fractur, ha? ha? It is not easy, ha?' He thrust a quill into my hand and rummaged in a box for a sheet of paper, then grinned at me as he laid it down before me. Thus challenged, I limned a neat little picture of four starving children with platters in their hands, standing meekly at the door of a house, where a benignant gentleman, the very spit and image of our present host, blinked down at them. Underneath, I wrote in my best penmanship with delicate flourishes and seraphs and an intricate rubric below, the first verse of the Souling Song as it is sung in my country by children from door to door at the vigil of All Souls'.

> A Soul, a Soul, a Soul cake!
> Pray, good master, a Soul cake!
> An apple, a pear, a plum, a cherry,
> A loaf or a cake to rest us merry:
> One for Peter, two for Paul,
> Three for HIM who made us all.
> A Soul cake!

Then it was he who slapped me upon the back, roaring with laughter that I had hit him off so luckily, and immediately shouted to his little cook-wench to bring us breakfast.

This consisted only of maize-flour stirabout, but since we had eaten nothing since our meal beyond the Susquehannah, fifty hours previously, we made a hearty breakfast. He eyed us with a quizzical expression, for we ate most voraciously; but abstained from asking us a single question as to our condition and destination. However, when we had finished, and he had given each of us a bowl of fresh milk he said solemnly: 'Gentlemen, I spy who and how you be. I spy your intention well. But I shall have nothings to do with you. For the sake of your good leader, who is mine brother in Fractur, I say as follows: "Depart now in peace"!'

I offered him money, but he would not accept of it, saying very obligingly that my little picture (which after breakfast I completed by giving the beggar children little scarlet coats) had paid our score. We thanked him warmly and withdrew to our usual hiding-place, the woods, where we remained for several hours.

'Well, Happy,' said Smutchy Steel, 'what is our next port of call?'

Broadribb told us that there was a gentleman, one of the King's Friends, who lived ten miles further on the great road leading to Pennsylvania. We should certainly receive entertainment from him. He was a native of Manchester in England and had grown very rich from the export of flour. Flour shipped on board at Philadelphia cost five dollars the barrel of 196 lb.; and, if it eluded the vigilance of the King's ships and privateers at the mouth of the Delaware River and won safe through to the Havannah, produced at least thirty dollars the barrel in hard money. Very many vessels were captured, but new ones were always in the stocks to take their places, and this gentleman had been more than usually fortunate of late. There was, I believe, scarcely a captain or even a common seaman who had not been taken six or seven times during the war—nor, for the matter of that, any merchant who had not been more than once rich, ruined and rich again.

When we arrived at this gentleman's fine mansion at dusk, we remained concealed in the orchard while Broadribb went ahead into the house. He soon returned and told us to follow him in by the side-door. We found ourselves in a most luxurious apartment, furnished in the English style. Tyce, Probert and Smutchy seemed ashamed to trespass into this elegance, clad as they were in sad rags, with cracked wet shoes on their feet and beards of five days' growth. But I determined not to be put out of countenance, and saluted the old yellow-wigged gentleman who rose from his wide elbow-chair to welcome us, as if I were in all the glory of full regimentals.

He bade us sit down at a fine wide fire until refreshment could be got ready for us. Then, in a most feeling manner he observed: 'You know the great hazard I run in receiving you as friends. It is now eight o'clock. I will let you remain under my roof till midnight. You must then depart. I will not ask your names, and if you know mine, I must ask you to forget it.'

'That we undertake, Sir,' I said.

A most excellent supper was then set before us by the old gentlemen's widowed daughter, who acted as his housekeeper. There was boiled ham, cranberry jelly, venison pastry, hot coffee with plenty of brown sugar as a sweetening; also apples, hickory nuts, wheaten bread and butter and plentiful cider out of silver goblets. The mahogany table glistened under the light of several white wax candles, and our instruments were ivory-handled Sheffield knives, and heavy silver spoons and forks. Our host asked us a number of questions relative to our experiences in the Carolinas and Virginia, which I answered at some length, for I could see that his mind was working upon problems of commerce and considering what new markets might lie open to him in that quarter, now that the Royal armies had removed. I was left to do all the talking, for my comrades had none of them sat at such a table before, and kept their mouths shut all the while except for an occasional 'Yes, your Honour' and 'No, your Honour' and 'That I cannot tell you, your Honour'.

The night proved very stormy, and the rain poured down like a deluge: we could hear it beating a continuous ruffle upon the roof of the portico outside. The hands of the tall clock drew nearer to midnight, and we eyed them wistfully, like the lady in the old wives' tale, who must leave the ballroom at that same hour lest the spell break and her fine ball dress be transmogrified into its original rags. But gratitude to our host forbade us to overstay our welcome. I asked a great favour of him, that he would write down for us a list of the King's Friends who lived in our line of march. This he did on condition that we learned the names by rote without taking the paper from him; and that we never, so long as we lived, revealed them to any questioner. 'Remember,' he said, 'that if by some great mischance the worst should happen, and by a treaty of peace the United States be granted their independence, these good people, unlike yourselves, must remain in America, where their fortunes lie. To be known as disaffected would prove as fatal then as now.'

We promised to abide by this condition, and I have ever since kept my word. Just before we braved the dark and boisterous weather, the old gentleman told us: 'Wait a minute, and we will drink a toast together.'

He brought out a very large bottle of rum from an armoury, filled up six Waterford rummers, and then, stepping up to a picture of General Washington which hung over the chimney, turned its face to the wall; so revealing to our admiring eyes another painting executed on the reverse of the canvas.

'To His Gracious Majesty, King George, gentlemen,' he said, and drank the glassfull down at one blow. We followed his example and gazed for a full minute in silence at the Royal features in the portrait. Then we saluted and trooped out.

CHAPTER XIX

THE NIGHT was so dark that we ventured to march on the main road to Philadelphia. The nearest of the King's Friends mentioned in the list lived near Hilltown, about seventeen miles away. We marched on hopefully, despite the increasing inclemency of the weather. We had not gone a mile before we were well drenched to the skin, and what made our journey yet more distressing was that the road was all puddle from the great fall of water. Broadribb began to murmur at the hardships which he endured, saying that his shoes were almost worn out and that the stones cut his feet. Indeed, all our shoes were in a wretched condition: we could scarcely keep them on our feet. Both my soles had come away from the toes, and to prevent them catching as I walked I had secured them with twists of wire.

We told Broadribb to be of good courage, enlarging upon the better aspects of the situation. Rain, we said, was at least better than snow, since it portended fine Spring weather. Besides, we had a good meal in our bellies and a recommended friend at the end of our march. We swore that we were proud of his company and would sing his praises very loudly upon our arrival at New York. Yet he stopped in his course, like a recalcitrant ass, and fetching a deep groan cried: 'No, comrades, no, I can go no further with you. You know that I am a deserter and a drunkard and a poor lost wretch, and you despise me in your hearts. Come, come, you can't deny your true opinion of me.'

Private Tyce put an arm about the wretched fellow and, 'Billy Broadribb,' said he, 'you take a delight in belittling yourself. You were a fine soldier once, and will be so again when you have shaken yourself free of your despondency. You, Sergeant Probert, weren't you present aboard the *Isis* three and a half years since, when we engaged the *Caesar* seventy-four, and didn't Captain Raynor, our

Commander, pick upon Happy Billy Broadribb, out of our whole Fusilier company, and call him a "damned cool soldier"?'

Probert clearly could not recollect any such occasion, but came out with an 'O yes indeed, I swear by damn those were the Captain's very words.'

This encouragement helped the unhappy fellow for another mile or two upon his journey, but then he stopped again, to observe with another groan: 'No, no, I have been thinking that perhaps all my hardships will be of no avail: when I get into New York I shall be denied my pardon and sentenced to the halberts. In my present weak state two strokes only with the lash would kill me.'

It still wanted an hour or so of dawn, but the rain now ceased and in the grey light we saw a small hovel on the road-side, and a solid house a little further on. I suggested that we should take shelter in it, and Tyce very nobly said: 'Yes, indeed, Billy Broadribb, I see now that your shoes are very bad. Suppose that you and I exchange, for as our guide it is only justice that you should be the best shod.' But it proved that the only man besides myself with a shoe of the right size was Smutchy Steel, so Smutchy devoted his to the common cause. I would have yielded mine, but they were in worse repair even than Broadribb's.

We pushed open the crazy door of the hovel, where to our great mortification we were saluted with the roaring and loud grunting of the pigs which were inside. We marched off at once, lest by their outcries they might alarm the people of the house, and Broadribb, who now understood how greatly we depended upon him, found a fresh complaint, namely that the coloured clothes he had received from the Scot were much thinner and more wretched than any of ours. Rather than that he should make an outcry as we passed the house, we undertook to give him, presently, the best clothes we had in exchange for his bad ones. At last we came in sight of a large barn. We had been cheated of rest on the previous morning and resolved to take shelter here; but were again disappointed, for as we drew nearer we saw that someone was inside with a lighted lantern. We heard some sheep coughing from the barn and guessed that here was one of those careful shepherds who sit up with their ewes in the lambing season.

Broadribb now began to whimper and sob and vowed that not another step would he march without rest and sleep. Behind the barn was a large dung-hill and, as the last resource to humour him, we agreed to lie upon it, covering ourselves with the loose litter. Here we remained about half an hour, but could not continue longer because of the extreme cold, and the shooting pains in our bones caused by the damp of the dung.

Smutchy Steel suddenly leaped up with a curse. 'Now, you wretch of a Broadribb, we have been subject to your megrims and fancies for too long. Why, you might be a breeding woman, not a Fusilier! For sixpence in old Continental paper, I'd break your lolling neck for you. Up now, you tapeworm, you poltroon, and lead forward or, by God, I will shoot you dead and bury you here in this charming muck-heap.'

This sharp speech had the looked-for effect. Broadribb started to his feet and declared himself ready to continue. The house recommended to us would not be far off, and morning was breaking fast on us. We reached the place after about a mile. It was a tavern, and as we approached we heard a neighing from the stable. I went forward to reconnoitre, but found to my unspeakable disgust that six army chargers were tied up in the stalls, with furniture which showed pretty clearly that the house was filled with American officers of rank.

I put a good face upon it, and returning to my comrades, remarked: 'The whole of General Washington's family appears to be sleeping in our beds. Do you proceed half a mile down the road while I get some liquor for us all, and if I am not back among you within five minutes, continue under Sergeant Steel's command, for I will be a lost man.' They moved off and I returned to the tavern.

As I approached, I was aware of two men talking behind a shuttered window—the one in thick drawling tones, and the other in the brisker accents of New York. I paused to listen. As nearly as I can recall the dialogue, it ran after this style:

'Captain Cuyler, I say you are a damned son of a bitch, yet I swear I love you.'

'Fie now, my dear Major M'Corde, I must take exception to that sentiment. Yet I forgive you with all my heart. For it is as plain as a cat's nose that you are altogether Addled and Awash.'

'How say you, damme? I want none of your plaguey Dutch forgiveness. I addled, sirree? Egad now, it is you who are addled. I am Sobriety's sweet self. You are, moreover, Boozy, Buzzy and Bepunched.'

'I deny that with blasphemous oaths, Major M'Corde, and will cap you, Tappahanock toper, throughout the English alphabet, if you dare. I say: you are customarily Cocked, Cock-eyed and Crocus, as my name is Cuyler.'

'I take you up, you dog! You are damnably Dagged and Drunk—yet I love you, I swear.'

'Dagged, am I? You are Ebrious.'

'And you, Fettered.'

'You, Glazed.'

'Hammerish, Sirree.'

'Intoxicate.'

'Juicy.'

'Knapt and Kill-Devilled.'

'Lappy, my trickish friend.'

'Mimbo'd, Mumbo'd and Momentous, my mighty Major.'

'Nimtoposical as old Noah.'

'Oiled, Sir.'

'Pungey with peach.'

'Raddled, Roaring and Rumfustianate, rascal.'

'Stingo'd, Stewed and Soaked, stinkard.'

'Tagged and tarnation Trammelled.'

'Unhinged and unusual Unsteady.'

'Vinous and Virginia-valiant.'

'Wine-logged and Whiskey-wet.'

'—Have at you, Major! To crown all, you are altogether X-Y-Zee'd. And there's my hand on it.'

'I kiss it, you most lovable rogue of a Captain. God's mercy, now, let us toss down another glass of I care not what—whether peach julap, or brandy-sling, or rank Boston kill-devil, or sweet sangree mantled over with nutmeg—to seal fast our enduring friendship, and drink damnation to Congress!'

A silence then falling, I passed on from below the window and pushed open the side door. Spying a man who proved to be the landlord, I said: 'Mr. ——, over by Hilltown, recommended your peach-whiskey to me. May I pray you to fill my can?'

He filled it without a word, refused the money I tendered, slapped me on the shoulder, wrapped a cold beef-steak in a newspaper, which he then thrust into my hand, and with an expressive command to silence, by squeezing his own lips between forefinger and thumb, pushed me gently out again into the yard.

With the meat and the peach-whiskey we managed to coax another few miles of travel from Happy Billy Broadribb. He led us off the great road and down the track which led to Valley Forge, where General Washington's men had shivered and starved during the winter that Smutchy and I had starved and shivered in the open huts at Prospect Hill. Near the cross-roads was a sign directing us to a shoemaker's dwelling, and there we had all our shoes repaired by a German workman and his apprentice while we sat by the fire in a corner. They were Hessian deserters, I believe, and showed more anxiety lest we be displeased than curiosity as to our history or intentions. For ten shillings we were all now tolerably well-shod but only Broadribb, and for another five we bought a new pair of shoes for him. We then returned into the woods and exchanged our good clothes for his bad, as we had promised. After another deep draught of the peach-whiskey he seemed determined for the present to continue with us to New York. That evening we made no mistake, but were nobly entertained in a mansion on the banks of the Schuykill by a lady who was a near relation of General Lee. She provided us with straw pallets in the attic of her house and then, after a lavish supper brought us by a negro, we slept like pigs for near twenty hours.

Her husband, a nervous and loquacious gentleman, dressed in a very dandiacal fashion, came up to discourse with us as soon as he learned that we had awakened; and enlarged upon his firm attachment to the Royal Cause. His observations, however, always came

round to the same point, namely what a monstrously dull city Philadelphia had become since the British had marched out. He said that
the subscription dances which had succeeded the fashionable balls
of those golden days were a mere mockery, that even the best-bred
ladies must now spend all their days in sewing shirts for Washington's rabble, that the odious French strutted and leered about the
fine brick walks of the City as if they were conquerors. 'Ichabod,
Ichabod,' was the burden of his song, 'the Glory has departed.' We
let him run on, listening sympathetically, though we could not feel
that in times like these a curtailment of his frivolous enjoyments war-
ranted so loud a howl. At least he had a good and handsome wife,
a fine house, attentive servants, money in both breeches pockets,
which he jingled all the while as he spoke, and, by his own boast, 'a
hale constitution, thank God'.

On the evening of March 8th, after we had eaten a very good
supper of turkey and cold meats, this poor, forlorn lover of pleasure
came to tell us that his canoe was at our disposal at midnight, and
that his servant would put us across the river. He gave us the name
and place of abode of a friend, a young Quaker, who lived a few
miles this side of Germantown and would assuredly take us in. This
Quaker, whose house we reached without misadventure, lodged us
in a loft above his stable. He happened to have been acquainted with
Major André, when that amiable and unfortunate gentleman was
imprisoned at Lancaster in 1776, and his children had taken drawing
lessons from him. He was as strict in his persuasion as my former
friend Josiah, and confirmed me in my good opinion of the sect.
He told us among other things that the Friends of Philadelphia had
a year or two previously passed a law to excommunicate from their
society any member who should pay a debt in depreciated Continental money; even though at this time it was treason to doubt the
goodness of the paper, and though they themselves must accept it
from their own debtors at its face value. They had also concurred not
to take part in any privateering or contraband trade; and our host
mentioned without self-glorification that he had been obliged by this
law to restore to the English owner his part of a prize captured by a

merchant ship in which he was interested. But he regretted that a number of his fellows had taken an active part in the war, forgetting their principles: so that he had been often accosted with 'Wilt thou take a gun?' and 'Can we expect thee on the parade to-morrow?' He told us that: 'Our poor *halting* brother, Nathaniel Greene'—the glancing reference was to the General's limp—'is of that company of backsliders.'

Upon leaving his house at midnight, we came about dawn to a creek, the name of which escapes me, that lay between Germantown and Bristol. It was swollen with the late rains. We chose to cross at a place where it was very broad, but only about four feet deep. Half-way over was a small island. No bridge or ferry or other means of passage offering, 'Come,' I said, 'there's nothing else for it but to wade over.'

'Ay,' said Smutchy, 'now to strip off our clothes and make bundles of them to tie about our necks! Heigh, you, Billy Broadribb, you have sleep still in your eyes. The cold dip will freshen you.'

Broadribb slowly removed one shoe and stocking and felt the water with his bare toes. He drew them out again with a cry. 'Now, in the name of Almighty God,' he complained, 'you cannot surely expect me to pass through this liquid ice before I have breakfasted?' He began to blubber. He had been so pampered by the gentleman of pleasure and by the honest Quaker, that he could not return to his former hardships. 'O, Sergeant Lamb,' he cried, 'my heart is almost broken, you know, with hardships. I am sure I will never survive if I wade into this river. And you can't deceive me about my pardon— the Commander-in-Chief will never grant it, that I swear.'

We proposed to carry him over on our backs, to give him half the money we had with us, which would have amounted to near two guineas, and of course renewed our assurances as to interceding for his pardon; but all in vain. He drew on his stocking and shoe again.

'Very well, then,' cried Smutchy, 'with Sergeant Lamb's permission, I will now carry out in earnest what I threatened before. I will beat the bad manners and cowardice out of you with the butt of this horse-pistol and then I'll shoot you out of hand.'

'You have my permission, Sergeant Steel,' said I, for this seemed the only means left of persuasion—the Quaker not having supplied us with any intoxicants, and our can being now empty.

Happy Billy Broadribb turned about in great terror and was off like a mountainy hare. We ran after him, but we were all bare-footed in readiness for the crossing, and could not pursue him far because of thorns and stones. He abandoned us there, taking with him his new shoes, our better rags, and the money we had advanced to him. We never saw him again, but agreed that it was good riddance: his cowardice had depressed our spirits.

We were already shaking with cold but, not wishing to postpone our trial further, waded in. That half-mile of water was indescribably cold. When we reached the island, we found that we had almost lost the power of our limbs. We rubbed and slapped one another to restore the flow of blood and danced about like Indians. Robert Probert, whose skin was bluish white in colour and his body shaken with a sort of palsy, cried in his sing-song Welsh voice: 'By Devil's damnation, no indeed, I cannot blame that poor fellow Happy. It is awful cold, I am. Indeed, I cannot blame poor old Happy.' Yet he was the first to wade into the second branch of the creek and the first to emerge. Smutchy gashed his foot very badly in the course of his passage, an injury which he did not discover until some time after leaving the water, all feeling being departed from his legs. We had to support him, for the next two miles of our journey, as he could not put his injured foot to the ground. Fortunately the house to which the Quaker recommended us proved hospitable. We were there concealed in the barn, and I was given salve and bandage for dressing Smutchy's foot. Our victuals, though plentiful, consisted wholly of corn-bread, honey and cider. Pennsylvania produces a remarkable quantity of honey, near every house boasting seven or eight bee-hives. It is said that bees were altogether unknown in America before the coming of the white men, as is proved by the name for the bee in most Indian languages being 'the Englishman's fly'.

Thus far we had been most successful. We were close to the great Delaware River, about twenty miles above Philadelphia. Somehow we must find a way across it into the State of New Jersey. Unfortunately our hostess, who was the widow of a former British officer, could give us neither assistance nor recommendation in this matter. She told us that it was as much as her life was worth to make fresh enquiries on our behalf: she was already highly suspect to her neighbours. We must act on our own initiative.

We set off at nine o'clock the same evening and passing a small house, observed a poor old woman chopping kindling wood in a shed. 'Depend on it,' said Tyce in an undertone, 'either the woman is a widow or else her husband is away. It is the men hereabouts who chop the kindling, and in the early morning.'

My experience having been that widows and other lonely women are seldom vindictive, and that they welcome company, I ventured to follow this one into the house. I asked her, could she direct me to the nearest ferry-house. She eyed me attentively from crown to foot and seeming to approve of her examination, replied in very genteel accents: 'Come in, with your companions. You will be safe. I can see that you are a British soldier by your walk and carriage. If you would pass for American you must relax the muscles of your neck and not pout out your breast so proudly; and in putting down your feet you must not crack down the heel first as if to wound the ground, but must use the ball of your foot.'

She had a bed-ridden husband upstairs, who had been in the service of the regal governor of Georgia, and her only son was at New York with Fanning's Provincials, in the King's Service. We were entertained very kindly and insisted upon paying her for her bacon and stirabout, when we left her in the morning and went to the ferry-house two miles away.

We had hardly entered the building before we found that we had run into a nest of hornets. Eight boatmen had just come in from the river to refresh themselves with apple-jack. They were from the neighbourhood of Trenton, forty miles up the river, and were bringing a raft of seasoned timber down on the flood-water to Philadelphia for use in the shipyards. Two of them carried rifle-guns. One, who had already, as we watched, drunk off two gills of apple-jack in succession, and now called for more, sang out: 'These four scarecrows keep very mum. Why don't they speak? Why don't they declare themselves? I'll be blamed if I don't believe that they are on the other side of the question. How say you, neighbour Melchizedek?'

The landlord spoke up: 'Now, now, boatmen, don't seek trouble for yourselves or this house. They are poor, honest Germans, I warrant, who haven't the gift of English. *Kommen Sie, mein Freund,*' he added, addressing me. *'Trinken Sie etwas?'*

I thought it best to appear cheerful and undismayed, and adopting a North of Ireland accent, which came easy, I called for four gills of apple-jack and told him that 'we Londonderry people aye keep our own company'. Then I added fiercely: 'Drink up, Phil, drink up, Corny and Sandy and you too, you big lump of a Robbie, before any good liquor be spilt. If these impudent tarry-faced rogues mislike our company, they must mind themselves.'

At this they rose with one accord and went into an inner room, the landlord running after them, I suppose to deter them from violence. Smutchy said: 'I have my pistol, but that will only be good for a single shot.'

'Let us sell our lives very dear,' cried Probert with all the ardour of a Fluellen.

'I believe that no buying or selling is necessary,' said the imperturbable Tyce, 'if we now seize the ferry-boat and make across the river. How say you, Sergeant Lamb?'

He was right. I bade them go ahead to the ferry, since Smutchy was delayed by his bandaged foot, while I called the landlord out and discharged the reckoning. I protested very angrily to this Melchizedek at the uncivility of the boatmen, and vowed to be revenged on them, soon as the remainder of my party of ten men came along the road. This speech covered our retreat in good order. I then sallied out and hurrying down to the river found my companions already in the boat, and Smutchy sitting behind the terrified negro-boatman with the pistol pressed against his black nape. I leaped in, we cast loose, Tyce seized the spare pair of oars and we were half-way over the river before the alarm was given. We were within range of their rifle-guns but Smutchy halloed at them as a bullet whizzed by us: 'Another shot, and by God, we kill your old mungo.' They then desisted.

Soon as the boat touched the opposite shore, we ran into the woods and were before long secure from our pursuers, as we had above a mile and a half start of them.

It would be tedious to continue detailing our travels in the same particular style: it is enough to say that in all the different places in America through which I have marched as a soldier, been carried as a captive or travelled in regaining my freedom, I never found people more strongly attached to the British Government than the inhabitants of New Jersey. I aver this with the most awful appeal for the verity of my words, despite the malignant assertions of the historian Belsham that 'such havoc spoil and ruin' had been made in this very part of the country by our licentious soldiery, particularly the Germans, under General Howe's personal inspection and command as 'to excite the utmost resentment and detestation of the inhabitants'. A historian ought to record the truth, and the truth only, whether of friend or foe. It must be admitted that the Hessians were addicted to plundering in the European style, so that their officers found difficulty in curbing their petty thieving of poultry, forage and the like; and that even so fine a corps as The Thirty-Third, when short of fuel in wintry weather, had here distrained upon the fences of the Whig farmers. I will also grant that there are rogues in every army, whose occasional crimes discredit their comrades. But had the British troops in America coolly and deliberately murdered Mr. Belsham's father, mother and all his relatives before his very eyes, he could hardly have been more rancorous or uncandid in attributing to British officers the direction or encouragement of atrocities. The officers who served in these campaigns were gentlemen, or noblemen, of the first families in the Empire for wealth as well as honour: men without any earthly temptation to the acts charged against them, and whose high spirits would have revolted at the bare mention of petty plunder and rapine.

But to return to my narrative. For the next week these good people of New Jersey ventured their own lives and property to secure ours, and smuggled us on from house to house in short stages, as the slipper is passed from haunch to haunch in the children's game of 'Cobbler, Mend my Shoe'. This country was full of troops, and the nearer we came to New York, the more numerous they grew. We went by way of Moonstown, Mountholly and Princeton, at which last place we were actually hid overnight by one of the masters in Nassau College. It was a fine, plain stone building of four storeys and a wide extension, but seemed to us rather a grammar-school, than an University College. We were concealed in the College Library. It surprised me that the books consisted almost wholly of old theological works, some placed in the shelves upside down, and all without any regularity, and having no scientific, historical or geographical treatises among them that I could see. At one end of the Library stood the famous Mr. Rittenhouse's orrery, but a year or two previously it had been hurriedly taken in pieces and removed from this place by the Americans—for fear, I suppose, that our officers would wish to add it to their plunder! Nor had anyone been found to restore it to working order. At the other end of the room were two small cupboards, named 'the Museum'. They contained merely a couple of small stuffed alligators and some curious fishes: which presented a very dilapidated appearance from having been the constant playthings of students at the commencement festival each year. No studious youth with a taste for the sermons of Attenborough, South or Bishop Berkeley came to disturb us during the hours we were here.

Since writing the above passage I have heard it asseverated by an American gentleman of some credit, a graduate of Nassau College, that the smallness of the library as I found it was due to the depredations of the rude Hessian soldiers quartered there, before General Washington's victory, at the close of the year 1777, dispossessed them of the place. He added with indignation that scores of the choicest volumes were used for fuel by them in the Franklin stoves. I sympathized with him that by perfect exactness of stupidity these boors had rejected all the dead and dry tomes as unsuitable for burning, while choosing only the greenest and least combustible timber of the tree of knowledge.

The last stage of our journey was to the town of Amboy, which lay opposite Staten Island, divided only by a river from the British outposts. We arrived within two days' march of it on March 19th. We had a guide with us, whom we believed to be worthy of trust. He took us to Elizabethtown at eleven o'clock that night, and pausing outside the place told us that we might safely march through, as the inhabitants were in bed and no Americans were stationed in it. However, the news had that day reached us, published in a Philadelphia newspaper to the following effect: 'William Broadribb, an acknowledged English deserter, was on March 9th taken up at Germantown by an Officer. He was tried the next day by a Military Court at Philadelphia on the charge of conducting four men, supposed to be British soldiers, towards New York; and the fact being proved he was summarily condemned to be hanged. The sentence will be publicly carried out *in terrorem similium,* in the usual place of execution, punctually at noon to-morrow, unless it rains.' This warning struck terror in our guide's heart. He now said to us: 'Lest I should happen to be seen with you, and they serve me as they served this Broadribb, I will make a circuit. Let us meet on the great road at the top of the next hill beyond the town.'

The people of Elizabethtown slept soundly and we were not challenged; but our guide was not to be found at the place appointed. We waited two hours for him and then gave up all hopes. We saw clearly that he had given us the slip. There was a piercing north wind which whirled heavy snow with it. We could not support the notion of waiting longer, our clothes being in tatters and our shoes having broken open again in our recent marching—for the leather was too rotten to hold the stitches of the German cobblers. We at last resolved to proceed by ourselves, though we had no notion upon what point of the compass South Amboy lay. The snowstorm abated and we saw the North Star shining rather bright; we knew we could not be materially wrong if we steered due north. We marched on, very hard, over broken, uneven ground, sometimes on the road, and sometimes through the woods.

At four o'clock in the morning, Smutchy Steel suddenly stumbled and fell prone on the rutted ground. He exclaimed in a very weak voice: 'Gerry Lamb, I have endeavoured to keep my troubles to myself and not let out a cry. But I have long overpassed the limit of my possible exertions. The pains of Hell are in my wounded foot, which is greatly inflamed, and not another step can I go.'

I knew that Smutchy was no 'malingerer' or skulker: if he said that he could not march another step, that was the mere truth. I therefore said to the other two: 'Come now, comrades, I know your feet are all very bad, but we must not abandon our friend so close to our goal. Come, hoist him up on my back, will you? We can carry him by turns until daylight. Then we will rest.'

'No, Gerry,' said he, 'leave me here! You are yourselves at the very end of your tether. Better that one should die than all be lost. If I live till morning, I will strive to creep to the next house; and if I have luck, I will follow you in a day or two.'

We tried to take him with us, none the less, but he was a heavy man and we could not support his weight: we fell down under it. We saw that we must after all leave him, and this was peculiarly distressing to me as his comrade in so many hazards. But for Tyce and Sergeant Probert being dependent upon my leadership, I should have elected to remain with Smutchy. He gave us his pistol, we wrung his hand, and marched on.

The whole of the next day we spent marching through the snowy woods. We were quite without provisions, nor did we break our fast before two o'clock of the following morning, which was March 22nd. Then we stopped at a house on the side of a narrow road, which was unconnected with any other building. We heard voices downstairs and rapped at the door. An old man quickly opened and, said he: 'I don't know who you may be, but step inside if you are a good man, and stop outside if you are not. My old woman and I are lonely old folk, but select in company.'

I said: 'Pray, Sir, I believe you are a Dubliner by your manner of speech. It is long since I heard the true Dublin speech from other than soldiers. May I ask from what part of the City do you come?'

This bold questioning drew a hearty laugh from the old man

and a cackle from his old wife. 'Glory be to God,' he cried. 'Do you mean, after all, that thirty years in this land of sharp speech have not cured me of my soft voice? Now, tell me, you night-prowler, whom in the name of Nick do you resemble? I have seen those eyes before now, and that manner of widening them as you speak. Well, I'll not think—it will come the easier to me, the harder I thrust the thought away. But I'll tell you, my fine, large man, that my abode was by Bloody Bridge, and that I worked about St. Patrick's Cathedral, for the old Dean, the dear man.'

I told him: 'The Cathedral was having that grand spire added to the steeple about the time you came away, was it not?'

He looked very grave: 'Truth, and I came away on account of that same spire. I had the misfortune to drop a hammer on the skull of a drunken, lying mason who was walking beneath me, and they all misdoubted it an accident: for I had the good fortune a few days later to marry my Molly here, whom I widowed. They gave me black looks in the Cathedral, did my fellow masons, and I came away here. Tell me now, isn't it true that there have been many fine churches and other edifices built or rebuilt in Dublin of late years? Answer me now, quickly, for I'm dying to hear.'

I here begged permission first to bring in my comrades; though I did not yet declare who we were. This he granted, and with a brisk nod at them immediately began plying me with numerous questions relative to these new churches—their style, materials, decoration and capacity. His wife chid him for his lack of hospitality to a fellow-countryman and began hastily to peel about twelve pounds of fine potatoes and made her husband mend the fire with the bellows, which she thrust into his hand.

It is very hard for a man caught in a hostile wilderness and near fainting with cold, hunger and sleeplessness to be obliged to read a lecture upon the ecclesiastical architecture of Dublin! Yet I was equal to the task, for I knew how much depended upon it. He was a choleric old man and would not be crossed. I told him of the elegant symmetry of St. Werburgh spire—a fine octagon supported by pillars and terminating in a gilt ball, and of the re-edification of St. Catherine's in Thomas Street, and of the new St. Thomas' church, the latest foundation of that kind in the City; and of the handsome front of hewn stone with columns and pediment which was added to St. John's in Fishamble Street about the time I left the City.

From churches I was obliged to proceed to the new Royal Exchange, which was a fairy-tale to my host, and to the rebuilding of Arran Bridge (now Queen's Bridge) which was destroyed by the floods in my eleventh year and soon after rebuilt in hewn stone. He suddenly smote his knee and cried: 'Now, isn't this an agreeable packet of news? Come, Molly, my duck, the whiskey! Here are two Irishmen who would be sociable together.' The potatoes were now bubbling in the pot and demanded eating, and had it not been for thoughts of poor Smutchy Steel, as another Dubliner, it would have been a truly merry evening.

My host informed us, as if accidentally, where were the American posts on the banks of the river, which flowed only two miles away. But he made no clear profession of politics, and neither did his old wife. She kissed me very affectionately when we presently left their abode.

Off we went, avoiding the American posts, and as soon as daylight dawned, we saw the woods of Staten Island in the distance, but a deep and broad river rolling between. We wandered up and down the shore in search of a canoe or boat, but found nothing. The broad appearance of day much alarmed us, and after a hurried consultation we agreed to return to my fellow-countryman's house, discover who we were and throw ourselves upon his protection.

He came running out of the house to meet me, snapping his fingers and crying: 'I have it, I have it!'

I tried to address him, but he would have his say first: 'Tell me this, my poor, ragged friend: who was the fine man with the pale blue eyes like yours who kept a marine store convenient to Arran Bridge?'

I replied, laughing: 'Now, why wouldn't his name be Lamb, the same as his son's?'

'That's the name, by Jesus God! It was from him I bought my seaman's clothes when I took ship for this country. He widened his pale blue eyes at me in the same way as yourself. Now, Mr. Lamb, I am yours entirely. You are British soldiers, are you not? Be guided by me. I love King George as much as any man.'

It was late that evening that we entered a small row-boat, owned by two friends of our Dubliner, and put off from the shore. We had agreed to pay them for the passage all the money in our possession. The river here was more than three miles broad.

The men had not rowed a quarter of a mile when the wind, which had hitherto blown fair for us, changed around and blew very fresh. The boat made a great deal of water, which alarmed the boatmen: they immediately brought the helm over and made for the shore whence we came. There was an English sloop of war that constantly cruised at night in these waters to intercept American privateers and other craft, but we had not yet caught a sight of her. We ordered the boatmen to turn the boat again and either attempt to gain this sloop or, failing that, row us at all events across to the Island. They declared that a boat could not live in such a wind and that we should all be drowned if we persisted. At this I pulled Smutchy's pistol from my shirt and peremptorily ordered them to do as I said.

After beating against the wind and waves for near two hours, and being almost perished with wet and cold, we espied a square-rigged vessel at half a mile from us. The boatmen declared her to be an American privateer, but as our boat was within a few minutes of sinking, despite vigorous bailing, we resolved to make towards her. Tyce could not swim at all, and Probert very ill. We must take the risk, I said. As we approached, we were hailed and ordered to come alongside. To our unspeakable joy, when a lantern was shown, we saw British soldiers standing on the deck.

They hauled us aboard and, as the leader of the party, I was ordered down to the cabin to give an account to Captain Skinner, her commander, who we were. Arrived before him, I could only gape, having lost for awhile the power of articulation. However, he humanely ordered a large glass of rum to be given me. This soon brought me to my speech. 'Thank God,' I cried, 'we are back among our own people!'

CHAPTER XX

THE AUTHOR has conducted his readers over varied fields of adventure and trouble, marching and sailing them some four thousand miles from his first enlistment at Dublin to his half-way house at Boston; and perhaps another four thousand miles on his complicated journeys, by way of New York, through the Southern and Middle States and back to New York again. However trying these scenes have proved, he hopes that the faithful local description contained in them will convey a certain degree of amusement and interest, as being the work of an eye-witness. Now, having almost reached the close of his career as a soldier, the author will make a quick exit from the literary stage, aware that the awful blaze of war alone could footlight so obscure a character as himself into public notice.

Captain Skinner set us ashore on the next morning with a letter to his father, the Colonel of a regiment of Loyal Americans. We waited on Colonel Skinner, who immediately ordered a boat to convey us to New York. Our appearance astonished the soldiers of the Garrison as with cheerful steps we marched up to Headquarters. Never had sergeants of the Royal Welch Fusiliers appeared in such scarecrow wretchedness. Sir Guy Carleton, whom we found to have superseded Sir Henry Clinton as Commander-in-Chief, received us with great kindness, and we communicated to him all the information we possessed that could tend to the good of the service. But it was with a pang, as I stood in the parlour, that I thought how I had stood here last in much the same pickle and how familiarly and sweetly poor Major André had talked with me. There were some framed sketches and silhouettes by his hand still hanging upon the walls. His appointment as Deputy-Adjutant-General was now held by Major

Frederick Mackenzie, who had been adjutant of the Royal Welch Fusiliers during the siege of Boston, and therefore took great interest in us. He desired me to write out a narrative of our escape, and then sent us to the officer who should pay us the usual bounty. This officer, after he had entered my name in the book, turned his eye to the top of the first page. 'Why,' said he, 'the Lambs are famous for this sort of work. Here is another Roger Lamb, a sergeant of The Ninth, one of the first who made good his escape from General Burgoyne's army, in the winter of 1778.'

I answered: 'I am the same man. I afterwards entered the Royal Welch Fusiliers.'

'Indeed, then,' he said, 'if you can prove that you are identical with the other, I have good news for you. Colonel John Hill who was exchanged and went to England has left here all your arrears of pay.' The proof was not difficult, there being officers of both regiments in New York at this time; and the money was paid me, amounting to forty pounds.

Major Mackenzie then recommended me to General Birch, the Commandant of New York, who appointed me his first clerk, at a good salary. Nor did the Major's kindness stop there: through his interest I was later made adjutant to the Merchants' Corps of Volunteers who were on permanent duty in the town. With them for two months I enjoyed the only repose, I may truly say, which I had during the eight years I was in America! Sir Guy Carleton, it may be remarked, had been appointed to his command by Lord Rockingham (whose Ministry had displaced that of Lord North) largely as being an honest and vigorous administrator who would root out from their seat at New York the parasites and plunderers who, under the negligent eyes of Generals Sir William Howe and Sir Henry Clinton, had sucked such immense private fortunes from the war. Sir Guy at once instituted a General Court of Inquiry and soon sent packing a number of officers, commissaries and contractors.

Later in the year when the preliminaries of peace were signed between Spain, France, America and Great Britain, I was at King's Bridge in charge of the recruits of the Royal Welch Fusiliers who were doing duty there. I heard the news with a sort of apathy, but high indignation was expressed by very many Loyalists and British. They were aware that General Washington's army were as naked and destitute as ever, and incapable of making a march of one day, even often plotting mutiny and held down only by the shooting of their ringleaders. General Washington himself afterwards confessed that his people were in a sort of stupor, that had we been permitted to march we could certainly have taken the Highlands above Hudson's River. The terms of the peace conceded the United States total independence; the great back-country territories from the middle Mississippi northward to the Great Lakes, formerly a part of Canada; the enjoyment of the cod-fisheries on the banks of Newfoundland; and the retention of the confiscated estates of the Loyalists. The Loyalists, twenty-five regiments of whom had served in our armies, now tore the British facings from their coats and stamped them under foot. They had lost all.

Thus ended a contest which had dismembered England of much more than half her territory. How far her commerce and her true interest as a nation were affected by it, was a point upon which it was then useless to speculate, and upon which innumerable and contradictory opinions have since been given. This at least can be written without fear of contradiction: that for the sake of enforcing duties upon tea and other commodities, which would only have brought in a few thousand pounds sterling—even had the expense of collection not greatly outweighed the receipts!—a war was precipitated which added no less than £120,000,000 to the National Debt, already very heavy, and doubled the burden of interest upon it. (The French, by the bye, were also £50,000,000 out of pocket as a result of this same war.) However, money is dross, and much money is much dross, and in the long run I believe it to have been for the best that the two nations were thus at last separate, in fact as well as by a fiction. It may even come about some day that, remembering the ancient ties of affection and language that, despite all, yet bind the two nations, the Americans will join in armed alliance with us against the French or other relentless foes who threaten our common liberties. However, from the loss of their Tories, they have been unhappily slow in settling down as a nation upon an even keel; and in this very year in which I write* we have fallen foul of them again, and been forced to land troops who have burned down their new capital city of Washington.

I have hoarded up two happy surprises for the reader; and may now disclose them. Sergeant Collins and his party came safe into New York about the end of April. They had endured the same great hardships as ourselves, and had been unfortunately taken prisoners in Jericho Valley as they prepared to cross the Delaware River a few miles below Trenton. They were confined in the famous Reformatory Prison of Philadelphia. There the treatment of prisoners was wisely designed to eradicate vice and make them look forward to their re-establishment as honest members of society: by allowing them to continue at their trades during their servitude, or teaching them trades if they were ignorant of any. Sergeant Collins and his party did not own to the knowledge of any trade and were therefore all together instructed in nail-making; just as ignorant females were commonly set to beat hemp. Had my comrades, who preferred liberty to reformation, been made into hemp-beaters they would have stolen strands to twist into light rope for their escape; but as nail-makers they stole iron bars instead and escaped by undermining the foundation of their cell. They smuggled themselves aboard a trading vessel at the docks and were rescued, as she sailed out of the river, by a British privateer.

We celebrated our banquet of reunion, as agreed upon, with the same choice viands that we had named as we crouched in the snow by the Susquehannah River, though we had to forgo our pineapples as unobtainable. The expense, I can assure my readers, was no paltry one, for in New York market at this time a leg of mutton sold for a guinea, a fowl for six shillings, a good egg for threepence, and the other articles proportionately. Liquor also stood extravagantly high. I proposed a

* 1814

silent toast to 'An absent face', meaning of course Smutchy Steel, and as we raised our glasses to our lips, then pat, as if by a theatrical cue, someone knocked at the door. 'Enter,' we cried. A well-known head craned in and a well-known voice enquired: 'Is the table set for eight or only for seven? And where is my great trencherful of potatoes that you promised me?'

'Why, Smutchy!' we cried, and ran to him, pressing him to our breasts. 'How came you here?'

He said: 'By the same way as you did, Gerry. I had the luck after you left me by Elizabethtown. The guide had not deserted us, but by an error waited at another hill closer to the village. When he found his mistake he went after us, and came upon me lying insensible by the roadside. He revived me with some warm rum and carried me to a friend's house, where I remained for three weeks until my foot had been healed with poultices. My next stage was the house of an old Irishman by the river who wished to be kindly recommended to you; and so across to Staten Island by boat with a fair wind and a starry sky.'

You may well imagine what a night was that!

In May, 1783, Captain de Saumarez, who was one of the twelve captains who had drawn lots for their lives at General Washington's order, led the Royal Welch Fusiliers, unbroken in spirit, back to the army in Staten Island. Colonel Balfour was already at New York, Charleston having been evacuated by the British some months before; I added my recruit company to the Regiment and on December 5th we sailed all together from Sandy Hook. As I watched the coasts recede, I remarked to Sergeant Collins who stood by me: 'Pray, Collins, how do you feel on this solemn occasion?' He replied: 'Well pleased at having seen so many interesting sights and scenes, but without the slightest desire ever to revisit that shore. I have had my belly-full of fighting too. Dr. Franklin was not far out when he declared that there was never a good war, nor a bad peace. Let the Americans keep America, I say: it will be both their reward and their punishment. They are a lively, sensible and not ill-natured folk: but if the Archangel Gabriel himself descended from Heaven to govern them, they would the next day indict him as a bloody tyrant, a profligate and a thief—so jealous are they of their liberties.'

When Sergeant Collins had gone below, the words of Richard Plantagenet in Shakespeare's *Henry the Sixth,* in which he mourns the loss of British possessions in France, came involuntarily to my lips. I declaimed in a melancholy voice to the gulls that sailed in our wake:

> Is all our travail turned to this effect?
> After the slaughter of so many peers,
> So many captains, gentlemen and soldiers
> That in this quarrel have been overthrown,
> And sold their bodies for their country's benefit?
> &c., &c.

After a short and prosperous voyage we landed at Portsmouth in England. From Portsmouth we marched to Winchester, where I requested my discharge, though I had very great privileges allowed me in the Army and was making money fast. Colonel Balfour kindly and humanely reasoned with me, in order to prevail on me to remain in the Service; but I had a notion to return to my own land.

He regretfully signed my discharge and with a number of my companions marched up to London in order to pass the board. Here I was considered too young to receive the pension, and likewise, it was judged, had not been long enough in the Service. I left the Metropolis, which I visited for the first and last time, on March 15th and four days later landed in Dublin, to the inexpressible joy of my aged mother and two surviving sisters.

The Ninth Regiment had also returned from captivity in the Spring of 1783, but sadly shrunken in numbers. They were soon brought up to strength and given the title of the East Norfolk Regiment, but they are now more generally known in jest as 'The Holy Boys'. They are still rough and ready; for the characters of regiments do not change. How heroically and steadfastly both they and the Royal Welch Fusiliers have conducted themselves in the wars against Napoleon Buonaparte is common knowledge.

Jane Crumer and her husband remained at Little York together with a number of married villagers. However, as it proved, I was later to renew my acquaintance with this very admirable woman.

On my arrival at Dublin I had determined, after long cogitation, that my duty to my Country had by no means terminated upon the battlefield, and that the frequent solicitations made me by Americans to remain in their townships in the quality of schoolmaster were clear signs of the destiny that Providence had marked out for me. Returned to Ireland, I would devote the rest of my life to educating the poor children of my fellow-countrymen in moral virtues and the simpler requirements of the useful citizens: viz. to read, write a fair hand, and cast accounts.

My affectionate recollections of Sergeant Fitzpatrick, to whose children I had first served as a teacher, suggested that I should undertake the charge of a new free school at the Methodist Chapel in White Friar Lane; where I soon had forty boys confided to me. We met daily in the Chapel lobby until, after some years, a school house was by subscription erected for me at the back of the sacred edifice. In the autumn of 1785, Mrs. Jane Crumer returned to Dublin. I met her again at the house of Sergeant Fitzpatrick's widow, her aunt. Poor Crumer, her imbecile husband, had been killed in Little York by the fall of a rotten pine. Since she and I agreed very well together, we were married by banns on January 15th, in the following year, in the Parish Church of St. Anne's, Dublin. We have had together a numerous progeny, many hard trials and much to be thankful for. I may add that my wandering feet have long ceased to travel. I have now taught in the same crowded school, with, I believe, an equal fidelity to that I gave my Regiment, for more than thirty years.

Before my marriage, I revealed to my dear wife the story of Kate Harlowe and the lost child; and was glad in the event that I had done so. For, ten years later, a handsome young female sought me out, having obtained my address from a soldier of The Ninth, and declared herself my child! She had with her my silver groat, wrapped in a paper on which was written:

The gift of Roger Lamb, Sergeant of the Ninth Regiment, to his daughter: Eliza Lamb.

K. H.

This charming young creature whose face and form recalled that of Kate at her most enchanting, had, I learned, been taken from the Indians by an American officer who wished to adopt her as his child. But the *bardash* Sweet Yellow Head, of whom I have written in my previous volume, sought her out and carried her back to his Chief, Thayendanegea, or Captain Brant, who brought her at five years old to the house of the Quaker Josiah, that she might be among people of her own race. Upon the Quaker's moving to Montreal she had been brought up in that city until the good man died, bequeathing her a modest competence. Shortly after her arrival in Ireland she married, with my consent, a man in the band of a militia regiment and soon made me a grandfather.

From my daughter I had news of Thayendanegea. She told me that he had visited London again in the year after I came to Dublin, and was presented to the King—but from some scruple of honour declined kissing his hand; observing, however, that he would gladly kiss that of the Queen. The Prince of Wales took a delight in his company and my daughter had heard Thayendanegea remark that the Prince sometimes took him 'to places very queer for a prince to attend'. While in London he had attended a masquerade in the Prince's company, at which were many of the nobility and gentry, appearing in war paint with one side of his face adorned with a black hand and his nose incarnadined. A member of the Turkish Embassy was so much struck with Thayendanegea's appearance that he ventured to touch his nose, to satisfy curiosity. No sooner did he do this when Thayendanegea, much amused but simulating a rage, uttered a tremendous war-whoop and flourished his tomahawk about the ears of the terrified Ottoman. Men shouted and drew their swords, ladies screamed and fainted dead away; and His Royal Highness could scarce contain himself for laughing. This was the same year that Thayendanegea published the Gospel of St. Mark in the Mohican tongue. After a war against the American General St. Clair, whom he defeated and killed in the year 1791, at the battle of Miami, Thayendanegea settled down to farm his rich estate at Niagara, on the Canadian side, having thirty negroes under him, whom he treated with the utmost rigour. He died in the year 1807.

POSTSCRIPT, 1823

I was hob-nobbing with Smutchy Steel, a few days since, at his respectable tavern in Parliament Street. He asked me: 'Now, Gerry, why do you look so pensive, and neglect your good porter?'

I replied that I was meditating on the fates of the few American generals opposed to us who had come out of the war with honour. General Nathaniel Greene had died of a sun-stroke, on the fine estate presented him in Georgia, but before he could enjoy it; and General George Washington, by his surgeons over-bleeding him. This was after two difficult terms as President of the United States; during which popular rancour had forced him to relieve his character from the charge of peculation, and he was accused of 'polluting the Presidential ermine to an extent almost irremediable'.

'Now what happened to that whipper-snapper of a Frenchman, that Marquis de La Fayette?' Smutchy asked.

I informed him: 'When the Revolution that he had fostered in America spread to his own country, the National Assembly declared him a traitor. He was immured in a fortress. Efforts were made to procure the intercession of England on his behalf, and the King himself was approached; but his Majesty cut the speaker short with but the two words: "Remember André!"'

'Ay,' said Smutchy. 'But, as you have shown, those that condemned the poor Major to hanging, never had much luck after. I wonder they had the heart to tuck up so handsome, so sentimental, so officer-like a gentleman. Our people would never have done so, had he been a dog of Rebel. We were ever too soft-hearted in such matters.'

'Yet even Major André's melancholy fate,' said I, 'was preferable to that of the man who occasioned it: General Benedict Arnold. He sought to end the war at a stroke and without bloodshed, for the betterment of his country. Had he succeeded, he would have won imperishable glory and the thanks of posterity. He failed, and was constrained to carry fire and sword against his own people. The war ended, America was lost. He came to England, and though he was brought into the Royal presence leaning upon the arm of Sir Guy Carleton, was avoided by the best society, and publicly hissed when he entered the playhouse. He died twenty years later, bitter, broken and debt-ridden.'

Then said Smutchy: 'Yet I would rather a thousand times have been in General Arnold's shoes than in another's—a hearty, well-intentioned, bustling man whose standing upon a point of honour plunged two worlds into death and disaster—who becoming aware of the incestuous alliance of his favourite daughter with his natural son went mad; and was put away for many years; and was daily whipped by his keepers; and went blind, and lingered on and on among the wreck of his hopes, and could not die——'

'His gracious Majesty the late King George, ay, truth,' I said, fetching a deep sigh, 'in whose service we suffered terrible things. I believe that even the Americans who wrote with such detestation of him in their Declaration of Independence must have forgiven the poor Royal creature before he died.'

THE ROBERT GRAVES PROJECT

In an unprecedented publishing initiative, Seven Stories pays homage to Robert Graves, one of the English language's greatest practitioners as poet, memoirist, classicist, novelist, and children's book writer. Working in close partnership with Graves's estate, the press is bringing back fourteen major, previously out-of-print titles that express the full range of Graves's restless creativity, most with new introductions by noted authors:

ANN AT HIGHWOOD HALL
POEMS FOR CHILDREN
illustrated by Edward Ardizzone

COUNT BELISARIUS
with a new introduction by Lydia Kiesling

THE GOLDEN FLEECE
with a new introduction by Dan-el Padilla Peralta

HEBREW MYTHS
with a new introduction by Adam Lewis Greene

HOMER'S DAUGHTER
with a new introduction by Michael Wood

THE ISLES OF UNWISDOM

LAWRENCE AND THE ARABS
with a new introduction by Dale Maharidge

MYTHS OF ANCIENT GREECE RETOLD FOR THE YOUNG

PROCEED, SERGEANT LAMB
with a new introduction by Madison Smartt Bell

SERGEANT LAMB'S AMERICA
with a new introduction by Madison Smartt Bell

THE READER OVER YOUR SHOULDER
with a new introduction by Patricia T. O'Conner

THE SIEGE AND FALL OF TROY
with a new introduction by Dan-el Padilla Peralta

THEY HANGED MY SAINTLY BILLY
with a new introduction by Catherine Pelonero

WIFE TO MR. MILTON